**"You're serious?" Pete challenged. "Someone's trying to kill you and you want me to leave you here, defenseless?"**

"And I appreciate you saving me. Twice. But I can't tell you anything else, so isn't it more important to catch that creep and find clues at the accident?"

"The scene and *Suit Man* aren't my priority. *You* are."

His blue eyes searched hers. If she'd known what he needed to hear, she would have said it. But she was a little frightened or worried or maybe just confused from the blow to her ear.

What was she thinking? These men had rammed her car off the road with the intention to kill her. And in all probability they had killed the man she'd been trying to help.

"I'll concede that you don't know me, but I'm not defenseless." The soreness in her jaw screamed otherwise. "I can take care of myself."

"Not tonight." He stepped back, one hand pushing through a thick head of short, light brown hair. "I'm escorting you home until someone decides what to do with you."

# THE SHERIFF

---

## ANGI MORGAN

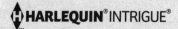

HARLEQUIN® INTRIGUE®

Thanks so much, Jan, you've been a
rock star this year. Jill and Allison,
your understanding and support is
unsurpassed.

ISBN-13: 978-0-373-69808-0

The Sheriff

Recycling programs
for this product may
not exist in your area.

Copyright © 2015 by Angela Platt

Printed in U.S.A.

www.Harlequin.com

**Angi Morgan** writes Harlequin Intrigue novels "where honor and danger collide with love." She combines actual Texas settings with characters who are in realistic and dangerous situations. Angi and her husband live in north Texas, with only the four-legged "kids" left in the house to interrupt her writing. They recently began volunteering for a local Labrador retriever foster program. Visit her website, angimorgan.com, or hang out with her on Facebook.

## Books by Angi Morgan

### Harlequin Intrigue

*Hill Country Holdup*
*.38 Caliber Cover-up*
*Dangerous Memories*
*Protecting Their Child*
*The Marine's Last Defense*

**Texas Family Reckoning**
*Navy SEAL Surrender*
*The Renegade Rancher*

**West Texas Watchmen**
*The Sheriff*

## CAST OF CHARACTERS

*Pete Morrison*—Acting Sheriff of Presidio County, Texas. Adopted by a deputy who became sheriff, he was raised at the department and has been in law enforcement since high school.

*Andrea Allen*—Working on her PhD in Star Studies. A daughter who would like to succeed without the help of either of her very successful parents. If she finishes her paper, she can secure a job at one of the top observatories in the world.

*Joe Morrison*—Retired as sheriff after suffering a heart attack. He adopted Pete twenty-five years ago. Everyone in Marfa knows and loves him. But everyone has secrets.

*Honey & Peach*—Sisters who dispatch for the Presidio County Sheriff's Department.

*Commander Tony Allen*—Andrea's father, a former astronaut working for Homeland Security's Customs and Border Protection Office.

*Cord McCrea*—Texas Ranger and ranch owner, head of the newly formed West Texas task force tracking drug and gun runners.

*Sharon*—An undergrad working at the McDonald Observatory.

*Patrice*—A woman who delivers messages for the drug/gun runners.

*Mr. Rook*—A sadistic man of perfection who plays chess like he's playing with people's lives.

# Chapter One

"This is not happening. Aliens are landing and I can't find the camera."

Lights moved in an erratic pattern low in the sky. Not aliens, but it was fun to think so. Someone on the ground? No. The lights were moving too swiftly. It had to be a chopper. It could not be a phenomenon. And especially not a UFO.

Andrea Allen was very familiar with everything that flew. She had to be when she was the only child of an astronaut and a pretty good pilot herself. It was definitely not a plane. It didn't look like a chopper, but it had to be. The lights weren't in the correct place. It hovered and disappeared.

Pulling the cords from her ears, she heard the faint drumbeat of "Bohemian Rhapsody" rocking in the background, but no mechanical sounds echoing in the distance. She rubbed her eyes and found the hovering object with the telescope. Whatever it was, it just wasn't producing enough light to distinguish an outline above the desert with a mountain ridge in the background.

Normally, she was bored out of her mind with the study on the Marfa Lights. Even though several tourists had posted seeing activity recently, no one with credentials had verified anything. Tourists posted all the time. Didn't they know it was just an occurrence similar to the aurora borealis? Everyone had heard of the northern lights, right?

The UT students studying the local phenomenon from the McDonald Observatory got excited, clamoring for a turn to watch the uneventful sky. Three nights later with no activity, everyone assumed the sighting had been tail-lights from the highway and then they all wanted the weekend off for a party.

Bored. Tonight had been no exception.

Nothing happened in this West Texas desert except lots of star time. Which she loved. She loved it a lot. Much more than she missed friends and family. Staring at a clear night sky was something even her astronaut dad didn't understand.

Since it hadn't been her night to stare through a telescope at the far distant universe, her coworker Sharon had begged Andrea to take her place on the university study. Sharon wanted the night off because she had a hot date with her boyfriend, Logan. Granted, the young student had been here three nights in a row, since it was part of her class assignment. Andrea didn't mind. She needed to switch sleeping to days anyway.

Another sparkle of red twinkled. Just a bit closer than the last spot.

With her spare hand she dug around in the disorganized bag her coworker had dropped in her front seat before leaving the observatory. "Where's that silly camera?"

She lost sight of the floating light through the scope and bounced her gaze to the horizon. Nothing. Had it disappeared?

If the darn thing came back, she needed the camera to record it. Dumping the satchel upside down, she searched through the assortment of items that resembled a loose picnic basket. Snacks, bottles of water, gum wrappers, a notepad, a small tripod, a spoon to go along with the empty yogurt containers, three different bags of candy—the butterscotch made her pause and unwrap a piece to stick in her mouth. No video camera.

She scooped everything back into Sharon's UFO-watching sack.

*Where's the camera? It was just here.* She closed her eyes to visualize getting in the car. Sharon had run outside with the bag in her hand as the car backed out of the parking space. The window had been down. "Passenger side. It must have fallen under the seat."

"My gosh." The adrenaline rush grew each time she saw the light a bit closer. A burst of red. A burst of blue. A plane would have red or green running lights on its wings and a white strobe light would be a consistent flash. A chopper, same thing. There were ways to identify what was in the air. Flight patterns.

Amazed, she just stared.

"Camera!" She ran to the car, pausing when she caught sight of the red flash again. She still couldn't distinguish an outline of what was flying haphazardly and low to the ground. It couldn't be a UFO. There were no such things.

Did she really believe that? No life in the universe other than on Earth? No time to debate, she needed pictures. Lots of pictures and evidence.

No one was around for miles to break into Sharon's tiny compact car, so it wasn't locked. The keys were still even in the ignition. Andrea yanked open the door, immediately feeling under the seat. "Gotcha!"

The strap was caught on something. The sky behind her was empty as she switched to the backseat, dropping to her knees again to get low enough to search.

If she could obtain evidence of the Marfa Lights, she could publish in addition to her PhD, make a name for herself as an astronomer. Finally be worthy of her Allen heritage. It all hinged on concrete evidence. Could it happen?

She recognized the sudden nausea and shakiness as fear. Fear of jumping to conclusions and being discredited. She'd verify the facts.

"What am I thinking? I have my own study to finish. I'm not chasing another subject. This is university work. I. Can't. Switch. Again." Her teeth ground against each other in frustration—not only with the silly camera strap, but also with the lack of focus her parents had accused her of. "What is this stuck on?"

The flashlight was back on the viewing platform with the UFO bag, and the dome light had been out for months. She couldn't really see anything under the seat, even bent at another awkward angle. But she finally came up with the handheld video camera, pressing Record and immediately scanning the sky for her mystery lights.

Andrea maneuvered from the tiny car, resting the camera on the door frame. "I don't know if it's appropriate to talk while recording, but I think it's better to describe what I'm seeing. Mainly because I don't know what I'm seeing. Five minutes ago there were flashing lights. Nothing about it suggests standard aircraft. And yet nothing suggests the Marfa phenomenon."

The corner of her eye caught a blur, something running from the darkness in her direction. She swung the camera toward it.

"I can't tell what that is. For the record, I'm Andrea Allen and alone out here. There's nothing close at hand to defend myself from wild animals or— Good grief, what is that?"

She kept recording, squinted. Still couldn't make it out. "The lights have disappeared. I don't know what's weaving toward me, but I think I'm going to get back in the car and roll up the windows."

Proud of herself for continuing the recording, she felt with one hand until finding the window handle. It was the first time she was grateful she'd paid extra for electric windows. But she wasn't in her car, she was in Sharon's old sedan. Backseat ready, she pushed the lock and shut it, then moved to the front door.

During the transfer, she lost where the movement was, spotting it again when she found the handle. Closer. More in focus. A man. Staggering.

She dropped the camera on the seat, using both hands to tug at the window stuck on the old car. "Not now. Uh. Give me a break."

"Help."

"Help? Not likely." She ran to the driver's side. If she couldn't get locked inside her car, she didn't have to stay there.

Marfa was nine miles away. This was a police matter.

"Please. Help. Night of aliens."

She heard him loud and clear as he tripped and stumbled into her. Shirtless, his skin horribly dirty. His lips parched and cracked. With his short-cropped military cut, she could see the gaping wound on the side of his head. There were cuts and bruises all over his arms. Some fresh, some old.

Where was the nearest hospital? Alpine. She couldn't leave him.

He fell into her arms, knocking her into the car frame. She kept him moving, guiding his fall onto the backseat. She pushed at his legs, tried folding them so the door would close.

"Come on, man. Help me…out…here." He was unresponsive and most likely unconscious. She ran to the other door, forgetting it was locked, wasting precious time reaching through the window. She yanked and pulled until he budged enough to bend his knees on top of his body and shut both doors. It had to be uncomfortable, but the man wasn't complaining.

"Hospital!"

She left everything on the viewing platform, including

her cell phone, only having a moment of disappointment about not documenting evidence. This guy was clearly not from a UFO. It looked as if he'd been in the desert for days.

There was no question the man's life was much more important than any research. She pointed the car east toward Alpine. Marfa was closer and had a doctor but no hospital. The dashboard lights showed smudges of the man's blood on her hands and forearms. She felt the stickiness of a heavy damp saturation just above her hip.

"Are you bleeding to death?" she screamed at the unconscious stranger and threw on the brakes. "Were you attacked by coyotes or something?"

Twisting to look at him closer, she searched the middle compartment for anything, even napkins. There was nothing here to stem the loss of blood. She pulled her long-sleeve shirt over her head and shifted to reach his body, searching with her hands until she found a wound. Her fingers found a distinct puncture. She'd never seen one in real life, but there was no mistaking the bullet hole.

*Dear Lord.* "What happened to you?"

She pressed the shirt into his side, moving his arm into a position to hold it in place. He moaned.

"Thank God you're alive, but who knows how long that will last."

The lights were closer, then gone again.

Using all the training her father had taught her about control, she forced her thoughts to slow and hold herself together. She readjusted in the seat and buckled the seat belt in place before putting the car in Drive.

One at a time, she swiped her hands across her jeans to remove the man's damp blood before pulling out of the parking lot. She dipped her head to her shoulder, trying to push a loose piece of hair, stuck across her cheek, off her sweaty face.

What in the world was she getting involved in? A secret

chopper? Maybe a new stealth plane? "Are you military or something? I sure hope you're not a fugitive or a drug runner. But whoever you are, you're dying and I have to get you to a hospital."

Nothing was around for miles. No homes, no businesses, no help. *Help?* She should call for help. Where was her stupid phone?

Oh, no. It was in the chair where she'd dumped Sharon's bag. She needed to call, tell someone she had an injured man and get directions to the hospital in Alpine. She turned in the small lot, prepared to jump from the car and dial on the way back. A one- or two-minute delay was better than getting lost. Maybe they could send an ambulance to meet her.

Bright spotlights blinded her in all her mirrors. She couldn't see and tilted the rearview up. *Forget the phone.* She punched the gas and could smell the smoking rubber of the slightly balding tires.

"It's following us!" Whatever *it* was, it was practically on top of the trunk.

The road was straight so she couldn't stop or it would crash into her. There was no way to outrun it in an old four-cylinder economy.

"Now what?"

Colored lights flashed. The inside of the car looked like a blinking neon sign. She could barely see the two-lane highway, and then whatever followed rammed the little car. Andrea's neck jerked back. Her body smashed against the seat belt. Her wrists slammed into the steering wheel. Her father would be proud she didn't scream—as much as she wanted to let out a string of obscenities at whoever was flying that thing.

Another hit. The thing had to be a chopper. The man in her backseat had to be in serious trouble and now so was she.

The car skidded sideways onto the shoulder and beyond. She maintained her grip, steering through the grass on the side of the highway. The chopper blocked her path back to the road. They bounced a few seconds before she aimed at the wire between fence posts and gunned the little engine again.

She had no idea what was out here. She could be headed straight to a small boulder or a ravine. The unknown was definitely frightening, but not as much as the chopper on her tail.

As suddenly as the thing appeared behind her, it was gone. No lights. No sounds. She wanted to slow down, but it wasn't safe. Too late she wished she had when a slab of broken foundation forced the car sideways.

It rolled.

She screamed.

# Chapter Two

Driving this empty length of pavement could put him to sleep if he wasn't careful. Pete Morrison stretched his neck from side to side, turned the squad car's radio up a bit louder and rolled down the window for fresh air. A quick trip out to the Lights Viewing Area and back to the office for some shut-eye.

Probably just a plane and a waste of taxpayer gas.

"I saw some strange stuff out there," a trucker had told Dispatch. "I don't believe in UFOs or nothing like that, but if it is, I want the credit for seeing it first. Okay?"

"Sure thing" had been the standard reply to every driver who thought he'd seen a UFO. And each report had to be checked out. It was Marfa, after all.

Griggs would get an earful in the morning about honesty and the law. This was the third time in two weeks Pete had covered the son of a gun's night shift at the last minute because of *illness*. Everyone knew the deputy had gone to Alpine to party. If he wanted to change shifts, he just needed to ask. There were twelve other deputies on the payroll, and yet Pete was covering. Again.

Partying hadn't been something he'd personally wanted to do for the past couple of months. But since Griggs had transferred from Jefferson Davis County, he'd been covering his shifts a lot. Covering wasn't the problem. He got extra pay and could normally sleep on the back cot. Nothing ever happened in Marfa beyond speeding citations and public intoxication.

Tonight was one of the exceptions. He'd make a quick pass by the official Marfa Lights Viewing Area, drive back and get some shut-eye.

"Dispatch, I've got an all clear. Not seeing anything unusual. But I might as well make a run to the county line."

"Okey dokey, Pete. This is Peach. See you in a while."

He laughed at Peach's official acknowledgment. No sense trying to get her to change. Everyone called her Peach. She insisted on it. Her sister, Honey, got the day shift since she was older. He supposed nicknames were better than Winafretta and Wilhilmina. They'd been in Dispatch for as long as his dad had been a deputy or sheriff of Presidio County. Or longer. His dad swore no one could remember hiring either of them. They'd just shown up one day.

When his dad officially retired, the new sheriff could request replacements for them, but he'd like to see anyone tell Peach she was too old to handle things at night around the office. A shot of regret lodged like a clump of desert dirt in his throat. He'd have to withdraw his name from the election so someone else would step forward. Galen Rooney had only been on the force for a couple of years and just didn't have the experience needed to run things.

No matter who the county elected, they'd most likely keep him on as a deputy. If not… Unfortunately, he hadn't thought past quitting the race. The idea of withdrawing gnawed at his gut like a bad case of food poisoning. He'd never quit anything. His dad—he couldn't ever think of the man who'd raised him as anything else—wouldn't be happy.

"Crap. What the hell was that?"

He successfully dodged a long object in the middle of the road. He swiftly U-turned the squad car, flipped his lights on and drove a couple of seconds. Parking across the road, he turned the floodlight until it shone on a black bumper resting on the yellow line.

Joe Morrison had raised him riding shotgun in a squad car. The mental checklist of what he did exiting his vehicle was as natural as walking. Even if Peach wasn't a stickler for the rules, he still needed to let her know exactly what he was doing.

"Dispatch, I swung back west to pick up some road debris. Guess a bumper dropped from a car and the driver didn't stop to take care of it. Almost sent me off the road."

"Wow, Sheriff Pete. It's a good thing we got that call to take you out that way tonight, then," Peach replied through the speaker. "What if an eighteen-wheeler had hit that thing? Oh, gosh, and what if it had been transporting fuel or hazardous waste? It might have spilled and leached into the water supply. We could have had deformed livestock or mutant wolves running around for years without anyone knowing."

"You reading another end-of-the-world novel, Peach?"

"How did you know?" she asked.

"Lucky guess." He laughed into the microphone. Peach and Honey's theories of espionage and Armageddon changed daily with each book they read.

"Well, I'm at a good spot in the story, so I'll let you clear the garbage. Shout out when you're heading back," she said.

"You got it. And, Peach, will you stop with the sheriff title? You know I'm the acting sheriff until the election."

"I feel the same way about my dispatch title."

"Point taken."

Picking up the plastic bumper from a small car, he noticed some skid marks on the asphalt. He flipped his flashlight on and followed their path to the gravel and farther into the flattened knee-high grass. A vehicle had obviously gone off the road. He tossed the bumper to the side and started walking.

About twenty yards away, the fence wasn't only down, but a section had been demolished and disappeared. There was nothing in range of the flashlight beam, so he shut off the light and let his eyes adjust to the well-lit night.

He finally spotted the car, the underbelly reflecting the starlight about four hundred yards into the field. He ran the short distance to the vehicle. The driver might need a hospital. A serious injury, he'd need to transport himself.

"Dispatch." Back in his car, he pointed the spotlight directly in front of the hood and followed the path through the fence. "Peach?" He raised his voice to get her attention.

"I'm here, just finishing the chapter. You heading back?"

"Looks like a vehicle went off the road about half a mile east of the Viewing Area. I spotted it. Driving there now. Check if there are any cattle around that could get loose, and notify the owner."

"Time to wake the sheriff."

"Don't wake Dad. He's officially retired."

"You know that's not going to stop him. Neither could a heart attack."

"Give me five minutes to check out the vehicle, Peach." And do something on his own without his dad shouting instructions in his ear. "I need to find the driver and see if we need assistance."

"He's gonna be mad," she sang into the radio. "You know how he hates to be the last told."

"My call."

"But you know how he is," she whined.

"Remember that he's retired. Five minutes."

"Yes, sirree-dee, Acting Sheriff Morrison."

*Yeah, but for how long?* He watched the land closest to him, searching for ditches or large rocks. Closer to the vehicle, it was apparent it had hit the foundation of an old building. Whoever had been driving the car had been traveling at a high speed, hit the broken concrete and flipped the vehicle.

He approached with caution, flashlight in hand, gun at his fingertips. "County Sheriff. Anyone need help?"

No answer. Nothing but the cool wind.

He switched the flashlight, looked inside the car. One body. Nonresponsive.

"Sir?" He felt the man's neck for a pulse. "Damn."

Dead.

The body was mangled pretty badly. "You should have buckled up, stranger. How'd you end up in the backseat?" He'd seen weirder things happen in car accidents than the driver being thrown around.

Back at his car, he pulled his radio through the open window. "Peach, send for an ambulance. We have a fatality."

"Poor soul."

"Yeah." He tossed the microphone onto the seat.

"Unit says they're about an hour out, Pete," he heard through the speaker. "There was an accident in Alpine and since it's only a pickup they aren't in a hurry."

"Not a problem."

No shut-eye anytime soon. He was stuck waiting here an hour unless Peach called him for a Marfa emergency. Fat chance. He'd get the pics they'd need for their records and maybe catch a nap after. He grabbed the camera from the Tahoe.

Careful not to disturb the body, he started snapping away, including the outside of the car and the tags. When he reached the driver's-side door, he noticed blood on the outside and then the tracks, patterns in the dirt as if someone had crawled from the car.

"Anyone out here?" he yelled, tilting the beam as far as it would project and following distinct shoe impressions. "I'm with the Marfa Sheriff's Department and here to help."

He shoved the camera in his pocket and picked up his pace. Two or three minutes passed, the footprints grew more erratic and then the bottom of a shoe came into view.

"Hello?" He ran to a woman lying facedown in the sand. She was visibly breathing, but unresponsive to shaking her shoulder. He verified no broken bones and no wounds, then rolled her over.

There was a lot of blood on her white tank, but no signs of any bleeding. He dusted the sand from her young face. Smooth skin. *That won't go in the report.* Caucasian. Short brown hair. Blue eyes, responsive to light.

"Ma'am? Can you hear me?"

The accident couldn't have happened that long ago. The hood of the car had been warm. Should he move her? There could be multiple things wrong with her. He ran his hands over her body checking for broken bones. She wasn't responding to stimulation. She needed immediate care and the ambulance was an hour out. That sealed it. He scooped her into his arms and rushed her back to his car.

Once he had her buckled, he picked up the microphone. "Peach!"

He returned along the same tire tracks, picking up his speed since he knew the path was clear.

"Bored already?" Peach asked.

"I'm transporting a survivor to Alpine General. Found her fifty yards or so from the car."

"Lord have mercy. I'll let them know you're on your way."

The car hit a bump and he heard a moan and mumbling from next to him. Good sign. "Hang in there, ma'am."

Slowing as he hit the road's pavement, he could swear the woman begged him not to let the aliens get her.

The Marfa Lights sure did attract a lot of kooks.

## Chapter Three

"I've told you several times now, I'm not sure what rammed me off the road. It had to be a chopper, but the lights blinded me and I never got a good look at what model."

Everyone seemed to know the man who had brought Andrea to the hospital. He leaned his broad shoulders against the wall closest to the door. He'd scribbled notes and asked questions while the doctors looked her over. And almost every other sentence had been spent correcting someone congratulating him for his new position as sheriff.

Pardon, *acting* sheriff.

A sprained wrist, a minor concussion and dirty clothes, that was the extent of her accident injuries. Her favorite jeans were ruined. Not to mention Sharon's car.

The nurse said she could get her a hospital gown, but the good-looking deputy hadn't offered to leave the room while she changed. Ruined and filthy clothes would just have to do. She'd feel too open and exposed in front of *Acting* Sheriff Pete Morrison.

It was hardly fair to have such an attractive lawman interrogating her. It made her mind wander to forbidden topics, so it was much safer to remain completely covered.

"How tall are you?" he asked, flipping another page in his notebook.

"Five-nine. How could that be important?" As tall as

she was, she'd have to tiptoe to kiss him. What was wrong with her thinking? Had she hit her head a little too hard? Of course she had. Hello. Concussion!

"Just being thorough."

She watched him sort of hide a grin, draw his brows together in concentration and drop his gaze to her chest. So he'd noticed the pink bra? No worries. Why? *Because he's extremely cute, that's why.*

"You're certain you didn't hear anything? The man who 'came from the desert,' as you put it, he didn't say anything?" he asked.

"I don't think so. By the way, how is that guy doing? Is he still in surgery? I keep asking, but no one seems to know anything about him. This is the only hospital, right?"

The nurse looked confused when Andrea had asked earlier. This time she turned to the sheriff, who shook his head, then shrugged. Everyone coming into the room had looked to the young sheriff for permission to speak and been denied.

"Can you tell us who your friend is?" he asked, flashing bright blue eyes her direction.

"Check your notes, Sheriff Morrison. I'm certain I told you he wasn't my friend. That was sometime between having my temperature taken and my wrist x-rayed."

"Yes, ma'am, you did say that." The sheriff looked at his notes and flipped to the previous page. "No need to call me Sheriff. Pete will do."

"Guess there's nothing wrong with her memory, Pete," the nurse said as she continued to wrap Andrea's left hand, pausing several times to smile at the hunky man.

Andrea had regained consciousness in the emergency room with a horrible smell wafting under her nose. It wasn't her first time for smelling salts. She'd gotten rammed a couple of times as a shortstop on the softball field in college. She could just imagine what her mother would say when she told her parents about this sprain. Peggy Allen would be glad her daughter was uninjured and it was simply a miracle how her middle daughter had managed to avoid a car accident until the ripe old age of twenty-six.

Not a miracle to her father, who had taught her how to drive like a naval aviator late for a launch at NASA. That was a phone call she dreaded. At least it could wait until morning. No sense worrying her parents tonight.

"How's that, Miss Allen?" the nurse asked, securing the last bit of elastic bandage around her wrist. Miraculously—to use her mother's word—the slight ache was the only pain she experienced. Other than a headache from the concussion.

"Great. Thanks. Can I go now?"

"I just need to get the doctor's signature and I can get your discharge papers." The nurse put her supplies away, smiled prettily again at the annoying officer. "See you, Pete."

"What's your hurry?" the good-looking man asked as she left.

At first she thought he was flirting with the nurse. He dipped his dimpled chin, raised his eyebrows, expectantly waiting…

"Oh, you mean me? I'm not overly fond of hospitals." Oh, Lordy, he really had a dimpled chin. She was a sucker for that little cleft under rugged, nice lips. *Whoa.*

How could his straight brows rise even higher? It was as if getting asked a question made him feel guilty for not answering, or he assumed she'd seen a lot of hospitals. Either way, she immediately regretted giving the officer any insight into her character. "The answer to your question, Sheriff, is no. I haven't escaped from a loony bin. I told you, I'm a PhD candidate working at the McDonald Observatory."

"I didn't say a word."

"Your face says enough without your lips moving." She covered her mouth with her good hand to make herself shut up. The annoying man just laughed and grinned even bigger. "What are you waiting on, anyway? I told you I can phone and get a ride home. The student I was covering for is already in Alpine. Somewhere."

He pulled a cell from his pocket. "Use mine."

She held her hand out, wincing at the soreness already setting into her muscles. It didn't matter, she had no idea what Sharon's number was without recovering her cell from the Viewing Area.

"I don't know her number."

She hated to think what a cab ride to the north side of Fort Davis would cost. If they even had cabs in Alpine, Texas, that traveled the fifty miles or so outside the city. She'd probably have to bribe the driver by paying him double.

"We tried to locate the owner of the car, but the listing is in Austin."

"I did mention she's a student."

He stood straighter, slipping the cell back in his chest pocket. "To answer your question, I'm still here because I need your official statement and I thought you might need a ride back to wherever you're staying in Fort Davis."

"Oh. Thanks. That's very considerate of you. I'm at the observatory, actually. I guess you do things differently here."

"Spent a lot of time with the law back home?"

She just stared at him. The man was actually being extremely nice. And seemed to be charming. Part of his expressive nature, she surmised.

"We'd never get along." She clamped her hand over her mouth again.

"I don't know about that. I like a woman who speaks her mind. Kinda refreshing."

"They gave me a pain pill. It must have gone straight to my mouth."

He nodded and covered a grin by rubbing long fingers over his lips. "I was here before the pain pill. You weren't exactly holding back then, either."

For some reason she wanted to push her hands through his slightly mussed hair and see the sandy waviness up close. *Wow.* What had the doctors given her to make her think like this? She had to remain professional.

"Do you think I did something wrong, Sheriff?"

"Miss Allen—"

"Please, my name's Andrea." She checked out her torn black jeans and ragged undershirt still stained with blood, not feeling like a Miss anything.

"Andrea. We've done some checking."

"Don't tell me, there weren't any planes or helicopters flying in that area. So I actually saw a UFO." She was trying to be cutesy or sarcastic or just funny. A giggle even escaped, but the expression on the officer's face didn't indicate that he was laughing with her. In fact, he looked dead serious. "I'm joking, you know."

"You did mention that aliens were chasing you."

"I was referring to illegal immigrants. Or maybe I was just delirious from being knocked out cold. I never once seriously thought I was being chased by an extraterrestrial, something foreign to this modern age of flying machines. I study the stars. I don't live in them." Exhausted, she wanted to lie back on the examining table and sleep. "I'm here working on my last dissertation."

The room tilted. Or maybe she did. It was hard to tell. She was conscious of falling, knew it was about to happen before it did. The heaviness of her arms prevented her from stopping herself. She didn't hit the floor.

Instead, a firm grip kept her in place, then lowered her to the pillow.

He had the best hands. Strong, short practical nails. Firm. And she shouldn't forget how quick. He'd taken a step and caught her as she swayed.

"Maybe we should talk later?"

"I'm sorry, Sheriff." She rubbed her head and winced at the little bump. "I'm…sort…of…woozy."

"Not a problem. I'm not going anywhere. And it's Pete."

"I'm Andrea." She could really get into liking that mouth of his. "You have a super-cute smile. Did I—" A yawn escaped and she almost couldn't remember what she was saying. "Oh, yeah. Did I tell you I like your smile?"

"I think you did, Miss Allen. I think you need to get some shut-eye."

She turned into his hand, still holding her shoulder. She caught a clean, musky scent before letting her heavy eyelids close and stay that way. "Can't think of a better place to do it."

THE SHERIFF WHO'D taken Andrea's statement stood outside the door, which was open just a crack. The person he spoke to was in scrubs. Maybe the nurse who'd checked her out earlier, maybe someone new. Shoot, it could be the doctor there to discharge her. She didn't know. She grabbed the side of the bed and began pushing herself upright, jerking to a stop as a hiss of pain whistled between her teeth.

"Wow, that really hurts." Her wrist was bandaged. Funny, she could remember everything except that her wrist was sprained.

"I'm headed back to the scene," Pete said. "I'm waiting on the local PD who are going to stay with Miss Allen until we have a few more facts."

"What if we need the room?"

"Mrs. Yardly, it might be a Friday night in downtown Alpine, but when was the last time the ER filled up?"

The casual stance and charm disappeared quickly as a

balding man approached, flipping open a flat wallet. The kind she'd seen many times before.

The Suit Man seemed to have no personality. He wasn't attempting to make friends. His straight, thin lips never curved into an approachable welcome. "Steven Manny, Department of Homeland Security. I'm here for Andrea Allen."

"I was told local police would be here to escort her to the observatory," the sheriff answered, shifting his right hand near the top of his gun.

"I have a few questions and will make certain she gets returned to her residence. You're relieved." A light knuckle tap on the door and Suit Man walked inside. "Miss Allen, are you ready?"

She nodded but locked eyes with Pete, silently imploring the sheriff not to leave her alone. Before she verbalized the words, he stepped into the room behind the new guy and closed the door.

"She passed out a few minutes ago and they're not ready to discharge her."

"We understand your concern, but we're moving. Now. Miss Allen." He gestured for her to head to the door.

As anxious as she was to escape the hospital before landing in Pete's arms, she was scared to leave without him. The guy demanding she put on her shoes wasn't the average government-issued suit.

"Where are we going?" she asked.

"That's classified."

"I won't tell anyone." Pete seemed taller, firmer. He waved his hand for her to stay put. "Think you can give me another look at your badge?"

When Pete took another step, ready to do battle, the Suit shoved his forearm across the sheriff's windpipe. Andrea jumped to her feet to help but received a backhand with the Suit's free arm, knocking her across the small emergency room bed.

Pete was no slouch. He was younger, three or four inches taller and in really good shape. His strength kicked in and he shoved Suit Man straight into the path of her hospital-socked feet. Without shoes she couldn't do much damage, but she did put a heel in Suit Man's gut, hurtling him into the supply cabinet.

Pete was there, swung his left fist and connected with Suit Man's jaw, sending him flying backward into the door. Her rescuer swung again, connected a second time. She recognized the panic in Suit Man's eyes. He knew he'd failed.

Suit Man had something in one hand and the other hand on the door handle.

"Watch out!" she yelled.

Pete ducked, but she couldn't get out of the path. The metal hit her square in the ear, and she tumbled to the linoleum.

There was some yelling, really close to her ear, but the world was spinning sufficiently enough that it didn't register. She saw the blur of black dress shoes running from the room. It was all she could do to focus on not passing out. Then the strong arms she admired lifted her to the table.

"Everything okay in here, Pete?" the voice she'd heard earlier from the hall asked through the intercom.

"Yardly, I need a doctor, and where's security?"

"It's just a bump. My ears are ringing. That's all." She'd seen double for a few seconds, but that had already passed. "What are you waiting for?"

A nurse and then a doctor entered. Pete slipped out, but she could hear his raised voice in the hall. She saw his phone to his ear. Watched him pace in front of the rectangle of a window and then speak with the doctor before coming back in the room.

"Why aren't you chasing Suit Man?" she asked between the blood pressure cuff and insisting she was fine.

"You're stuck with me while I ensure your safety. That's your best option." He didn't seem at all satisfied being saddled with the position of her protector.

"I can wait for the police. There are plenty of people here. So go."

"You're serious?" He followed the nurse to the door, looked down the hall and slammed it shut. "Someone's trying to kill you and you want me to leave you here, defenseless?"

"And I appreciate your saving me. Twice. But I can't tell you anything else, so isn't it more important to catch that creep and find clues at the accident?"

"The scene and *Suit Man* aren't my priority. *You* are."

She watched his Adam's apple bob nicely as he swallowed hard. His blue eyes searched hers. If she'd known what he needed to hear, she would have said it. But she was a little frightened or worried or maybe just confused from the blow to her ear.

What was she thinking? These men had rammed her car off the road trying to kill her. Okay, technically, it was Sharon's car. And in all probability, they had killed the man she'd been trying to help. She'd been knocked silly-unconscious by a complete stranger with really good counterfeit DHS credentials who also wasn't afraid to show his face and try to kill her with security cameras everywhere.

"I'll concede that you don't know me, but I'm not *defenseless*." The soreness in her jaw screamed otherwise. "He caught me off guard. That's all. I can take care of myself."

"Not tonight." He stepped back, one hand going to his hip and the other pushing through a thick head of short, light brown hair. "I'm escorting you home until someone decides what to do with you. The local authorities will find Suit Man."

"Are you sure about that?"

She'd lost her chance. He'd made his decision. And it was probably best. The only personal possessions she still had were her earphones. They'd hooked around her neck and somehow not fallen off. If she'd been alone when the *Suit* attacked, she would have been dead before she could press the nurse call button.

Or maybe worse. She might have actually been woozy enough to leave with him. Then what?

The sheriff opened the door. "Yardly!" The nurse he'd been speaking to came running. "We're not waiting to give an incident report. We're leaving. Do what you have to do to get us out of here. *Now.*"

"Well then…it isn't just another boring Friday night, after all."

# Chapter Four

Pete kept Andrea Allen in sight through the sliver of an opening in the door. There weren't any windows in the exam room, and he needed to keep an eye on her. Victim or perpetrator. He didn't know if that was an unsuccessful rescue attempt or an averted abduction.

Whichever, something didn't sit right and he wanted to know what she was doing. She was the prime suspect or witness in a man's death.

"I've got things under control, Dad. I don't need backup at the hospital. I'll be gone before anyone can get here. We're just waiting on a prescription. There's nothing you can do. I know you're already at the office. Just stay there and handle that end of things. When exactly did Peach call you?"

"Now, son, it's no reflection on your abilities that she called. We've been working together for a couple of decades."

When were any of his instructions going to be followed?

He'd been at the hospital almost three hours waiting on Andrea to be treated and discharged before Suit Man—it was as good a description as any—had shown up. And to get the okay for her to leave was taking a lot longer than he'd anticipated. The murderers seemed to be a lot more organized than the hospital staff, who couldn't get them out the door.

"Who am I kidding? Peach called the *real sheriff* as soon as I reported the dead body. Right?" A guy who went missing by the time the ambulance showed up twenty minutes later.

"You are the sheriff now and never mind how long I've been here," his father said, sounding wide-awake and probably on his third cup of coffee. He'd dodged answering like he usually did. "The picture you sent popped a red flag. I'm waiting on a call from the DEA and DHS."

"You think this guy was working undercover?" His charge was lying on an ER bed, ice bag on her ear.

"Could be, Pete. They're waking up some top-dog bureaucrat to get instructions. I don't want the call to drop on my way out to the Viewing Area. But I want to take a look at that car before it disappears, too."

"So you believe our Sleeping Beauty's story about the flashing lights?" His dad would take over the crime scene while Pete babysat the witness. This night just kept getting better and better.

"Well, something's not right. Dead bodies don't just walk away. The paramedics are sure there was no sign of animal involvement?" his dad asked.

"They actually accused me of yanking their chain when they returned to the hospital." A quick look into the room confirmed Andrea was still asleep, secure and safe.

"Then whoever was in the chopper chasing our witness didn't want the body found."

"Did Peach get anyone at the observatory to verify her ID?"

"Yeah, the director confirmed everything. She's lucky you got there as soon as you did or she'd be dead twice over now. Don't let her out of your sight until we get this thing figured out."

"I hadn't planned to. I know my job, Dad." He wasn't normally a pacer, but he couldn't lean against the wall much longer. He looked at the nurses' station, where there was still no sign of activity.

"You'll make a fine replacement. I'm looking forward to sleeping in," his dad said.

"That'll never happen. You'll just be at the café for breakfast earlier." He left the replacement statement hanging. He couldn't get into a conversation they'd been avoiding for almost six weeks while in the middle of what was becoming a major mess. "Listen, you know you're supposed to take it easy. I'll stop by the crash site on my way back."

"I'm not an invalid."

"You should be after a quadruple bypass."

Andrea yanked the door open.

"He's dead?" She was obviously panicked, more upset than she'd been earlier after the Suit had backhanded her jaw. "The man who stumbled out of the desert is dead? Did he die in the crash? Did I kill him?"

"Gotta run, Dad. Get a deputy there to pick you up. You shouldn't be driving." He slid the cell into his pocket and faced her. "I'm sorry you had to hear like that. How he died wasn't clear when I viewed the body, so I don't have the answer to your question."

"I need another shirt. Now."

He witnessed her realization she still wore the man's blood. Her chest began rising and falling more rapidly, and she was about to completely lose it. Good or bad? He didn't know. They didn't get too many cases like this bizarre situation in Jeff Davis County.

One second he was sticking his head out the door calling for clean scrubs and the next he saw Andrea tug the back of her shirt over her head.

"What are you doing?"

She threw the shirt across the room. "I think that's

self-explanatory. What? You've never seen a woman in a bra before?"

"Here." He shifted the pillow from the bed to block the view of her breasts.

"I'm not claiming harassment, if you're worried—"

"This is a small town and people will talk no matter what you claim."

"Someone's trying to kill me. I have no idea why. And you're worried about seeing me in my bra." She stared at him, hugging the pillow to her stomach.

She wanted a logical explanation. There wasn't one. "They're covering their bases."

"But I don't know anything," she whispered.

"They don't know that."

The door swung open, and Ginny held a pair of pink scrubs. She handed them to him without a word and turned to leave.

"Wait." He stopped the nurse after the disapproving look she shot his way. "I'll leave and you help Miss Allen get cleaned up and changed. Bag all her clothes, will ya?"

"Sure, Pete." Ginny smiled, raising an eyebrow to match the questions in her voice.

He stepped outside and pulled the door shut behind him, leaning against the wall and refusing to beat his head against the drywall. He was attracted to Andrea Allen in a major way and needed to set it aside until this mess was cleared up.

It didn't matter that her belly had been faintly stained with blood. He'd barely been able to think like a sheriff while admiring her other…assets. His red-hot American boy shouted at him to take notice.

The woman he'd been watching closely was completely in shape, sleek muscles in spite of being a scholar. That is, they still needed to verify her identity. They hadn't found any ID at the scene. Nothing on the viewing platform the way she claimed. And if he hadn't seen the dead man himself, they'd be questioning her story about that, too.

Maybe that's what she'd intended? Get him distracted so she could slip out of the hospital. Andrea Allen might just be a legitimate name she acquired so she could pretend to be someone from the university.

She was either the most carefree, speak-her-mind woman he'd ever met or the best con artist he'd ever witnessed. Being a looker helped. Spirited. Easily embarrassed on one hand and then contradicting it by stripping her shirt off without blinking an eye. Dark brown hair, skin that hadn't seen sun in a while and at least five necklaces, varying in length, drawing his stare to a pair of perfectly shaped breasts.

Ginny closed the door behind her. "She sure is upset that mystery guy is dead. You better watch her, Pete. No tellin' what you've stumbled across now. Guess that's the breaks when you're the sheriff." She dragged a finger across his nameplate. "Give me a call the next time you're in Alpine."

That ship had sailed a long time ago. "Thanks. Got an estimate on that prescription?"

"I'll go check for you."

He knocked on the door. Andrea sat on the bed, tapping the nails of her right hand on those of her left.

"So they think I'm crazy or lying. What do you think?" She had a pretty pout.

He shrugged and leaned on the wall again. "Maybe the man isn't dead after all. Maybe he came to and wandered into the desert. Search party will find him or evidence. They're usually good at that."

He cleared his throat, shifted his stance and forced his thoughts back to this case. A real case. A case that would prove he could be sheriff on his own merit. Not just because his dad had to step down after his heart attack. A case that would cinch an election.

He could hear questions being asked in the hall and no answers given to Ginny. But as much as the nurse kept her mouth shut here, he knew from firsthand experience she'd be sharing that he hadn't left the room. It would be all over the county as soon as she got on her social media devices.

So be it. Her gossiping was one of the reasons they'd stopped dating. Among other things.

If the woman he'd found had been caught in the wrong place, she needed protection. She could be a witness to a mysterious crime. Or part of it. He didn't know, but he would be discovering the truth soon.

Whatever was going on, until he figured it out, Andrea Allen was stuck with him.

BEING LOOPY IN the same room with a handsome man in uniform was humiliating enough. Then Andrea had taken her shirt off. *Oh, my gosh.* And he *was* handsome. She melted a bit when he put his hat on while leaving the hospital. *A cowboy? Really?* She was a rock 'n' roll girl all the way. Classic rock and definitely not country. This guy wore boots. Real boots. Still, she wanted to find out what kissing him was like.

She absolutely adored cleft chins. Especially this one. Then there were his eyes—kind and serious, or embarrassed and sweet.

"In case you're curious, we're heading down Highway 90 to Marfa instead of directly back 118 to Fort Davis. Just in case Suit Man is waiting with friends. There are plenty of cops on 90 tonight."

"Thanks."

She refused to further embarrass herself by making small talk. Her mouth had a habit of saying exactly what she was thinking, and the more time she thought about a subject, the more she'd end up blurting out trivia about herself.

"You warm enough?" he asked.

An innocent question. Small talk. She nodded, refusing to verbalize anything. It would open a floodgate of words that would inspire an entire conversation. And what if she ended up really liking him? How could he think of her as anything but a lunatic after what had happened?

"Sorry, is that an affirmative?"

"Yes." *Keep your cool. Maybe pretend to fall asleep and he won't ask anything.* She closed her eyes and leaned her head against the cool glass of the window, trying to see the stars and constellations.

"It's okay to talk, you know. Why don't you tell me about why you're in West Texas."

Was he just making conversation? Being polite? Or pumping her for information? Did it really matter? "I don't think I should say anything. You're treating me like a suspect."

"Do you feel like a suspect? I thought I was treating you like someone who needed a lift home. I do that. It's part of my job."

"I don't know why I'm being so paranoid."

"Maybe it has something to do with a dying man falling into your arms in the middle of nowhere or being chased by unknown assailants?" He scratched between his eyebrows for a brief second. He'd done that several times as he'd dipped his chin. "Or maybe it was the guy posing as Homeland Security who attacked you."

"Yeah." She laughed for a second, surprising herself. "That might have something to do with it."

"Pretty good badge, too. Had me fooled, even down to his shoes. Most of 'em forget the shoes."

She covered her eyes, sliding her hand over her mouth. *Small talk, remember the small talk consequences.* She did not want to reveal who her father was or who he worked for. His job title was a red flag, warning off guys too frightened to stand near him. Or others would fall into hero worship when the former astronaut showed up. Either of her father's personas would make her feel like the background, and she'd lose interest in a potential relationship.

"You can rest if you want. Use the blanket I took from the trunk for a pillow. I promise it's clean."

Rolling the dark cotton into a cylinder, her brain jump-started as the road veered directly west again. They were getting close to the Viewing Area. She could see warning lights down the road, still miles away, but bright for a clear night on a flat piece of earth. Not anything like what she'd experienced earlier.

"I probably should just keep my mouth shut, but I don't want to forget this." She pointed at the hills to the south. "The lights I saw first appeared back that direction. There was something strange about them."

"People see lights out here all the time."

"Don't dismiss me like a tourist."

"Pardon me, ma'am. I forgot for a minute you were an astrologer."

"Astronomer, but you already knew that. Trying to insult me?" From him, it didn't come across as an insult. "Can we stop to get my things, Pete? I think I'm clearheaded enough to have a discussion with your colleagues about what happened. And I'll never get to sleep if I don't have my music."

He tugged at the front of his shirt, shifting behind the wheel. "I don't think that's a good idea."

So when Pete didn't want her to know something or he was holding back, he kept a straight face and couldn't smile. Interesting. He was definitely holding back. She'd seen a lot of guys in uniform in her lifetime and they all stood a little straighter, forcing the confidence to come through as the truth.

"I don't really want to see Sharon's car or have that memory with me forever. But isn't it better than wondering about it for the rest of my life? Which is worse?"

"I can't answer that, Miss Allen." He pulled to the shoulder of the road and put the car in Park. "What I can tell you is that nothing was there except the car."

"You aren't taking me back to the observatory. Are you?"

"No, ma'am."

"So you think I murdered that man and wrecked my friend's car and made up a story about weird chopper lights to cover everything up? He was shot. Did you find a gun? And really, I came into the desert without anything? No cell, no purse, no shovel, no identification whatsoever to get rid of a dead man?" She'd started talking and couldn't stop. "Granted, if I were getting rid of a dead man, I probably wouldn't carry my ID. But alone? Get real. And if you knew me at all, no snacks and no water? Well, that just isn't going to happen."

"Wow." He draped his arm over the steering wheel, turning more of his body toward her and smiling once again. "That's impressive."

"I have a vivid imagination and think really fast. My dad rubbed off on me. I don't understand how you can assume that I'm guilty without any proof. There isn't any proof. Right? I mean, I'm not being framed, am I? Lots of people knew where I'd be tonight."

"Just hold on a minute." He straightened the arm closer to her, reaching out to pat her shoulder. "If you can take a breath and slow down to my speed, I can explain what's going on. To a certain degree."

She faced forward and shoved her fingers under her legs. Watching his sincerity was clouding her ability to analyze the situation correctly. She'd allowed him to distract her far too long and should have called her parents immediately. She knew *that* number by heart. "Okay, I'm breathing."

"You've been in protective custody since I got a phone

call from the paramedics that there wasn't a body in the vehicle. No one's arresting you."

"But you saw him? I'm not…" She'd been about to say *crazy*.

He nodded. "I have pictures of a man at the scene matching the description you gave me earlier. Neither of us imagined it."

"Thank goodness." The sigh of relief was more than just verbal, it was liberating, and she physically felt lighter. For a moment, she'd doubted if she was experiencing an actual memory. Part of her imagination could have been distorted from the concussion.

Was that a possibility? She had definitely passed out after the accident. Could she have warped what really happened? Should she throw that scenario into the mix? No. She wasn't paranoid, just overthinking as usual. It was better to wait on the investigation and not doubt herself.

"Look, Miss Allen. Until we know what's going on, everyone believes it's better for me to stick close."

"I can't do my work just anywhere. Even under protective custody at the observatory would be difficult. Don't I have to consent or something? And who's everyone?"

For once, the man with all the answers seemed at a loss for words. It couldn't be plainer he was choosing his words carefully.

"I'm not trying to scare you, but being new around here you may not know that we've had a lot of drugs and guns crossing the border recently. Strange activity involving a helicopter and a disappearing body seems more than a little suspicious. It's better to be safe."

"And better to keep me close while you verify that I don't have anything to do with it."

"Hmm, there is that."

He grinned again, and she realized that there wasn't anything calculating about it. He seemed to be a good-looking, concerned officer who took his job very seriously to help her feel safe and at ease. Correction, he was absolutely terrific-looking and naturally charming. And off-limits?

Pete Morrison should be off-limits. She was completing her study and then getting a job halfway around the world. No reason to get involved. It wasn't logical. She didn't have time for a relationship.

Satisfied he was there to help and she needed to curb her attraction, she slapped her thighs, ready to cooperate. "I have a passport to verify who I am. It's at the observatory housing where I'm staying until I get my telescope time. I'm only here for three weeks."

He put the truck in motion. "So it was just coincidence that you were at the Viewing Area looking for the lights? Tourist or PhD work?"

"Filling in for a student. It's an ongoing study by UT. That's why I was driving her car. I hope her insurance covers accident by strange helicopter. She's going to kill me."

"No comment. I don't let people borrow my truck." He put the patrol car in Drive. "Not even my dad."

The circular building where tourists stopped to watch for the Marfa Lights phenomenon passed by amid several parked vehicles, including another squad car identical to the one she was inside. The radio squawked, and Pete lifted the hand microphone to his lips. It certainly was easy to think of the man by his first name.

"Yeah, Dad?"

"And what if it hadn't been me?" answered a gruff voice through the static.

"It's always you." Pete laughed after he'd released the talk button and couldn't be heard. "Remember that I have a ride-along."

"I ain't that old, buster Pete. Not much new here, but DHS wants you to meet them at the station with the witness."

"Headed there now. Out."

He stowed the microphone, and she waited for an explanation, but waiting wasn't really her thing. She was more of a straight-to-the-point, fixer type of person and yet she really didn't want to explain right now.

"Real DHS?" she asked, gulping at the potential conversation she'd be forced to have soon.

"The Department of Homeland Security. Looks like our missing body rang some official bells."

"Dang it." *Are they here for a missing body or because of my involvement?* It didn't take much to come to the conclusion it was about her. "Did they mention why they want to talk to me?"

"They probably need your statement. This is a good thing. They'll move the investigation forward a lot faster. You should be glad. We'll be out of your hair that much sooner."

Her instinct and her luck shouted differently.

"Not likely. Why is this happening now? Oh, I know you mentioned the guns and drugs and border thing. But I'm so close to finishing this dissertation. Shoot."

They entered Marfa and turned north toward the county jail. Pete let his department dispatch know they were on their way in.

"Did they say who would be coming here?" she asked.

"You know someone at Homeland Security?"

Hopefully, she wouldn't have to explain herself. She'd give her interview, they'd say everything was a huge mistake, no one's actually trying to kill you and she could return to finish her short time in the Davis Mountains. "I'd rather not get into it."

"Andrea, you're the one who brought it up."

"And I'm the one who's not going to talk about it." *Not unless I really, really have to.*

## Chapter Five

Close to nine in the morning, an official government vehicle pulled in front of the Presidio County Sheriff's Department. One uniformed man got out. Navy, lots of rank. He openly assessed the street, then spent several minutes checking his phone.

Pete watched everything, but his main focus was Andrea. Her posture changed. She looked defeated. After she'd said she didn't want to discuss the DHS, she didn't discuss anything. Gone was the chatty, confident woman who spoke her mind. Now she was withdrawn, closed off, silent, and stood with her hands wrapped around her waist.

The officer acknowledged Pete, but his eyes had connected with Andrea and he wasn't looking anywhere else.

"Commander," Andrea said on a long, exasperated sigh and led the way to his dad's office. She clearly didn't want the DHS representative to be the man who'd walked into the sheriff's office.

"Andrea," the DHS expert acknowledged with a similar annoyed exhale. He shut the door behind him, leaving only silhouettes against the opaque window—letting Pete know they were on opposite sides of the small room.

Interesting. His witness recognized military rank and the DHS officer seemed to know her. She'd been tight-lipped since they arrived at the station. Either pretending to be asleep on his cot in the back or flat out refusing to answer any questions.

"Do you want something to eat, Pete?" Honey asked.

The shift change had occurred at eight o'clock sharp, just like every normal day. Peach and Honey insisted on working seven days a week, knowing his dad would let them off anytime they wanted. They liked staying busy, but they liked staying out of each other's hair more. They'd each confided in him—and probably everyone else in town—that it was the only reason they continued to live in the same house.

"No, thanks, Honey. I thought I'd take Miss Allen to the café when she's done."

"Are you sure she's not going to be whisked away by aliens or a secret government agency?" The older woman laughed, making fun of several theories Peach had shared before leaving. "The sheriff is hung up at the scene for at least another hour, Pete. He wanted me to let you know."

He could guess why his father hadn't spoken to him directly. Most likely to keep his cool at the lack of cooperation. "He still fighting for information?"

"I can only assume so," Honey said, picking up her pen. "You know those government types. They never let us in on the fun."

"You adding this to your novel?" he asked, and was ignored since she was already engrossed in writing her sentence.

Peach came up with the stories and Honey was the aspiring writer who wrote them down. They'd kept the local women busy debating the realism of their tales for several years. It was obvious even to strangers that they were best friends who happened to be sisters.

A yawn escaped him. It was the first double shift he'd completed without a wink of shut-eye in a long while. But he couldn't head back to the ranch until DHS instructed them on what was to happen with Andrea. His dad would be at the scene awhile. That left him with nothing to do but catch up on paperwork and wait for their guests to finish. He'd be lucky if he could go home afterward.

"Since things are covered at the moment, I'm going to grab a quick shower in the back and wake up. Alert me if they," he said, hooking his thumb toward his dad's closed office door, "finish up."

"I have a feeling they're going to be there awhile," Honey said. "Don't you think it's a bit strange that he's here to interview a witness and didn't even introduce himself?"

"I suppose you have a point. I'm not certain what protocol is for something like this. We normally don't share murder jurisdiction with anyone."

"You certain there's not going to be another murder soon?"

Voices were definitely rising on the other side of the window, but the old building had walls thick enough that he couldn't distinguish the words. Should he step inside and allow them to cool off? If he was closer, maybe he could understand what the argument was about.

"Do you think you should join them and referee?" Honey asked.

Pete took definite steps toward the arguing and stopped. It only took those three steps to realize he'd been waiting on encouragement from Honey so he could barge in and rescue Andrea again.

*Son of a gun.*

He was more interested in this fascinating woman than the murder and the disappearing body. He pivoted and headed into the back.

"Ten minutes. That's all I need for a shower."

"*I* could eavesdrop?"

"Get back to your writing, Honey."

"Yes, sir."

The door slamming had nothing to do with his actions. They'd been meaning to fix the mechanism that slowed the heavy door from crashing shut. He hadn't thought about it until the loud crash echoed in the concrete hallway. He threw his stuff into the locker and jumped under an icy spray, not giving the water time to warm.

Holding cells and the jail were on a different floor. He needed to put some effort into this case. His thoughts were centered more on Andrea's relationship with Homeland Security than getting his notes together for the investigation or why someone would steal the body of a dead man.

He'd offered to try to identify the missing man but had been specifically instructed not to even print pictures from the camera. Normally, he hated being shut out and treated like a wet-behind-the-ears rookie. Today, it had hardly crossed his mind. But it had, and soon after, he'd copied the pictures to a memory stick and stuck it in his pocket.

On the flip side, he couldn't *stop* thinking about Andrea Allen. He had no reason to book her and no criminal record he could find. DHS had just asked her to be held until they arrived.

Who was she? Where was she going after the observatory? What was her life like? Where had she been? How had she gotten that jagged old scar under her chin and the small one just above her collarbone?

Three weeks wasn't a long time to get the answers. Might be even less time. She'd mentioned three weeks total but had never mentioned how long she'd been here.

Pete toweled off and stuck his legs in his pants as quickly as a surprised rattler about to strike. He wasn't about to miss the opportunity to speak with the officer when he left. He considered shaving, but it would take too much time.

Looking in the mirror one last time, he shoved his

hair straight back and caught movement behind him. His weapon was still secure in his locker, so he spun, ready for—

"Andrea? How'd you get back here? I didn't hear the door."

"Some of us know how to close one without slamming it. They probably heard you come through it on Proxima Centauri."

"Prox what?" He leaned against the sink, crossing his arms and just enjoying how she could look so dang sexy even in teddy bear scrubs. The meek, insecure side of the woman he'd been admiring was gone. Spunky, speak-your-mind PhD candidate was approaching him one sure step at a time.

"It's the nearest star to earth, with the exception of our sun, of course. But it's not my favorite."

"The sun? I'm sort of fond of it."

"As I can see by your tan. No, Proxima Centauri. It's such a stuffy name."

She halted within arm's distance. A dangerous distance. Close enough to see his attraction reflected in her soft blue eyes. The desire to put a hand on each of her hips and draw her to him was tremendous. He had to clear his throat to think of something other than the pink lacy bra he'd seen earlier.

"I should go speak with the DHS officer." He took a step to move past her and ended with a slender hand on his chest.

"The Commander's gone to the scene. He said to stay put until he returned. Looks like you're stuck with me, Sheriff Morrison."

"*Acting* sheriff. Why don't you call me Pete." Was he insulted? Or too dang excited he didn't need to dart off to talk shop? *Excited*.

"I need to show you something."

"I don't think that's appropriate."

She threw back her head, laughing. He barely heard it as he admired the bend of her neck. "Silly. Do you have any gel?"

"Huh?" *Silly* wasn't the word filtering through his mind.

"Styling gel."

"I used it already."

"Not enough to do anything." She reached around him, brushing his arm as she squeezed goo into her hands.

Stunned into silence? Choking on his words? Cat got his tongue? He didn't know which, and if she asked, he couldn't hear her. He was focused on her hands rubbing together and then her arms lifting to reach his head.

"Get shorter." She tapped the inside of his bare feet wider apart, leaving enough room between them to breathe without touching.

"So, what *is* your favorite star?" he asked, closing his eyes and enjoying her fingers lightly massaging his scalp as she liberally put gel on every strand. He couldn't look.

"Wolf 359. Isn't that an awesome name for a star?" She took the tube a second time. "Just a bit more. Your hair's really thick and wavy."

He was dang lucky he'd put his pants on quickly. If he hadn't…

"See?"

All he could see was the roundness of each breast under the thin layer of hospital garb.

"All you have to do is squeeze some on your hands and rub it around like this. Then it should stay looking deliberately messed up all day." She wiped her hands on his towel and admired her handiwork. "That will look much better later when it's dry."

She twisted one last piece of hair and placed her hands on his shoulders. It seemed like the most natural gesture in his memory for his fingers to move and span either side of her waist. Drawing her closer to him was just as easy.

They were forehead to forehead. Her slow, warm exhale smelled sweet like the cola she'd insisted on before the officer had arrived. She'd called it her wake-up drink of choice. He, on the other hand, loved coffee and lots of it.

Concentrate on the job. What job? All he had to do was hang around here, keep her in sight till she was someone else's problem. Maybe even escort her home.

"I'm not a rule breaker, Andrea."

"Then why are your hands still around me?"

Kissing her was destined as soon as she'd told him they'd never get along. "What's about to happen probably shouldn't. But you won't find me apologizing for it later."

"You better not, Pete. Bad first kissers don't get a second chance."

He liked her. A lot. Too much. Too fast.

He leaned his lips to touch hers for the first time. Soft and wet, they parted just enough to encourage him. His hands spread up her back, noticing the firm muscles.

There wasn't anything between them now except a thin layer of cotton. He stopped himself from getting the shirt out of his way. This was their first kiss but sure didn't feel like it.

Their lips slid together, teasing, seeming to know their way without conscious effort. A perfect fit? Practiced. Confident.

He wanted his hands to wander but forced them to stay put. Andrea's arms encircled his neck, shifting her body next to his. Her tennis shoes snuggled next to his size-thirteen feet. That one layer kept him both sane and drove him crazy at the same time.

He wanted it off. Wanted her bare skin under his flesh. Wanted to forget exactly where they were and remember everything much too late.

The attraction turned to mutual pure hunger and he liked her even more.

# Chapter Six

Maybe it was defying her father, the Commander. Maybe it was a bit of the rebellious daughter in her that forced the need to push him at every turn. Or maybe she saw something in this man that she recognized as rare. A part of him that was wise beyond his years.

Attraction or defiance. It didn't matter for Andrea. Not at this moment. She was totally enthralled by Pete's kissing abilities. Something she hadn't experienced in a long time, if ever.

"Did I pass?" he asked when they came up for air, continuing small kisses and nips down her neck.

"I think you've earned a second audition." She tilted her head back to give him better access.

A few light touches of those incredible lips across her shoulder where the large scrubs top fell to the side and then he stood straight. She was close enough to notice the tiny gold flecks in his dark brown eyes. Hard chest, hard shoulders, hard biceps. This man was all man, yet playful. And those dimples were just killer.

She liked him. He was perfect for her plan to ignore her father.

"And just when is this second audition to take place?" he asked, his voice rich with the desire displayed in his eyes.

"How long does it take to get back to the observatory?" She had to entice him into taking her home.

"I thought you were ordered to stay put?" His hands slid under her loose top, warming her bare back and exposing her belly as the top inched higher.

"Technically, but I'd be safe with you. We came to an understanding." She did a little of her own exploring, dragging her nails across his well-sculpted muscles.

"I think you may have gotten the wrong impression about me." He gently circled her wrists with his fingers and returned their hands to their sides.

"Why do you say that?" Andrea painted the words with innocence.

He took a couple of steps backward and opened the door. "Honey?"

"Yes, Pete?"

"Did the Commander leave any parting words?"

"You mean when he said, 'I expect my daughter to be here when I return'? That's pretty much everything."

When Pete smiled a really healthy smile that made it all the way to his eyes, he had dimpled cheeks to match the one in his chin. She truly was a sucker for dimples. He let the door close, crossed his arms and leaned that bare back against the gray paint. "So he's your father. How did you understand those specific instructions to include a drive up the mountain?"

"Are you going to let him order you around? You aren't in the Navy. Technically, he doesn't have any jurisdiction. He's only here because I'm involved." Her dad was assigned to the Customs and Border Protection Office, reporting directly to the DHS. He had every right to ask the local sheriff for cooperation in a case. But he hadn't. And forcing her to stay at the county jail wasn't about any case. It was about controlling her life.

"To use a word you seem to love—*technically* he's with Homeland Security. I haven't been filled in yet, but he does have some authority around here. Your dad wants you to stay put and be safe. My dad wants me to stay put and see that you are." He pushed off the door, twisted the combination on a lock and lifted the latch of a locker. He pulled out a crisply starched uniform shirt and shoved his hands through the sleeves.

"Your jerky movements may be revealing your true feelings. Or they could be showing me your true nature."

"Maybe I just failed the second audition." After turning his back, he pushed the tail of his shirt inside his pants.

"I know my rights. You can't keep me here against my will. You certainly can't use the excuse *her daddy made me do it*. It will all be on you when I sue the county."

"At the moment, I'm too tired to care. I've gone without sleep for a couple of nights and haven't had the privilege of napping like you. So let me spell this out real plain like. You have two choices. Spend your time here in protective custody locked in a cell or walk down the street and have breakfast with me. Simple. You choose."

"You won't change your mind about that audition?" She added a wink, teasing him.

"I'm too hungry to change my mind." He stretched his neck, swiveling his head from side to side.

She made a grand gesture to follow him. "Lead on."

"Be right there. I walk better in my boots."

If she could get through the door before he buckled his gun around his hips, she might have enough of a head start to ditch the impromptu bodyguard her father had assigned. Then what? Downtown wasn't filled with public transportation and there certainly wasn't a taxi waiting on the corner.

The heavy door to the restricted area slammed behind her. She'd at least wait in the comfy chair in his office. Getting far away from his dimples seemed a good idea. The more he smiled at her, the more she was willing to change the venue of his *audition*.

Who was she trying to fool? Pete had already passed any audition with flying colors. She had one more Saturday night in West Texas and hoped this was the last time she thought about being bored.

Before she could sit, the restricted door slammed again. Pete scooted through, one boot on and one boot in his hand. With the office door open, she could watch his head turn, searching and landing on the receptionist.

He looked straight at her, let out a deep breath, showing his relief, and pulled on his second boot. "Good. I'm too tired to run."

"Don't get comfortable. There's been a disturbance near Doug Fossen's place. A burning vehicle on the side of the road near the state park."

"That's Davis County jurisdiction. Give Mike Barber a call."

"They know that but think you need to see it."

"Send Griggs, then."

"He hasn't reported in this morning and they're asking for the sheriff. That's you."

"What the…" He took a piece of paper from the woman. She looked a lot like the receptionist who had been at the front desk when they arrived. "Honey, please call Peach and see if she forgot to give me a message about Griggs."

"Pete, you know she didn't forget. I can get Joe to write Griggs up if you don't want to do it. But right now we have a problem at the Fossens'."

"I have babysitting duty."

Andrea stuck her head out the office door. "Don't mind this baby. I can sleep in that nice jail cell you suggested. I'm sure the Commander would prefer me safe and sound, guarded by a senior citizen." She nodded toward the receptionist. "No offense."

"None taken," Honey said, bringing the ringing handset up to her ear. "Presidio County Sheriff's Department." Honey wrote more notes. "We'll get someone out there shortly, Mrs. Fossen." She waved the slips in the air.

"I'm not heading anywhere, Honey. I smell a mess brewing and there's no way I'm taking anyone with me on a call." Pete reached for his hat on a nearby desk. He almost shoved his hair off his forehead. He stopped, tapped the styling gel now hardened in place and then scratched the bridge of his nose.

"Sounds like you need to get a move on." She raised her wrists to him. "Do your duty, Sheriff Pete. Lock me away."

His moment of indecision played on his handsome face. Then it was chased away with confidence. "Honey, get my dad or somebody from the accident last night on the radio."

"Yes, sir," the receptionist said.

"I'm not doing it. Send Dominguez and Hardy." He muttered something under his breath. "Come on, Andrea."

"Mind if I take the jacket from your office?"

"It's not my office, but I'm sure the sheriff won't mind."

With Honey answering the ringing phone and Pete rubbing the bridge of his nose, she walked to the coatrack in the corner. All the framed pictures on the wall were of Pete growing up. There was no mistaking the cleft in his chin or the tall, lanky frame. They were snapshots from his life of sports, school and graduation. One caught him shoving his hand through his hair and setting his hat on his head.

"That one's my favorite. He looks so uncomplicated, don't you think?" Honey stood in the doorway, arms crossed over her Davis Mountains souvenir T-shirt.

"I imagine he's rarely uncomplicated."

"You're a smart woman for picking up on that so quickly. He went for breakfast or he's using you as the excuse to fill his belly. We didn't get to officially meet earlier. I'm Honey, part-time dispatcher and unofficial receptionist around here. You met my sister, Peach, when you arrived earlier."

"You look alike."

"Don't tell her that." Honey laughed. "Do you have everything you need?"

"Yes, thanks. Sorry if the Commander offended you earlier. I wish I could say he was stressed and this wasn't his usual behavior, but today is just business as usual. I love him, but sometimes he's rather rude."

"I totally understand, sweetie. I hope you like breakfast burritos. That's just about all Pete ever has time to grab from that café." Honey crossed her arms over her heaving bosom and planted herself in the middle of the doorway.

"Anything's fine. Some of these pictures are really good. Have you known them long?" She quickly received the message that Pete had gone to the café alone and she was staying put. She might as well glean useful information about her adversary.

"Pete's worked with his dad since he was— Actually, I can't remember a time Pete wasn't here in this office. The sheriff prior to Joe paid him to empty the trash and sweep up as soon as he could hold a broom."

"Was his mom behind the camera in all these?" Andrea pointed at the wall, noticing that there weren't any with women.

"No. One of Pete's parents was a second cousin or something to Joe. They died and Pete came to live in Marfa. Poor man never considered marrying, but adopted a three-year-old without missing a beat. Peach and I moved here close to the same time."

"I'm glad Pete found someone and things worked out for him. And thanks. I would have really stepped in it asking about his mom if you hadn't shared."

"The whole community's been contributing to that wall. He's like one of our own, you know."

"I sure didn't want to spend all morning locked in that cell. Maybe we should go back to your desk." She got close enough to hug Honey—even though that was the furthest thing from her mind. She gestured to move out of the room, and then it hit her. "I get it. You're supposed to watch me until Pete gets back. Aren't you?"

Honey smiled, crossing her arms and planting her large frame in the doorway. "He reminded me that it's part of my job responsibilities designated under 'other.' I offered to get his breakfast, but he said he needed a break. Sorry, but you aren't going anywhere until Pete comes for you. He's smarter than he is cute."

"Ha, he is pretty darn cute. This doesn't have anything to do with him. Not really. I'll lose two years of work if I'm here when the Commander comes back. He'll haul me to Austin or worse, DC. I'll be unable to finish my thesis and…" Trying to talk her way out of the office wasn't working. "You don't care one rogue meteor what this is going to do to my life."

This couldn't be happening. She only needed six more days.

"Take a seat, Miss Allen." Honey crossed her arms and stood as straight as her aged body would allow. "I do know that *caring* about prisoners is not in my job description."

For a split second she considered making a run for it out the restricted door through the back exit. But there was nowhere for her to go. Staying with Pete wasn't a bad idea. He was the only one who could solve her current problem. She had to avoid her father and stay in West Texas for at least six more days.

# Chapter Seven

"I can't be here when my father comes for me."

"You won't be. Let's go." Pete waited for Andrea to follow, cell phone still to his ear.

"Some days are busier than others. Enjoy your ride." Honey answered her ringing phone.

He escorted Andrea to the Tahoe without any instruction. She hopped in and quickly dropped her head against the headrest, closing her eyes and looking completely relaxed.

Pete knew different. He recognized the compliance she thought was necessary until she could talk herself into a different position.

Pete tapped his smartphone and left another message for his dad. "We didn't finish our conversation. Be prepared. I'm dropping Miss Allen off with her father and returning with you. I will lock you up to make you rest. Honey's plumping the pillows in the holding for you. No scene or I swear you won't like being cuffed and thrown into the backseat of your old service vehicle."

He disconnected, debating the logic of moving his witness. She was safer here, in a building filled with law enforcement officers. Yet Commander Allen had been adamant when they spoke. His daughter would be brought to him at the Viewing Area immediately. A chopper was on its way to airlift them home. The directive had included instructions not to inform Andrea where they were heading or why.

Prisoners were kept better informed than this guy treated his daughter.

"When did he call?" Andrea asked as soon as he sat behind the wheel. Questioning arched brows, innocent open eyes and an impish suggestive grin—she looked totally in control.

"Who?" That wouldn't fly. She knew that *he* knew who she was talking about.

"The Commander. I've seen the look of having to swallow his orders many times."

"What you witnessed was me leaving a message for my dad."

"Oh." She looked at him and then her chin went up a notch with her aha moment. "You aren't denying that the Commander called."

"No, I'm not. Why do you call him Commander?"

"I've always addressed him by his rank. Well, at least since I was a teenager. It was easier. He answered to it faster when we were in a crowd and he's never seemed to mind. Since you aren't sharing our destination, I suppose he told you not to tell me. Afraid I'd pitch a fit or something?"

"He didn't mention fits of any sort. In fact, he didn't explain his reasoning with me at all. He seems very concerned about your safety. Why is that exactly?" It had to be finding that man from the desert. Whoever he escaped from—that didn't take a genius to determine—knew he'd made contact with Andrea and they thought she knew something. Including her father.

"I don't know what you mean. I spent all of five minutes in his presence. How does that make him appear concerned?"

"We can skip all the tippytoeing around." He took another look behind them and yet another along the horizon, searching for he didn't know what. "Your father asked me to bring you to the accident site. I disagreed. If men are after you, then you're much more vulnerable alone with me in this vehicle. Doesn't matter that it's only nine miles to their location."

"Did he mention why he wants me there?"

"To leave."

Either Andrea had seen or heard something from her passenger or these men were so well connected they knew she was the daughter of the man investigating them. That would account for a DHS impostor trying to remove her from the hospital.

Her fingers curled into her palms. "I've said this before, but I'm an adult and he has no right—"

"Pete?" Honey's shaky voice broke through on the radio. "Pete, are you there?"

He could tell she was upset. "What's wrong?"

"Jeff Davis County just called. They found our missing deputy's car abandoned near the state park. You want me to send one of the new guys to check it out?"

"Negative. Ask Hardy to head over." He released the button on the microphone.

"You need to go and I'm in the way," Andrea said. "You can drop me off with Honey. I promise to be good."

He pulled the car to the side of the road. "The Viewing Area is still three or four miles. I could drop you off, then hightail it back north."

"Or?"

Something hadn't been sitting right about the facts in this case. Too many coincidences. Too many orders issued. Too many gut feelings that he needed to be doing something active instead of reactive.

"Did I lose you, Pete?" Honey asked.

He spun the vehicle around and brought the microphone

up to his mouth. "I'm here. Tell Jeff Davis County I'm on my way and ask if they can wait to move anything."

"That's what they wanted to hear, Pete. They're searching for our deputy as we speak." The radio clicked off and back on. "You still babysitting?"

Andrea rolled her eyes and shook her head. A laugh escaped as he answered, "That's an affirmative."

Honey laughed into the microphone. "Think they'll find our deputy passed out on a park bench?"

"I'll write the reprimand myself. On my way."

Pete's rash decision about bringing a witness to a crime scene would come back and bite him. He was certain about that. He was also certain she'd done her best to manipulate him with the make-out session and talk about second auditions. Andrea Allen sat next to him because *she* wanted to be there. She might have just hypnotized him or something with those large, dark blue eyes. Yep, this decision would definitely bite him in the end.

"I never stood a chance," he mumbled aloud.

"Did you say something?"

"Yeah, stay in the car when we arrive until I give you permission to get out. Or I'll put you in cuffs for your own protection."

"Sure thing. That was a good breakfast burrito."

Was she agreeing just a little too quickly? Changing the subject even quicker? If she wanted it changed, he could roll with that.

"Always is from the café. I'm thinking you should tell me what's going on between you and your dad. Why are you afraid he's going to take you home? You're a little old for a runaway."

"That's funny, but not far from the truth. I've been running from my parents since I was twenty and wanted to change my major the first time."

"You've changed more than once?"

"Not really. I let them talk me into completing three."

"So you're an overachiever. Will this be a fourth?"

"Not an overachiever as much as… Well, I feel more like a compliant child. I'm working on my doctorate in space studies and need to be here to finish up."

"Sounds like a complicated relationship."

"You know how parents and college are," she said casually.

"Not really." He repeated her words, wanting to avoid his life history as much as possible.

"You didn't have to go to become a police officer?" She looked genuinely confused. "You're looking at me like I'm a cat with two heads."

"My dad has been sheriff in this county since I graduated from high school. He was a deputy before that. I've been around that office my entire life. I didn't need any references or education except what he could teach me."

"Is this all you ever want to do? Be sheriff?"

"You say that like it's a bad thing."

"No, I'm sorry. I always have an uncanny ability to say exactly what makes people uncomfortable or just end up insulting them."

"Well, now that you mention it…"

"Seriously, I apologize. I just meant…is being sheriff your dream or your father's?"

"Both, I guess. I haven't ever given it much thought. Everyone just assumed I would be."

He hadn't given it much thought until his dad's heart attack and he'd been asked to step in. It was always one day in a future he assumed was way down the road. Now? His father's bombshell had exploded and was a constant distraction.

He couldn't dwell on that problem. Andrea was enough distraction for any man to handle.

"Not too many people have wanted the job. It's a lot of territory and a lot of nothing. It's just so excitin' and all."

"Now you're just teasing. You've had alien visitors, a missing body, an attempted homicide and Homeland Security taking over an investigation all in less than twelve hours. I am very confident that everyone wants to be in your shoes." Andrea smiled, teasing him at every turn.

"Yeah, I see what you mean." He did have a decision to make about the election. Soon. But not before he needed to find a missing deputy and determine what was really going on in his county. And if he let this woman go before he had some basic questions answered, they might go unanswered for quite a long while.

He drove. Quickly, efficiently. He knew every shortcut not only in his county, but also to the north and east.

"I've always been told I'd achieve certain things. There are only problems when I assume I can go about them in my own fashion..." Her voice drifted off and she looked out the window.

"Sheriff, this is Honey. Where are you?"

He picked up the car radio. "About three miles south of Fort Davis."

"They found Logan."

He heard the shakiness to her voice. She wasn't irritated—a tone he'd heard plenty of times from her being interrupted. She'd been crying. "What aren't you saying?"

"It's not good, Pete."

"Are you talking about Logan Griggs?" Andrea asked, gripping his arm.

He nodded. "Why? Do you know him?"

"That's Sharon's boyfriend. She's the woman I was covering for last night. They had a date. Do you— Do you think...?"

He knew what she didn't want to ask. If they'd been

returning from Alpine and were stopped by the same men who had tried to kill her...

"Both of your fathers are headed there now. Should I tell them you're on your way?"

"Negative. They'll find out soon enough. Inform the searchers there may be a woman missing."

"Come again?"

"A UT student may have been with Griggs. Tell them and keep me posted."

*What a mess.*

"Before you try to convince me to take you someplace other than to meet your father, we need to stop the secretiveness."

"Absolutely. Do you really think Sharon was with him?"

"There's more to your accident than you're telling me. Homeland doesn't send teams to investigate car accidents for six hours. Not even when daughters are involved. Now, what's going on?"

"I...I swear I don't know. Sharon asked me to cover for her at the last minute. That's all. She had a date, didn't want to watch for the lights, asked me to take pictures if anything happened and even let me borrow her car." She raised fingers as she went through her mental list.

"Did you take pictures?" That had to be what they were after. "Where is the camera? I didn't find one in the car."

"I...I dropped it in the front seat when I dragged the man into the back. It had to be in the car. Do you think it got thrown out during the crash?"

"I made a cursory search in the dark, then followed your tracks and took you to the hospital."

"Then those men followed you to the hospital."

Pete turned the Tahoe into the state park entrance, eager to confirm that this accident was connected to the other. Dreading the sight of one of his deputies—and friend— being the victim of a homicide. Dreading more that he knew it wasn't an accident and that he needed to warn the woman next to him.

"Andrea, as more information comes to light, I have a gnawing feeling that none of this has been coincidence. I don't think anyone followed me to the hospital. I think they were prepared for the possibility you might get away. That they expected you to be at the Viewing Area last night."

She stared at her hands, shaking her head in disbelief. "No way."

"Do you think they could be setting a trap to get rid of your father? Has anything like this ever happened before?"

"He's only been DHS for a year or so, but no. Never."

"You're staying with me. I'm responsible for you. You will listen to me, understand? I tell you to stay in the car, you stay in the car. I tell you to do anything, you do it. Got it?"

A man had tried to abduct her, had knocked her across the room just hours ago and she hadn't looked as worried as right now, staring at him.

"You can't be right about this, Pete. But even if you aren't, you're beginning to scare me a little."

"Well, damn. I meant to scare you a lot."

# Chapter Eight

Andrea waited in the car as instructed. Not because Pete had sworn her to obedience or issued orders. If waiting in the car hadn't been the safest place physically, it was the safest place mentally. Logan's body had been found not far from the car on the other side of the hill.

The car fire had brought the park rangers to the main road. They'd extinguished the dry brush before it had gotten out of control about the time she and Pete arrived. She'd put her face in her hands and refused to watch after Pete parked. She didn't want the image of a wrecked car, possibly with charred bodies, forever in her memory. The fake ones in movies were bad enough to fuel her imagination.

The sunlight began chasing shadows away at the bottom of the nearby hills where officers searched for evidence. And for Sharon, who hadn't returned to the observatory housing last night.

Plain, simple, old-fashioned apprehension had her short, practical nails digging into her palms. It built in her chest, clogging her throat until she wanted to jump from the SUV. She pushed the door open and was greeted by the horrible acrid smell of burning plastic. Dark smoke continued to billow into the sparse trees.

The guilt and uncertainty of what she should do played

with her mind. Pete had scared her with his declaration before jumping out of the truck to identify Logan's body.

Was she in danger if she stayed to finish her study? She swiped the tears trickling down her face. Sharon had been so full of life...

Had her young coworker died because those monsters thought it had been Pete returning her to the observatory? Was this her fault? What was she supposed to do now? Or had Sharon set her up to be kidnapped so they could manipulate the Commander?

After what they'd been through at the hospital, she trusted Pete to defend her and do it well. She respected his honesty along with his ability. She also appreciated that he wasn't bossing her around because he could. He had every right, and he could have left her in a jail cell waiting on the Commander. She knew what her father would do. A decree would be made and if she didn't follow his instructions to the letter, an agent or officer she didn't know would enforce his orders.

Parents shouldn't have that type of authority over their twenty-six-year-old children. Especially since she'd been paying her own way since her first degree. And most didn't. She was the only person who gave her parents the authority. This was her life, but she had the feeling it was about to spin completely out of her control.

Six days was all she needed to finish her dissertation and get the dream job halfway around the world. Far away from Commander Tony Allen, former astronaut now working for the Department of Homeland Security. And farther away from Dr. Beatrice Allen, wife, perfect mother and foremost authority on the Brontë sisters in the United States.

Even with three degrees behind her, Andrea felt compelled to argue for a thesis on a once-in-a-lifetime star. She'd fought for her allotted time tracking it over the next week. Even though the observatory had been perfectly willing to record what the telescope found and send it to her, she'd insisted on being here. Personally overseeing the collection of data, trying to impress experts halfway around the world.

If she failed...what then? Another degree? In another subject? Another direction? Give in and teach with her mother? Hear all the reasons she'd failed because she'd chosen a terrible topic or that she must not have applied herself enough?

Her parents' voices saying "I told you so" rang through her head. They'd been right too many times to ignore.

This was her last shot. One star was certain to rise over the next six days. The question was if she'd watch it from behind an international telescope or if she'd see it on TV designated by her father as secure.

Pete tapped on the driver's window, and she unlocked the doors. "No, she's with me and staying with me. Especially now." He carefully set his hat in the backseat, kept the phone to his ear and made a motion for the keys.

While he was gone, she'd kept them in her hand. She placed the key in the ignition and started the car. Pete looked at her strangely and agreed with whomever he was talking to. Cell still to his ear, he put the car in gear and took off quickly, a cloud of dust billowing behind them.

"Two males. About a hundred yards from the vehicle. No, that's not in question." He paused, listening. "No, she's not staying. I agree, not over the phone. I assume someone's listening and I won't risk it."

"What's not a problem?" she asked, but he hadn't hung up and just waved her question aside.

"Yes, sir. I understand, sir." Pete stuck the phone in his shirt pocket.

"I can tell that was my father. What are our orders now?"

"Your transport is meeting us at the observatory."

"And I have no say in it." She wanted to fight for her right to stay and yet…two men were dead.

"No, Andrea, you don't. It's obvious to everyone now that *you* were the target. The man beside Griggs in that ditch is the same one from the car."

"And Sharon?" She'd barely known the young woman, but her heart sank under the guilt. Sharon was probably dead because Pete had taken her to Marfa instead of to the observatory. If it hadn't been for Pete finding her when he did, she'd be dead, too.

Pete's phone rang, squealing a hard-rock tune she loved before he tapped it and raised it to his ear. "Come on, Dad. Take it easy on the man and work with him. Right. You, too. See you at the ranch."

Question after question rammed their way into her mind and needed to be asked as soon as Pete set the phone down.

"They thought they were us. That could have been you. Oh, my God, I can't believe— I mean, I know what that suit tried to do last night, but it all sort of seemed surreal. You were there to stop him. What do we do now? I mean, I heard what you said, but are you taking me to the Commander? He's going to ship me home on the first plane headed in that direction. Or any direction, for that matter."

"Honestly, Andrea, you throw out so many questions that I don't know where to start. They haven't found your friend. Were you close?"

"Not really. I just can't believe she's dead."

"The body from last night is an undercover agent working for your father." His grip tightened on the wheel. He was obviously upset, too. "I'll wait with you until your father's helicopter arrives. He's ordered—"

"I'm not leaving."

"Someone's trying to kill you. Two people are dead, maybe three. What do you mean you aren't going?"

"I've waited two years for this one week. This one specific week. I'm scheduled to use the telescope for the next six nights. If I don't, all of my research is useless."

"And that's more important than your life?"

"I have one shot at this star."

"In the right wind, one shot's all any sniper needs."

"You really believe that my life is in danger?"

"Yes. Or worse," he mumbled, but she heard him loud and clear.

"Then I'll go." She really had no choice. The longer she stayed here, the more people she put in danger. Her father had loosely warned about threats a year ago when he was transferred. Until that very moment, she'd never believed anyone would actually threaten her.

Now she was indirectly responsible for at least one man dying. She couldn't handle another—specifically Pete—losing his life, too.

"You're not just saying the words that I want to hear. You're going to leave when the time comes?" He reached out and tipped her chin upward. Her eyes raised from her hands and focused on the dimples apparent in his cheeks.

His smile relieved the apprehension, lessened the guilt, made her want to spar with him again. "Do you need me to pinkie-swear or something, Sheriff?"

"Acting sheriff, and no." He rested the crook of his arm on the back of the seat between them. "So…um…I guess this will be it. I don't suppose you'll be back for another look at the stars anytime soon. I was sort of looking forward to that second audition."

"Yeah, me, too."

## Chapter Nine

"If you know where this woman will be, why not just let the men shoot to kill?" Patrice Orlando strummed her extra-long nails against each other in a ghastly rhythm. "Homeland Security will surely bring in extra patrols we'll need to avoid."

"I'd like to find out what she knows before we disrupt months of planning." He disliked repeating himself, especially to the same person.

He moved around his library, passing the multiple chessboards along one wall. If Patrice would satisfy her thirst—either for his wine or her delusion that she had any part in the decision making of this operation—he could achieve checkmate in three moves with board four. He contemplated his next play on chessboard one.

"But Homeland is involved now," she whined.

He hated whiners, but she was necessary for a major component of his plan.

"Yes, it does present a challenge that needs a complex solution. And yet I've dealt with complicated problems before, if you recall."

"Not like this."

"My dear, why do you continually doubt my ability? Didn't you say that the last time we faced an adversary?"

"Getting rid of two Texas Rangers is not the same as the

Department of Homeland Security. Why would they send a man undercover into our operation, anyway?"

Explaining oneself was the tedious part of working with expendable assets. Yet sometimes it was necessary to ease their minds and clue them in to the big picture, as someone once reminded him. He might be able to see several moves ahead, but he did have a propensity to forget others could not.

"I'll begin with your question. One small reminder, Patrice, that Homeland is in charge of our borders. We have outwitted them on several occasions regarding our gun trade. And we are a major drug supplier in the south. Soon to be number one, I might add. Therefore, it makes perfect sense for DHS to weasel an operative into our business."

"Can't you stop talking down to me, Mr. Rook? I get all that. I'm not a dummy." Patrice guzzled the remainder of the California pinot noir.

She might not be a "dummy" about certain components of their business dealings, but when it came to wine, she needed a great deal of schooling. After four years of her visits, he didn't bother any longer. "I meant no offense, dear."

"Just spell it out. We've been lucky. I just want to keep that trend trending."

*Luck?* Dozens of plans had been considered and one had been carefully chosen, then manipulated into action. There had been no *luck* involved.

"The Texas Rangers were out of the picture for almost four years because of one of my simple plans, as you referred to it." He sat at board number two, wanting the intricately carved pieces to fill his vision instead of Patrice's continual pacing around the room. "Once they reappeared, they were distracted with their wild-goose chase. Patrice, come sit down."

"We're wasting our time and resources. I don't want anything to go wrong. What's the point of capturing this woman who happened to see the crew last night? Don't we already know she switched at the last minute?"

"Patrice, Patrice, Patrice." He rose and placed his hands on her shoulders, patting them like a pet dog.

He'd never had a dog. He couldn't abide the shedding, drooling or constant neediness. He'd tried a cat once, but soon disposed of it. He supposed the people who worked for him were pets enough, but he preferred to think of them all as pawns.

"Why can't you appreciate the fine chessboard that I've set into motion? This is the part I enjoy."

"Chess has never been my thing." She smiled uncomfortably. He saw her reaction in one of the many mirrors he had strategically placed around the room for just this occasion.

"And still you've accomplished so many aspects of a refined chessman," he complimented her, forcing the words he barely could say, squeezing her shoulders a bit. Patrice was far from a disciplined chess player. "You are very good at guile, manipulation and distraction. Dispatch four of your best, dear. I want this accomplished this morning."

"Four of my best?"

"If you want to achieve your goal, then you must be willing to sacrifice your players." He moved his queen's bishop, knowing the piece would be captured. He'd left his opponent no choice. The sacrifice would be seen as a potential deadly mistake, but in the long run it would help him achieve his goal of checkmate.

"That...that...hurts—"

"They are easily replaced. More can be trained."

He applied even more pressure, certain her skin would be bruised the next time he saw it.

To her triumph, she didn't pout or ask him to stop. "Where should she be taken?"

"I will make the arrangements. Notify me when the

deed is done." He released the pressure and petted the bruised flesh.

"Yes, sir." She carefully wiped a tear from the corner of her eye.

Pain could remind pawns faster than any words.

"We shall give the authorities another bone to dig their teeth into for a while. It appeases the American taxpayers and we go on our merry way for some time before they drag their hungry behinds back to the border for more."

"And what is this bone?"

"Andrea Allen."

## *Chapter Ten*

Andrea's bags were packed and would be shipped later. Her laptop and change of clothes were in her shoulder bag. She looked around the observatory with a feeling of desolation. Everyone around her was determined she'd leave on that helicopter with her dad and...

*That* was the problem. There was no "and." If she left the McDonald Observatory and her research, there wasn't an option left for her. Nothing except a second-rate teaching job at a university already overstaffed with more than enough astronomers twiddling their thumbs. Well, it might not be that horrible.

But it wasn't her dream job. Nor did it sound exciting at all. Definitely not as exciting as working in Germany, Australia or South Africa.

"You don't look too happy."

"You think?" she smarted off to her rescuer turned guard. "I'm sorry, Pete. It's just that my dad is so overprotective. Because of his position and authority, everyone just falls into line with any decision, complying with his every wish."

"Got it."

Sheriff Morrison opened his stance and placed himself back to the wall, facing the entrance, staring straight ahead. Straight over her head. He probably didn't realize his hands rested on his belt, his right very near the hilt of his pistol. He was ready for whatever might come their way.

It was just plain selfish of her not to acknowledge the risk he was taking or the friend he'd just lost.

"I'm sorry, I realize you'd rather be investigating your friend's death."

"My job's right here." He continued his guard duty, never meeting her eyes, looking anywhere—everywhere—but at her.

"Forget it. I'm not running away. I know I have to leave. I can't let anyone else get hurt because of me." *Or murdered.* She saw the words on his face with the minuscule clenching of his jaw. "I appreciate you staying with me until the Commander arrives."

"I gave my word," he said matter-of-factly, without much inflection or a shrug. He looked like every soldier who had ever stood guard over her growing up.

"Of course you did. I'm appreciative nonetheless." Not only did he look the same as those soldiers, he acted the same, too. "They should be here any minute. I think I'll wait outside."

"I don't think the patio's a good idea."

"I don't really care what you think. I can't stand it in here another minute." On her way through the door, she punched the release bar a little too hard, causing her injured wrist to sting. It was just enough to make her eyes water. Or make her realize they were watering. And once they started there'd be no stopping the tears.

"Hold on," Pete said, coming after her. "If someone followed us, they could be waiting for you to show yourself."

"You're right again, Sheriff." She let her hands slap her thighs, frustrated she couldn't do anything right. More frustrated that he was about to witness a meltdown. She rubbed the protective bandage, determined he'd interpret that as the reason for the tears.

"Come on, Andrea. This isn't my fault."

She knew that and was about to blab it to him. The words weren't going to stop and she wouldn't be able to pick and choose which she said out loud.

"Dang it, I'm not blaming you for anything. I've lost the only job I've ever wanted because I was…I was bored on a Friday night. It's all my fault. I know that." She swiped at the silent tears. Tears for Sharon and a deputy she'd never met. For an injured man who walked out of the desert and died anyway when she wrecked the car. And selfish tears for her lost career. Crying for herself seemed petty, but she couldn't stop.

Before she knew it, Pete had his arms around her, turning her face into his shoulder. His name tag poked her cheek, but she didn't care. She could smell the starch used on his shirt. Feel the rock-hard muscles again under her palms. It was so easy to be safe wrapped in his arms. It defied logic, but there was nothing logical in anything that had happened since yesterday evening.

Nothing logical at all.

"You can't blame yourself, either, Andrea. If you hadn't volunteered to take Sharon's place, they would have found another way to get to you. It could have been here, surrounded by tourists with lots of kids running everywhere."

Since the fire he'd been professional to the extreme. She preferred him closer with his words a warm whisper against her ear. His hands a steadying force cupping her shoulders. Standing in the circle of his arms seemed both natural and enchanting in spite of the circumstances.

"I wish I'd met you two weeks ago," she said softly into his uniform.

"You might not have found this place so boring." He gently moved her away from hiding her face in his shoulder.

Her chin momentarily rested in the crook of his index finger before he quickly extended his others to circle the back of her neck. Angling her lips closer to his, sweeping down to make a claim.

His lips captured hers, or hers captured his. She didn't care. They meshed together while their bodies screamed to get closer. He was right yet again. If she'd met him when she first arrived in West Texas, she definitely wouldn't have been bored.

"I don't know how many rules we're breaking. At the moment, I'm not really sure I want to know." There was nothing soft about Pete's kiss.

No auditioning necessary.

He was an easy person to like, to admire. Maybe it was a good thing she wasn't sticking around, because she could fall for him. Easy.

The sounds of a helicopter bounced through the mountains. Her father would be here any minute. The Commander hadn't revealed what location she'd be whisked off to. If she was the only person this situation affected, she'd be kicking everyone controlling her life to the curb.

Including the handsome young sheriff holding her in his arms.

"I don't want to go, Pete. I'm not saying that because of the Commander or my dissertation. I haven't wanted to stay with anyone in a long time." She searched his eyes and melted a little more when his dimples appeared. "Have you?"

"I thought that was a pretty good second audition, if I do say so myself." He caught her lips to his again but quickly released them, too. "Just makes me want you on that chopper that much more. You aren't safe here."

"At least give me your number. Do you have a card or something?"

He laughed and shook his head. "You know how to reach me, Andrea."

"True, but Honey doesn't like me. She might not give

you the message." She had to joke. They were talking about a call that would never happen. She'd never be allowed to come back to Fort Davis or see the Marfa lights. No matter what position her father held, he'd put her under house arrest before she got close to the border alone.

"Your ride's here." He casually dipped that chiseled chin toward the chest she'd just cried her heart out against. His Adam's apple dipped as he swallowed hard. The brim of his hat cast a shadow over his tanned cheek.

Before he could release her, she leaned in for one last kiss. Pete didn't disappoint. Their lips connected and there wasn't a thought of what they should or shouldn't be doing. Just feeling.

The sad goodbye got her hotter than the desert sun. Then the chopper approached and she recognized the sound. She'd heard it the night before. She'd been racking her brains trying to match the distinct *whomp, whomp, whomp* that had been chasing her. Mixed as it was with the engine noise of Sharon's car, she hadn't been able to distinguish its distinctiveness.

But she knew helicopters and planes. She might not have had much in common with her father…but she had that. It had been their game. They knew their engines.

"That's not my father." Andrea pointed in the direction the chopper was approaching. "You have to trust me, Pete. That's a Hiller, a training helicopter. My dad wouldn't be traveling in anything that small. It only holds three people."

"You know what kind of helicopter just by the sound?"

"What do these idiots want? I can't believe they're coming here in broad daylight with my father ten minutes behind them. It's insane. Do they think they're going to swoop in and—"

Cut off by a shotgun blast, Pete pushed her between him and the building. People eating snacks at the table ran, ducking for cover behind the low brick wall separating them from the field.

"Pete! They don't care who they hurt!"

The doors were a couple of steps away. Another shot burst the brick just above their heads. She ducked to the side, but Pete kept his head down and drew his weapon, retreating to the people pinned down outside.

The gunfire shifted to the other side of the building. Pete searched the direction of the field, stood and helped a family inside the building.

"Everyone back from the windows! Go!" He waved people away from the doors made of glass toward an open classroom. "Get those kids into the classrooms. Everybody stay low. You'll be safe."

"What's going on?" an older man yelled from behind the information desk. "Who's attacking?"

"I'm Sheriff Morrison, Presidio County. Get on the speaker and tell everyone to get to an inside room. Stay away from the windows. No one goes outside. Anyone outside needs to stay in their vehicles."

Pete had her backed up against a wall, literally. He directed people, having holstered his weapon when the threat didn't follow him indoors. He pressed her against the paneling well away from the outer doors.

"I can help. I'm a pretty good shot," she offered.

"You don't leave my sight. That's what they want. Chaos and for me to lose focus. You're the prize, Andrea. They want you for leverage and are obviously willing to risk an open attack."

"I can call the Commander."

"They're listening to the police frequency, maybe even my phone. It's the only way they could have known you were here or that your father was sending a chopper for you."

His body completely blocked her view. She shifted to her right and so did he. Hand on his weapon, ready to go.

"How did they even know who my father is? Oh, God, my ID. They have my name and found out who I am." It really was all her fault. A stupid series of mistakes or events that were ending with innocent people's deaths. "If they are listening, the sooner my father says he's coming, the faster they'll leave. Please, Pete. I can't let anyone else get hurt."

"Here." He shoved his cell between their bodies. "Make it quick. The men after you are aggressive bas—" He cut himself off while two women herded kids into the classroom, shutting the door behind them.

She punched in her father's cell number. "No luck. There's no reception here." She tried to wriggle free from behind Pete's back. "I need the observatory phone."

"Stay where you are, Andrea. Wait, you should get into the classroom with everyone else. You'll be safer and can make the call from there. It sounds like they're landing." Pete moved along the perimeter of the room, closer to the glass patio exit.

She felt exposed, even though she was safe from any gunfire.

"Where are you going?"

"I can't let them enter the building."

She ran across the room to the information desk. "Where are the keys to the doors?"

"Right here," the volunteer answered, slapping the keys on a pile of Star Party pamphlets. "But I ain't getting paid to risk my life."

"Of course not," she said, soothing his hand and looking at his name tag. "But, Ben, can you dial 911? Tell them to find Commander Tony Allen to let him know what's happening. I swear he'll help us."

"Don't even think about locking those front doors, Andrea. That's what they want," Pete instructed, handgun finally drawn and in a ready position. She recognized the stance as the same one her father had taught her. Her gun was inside her travel bag and the bag was on the patio.

"Hurry," she whispered to Ben, who had the landline in his hand but hesitated to reach for the base to dial. "Please."

"It's too dangerous."

"I can do this, Pete. Are they on the ground yet?" She'd feel better if she could get to her gun on the patio.

"What the hell do you think you're doing?" Pete said beside her, taking the keys from her hands. He stood and pulled her back behind the information desk.

"Trying to slow them down."

"Locking the doors won't do that, hon. We don't know what's out there. And I won't let you—or anyone—risk being exposed." He jerked his head at the volunteer still holding the phone. "Get into the classroom and bar the door with anything you can find."

"Yes, sir." Ben crawled extremely fast for an older gentleman.

"Hello?" a voice coming from the receiver yelled. Pete clicked a speaker button. "Morrison here. Did you get through to Commander Allen?"

"They're still trying to locate him. Sheriff and deputies are about twenty minutes out."

"That's what I figured." Pete raised himself far enough to see over the counter. "He's probably with my dad. Try his cell. Tell them we're pinned inside the Observatory Visitor Center. I'm leaving the line open."

Andrea tried to peek over the counter with him, and he shoved her shoulder down before she could get a look. There was nothing to see anyway. Chairs had been knocked over, but the center was empty. This was the first time she actually wished her dad was closer.

PETE SEARCHED THE WALL. Maintenance. Office. Auditorium. Café. He needed someplace safe to hide Andrea before an unknown force burst through the unlocked doors and over-powered them. He wasn't wearing his vest. His dad would tan his hide…if he had one left to hang out to dry.

The extra protectiveness and responsibility weighed on him. It had nothing to do with giving anyone his word. Had nothing to do with his job responsibility. He flat out liked this woman. Everything about her shouted that she was special.

He'd never forgive himself if she was shot or—worse—abducted.

"We've got to get you out of here."

"I am not helpless, Pete. I've been in self-defense courses my entire life. And I know how to shoot. My gun's in the bag we left outside."

Good to know, but he wasn't letting her near that bag. He dropped the key ring on the floor near her hands. "Find one that looks like it's to a regular inside door. Like a broom closet. I'm going to lock you inside."

"Are you sure they're still out there?"

"The chopper's on the ground. The blades are still rotating. No telling how many were already here ready to ambush us." He watched two shadows cross the patio. "Let's move. Next to the snack bar, there's a maintenance door. Run. I'll lay down cover if we need it."

They ran. He could see the shadows but no one followed. Hopefully they didn't have eyes on him or Andrea. He heard the keys and a couple of curses behind him, then a door swung open enough for his charge to squeeze through.

He saw the glint of sun off a mirror outside. They were watching.

"Can you lock the door? Will it lock without the key?"

"I think so."

"Keep the keys with you. I don't need them. Less risky." Bullets could work as a key to unlock, but they might not risk injuring Andrea. He was counting on that.

"But, Pete—"

"Let me do my job, Andrea. Once you're inside, see if you can get into the crawl space. They just saw you open the door. Hide till the cavalry arrives."

"You mean the Navy. He won't let us down," she said from the other side of the door. "This is his thing, after all."

Pete had done all he could do to hide her. Now he needed to protect her. He turned the café tables on their sides. If he had to run, it would give him some cover. The thickest defense was the café counter itself. He plunged over the bar—taking the condiments with him—just as the first shots pierced the windows.

He heard the shouts—in Spanish—and the entrance doors open. More shots, from a machine pistol. The cartel's weapon of choice. Another burst of fire hit the café's menu.

"We know the *chica* is in here. You give her to us and nobody gets hurt."

Pete answered in not so flattering Spanish and blindly fired two rounds toward the front. He was answered with another burst from a machine pistol and plenty of curses.

Static over his radio. Maybe the cavalry would arrive sooner than he'd anticipated. He couldn't make out any words, but he turned the volume down so none of his adversaries would hear them when he could. He spoke into the microphone with a low voice. "This is Morrison. Pinned in the café. Numerous civilians in the classroom area. No eyes on multiple hostiles with machine pistols."

"We know it's you and you be all alone, Sheriff. We got no problem with you, man. We just want the girl."

"Didn't hear me the first time?" He popped off two rounds over the counter again, preserving his ammo. Cursing exploded from his opponents, followed by scrambling. "Why her?"

"No help's getting up the mountain."

So did they know about Commander Allen's helicopter

or not? He knew how many rounds he had left. There wasn't much he could do until they made a move on the door.

Rapid fire pinned him to the floor, ricocheting off metal objects in the kitchen. His biggest worry yesterday had been if he'd have a job after the election. Today the only future he was worried about was surviving the next couple of hours.

And making certain Andrea did, too.

## Chapter Eleven

Andrea could hear them through the door. Balancing on the mop bucket wasn't easy, but it did get her close enough to the ceiling to push the tile to the side. Her wrist ached before the men trying to kill her had landed. She was extremely aware of every tendon as she did a chin-up into the ceiling.

Her muscles shook with the strain. She bit her lip to silence the grunt of pain. She spread her weight over the steel supports, breathing hard, wanting nothing more than to roll over to her back and rest. But that wasn't an option.

Silently, she moved the tile back into place. Shouting. More gunfire sounding like a machine gun. *Come on, Commander! Where are you?*

The ceiling wasn't the safest place. One wrong move and she could fall through. One wrong sound would alert the men with the automatic weapons that could penetrate the tiles hiding her.

So she needed a way out.

They both did. That rapid fire would cut through Pete in a matter of seconds. She heard him, heard his weapon. He was still alive, but for how long? She could do this. She wasn't your average astronomy PhD student. She'd never been average, with a dad who trained her well. She could shoot and hold her own in a fight. If those men were on the inside of the center, then she needed to get to the outside and her gun.

"PETE, PETE, ARE you there? We're in the parking lot. You doing okay, son?" His dad's voice was a welcome reprieve from the bullets flying over his head.

"Just great."

"Let's assume they're tuned in to our frequency, son. Let's change it up. Remember the colt's birthday last month?"

"Do it."

Pete changed frequencies on the hand radio. They wouldn't have long before the men sitting on top of him would circle through the numbers and overhear.

"Pete? You know what these guys want?"

"Yeah, Andrea. Is Commander Allen with you?"

"Separate entry point. How many?"

"Four that arrived by chopper. I don't know about outside."

"We've cleared the parking lot and are ready to evacuate the classroom through the emergency exit. Change frequency to Peach's birthday."

"Got it." Pete twisted the dial again. It was another date easily remembered. They had just celebrated it last week.

"Sit tight, Pete. Just sit tight. We'll have you out of there in two shakes."

He checked his rounds. Three remained.

He'd left his extra clips in the truck and hadn't been prepared for a shoot-out.

*Sit tight.* As if he had a choice. He heard low grumbling in Spanish, words he couldn't distinguish other than complaints about a madwoman. Shuffling.

"Who's out there?" one of the men asked in English.

Pete slid to the edge of the counter and peered around,

expecting one of the Jeff Davis deputies to be in a position to take these guys down. Shocker of shocks. Andrea drew her hand out of her bag and raised a weapon.

Three shots. That was all he had to get to her. He couldn't stay put. She fired, and he ran straight through the shattered door under her cover. She stood at the ready, waiting for him.

A fifth man came around the brick wall, a large gun barrel pointed at them. "Down!" Pete shouted. He reached Andrea, they spun, the man fired, Andrea fired.

The bullet seared Pete's flesh and knocked him sideways. Their assailant fell to the patio concrete. Pete managed to stay on his feet and kept them moving forward. "Run!"

They both took cover at the wall of the ramp leading to the closest telescopes. A five-foot-wide path bordered on either side with a three-foot-high brick wall that was one foot thick. It would stop a spray of machine-pistol bullets.

Too much space. Wide-open fields. No cover.

But if he jumped the brick wall he could draw fire and possibly disable their helicopter. Andrea could make it to the front of the building and his father.

"Follow the sidewalk to the front. Deputies are on sight evacuating the civilians."

One of the men jumped through the glass, and Pete tugged Andrea to the ground behind the brick. He covered her with his body. They heard several rounds and saw red shards splinter into the air. The strength in his left arm where he'd been shot was waning.

"Where are you going?" Andrea didn't seem fazed. She spoke from under the protection of his body, taking everything that happened with a deep breath and calm logic.

"We need a distraction so you can get around front," he answered, breathing hard from the exertion. "I'm heading to their ride and you're heading to my dad."

"The helicopter? Can you fly that old relic? I can."

He shook his head. "But I can disable it. We go on three."

"But I said I could fly—"

When a new blast broke more of the brick into splinters, he ducked his head again, reaching around Andrea, tugging her closer, covering as much of her body as he could. If she wouldn't cooperate, he'd take her to the front himself. The men might be able to escape, but that wasn't his highest priority. Getting Andrea to safety was.

The burst ended and he moved past her, clasping her hand with his right to get her started in a low crouch below the wall and up the path. His left arm was getting harder to move, but he still had clear vision and a clear head. "I don't need your help. We need to move."

She tugged him to a stop. "You're getting my help, so don't argue. I don't want those men to get away. So, do you want to jump the wall or go around the far end by the telescopes? I'm thinking jumping is faster. I'll lay down a cover while you run."

"Hand me your gun." He stuck his weapon in its holster and covered her weapon with his hand. "I'll disable the chopper. You're going around front."

She placed the handle of her Glock in his. "We're wasting time. It's not a one-way ticket if I fly that hunk of junk out of here. Cover me."

Spunk or confidence or just plain stubbornness. He didn't know which. She stuck her head up, evidently didn't see anyone and took off, crossing the path and rolling over the brick wall separating it from the field. He didn't have the chance to stop her and didn't think he could have. He hadn't radioed his dad to say they'd left the building.

He stood a little slower than normal—probably the blood loss—he could see it soaking through the sleeve of his shirt. He backed to the opposite wall, keeping his eyes on the doorway to the Visitor Center. He heard gunfire, but from the opposite side of the building.

Those men would want to make their escape…fast. They'd be heading toward their escape, and Andrea was almost at the chopper. Dammit, all they had to do was sit tight as his dad had instructed.

A man came through the door again. Pete fired two shots, breaking the glass next to him. His aim was off, missing the man's body mass, but he'd forced him back inside. Maybe he was closer to passing out than he'd thought. The chopper was warming up. Pete ran, firing his last rounds that kept the machine pistol inside the building silent.

Now, if he could just keep his feet moving.

FORTUNATELY, THE HILLER wasn't that far and there wasn't anyone inside it to deal with. The man who had come up behind her had probably been left to stand guard. Andrea concentrated on getting ready to get in the air and let Pete deal with the men wanting to kill her.

Pete opened the opposite door and slowly climbed inside. "You sure you can fly this thing?"

He leaned on the door, so tired his head thudded against the plastic.

"Definitely. Buckle up." She didn't wait on him, moving the stick and lifting into the air.

They were away from the observatory in seconds. She could hear machine gun fire but didn't hover to see how many men or find out what they looked like. The former sheriff could round up the bad guys.

She was a bit rusty, but it felt good to be behind a stick again. She'd loved flying with her dad while she was growing up. He'd take her into the air with him as often as he could get private fly time. He'd been Dad then, back before he'd permanently become the Commander.

"Hey, I meant it when I said buckle up, Pete." She swatted his arm to get his attention. Her hand came back bloody. "You were shot? Stay with me, Sheriff! Don't you dare pass out."

He didn't answer. She took a quick glance at her passenger, who was seriously slumped toward his door. Shoot, she wasn't even certain he'd closed the thing correctly. He was out cold.

There were a couple of wild bumps as she jerked him closer to the middle. It was a nervous couple of minutes as she looped his arm through the seat's shoulder strap.

One thing missing on the Hiller was the radio. She couldn't call anyone. She couldn't reach Pete's cell phone and couldn't see his department radio.

"I guess I should put this thing down somewhere and try to keep you alive."

The controls weren't responding as fast as she would have liked. They were as sluggish as peddling through pudding. They had probably been hit by the last gunfire as they were taking off. She wouldn't let them crash. But wherever she set this thing down, they were going to be trapped there.

Stuck without medical supplies, food or water. Each minute they were in the air, the controls got worse.

"Hold on, Pete. We're going to land."

## Chapter Twelve

Soft lips. Pete wasn't too familiar with being awakened by a kiss, but he recognized the sweetness. He reached out with his arms to catch Andrea's body and hissed between his teeth instead. The pain in his left arm was manageable, but he'd rather not push it.

"I was shot."

"Yes, you were. I've been patiently waiting for you to wake up. But let me tell you, it was getting pretty boring around here again without your company."

"Can't have that." He sat up with a little help from Andrea. "We know what happens when you get bored."

"Ha. Ha. Ha," she said, plopping down next to him and crossing her legs.

He carefully lifted his arm without the same pain he'd experienced a few minutes earlier. The chopper was thirty or forty yards away, seemingly intact. Drag marks from his boots left a trail to where they currently sat. He'd be lucky if there weren't holes in his jeans.

"I'm sort of glad I wasn't awake for that." He nodded toward the chopper.

"We've been here awhile. I couldn't leave you baking in the sun. You lost your hat."

"It's late afternoon already." They had an hour, maybe

an hour and a half of light left before the sun was obscured by the mountains.

"That's right, tough guy." She swayed into his good arm before bringing her knees up and resting on them. "You finally got that nap you needed."

"No cell reception?"

"No nothing reception." She pointed to the department radio, then jumped up to retrieve it. "I thought for sure the Commander would be swooping in for the ultimate I-told-you-so. But I haven't heard anything except a cow mooing."

"Thanks for fixing my arm."

"I can't believe you were shot. Okay, never mind, I can believe it. I mean, there were a lot of bullets flying around. You should have told me when it happened. You might have at least tried to tell me before I ran to the Hiller. Though, honestly, I don't think I gave you time to tell me—"

"Andrea," he said, covering her hand with his good one. She was talking fast without taking a breath. Nervous or scared or maybe a little of both.

"Yeah?"

"You didn't shoot me. We got out of there and I doubt those men escaped. There was nowhere for them to run when you took the helicopter.

"Can I assume something's wrong with that thing?" He pointed toward the chopper.

"One of those men shot the engine before we got safely away. Well, almost safely away. We were very lucky, considering he could have sliced that trainer in half with his machine gun."

"Machine pistol. We've known they were smuggling those for some time, but it was the first time I'd faced one."

"How's your arm? You know, you were lucky. The bullet tore a hunk of your flesh away. You'll just have a wicked scar." She picked up a pebble and tossed it across the path. "But I got the bleeding stopped and didn't have to dig around with a penknife for a bullet. And believe me, I could have, too. My dad saw fit that I have lots of practical survival training."

"I see that. You're pretty good with a gun, too." He held her hand, resting it on his thigh. "Come on, just catch your breath and give me a minute to figure this out."

"Oh, sorry. I'm babbling again, aren't I? I do better when I'm moving. Less stressed." She tried to release his fingers with the intent of getting to her feet. "I'm not certain why you passed out. It bled a lot, but did you hit your head or something?"

"I'm fine. Don't worry about it." Pete kept a firm grip on her hand, wanting her next to him for multiple reasons, but touching her skin was the first one that came to mind. "Give me a second. Then we'll take a look around. See if I recognize where we are." He knew they hadn't flown far and were still pretty much close to nowhere.

"Oh, I know exactly where we're at," she said with confidence.

He knew the peaks, the general vicinity. "Maybe twenty-five miles northeast from the observatory."

"Very good, Sheriff."

"I've traveled these mountains enough to recognize the terrain. That puts us darn close to the Scout ranch. We'll need to get started up one of those trails if we want to sleep in a bed tonight."

"Is that an invitation?" She winked. "If so, I think you could at least buy a girl dinner first."

"I've already bought you breakfast," he teased in return. "But I'm sure your father will have strong words objecting to your spending another night in Marfa."

He groaned as he stood up. Feeling like he hadn't slept

in a week and that he was as old as sin. Andrea helped him until he was steady on his feet.

"You know, I am an adult. I make decisions all on my own."

"Maybe we should start with dinner after we determine exactly why those men would make such a stupid move today."

"I can go with that."

"No radio in the helicopter?" he asked as they passed it. She answered with a look and a long sigh. "Right. First thing you would have tried."

They headed up the trail. He was a lot weaker than he could let on, but they needed higher ground for cell reception.

"You okay?"

"I'll manage." He would.

"Mind if I stay close to make sure you do?" She shouldered up next to his right side.

"Going to hold my hand?"

"Maybe." She smiled.

"Why hasn't your father found you yet?"

"I've been asking myself the same question."

"I'll take your Glock back." He extended his palm.

She slapped her hand on his, wrapping her fingers tight and keeping hold. "No offense, Pete, but I think I'll keep it. You aren't quite yourself at the moment."

Perhaps she was right. She was definitely right about him not being one hundred percent. He'd seen her shoot. They'd both hit their target on the café patio and she hadn't fallen to pieces when the body hit the ground. He didn't know yet how he actually felt about shooting someone. It wasn't like they'd had much time to think about their actions. Their assailant had been attempting to kill them. They didn't need to think about it at the moment, either. There'd be plenty of time later.

"So, I've been thinking, since I haven't had much else to do all afternoon waiting on you to wake up."

Unless he wanted to walk home, they had another good fifteen-minute hike before they got a phone signal. They'd never manage a call at the bottom of one of these gullies, even if it was the easiest route home.

"What conclusion did you come to?" He was gaining confidence with each step. Up it was and then down the other side to the Scout camp he'd gone to in his youth.

She took a step away from him, angling toward a path cows and horses had beaten over time. "You can't be serious?"

He pointed toward the butte. "E.T. should phone home."

She faced him with both hands on her hips. "You are never going to let me live down that *aliens* were chasing me, are you?"

He laughed. Really laughed. There was something about the way she stood there along with the way she held her mouth and tilted her head. "No, I don't think I am."

She didn't ask if he was up to the climb, just took a step and looped her bandaged wrist through his right arm. One wobbly step at a time, he stayed on his feet.

"As I was saying, I've had a lot of time to think. When the *aliens* showed up at the observatory—" she used her original description of the men trying to kill her without skipping a beat "—it didn't make a lot of sense."

"How did they know you were leaving? And why are they trying to grab you?" They kept a steady pace on the inclined path. "After we make the call, we need to take cover. We can't be certain they aren't listening to my phone, but it's more likely they were monitoring the police bands."

"Right. So we're thinking along the same lines."

"You're a valuable asset just because of your father. But why risk losing men and a helicopter?"

"Exactly. They might think I know something, yet killing me would be the fastest, most reliable way to eliminate that threat."

He'd never met anyone like her. She wasn't upset or falling apart. "Does this happen to you all the time?"

"Hardly. I grew up preparing for it, though. I wanted to please my parents and did everything possible to make them proud."

"Like learning to fly helicopters?"

"That's actually fun. All of it has been to some degree, I guess." She squeezed his biceps. "You'll have to tell me about your treks into the mountains sometime. Right now, concentrate on breathing. We'll have time to get to know each other later."

He was surprised how much he wanted that to be true. "The aliens either think you know something or they wanted to hold you hostage in order to exchange you for something."

"That is the same conclusion I came to earlier. Unfortunately, neither of those reasons explains why they attacked in broad daylight using a helicopter. I mean, wouldn't it have made more sense to enter through the door, take us by surprise and then signal for the chopper once they were successful?"

He stopped and checked his pockets for the phone.

"Looking for this?" She handed him his cell after pulling it from her back pocket. "I turned it off to save the battery."

He turned it on, then continued their climb. He wanted this point to be high enough for a connection but it wasn't. They climbed in silence for a while, thinking. "You're right. Their attack doesn't make sense. They would have assured themselves of your location, been ready to get in and out, not hang back. They could have overrun me easily."

"Unless it's all a diversion."

"You're brilliant." She was gorgeous and brilliant. The

phone was ready. He pulled up his dad's cell number and tapped the speaker.

"Pete?"

"Hey, Dad."

"Thank God. Is Andrea with you?"

"We're both great. I think my cell might be compromised."

"We assumed communications weren't safe. Do you know your location?"

"Yeah, I could go for a Buffalo swim if it were open."

"Ah, gotcha. Nicely done, son. We'll be there ASAP." Andrea looked around, obviously wondering about his coded message.

"Sort of wondered why you haven't found us already," he asked his dad.

"We lost the helicopter soon after takeoff. Took us until about half an hour ago to discover that neither of you was with the last man who escaped to the south."

"Five men. Three in the chopper and two in a vehicle?"

"Correct and all accounted for. Commander Allen wants to talk to his daughter."

"Are you all right, Andrea?" her father asked.

"Yes, sir. Not a scratch."

"That's my girl. Mechanical difficulties?"

"Yes, sir."

"The search team got a late start. We'll steer them to you soon. You're certain you're fine?"

"She's brilliant, sir," Pete answered when he noticed the tears in Andrea's eyes. "We better save the battery, sir. Just in case."

"Certainly." He disconnected.

"He's not much for goodbyes." Andrea used a knuckle to wipe the moisture from her eyes. Pete might get the wrong impression…or the right one. Either way, she could break down later. Think about everything…later.

With the exception that Pete thought she was brilliant.

"This is a pretty good place to wait. If you hear the wrong helicopter again, we can dart down this side of the hill." He nodded behind her. "Closer to the road."

She squinted, noticing the buildings at the bottom of the canyon. There was a well-marked trail zigzagging down. "You mean I was one hill away from civilization?"

"Yeah, but to its credit, it was a large hill." He was still breathing hard from their hike, but smiling.

"We're resting. Sit." They chose one of the smoother rocks and kept their backs to the sun. It was quiet. A gentle wind was the only sound. If whoever was chasing her did understand Pete's description of their location, she'd be able to hear them straightaway.

"So, a diversion? That makes sense."

"Whatever happened this afternoon had to be a profitable enough deal to sacrifice five men and a helicopter. It wasn't rigged for the light show they used to imitate the phenomenon near Marfa. It sounded like this type of Hiller, but this one is bare bones."

"So they have another chopper."

"It's logical to assume so."

"Whoever's behind this discovered who you were and used the opportunity presented to them to their advantage." Pete wiped his brow. "Are you certain you don't have experience being a detective?"

"I had an hour and a half to myself, and deductive reasoning just happens to be my strength."

"So your switching places with Sharon last night was purely coincidental. If I were them, I might assume you work at the observatory. I don't think I'd assume you're the daughter of a director with Homeland Security."

"Sharon. Sharon knew. I talked about it last week. About

how difficult it was for me to convince the university to let me come, since my dad was opposed." She had to move, so she jumped to her feet. "Shoot. I forgot the first rule my dad taught me. He's been paranoid about my mother and me since he joined the DHS. Afraid someone would attempt exactly what they did today."

"Then we can't assume Sharon's switching with you was a coincidence. This might have been the plan all along."

"They couldn't have known I'd say yes. And what about the man in the desert?" She walked a few feet and tugged a long leaf off a bush, nervously tearing the ends off.

"He's an undercover agent who discovers the plan to abduct his commander's daughter. I can think of a lot of reasons he'd risk warning someone. So last night the aliens aren't smuggling drugs across the border, they're searching for an escaped hostage—your dad's undercover man. He's got details they can't let be exposed, but he finds his way to you. They run you off the road and would have abducted you."

"But you came along. They don't know that the agent didn't tell me anything, but they want to make certain."

"Somehow they know he's Homeland Security and send someone in posing as…"

"The phony agent," they said together.

"How would they have known he was DHS? Your dad's man from the desert was pretty beat up. They could have gotten the info from him." Pete stood, shaded his eyes and checked out the terrain behind him. "Then again, it makes more sense that they discovered him if he was trying to warn your dad about the danger you were in."

"If all of this is just coincidence, though… Why is Sharon still missing?"

Not answering said more than trying to soothe her guilty conscience. He thought Sharon was dead. Once they got the necessary information from her, they wouldn't need her any longer. "Do you think they killed Sharon or that she was working with them?"

"I don't believe these men think twice about eliminating anyone who stands in their way."

"I'm sorry one of those people was your deputy. Logan seemed nice."

"I had to cover for him a lot. Now I know why. He was a good kid. I didn't have much else to do. If I hadn't worked all night, I'd be up taking care of ranch chores. I'd rather ride on patrol."

He lifted an eyebrow, smiled and she knew the subject was changing. "Hey, you going to share how you got outside from the maintenance closet?"

She waved her injured wrist. "Let me tell you, it wasn't easy. Good thing I can pull my own weight, injured or not. Once I got into the crawl space and found a way to the roof, I climbed down the steel beams that formed the partial shade over the door. They were at a slant and got me close enough to the ground that I could drop."

"Is that the Commander's chopper?" he asked, facing the south to catch a glimpse. She nodded, and he dusted off his jeans with his good hand. "You're a very competent, capable woman."

"Tell that to my father." She followed him back the way they'd come. There was plenty of room for another chopper to land. "He's going to command me to leave. I doubt he'll hang around long enough to drop you by the hospital."

"I don't blame him."

"I'm not certain I'm leaving." There was too much unfinished business here. "I don't want to run away."

"Of course you should." He stopped, grabbing her upper arms, wincing at the sudden movement of his own injury. "Seven men are dead. You can't just shrug that off. It's dangerous for you here."

"Whatever reason they had to abduct me, it's gone now."

"You don't know that." His grip tightened, but it didn't hurt. It seemed he was fighting to keep her at arm's length. She would have preferred to be pulled next to his chest.

"But you agreed with me."

The chopper was getting closer.

"A good guess doesn't mean we're correct." His good hand cupped her shoulder.

"I know you're right." Then why was the first thought in her head how to ditch her new escort that hadn't even been assigned to her yet? Then find a way back to Pete's place. She didn't even know where Pete's place was. "What if I don't go back with my father?"

"But you agreed—" Pete searched her eyes and she wasn't certain what he saw, but he dropped his hands to his sides. "Come on, Andrea. What would be gained from staying? You have nothing to prove."

She didn't want to stay just for Pete. She barely knew him. But her heart dropped when he started back down the path, leaving her to follow again. "How are you going to catch the men responsible for Logan's death? What about Sharon? You said I was good at this detective stuff."

"Do you really think your father's going to allow you to stay? He was packing you off before the attack. There's no way he's saying yes."

That was true. She'd rarely stood up to her parents. Their advice was usually firm and logical. So there had never been a reason to question them. The exception was when her father had declared she couldn't come to West Texas in person. Perhaps if he'd explained his reasons instead of dictating, seven men wouldn't be dead and a young woman wouldn't still be missing.

"There's one thing that everyone around me keeps forgetting. You can't force me to leave the observatory."

## Chapter Thirteen

There had been many times throughout Pete's teenage years that he'd argued with his dad. During the past six weeks, he'd been holding back because of his dad's heart attack, but he was building up to a doozy of a fight. If he confronted him, he'd been thinking that all hell would break loose.

"They still at it?" Honey asked from her desk.

"I didn't know people could yell that long without a drink or shot of tequila," his dad joked.

Andrea and her father might not have the exact family problems, but they definitely had a lot of words to *share*. If he'd known, he would have taken them to the middle of the desert for this confrontation instead of his dad's old office.

The door flew open and the Commander marched out, eyes front without any acknowledgment as he passed them. Pete had no illusions. That was not the expression of a man who had achieved his goal—which was to get Andrea on the next transport home.

Commander Allen executed a one-eighty to be face-to-face with him. "You should get that wound seen to." His voice was void of inflection yet full of buried emotion.

Or maybe it was just Pete's own anxiety pushing its way onto others. He didn't need the responsibility of an attractive woman in his life or workplace. It was time for decisions.

"She's determined to stay," Allen continued. "And mad as hell at me because she's not."

"Yes, sir. I understand your frustration." She wasn't going to be his responsibility. That was good. Very good. His personal desire didn't amount to anything in this decision.

"I need coffee before round two."

"Does it matter if it's good?" his dad asked.

"I'm used to the worst."

"Around the corner and you'll smell the sludge," his dad directed but walked beside the Commander, who threw back his head laughing at something else his father had said.

Pete could only scratch his head.

"Everyone show up for their shift?" he asked Honey. "When will the Griggs family arrive?" Could he pull off business as usual? Swing by the café for a break without the rest of the town asking what the hell was going on? He needed a minute to take care of his responsibilities. Another minute to think. But where? His best bet for a reprieve was his house.

"Yes, and in about forty-five minutes," Honey answered.

No time to make it to the house and back. He needed a real meal, not just a package of pretzels from the vending machine, before he could face Logan's parents. He glanced up to see Andrea standing in the office doorway and then their dads rounded the corner with smiles on both their faces.

"Pete, would you join me a minute?" Andrea's father asked, gesturing to the office.

Did anyone lower on the totem pole ever tell this man no?

"We've been tracking a high number of gun purchases by a few individuals. We believe something big's in the works, that the cartel is tired of receiving their guns one or two at a time. Homeland likes your distraction theory, Pete," Commander Allen stated once the door was closed.

Pete kept his hands tucked in his armpits and his mouth shut. Andrea had let her father believe he had thought up the distraction angle. He was sure they both sort of followed that trail together.

"We checked out some satellite pictures and discovered a large number of trucks crossing the border at Presidio into Manuel Ojinaga. You were right. They wanted us focused on the attempted abduction instead of the payment delivery for a major drug deal. I think it's time I brought you onto the team, Sheriff."

There wasn't any doubt which sheriff their visitor from Homeland Security was directing his comment to. Pete caught himself swallowing hard, nervous. He knew his job and his county and didn't have anything to feel nervous about. Nothing except losing everything if DHS checked into his background.

Pete understood the sideways glance from his father. A look that said keep your mouth shut and let me do the talking.

Easy for his dad, who had kept his mouth shut for over twenty-six years. He'd kept a secret that could potentially destroy them both. Andrea sat in his father's chair, head down, not making eye contact.

"I'm setting up a task force and I need you to be a part of it."

Pete snapped his attention back to the Commander. "You need me. Why?"

"You're familiar with the area and think on your feet. We need some of that and someone to coordinate with the other county sheriffs or local police."

"Thank you, sir, but I have to pass. My plate's about as full as it can get right now." He ignored his dad's attempt to get his attention. "I have work to do. I'm actually in charge of a few things around here and need to get ready for Logan's family. Excuse me."

The two older men parted, and he passed between them.

"Maybe I should explain?" Andrea asked behind him.

"No, this one's my responsibility," his dad said. "Wait here a minute, will ya?" He followed him out the door. "Son, this is a great op—"

Pete bit down hard—teeth on teeth. He knew where the conversation was headed and didn't want to have it publicly, so he pushed through to the locker room. His dad caught the employee only door before it slammed in his face. Pete verified no one was there so they could talk freely. "You're really for me joining a Homeland task force?"

"Of course I am. It's a big step for you."

"It's a family power struggle. She wants to stay, he wants her to go. The last thing I need is to be around any of that mess." He lowered his voice. "Especially involved with the daughter of one of the top dogs in Homeland Security."

"She's leaving with her father. Besides, no one's going to uncover who you really are. You don't need to think of that right now."

"Hell, Dad, it's all I ever think about since you dropped this bomb on me."

"Keeping your identity a secret is for your own safety."

He dropped his hands onto his dad's shoulders. The muscle under his fingertips was less solid than two months ago. A lot less solid than two years ago. He shook his head. He wasn't a crying man—neither one of them was. But the only man he'd ever called family stared at him with his brown eyes about to overflow.

"I love you, you old coot. But I already know who I am and who my biological father was. I've just been waiting for you to tell me why it all happened."

"How did you find out?"

"I'm the sheriff. At least that's what you all are telling

me. It didn't take much investigating to discover where I came from twenty-six years ago or the identity of the man I assume was my biological father."

"We'll talk about that at a more appropriate time. Right now Commander Allen needs your help." Pride or excitement or envy weaved its way into his father's words. Maybe because of the times their department had been overlooked for opportunities like this one.

Would his dad be let down to know that it was Andrea's idea and had nothing to do with the Commander's need for help?

"What happens if he decides to run a background check on me? What then? How much trouble are you going to be in? You're right. This isn't the place to talk about forging our relationship with the Department of Homeland Security or why that's impossible. The best thing is to bow out and assist where needed."

His dad's face grew older under the fluorescent lights. "I know you have a lot of questions, but you're right. This is a talk more appropriate for home. I do wish you'd reconsider working on the task force."

"Not a chance. It's just a disaster waiting to happen."

"It can't be all bad, son." His dad winked. "I've seen the way his daughter looks at you."

"You haven't seen anything. And it'll never happen. It might have been fun while she was here, but I have no future. A woman like that needs a future." He couldn't risk the complications of becoming involved with the daughter of such a powerful man.

"What are you talking about? You have job security here. You're running unopposed."

"Let's drop it." Now wasn't the time to tell his dad he hadn't submitted the election paperwork to run for sheriff. He hadn't decided—yet—if he would. But he could set him straight on one thing. "I'm not getting involved with anyone, especially Andrea Allen. My babysitting days are long behind me."

OUCH. ANDREA WAS careful not to allow the door to slam, hearing a gentle clicking noise as it closed. She'd completely misread their friendship. Following him to apologize, ready to abide by her father's wishes and leave Marfa, she hadn't meant to eavesdrop, especially on a father-and-son chat that seemed very private. But now she was glad she'd overheard Pete say he wasn't getting involved with anyone...especially her.

Now she was having second or third or fourth thoughts. She'd lost track of how many times she'd changed her mind about staying here. It was as if her decision-making ability had evaporated with one look at Pete's dimples.

Pete's earlier look of disappointment had deflated her desire to be around him. She'd thought staying in the area worked to everyone's advantage. Before the shooting at the observatory, she thought she'd keep her promise to her father and get her dissertation finished and maybe allow a few distractions with the sheriff.

Not anymore. Not now that she knew those men were willing to kill anyone. And not now that she knew how Pete really felt.

It could be all business for her and not matter who stood guard outside the telescope. No. She was acting like a scorned lover. Staying meant putting more people at risk and she couldn't do that. She'd have to find another way to obtain telescope time.

It wouldn't be the end of everything if she finished up the thesis in Austin. But she could be disappointed for not being able to finish here. She couldn't stay. It would be horribly selfish. She hit the employees only door as she pushed it open again, catching Pete with a hand on the other side and a surprised look on his face.

"You aren't going to talk me into joining his task force," Pete said to his father, then turning to Andrea, "and neither are you."

"I came to apologize before leaving Marfa. But now…"

"Nothing to apologize for. Excuse me."

"Man, you really are something." She blocked the door. Pete could have moved her easily but seemed reluctant to.

"Can you leave us alone a minute, Dad?"

The retiring sheriff squeezed past. Pete clasped hands with her, gently pulling her to where the door could shut with a loud bang. She shook his hand free as quickly as she could.

"You don't need to be talked into anything." She knew what calls her father would make as soon as they all left the office. "The people who sign your paychecks are already being contacted. You no longer have a choice."

"Why is this so important to you?"

"Not me. I don't force myself on anyone. My dad's limiting the number of people who know about the incident. You're already a part of his small circle. It's logical—therefore, it'll happen."

"As much as I hate that logic, I understand it."

"Oh, and don't worry about having to be around me. You know you can assign anyone you want as my *babysitter*. It doesn't matter to me." Telling him she'd changed her mind and wouldn't be heading back was on the tip of her tongue. "I really don't understand why you're so reluctant to help the Commander. This is an amazing opportunity that could take you places. After this is over you could name your assignment."

"I'll make sure Commander Allen gets the help he needs. And who says I want to leave Marfa? That's a lot of presuming you're doing after knowing me for such a short time. I actually like it here."

He smiled, and her heart melted a little. He was delightful when he wanted to be, but right now was obviously not one of those times.

"You should use that wicked charm of yours more often, especially with strangers. I bet your father and the rest of the community who raised you gave in every time you smiled. Is that why you're so spoiled?"

"Me? You think *I'm* spoiled?" His deep voice rose a couple of octaves with that accusation. "Where do you get off calling anyone spoiled? Have you taken a look at the way you have your father wrapped around your pinkie finger? Never mind, I don't care to know the answer. It's not worth it."

"Man, do you have that wrong. I don't call him the Commander because of his rank."

Andrea didn't really think Pete was spoiled. She was hurt from his private remarks to his father and she was striking out. She wanted to apologize, take it back, tell him she didn't mean it. But she couldn't. She'd thought he'd liked her and the wound was too fresh.

Later. She'd apologize later. She'd calm down while looking into deep space or on the plane back to Austin. She was still uncertain which route was in her future.

"If you'll excuse me, I need to get in touch with the observatory. I've already confirmed that my telescope will be ready at seven-thirty and need to make arrangements." Arrangements for the information and her things to be sent to her, but she wouldn't admit that to him. She reached for the door. His arm stopped her. She spun to face him, landing against his chest, looking straight at that dimpled chin.

"You aren't going anywhere on your own. You can wait in the office while I make the arrangements."

"Fine."

"Okay."

Earlier today, being this close would have ended in some serious kissing. The disappointment she was experiencing that it was no longer a possibility froze her in place. She focused her stare at his chin, unable to meet his eyes.

His hands were snug around her waist and she was ready to forgive him and explain her harsh words. Ready for those kisses to take over and there not be a need for any explanations from either of them. Then he gently moved her to the side.

If she had looked at him, she might have known that he was trying to open the door. By the time she figured it out, she added embarrassment to the long list of emotions she was scrolling through.

"You stick with me or your dad until I find a deputy to escort you. Or you can wait in a locked office."

Without uttering a word, she veered left, choosing to stand near Reception instead of sitting in the chair waiting on her father to finish his calls. Pete went about his business, giving instructions, signing some papers…man-in-charge stuff. When he was done, the mayor or someone equivalent called to speak to him. He looked at the glass front doors and told Peach—the sisters had switched positions—to take a message.

A couple entered the front. The man's face looked confused and the woman cried into an old-fashioned handkerchief. Peach pointed to Pete without a word. He tapped on the open office door and brought a third chair inside.

"Sorry, Commander Allen, but I need this room for a bit."

Her father glanced at the couple and left, walking to a corner, placing another phone call on his cell while she watched Pete hug each of them before they sat.

"Logan's parents. They wanted to talk to Pete about what happened," Peach said softly next to her.

"I wish I'd known him better."

"He was a nice young man. They're still searching for the student he was on a date with," Peach stated, then answered the phone.

Andrea's guilt was growing. She'd been so caught up in her own world she hadn't thought about Sharon or that her body hadn't been found. Had she been abducted or murdered and her body dumped in a remote spot? They might never know, but she had to find out.

## Chapter Fourteen

"Is there another office my father could use, Peach?"

"Sure." She pulled open a drawer and handed Andrea a key. "Through the back hallway next to Pete's office, then second door on the right."

Andrea tugged gently on her father's sleeve, and he followed, arguing with someone else for a change. She sat in a straight-back chair and let him take a seat behind the desk, waiting for him to finish the call.

"I'm staying. I was going to return with you, until I saw Logan's parents. I meant what I said. I think you should come up with a plan and let me help find Sharon or whoever abducted or murdered her. Will you let me do this and include me?"

The office was empty except for the desk and chairs. No pictures of Pete on the wall to distract her.

"Why do you think you're qualified to help?"

"I don't, but those men were after me for some reason today. They might be again."

"Therein lies the problem. You aren't safe here," the Commander stated firmly. His men never argued with that tone, but it always brought out the rebellious teenager in her.

"I don't want you to be disappointed with me again."

"Why do you think I would be?"

"I thought… Well, you and Mom argued so vehemently

## OFFICIAL OPINION POLL

Dear Reader,

Since you are a book enthusiast, we would like to know what you think.

Inside you will find a short Opinion Poll. Please participate in our poll by sharing your opinion on 3 subjects that are very important to all of us.

To thank you for your participation, we would like to send you **2 FREE BOOKS** and **2 FREE GIFTS**!

Please enjoy them with our compliments.

Sincerely,

*Pam Powers*

# For Your Reading Pleasure...

Get 2 FREE BOOKS from the series
you are currently enjoying!

Free

# YOUR OPINION POLL
## THANK-YOU FREE GIFTS INCLUDE:

▶ **2 FREE BOOKS**

▶ **2 LOVELY SURPRISE GIFTS**

▼ DETACH AND MAIL CARD TODAY! ▼

## OFFICIAL OPINION POLL

**YOUR OPINION COUNTS!**
Please check TRUE or FALSE below to express your opinion about the following statements:

**Q1** Do you believe in "true love"?

*"TRUE LOVE HAPPENS ONLY ONCE IN A LIFETIME."*
○ TRUE
○ FALSE

**Q2** Do you think marriage has any value in today's world?

*"YOU CAN BE TOTALLY COMMITTED TO SOMEONE WITHOUT BEING MARRIED."*
○ TRUE
○ FALSE

**Q3** What kind of books do you enjoy?

*"A GREAT NOVEL MUST HAVE A HAPPY ENDING."*
○ TRUE
○ FALSE

**YES!** I have placed my sticker in the space provided below. Please send me the **2 FREE** books and 2 FREE gifts for which I qualify. I understand that I am under no obligation to purchase anything further, as explained on the back of this card.

❑ I prefer the regular-print edition
182/382 HDL GGDL

❑ I prefer the larger-print edition
199/399 HDL GGDL

FIRST NAME

LAST NAME

ADDRESS

APT.#

CITY

STATE/PROV.

ZIP/POSTAL CODE

against my coming out here." She looked at the secrets he hid beneath the stoic naval-commander expression. "Oh my gosh. You couldn't tell me the real reason you didn't want me to come."

"No, I couldn't. I'm not supposed to speak about it now. I had a man undercover and I knew how explosive this region is. I didn't want you in danger."

"I have to do this, Dad."

He reluctantly nodded. "My boss is twisting my arm to get you to cooperate. They want to use you for bait."

"It's not very appealing or noble when you put it like that."

He stood and pulled her to her feet. "Andrea, this is serious. You aren't trained to be an operative, and any number of things can go wrong. Probably will go wrong. We've already lost a very experienced agent."

"I know, Dad. I just don't think I could live with myself if I walked away. Could you?"

He shook his head. She liked it when Commander Allen left the room and he was her father again. "Whoever's arranging for this gun shipment to Mexico has to be high up in the cartel."

"I wish you'd reconsider." Her father's voice dropped so soft she could barely hear.

"You let me think you were the overprotective commander to try to keep me from coming. You've got to remember that I'm your daughter. I need to do this. The entire time I was growing up I heard you say how important it was to finish what you started, to be a part of a team and not leave anyone behind. How can you ask me to walk away from all three of the most important things to you?" She wanted to hug him, but they really didn't hug a lot in her family.

"The most important thing to me is keeping the two women I love the most safe from harm. What kind of father would deliberately let his daughter be abducted by drug dealers?"

"One who understands how much this means to me. I can make a difference. Please let me help."

He gave a reluctant nod. "For you. Not for the men twisting my arm. I do understand about not leaving a man behind. Responsibility can sometimes weigh you down. I should have a team with you every moment—that's what your mother would want—but we're shorthanded as it is. Would you consider a professional bodyguard…would you allow—I see by your expression that's not a possibility, either."

"You know a military detail or bodyguard won't allow these men to feel comfortable enough to act. I'll finish the study at the observatory. I promise I won't leave until you're ready for me to draw out these murderers again. I'll call as often as you need me to. I don't want to be a burden…"

"But that's not the most important reason you want to stay." He finally had his dad face on, the one she could relate to, the person she loved so much because he understood her. "You sure?"

"It's more than the study or potentially helping catch the murderers. Sharon's still missing. What if she was abducted because they thought she was me? That's on my head. Oh, don't you give me that look that it's your fault. No. You've warned me for years to be aware and on my toes, one step ahead of anything like this. I let my guard down, Dad. I feel so selfish—"

"It's okay, Andrea. This isn't anyone's fault except the men with no thought to human life. I completely understand why you need to stay here. I'll explain everything to your mother. But we do this my way. When my team is ready. Make everyone believe you're here only to finish your thesis. No one knows the truth except my liaison."

She remembered Pete's arm around Mrs. Griggs, wondering who the liaison would be. If not Pete, then she'd be forced to act like a selfish, spoiled woman with no thought for anyone else other than herself, lying to Pete.

"My men said the Hiller was a piece of trash. That was some nice flying this afternoon. Reminds me of our Sunday afternoon flights. That was a lot of years ago."

"Yes, sir. I miss them."

"We'll have to do it again sometime soon." He squeezed her hand. The closest thing to a hug she'd ever get in public.

"It's a date."

"For the record, I'm damn proud of you, Andrea. Very proud. And regarding the attempted abduction, you touched on several points that had already been considered by my team. They believe they're going to try again as another distraction. I'll be couriering a pair of earrings to you. Wear them at all times and I'll be able to find you."

They walked from the spare office and witnessed Logan's parents leaving.

"You don't have to do this." Her father spoke quietly, hope apparent in his voice. "You don't owe anyone anything."

"Yes, I do. For them, for Sharon and especially for me."

"Only one person will know the real reason you're staying. He'll be fully briefed and ready to move without my permission. You and I both will have to trust him with your life. I'll assign him to be in charge of your protection detail, but you can't tell him why you're really staying here. You can't tell anyone."

"I want Pete to be in charge."

"He's already declined my offer."

"I know that won't stop you. It would look more realistic for the sheriff to be in charge."

"I should lock you up and throw away the key."

She nodded and her father left her standing at the edge of the office. More like on the edge of reality. She couldn't believe she'd insisted on putting her life on the line. Something these men and women did daily.

Homeland Security. Texas Rangers. Drug Enforcement Administration. Presidio County Sheriff's Department. Pete would be another valued member of their new task force. But her role? She was the bait. She felt every bit exposed as if she were dangling midair on a small hook, holding on for dear life but her fingers were slipping.

Andrea was determined to stay, determined to help find Sharon, determined to put the creep behind all this confusion in jail. And like it or not, she was determined to find out why Sheriff Pete Morrison had no future.

It was a shame that to accomplish her goal she had to let him think her a selfish human being.

"I NEED TO speak with you, Sheriff Morrison," Commander Allen commanded, but remained outside the office.

No choice. He'd already received a phone call from the mayor ordering him to help in any capacity. He was sunk, but at least Andrea would be returning with her father and remain safe.

"Did they find your hat?" she asked out of the blue.

He was certain she had a look of mischief, just a slight tilt to those luscious lips and a twinkle in her eyes.

"I didn't check, but someone brought back the Tahoe. I imagine it'll turn up."

"This picture is great." She pointed to one his dad had caught of him shoving his hat on his head. "It'd be a shame to lose that hat."

"Andrea—"

"Were you on duty?"

"What? Oh, in the picture? No. I'd just been pitched from a bucking bronc at a local rodeo. Can you wait with Peach till I can get a protection detail together to take you back to the observatory?"

"I don't mind at all. The Commander actually threatened to arrest me to get me home. Fortunately, we came up with another arrangement. I want to help find Sharon. To do that, I had to concede to his terms. And if you're in here, that means he's given in to mine."

"What terms?"

"I hope you can forgive me, Pete. It really is the only way, but I'm not picking up my things and running home."

He was afraid to ask, and for some idiotic reason he felt like he'd been waylaid. He crossed his arms over his chest and backed to the door, wishing he had his hat brim to hide behind. "What terms?"

"I'm trusting you with my daughter's life," the Commander said through the doorway.

Why would her father state that she was leaving only to give in to Andrea's demands moments later? A quick glance at the enthusiasm on his dad's face, then a sharp stare at the woman who couldn't meet his eyes. A sliver of secretiveness was still there no matter how much she tried to hide it. And no matter how good an opportunity this sounded, Pete didn't think he would like working for her father.

She still hadn't answered his question. "One more time, Andrea. What terms?"

Victory was displayed in her smile as she finally met his eyes. "I'm staying as long as you're my personal escort and that you agree I'll stay at your ranch when not at the observatory."

"You mean, glorified babysitter." He turned to Commander Allen. "You said she was leaving."

"She was—now she's not. She agreed to stay put at the observatory and in your home."

Not only was he responsible for her every move miles away in another county, but she was supposed to bunk at their ranch? Live with him?

"You're willing to bring me onto your team so you can

order me to play bodyguard for your daughter? Seems like you could have just asked me to assign her a protection detail."

"I'm a bit surprised by Andrea's change of heart, but I assure you there's much more involved than protecting my daughter." Another couple entered the sheriff's office. "Looks like my state liaison is here. Please escort my daughter to the conference room, Sheriff. You're both needed for the briefing."

Pete recognized the Texas Ranger entering his building and directed to the office. The woman next to him looked completely out of place. With an expensive suit and heels that belonged on a television show—completely ridiculous and useless for West Texas.

"Commander Allen? Cord McCrea, Texas Rangers. Nice to meet you in person. Good to see you, Pete." He turned to the woman next to him. "This is Special Agent Beth Conrad, Drug Enforcement Administration."

"We've got the upstairs briefing room cleared out and ready to go."

Everyone turned toward the stairs, with the exception of the woman in high-end heels. "Where's the elevator, please?"

"I'll show you the way," his father said, draping her arm over his.

When everyone except Andrea had left, he asked, "Why?"

She shrugged and averted her eyes. "I need to finish my thesis. If you're too busy for this opportunity I'm dropping in your lap, you can always ask your father to take on the job."

"That's not the reason I said no. You aren't safe here."

His new charge was hiding something and he had a really bad feeling he knew what it was.

## Chapter Fifteen

Andrea followed the others upstairs to a vacant briefing room since Joe's old office was no longer big enough. Each person grabbed a chair and made introductions. Pete crossed his arms and leaned against the wall instead of taking the empty seat next to her.

The Commander was back in full force and sitting at the head of the table, definitely in charge. "I'm keeping this task force small for a reason. I would prefer we stay under the radar and not let our enemy know we're searching for him."

They all glanced in her direction, except Pete. "I'm not going to blab about it."

"We know. At approximately 2200 hours Friday evening, a severely beaten man came from the desert and—"

"If I may, Commander." Pete pulled his notebook from his back pocket. "McCrea and I are pretty familiar with this area. It might help to hear a detailed account of events."

"Then we're all up to speed. Sounds good," McCrea said.

The woman from the DEA compressed her lips and took out an electronic notepad.

"Andrea Allen was at the Viewing Area on Highway 90. People stop and watch for the lights to appear this direction—" he pointed to a spot on the map hanging behind him "—southwest toward the Chinati Mountains. A trucker reported seeing the lights at 2204. Andrea returned to her vehicle searching for a camera."

The camera. What had happened to it? She needed to ask her father, or maybe Joe would know. Pete recited the details of their adventure. She rubbed her wrist, which was still sore from all the climbing she'd done to escape that supply closet. She couldn't remember how she'd kept her wits to find her way out of the building. His mention of how she'd escaped got her a nod from both the Ranger and the DEA agent.

"Which brings us back to Commander Allen," Pete concluded. He remained standing and didn't look at her.

"The man who had been beaten was Lyle Moreland. He was one of mine. Trained to fly just about anything. McCrea had given us a tip that a new gang could be using helicopters to move drugs. We know that this has been done before, but whoever's in charge of this new group is smart and, unfortunately, patient."

"Did you know about this, Dad?" Pete asked.

"Not until I went to the car accident and met the Homeland crew."

"While you were there, did anyone find the observatory's video camera?" she asked quietly.

"Did you manage to record part of the altercation or anything Moreland might have said?" the DEA agent asked from across the table.

"I remember turning it on. Then he was there and unconscious."

"I didn't see it," Pete answered. Their fathers shook their heads.

"Perhaps that's why they believe Miss Allen knows something of importance," Agent Conrad surmised.

Andrea had just come to that same conclusion while waiting for a break to ask about the camera. The statement carried more weight with a real agent stating it as a possibility. Andrea knew how these things worked. It was like dealing with four "commanders." Only four because Joe watched them all chat, too.

Pete wanted answers as to why his department hadn't been included. The Ranger said, "Need-to-know basis." Pete seemed to keep his cool but didn't let the conversation end.

She quietly scooted her chair from the table. If she could get out of the room, she wouldn't have to lie about her real reason for staying in the area. She made it to the hallway without anyone asking her to take her seat again.

"Need a cup of coffee?"

"Oh, Joe. You scared me. Yes, I'd love a cup."

"I'm thinking you haven't had anything to eat. Want a bite, too?"

"No, thank you. I better hang around for my dad and I need to find a ride to the observatory."

"Pete's taking care of that."

"But—"

"No need to argue. He's already made up his mind. Tahoe's gassed and sitting out front." He waved his hand and started walking away but turned around, waving her closer to him and farther from the door. "There's a solid reason he believes he can't get involved with anyone. You should ask him. He might even tell ya."

Joe dropped this statement into her lap and headed down the stairs.

How did the man know that she'd overheard any portion of their conversation? It didn't really matter. Any connection with Pete would be based on the lies she promised to tell. After all this was over, he'd find out the truth and really have no reason to become involved with her. No matter how determined she'd been an hour ago, his reasons were none of her business. Period.

PETE NOTICED THE moment Andrea had crept out of the conference room. He wanted to stop the discussion, to follow her, but his dad had given him a thumbs-up and taken that job on himself.

Half an hour later she was still on a bench in the hallway. She might even be asleep.

"So we're agreed on a plan?" Commander Allen flattened his palms on the table, ready to push up out of the chair.

"Yes," everyone confirmed. Pete nodded his agreement.

He would funnel information to the Commander and the DEA through McCrea—who also had an informant in Presidio on the border. And as he'd been warned earlier, he'd been assigned the duty of keeping the witness safe. Although he'd never promised that he'd be with Andrea 24/7, he had agreed to provide her with a protection detail.

Beginning with him.

It was going to be a long night.

"Wondering if you should wake her?" her father asked from just behind him. He placed a hand on Pete's shoulder. "The answer would be yes. Back to that dang observatory and searching the stars for who knows what. Her mother can't understand her passion but I do. I was in the program at NASA for several years while she was growing up."

"You wanted to be an astronaut?"

"Damn right. Didn't you?"

"Afraid I wasn't at the top of my class." Close enough, but studying had never been his thing. "Are you staying the night, sir?"

"I did everything right, still didn't make it to space." Regret passed quickly over his face. "I'm confident that you've got this under control."

"You mean McCrea."

"I know who I meant." He patted his shoulder in a

fatherly fashion and passed through to the hallway. "Andrea, time to get a move on."

"You leaving?" she said midyawn.

Pete went downstairs, collected messages and checked out an extra shotgun. He secured everything in the Tahoe, including the fast food Peach had ordered during the meeting. A government vehicle pulled up next to him. The driver was on his phone and stayed behind the wheel.

"Thanks for the eats."

"I told Brandie to double your usual and put it on your tab. You know, one of these days you're going to have to learn how to cook."

"Peach, you know dang well I haven't been home since Thursday. When would I have had time to cook?"

"I'll let my book club know you're ready for some casseroles. Looks like you're going to need them with company at your house."

"Lord save me from a death by casseroles." *And a frustrating woman living in the guest room.* He put his hands together in prayer just in time for Andrea and her father to enter the hallway.

The Commander shook Pete's hand, then took his daughter's between his own before saying good-night and leaving.

Andrea turned to Pete. "Well, what now, Sheriff? Where's the escort?"

"You sure about this? I could catch your father before he pulls away. You were ready to leave with him this morning. I'm not certain I understand what's changed."

"Do you have a ride for me or not?"

"Right this way."

Five minutes down the road, he thought she'd given up the battle to stay awake again. Catching a nap before she worked all night seemed to be a good idea. He reached in his bag and pulled out a hamburger.

"That smells absolutely delicious."

"There's one for you."

He heard the bag rustle.

"Oh, my goodness. That's awesome. Thanks for thinking about me."

"Peach took care of it."

"Okay. Be sure and thank her for me," she said with her mouth full.

"I'll need to know your routine when we get there. And I need your word you won't vary from it."

"I promise. No playing, no hikes, no exception. Just straight to and from the telescope."

"I'm in charge of scheduling your escorts and protection. No one has authorization to make changes and I won't send a message via anyone else to do so. Not even my father. Is that clear? If you don't hear it from me, you can assume the message is bogus."

"That works."

Her tone was short and abrupt. She acted mad at him, but for what? She'd actually called *him* spoiled when she was the one using her father's position, demanding to stay to finish her research. But what did he know? They'd kissed a few times. He didn't know anything about her.

There hadn't been time for much else. And there wouldn't be. He hadn't just been spouting words that she deserved a man with a future to his dad to shut him up. Without his job, he'd work their ranch with the few cattle they currently had. They couldn't keep the place up just on his dad's retirement. Hiring out as a ranch hand was his best option to help make ends meet.

But right now he had a job to do. Get Andrea to the observatory and ensure her safety until she left next week. He could do that and do it well. She didn't have to like him.

"What's so important about watching a star?" he asked. His curiosity had gotten the better of him. "What made you change your mind about leaving?"

"I'm working with a University of Texas astronomer who verified the most distant galaxy in the universe using several telescopes. For me this study is more about securing time with the actual telescope than studying the stars. If I finish my thesis and publish, I'll have a good chance of obtaining a position with one of the best telescopes in the world."

"This is about a job you may or may not get?"

"The Chilean Giant Magellan Telescope will begin construction soon and will have nearly five times the light-gathering power of the best infrared in the world. We'll see more distant galaxies and watch stars being formed. Someday I'd love to get on a team studying reionization."

Under different circumstances he'd appreciate the enthusiasm in her voice, the excitement displayed through her hands as she spoke of something she truly loved. Another time he'd ask her what all that meant. At the moment, he was confused.

"You're willing to risk your life, not to mention the men on your protection detail, for a potential job? And you called me selfish." *You're an idiot, Morrison!* He could keep his distance without insulting her.

"You asked about my work. I...um...understand that Logan is dead and Sharon is still missing. I can't change any of that."

"*You* could be missing. Do you understand that?"

"Yes, I do," she admitted quietly.

Then it hit him. "Son of a gun, your father stated three separate times that you were a witness and not an active member of the task force. You're both lying. Aren't you?"

"I'm staying at the observatory to finish my study."

"And hoping that those maniacs will try to get to you again. Dammit." He hit the steering wheel hard enough to make his palm sting. "This is a stupid plan. I can't stand guard twenty-four hours a day."

"You aren't supposed to. They won't make a move if you're too close."

There it was, the admission. He was right and she was staying behind to draw the murderers out.

He jerked the car to the side of the road as soon as there was room to safely do so. "We're going back. Or I'm taking you to Alpine to catch the first flight to Austin. You can't go through with this. You have no idea what you're doing."

"You'd be surprised, but it doesn't matter. You don't have a say in the decision."

"Andrea," he beseeched, hoping her name and his tone could say more than the words that wouldn't form into sentences.

The closeness between them was strained. She'd pulled away after spending time with her dad. He knew why he had distanced himself, but why had she changed?

The soft gleam from the dashboard lights gave her a glow like one from a full moon. Perfect for someone who worked with the stars. He wanted to take her in his arms. Their attraction had them both leaning toward each other, until bright headlights interrupted and they both pulled back.

"I appreciate your concern, but I have to do this." She retreated as far as possible, wrapping her arms around herself like she was freezing to death. "This was my idea, Pete. But the Commander's superiors agree. Please believe me. Even my father's respecting my decision."

The nonstop nervous chatter he'd grown accustomed to had disappeared. This woman seemed completely in control. He faced forward, ready to continue to the observatory, wanting to know why it was so important to her yet holding back.

"You're right. It's not my call." Easing the vehicle back onto the empty road, he wanted to ask but couldn't allow himself to get closer to her. "Aw, hell, mind sharing why your dad insisted you weren't involved? Or why he wants the very task force he formed out of the loop?"

"It's better this way. Less chance of word getting out that it's a trap."

"I see. He said a couple of times that he didn't think you'd be part of the equation again. So no one's supposed to know except Cord. He knows, right?"

"Yes. Please don't think badly about my dad. He understands why I need to stay. Sharon's still missing, and if there's the slimmest chance…"

"I need to assign you a larger protection detail."

"No. Please, Pete." She leaned toward him. Close enough for him to see the strain on her face. "I have to do this."

"Not at the expense of losing your life."

"Again, it's not your call. If you refuse to help, then you're not part of the loop. You can step away, and we'll get the Jeff Davis County sheriff to help."

"Over my dead body you will."

"Nothing that extreme, please. Like I told my dad, I promise I won't make any detours. Straight to work. Straight back to your ranch. I won't ditch my guard or anything like that. But if there's a chance that Sharon's alive and they still think I have some information, I need to be here to help."

"I admire your determination and courage, even if I think you're insane for volunteering to do this."

"Thanks, I think."

He'd already planned to handpick her protection detail from both counties. He'd already spoken with his father about driving her and made arrangements for the house to be cleaned. It would be a pain driving her back and forth, but he didn't care.

Nothing would happen to Andrea on his watch. They might not have a future together, but she definitely had places to go and stars to discover.

## Chapter Sixteen

The operation had lost one helicopter and five men. Patrice would be upset. More accurately, her employer would be angry. Indeed, she was due here any moment. He uncorked her favorite California wine to let it breathe.

Homeland Security's spy had stolen from him and had the power to bring down more than what Patrice had lost. He was certain Andrea Allen had been given information at her car in the desert—whether she knew it or not.

Tomas had been too inquisitive. His intelligence should have given him away immediately as an undercover agent. But to his credit, he'd kept himself in the background operations for months. Unfortunately, their methods hadn't been able to obtain how he was making contact with DHS to pass any information back to his superiors.

If they hadn't learned of Miss Allen's importance, they might never have ferreted out the spy. He still wanted the young woman. Having her in his control was key to the next phase of operations.

It had been highly improbable Patrice's men would succeed in the abduction but well worth the try. The benefits far outweighed the losses. He heard the front door open.

"Miss Orlando, please come in."

"I told you it wouldn't work, Mr. Rook." She dropped her purse on the floor and stripped off her jacket, tossing it haphazardly across a brocade chair. She saw the wine, tilted some into a glass and gulped the fine red elixir too fast.

"Yes, you did." He bit his tongue to remain pleasant. "But I also informed you that it didn't matter to me what the cost was to you. The trucks made it into Manuel Ojinaga and we're on schedule."

"I'll need compensation for the men I've lost. Replacing them will cost me a bundle. I don't want to dip into my reserve, drawing attention to myself."

"Naturally. These men will be worth the higher price. Unless you'd like to reconsider?"

His fingers caught her exposed throat as she tossed back the last of the wine in the glass. She choked—partly on the wine, partly from the pressure of his grasp. The fragile handblown wineglass shattered on the floor. He should have waited until she'd set it on the table. Her fingers curled around his own, attempting to pry them away from her skin.

As her oxygen waned, her eyes grew enormous as she realized he controlled whether she lived or died. He saw the acknowledgment in her face, in the desperation of her clawing hands and kicking feet. Her dress rose to show the tops of her stockings.

Had she worn them for him today? Sex with her might be a satisfying distraction while he waited. He released his grip, immediately turning his back to give her a moment to recover.

As he was concentrating on board three, his next move presented itself. "Aw, thank you, Patrice. Nc6 is a very nice move."

She coughed and sputtered behind him, then began tugging on her dress. Yes, it was time to remind her who was in control. He gathered her things and offered his hand to help her stand.

"I'm in the mood to postpone the doldrums of business for a while. How about you?"

The fright in her eyes spurred his movements. He controlled himself, restraining from pulling her along. He glanced at the six boards, committing the pieces to memory. Ready to be inspired while Patrice was at his fingertips.

He opened the door, waving off his assistant. "Delay dinner an hour. Oh, wait, Mr. Oscuro."

Patrice's stylish dress had a visible zipper down the back. He'd noticed straightaway that she was also braless underneath. It had been a long while since he'd reminded her where her place was. He jerked her to a halt in the hallway, tugged the zipper and waited to see if she'd let the dress fall.

A small gasp of surprise was her only protest, and he'd let her have it. She dropped her arms to her sides and the dress amassed around her ankles with a gentle tug over her hips. He offered his hand again to help her step over the sleek red pile. She took it. The bruises on her shoulder and neck visible against her flawless skin.

"Marvelous. Simply marvelous. That's all, Oscuro."

He nodded to the near-naked woman. She brought a smile to his lips like no other could. But she needed to know he'd sacrifice her faster than a knight's pawn if she defied him or took his courtesy for granted.

## Chapter Seventeen

*There's a solid reason he believes he can't get involved with anyone. You should ask him.*

Andrea tried to work on entering new information into her database. She'd managed to eke out a couple of sentences on her dissertation during the past two hours. Useless. Her mind kept coming back to Joe's statement and wondering why he couldn't just tell her what the reason was himself.

"This is hopeless." She shut the laptop lid and rubbed her aching eyes. All her things had been moved to the Morrison ranch house, but she still had her assigned room at the dormitory where she could work. She'd come early today, hoping to get caught up without any distractions.

Distractions like Pete sleeping in the next room or working horses in the late afternoon. Yesterday from her window she'd seen him thrown from a horse. She'd wanted to run to him to make sure he was okay. Willpower hadn't stopped her. She'd been frozen to the windowsill watching him take off his shirt to shake out the dirt.

So she'd come to the observatory early in order to avoid those type of incidents today.

Studying, applying herself or stringing words together for a paper had never been a problem…until now. She'd never had trouble sleeping at odd hours before. You got used to that when you studied the stars. Who was she kidding? Sleep deprivation had nothing to do with it. Every thought centered on Pete and the cryptic advice his father had given her.

Just concentrate.

Three nights watching the farthest regions of the galaxy and she couldn't type up her notes. Learning the nuances of the 9.2 meter mirror on the telescope hadn't relieved her or excited her the way it usually did. And if she did manage to keep on track for a few minutes, the next person entering the room would ask her about the shooting or share how she and Pete had escaped. Or they'd tell her what they were doing during the shooting. She'd either commend them or apologize to them.

During the day, construction crews were down the hill at the Visitor Center repairing windows and bullet holes. The shattered glass had been swept up and thrown away. Pete's dad had tried to capture her would-be abductors alive, but they'd all chosen to fight to the death. One had escaped into the woods and been tracked for several hours until he also stepped in front of a bullet.

The manhunt was the reason authorities had delayed searching for them after she'd landed the Hiller chopper in the middle of nowhere. It was ridiculously hard not to think about the incident. Much harder not to think about Pete.

Her hands smoothed the laptop. Was she ready to open it and get serious? *No.* She wanted to stop thinking of Pete. Andrea stepped out of the main room of the dormitory.

"Hi, Bill. Need anything?" She spoke to the guards throughout each day, making a point to learn the names of the men who accepted the risk of protecting her.

Pete had warned the deputies not to take the assignment for granted. Joe reminded them each morning when dropping her off at the ranch about potential attacks. He stressed the danger without disclosing specifics about the task force or possible trap they could be setting.

"No, thanks, Andrea," Bill answered, tipping his hat and resuming his watch.

The crime scene and repairs had closed the main building and classroom. Neither was necessary for the star parties. From out here she could see the visitors lining up on the sidewalk, claiming their telescopes. It would be a beautiful night for stargazing.

The observatory was short on staff and volunteers. She'd received an email asking for all volunteers to help with the class tonight. Her telescope was set and she wasn't needed until much later. Why not help?

There was no reason other than writing or compiling data. If she wasn't going to do either of those, then she could give back a little. After all, she was the reason all the windows were broken.

Technically, she'd promised not to do anything other than study at the observatory and sleep at Pete's ranch. The Commander had forced a promise and then Pete had asked for one. But it had been two full days and three nights without another person making an untoward move against her.

The closed spaces were beginning to make her twitch. She needed to move, feel a little free.

Wasn't volunteering to help kids considered part of her job? She'd helped a couple of times her first week and loved it. The star parties were so much fun and, man, oh, man, she needed some fun. It wasn't like getting in her car and driving into town. She would still be at the observatory and keeping her promise.

She pulled on tennis shoes and practically ran down the hill from her dormitory room. Bill stayed close after jumping into his squad car and repeating ten times that she needed to wait. She slowed and took a deep breath of the crisp clean air as she got closer to the café patio and where Pete had been shot.

Last Friday afternoon, she'd taken the same walk to get to Sharon's car. On that journey she hadn't nearly been killed in a car accident, shot at on the observatory patio, stranded in the mountains or kissed by a sheriff. The very same sheriff who seemed to avoid her as often as possible.

His days were full of work—doubly so since he'd joined the task force. Her days were full of sleep. Her nights were busy with calculations and stars. His were surrounded by dreams. At least she hoped they were.

Stubborn man.

Right now, this very minute, was about sharing her love for the stars. Helping someone—child or adult—find a constellation or a crater on the nearly full moon.

*There's a solid reason he believes he can't get involved with anyone. You should ask him.* Joe's words orbited around in her mind like a moon around its planet. They were constantly there with no choice but to continue.

The next time she saw the sheriff of Presidio County… she was going to ask.

"THE SOURCE IS RELIABLE. They're going to use the cover of the UFO Border Zone to move something major." Cord Mc-Crea had been trying to stop drug trafficking since transferring to West Texas almost ten years before. He knew the area and could get information from a dried cactus.

The men who had followed Andrea to the observatory had inside information—from either the police radio or bugged cell phones. So he met Cord in an open area dead cell coverage zone between their properties. Making certain their conversations weren't monitored or overheard. Pete wasn't taking a chance with Andrea's life. Not a second time.

"How would they use the UFO convention? It's not like

there are crowds and crowds of people wandering everywhere. The thing draws a couple of thousand at best. And that's during the concerts. They've only been having the conference for a couple of years now." Pete caught himself shoving his hair back and resituating his hat. A habit Andrea had drawn to his attention when she'd arranged his hair with gel. His fingers had gotten stuck a couple of times in the stiff edges. After every shower now, he stopped himself when he reached for the styling tube.

"I don't know, Pete. All I can confirm is what my informant tells me. And that's all he's got."

"What's the deal with your task force? Do I need to be doing anything differently?"

Cord stretched his back. He'd been shot several years before by drug traffickers. All those men were behind bars or hadn't survived a second confrontation. "Naw. Just keep being the sheriff and keep Allen's daughter safe. You could let me know who you'll be sending to the aliens conference."

"You got it." Exactly what he'd thought. He'd been put on the task force only because of Andrea. "Cord, I know Andrea's being used as bait."

"I didn't think it would stay a secret from you long."

"Is that right? Why?"

Cord raised a curious eyebrow. "Come on, man. I saw the way you two looked at each other. The tension the other night could be cut with a knife. She insisted on staying at your place, having you as her protection detail. Allen wanted you in charge of the border detail."

So those were her terms.

Cord clapped him on the back. "I can see that brain of yours working, pal. That's right. Miss Allen wouldn't trust anyone else with her life. Just you. Go ahead, stick that chest out a little farther. Does that make you feel more important?"

They both laughed, but he did feel more competent.

"Just so you know, I'll be filling her in on our suspicions that something's happening. I want her to be prepared."

"Makes sense."

"Kate and the new baby okay? We haven't seen much of her around town."

"They stay close to the house, but they're great. Danver's a regular roly-poly. Kate's brother David is coming in at the end of the month, which is a code word for barbecue with the McCreas. Bring your dad."

"Sure. As long as this thing's over by then."

"You realize that we're never going to be done with drug traffickers trying to make a buck. We stop this group, another one is standing right behind it ready to take up the reins and harness a new set of horses. It'll never be over," Cord said sadly.

"Job security. What more can a man ask for?" He shrugged. At least Cord had job security. The position of sheriff—no matter how competent Pete felt—might be out of the question for him.

"There's more to life, man. I hope you'll find out what soon." He tipped his hat. "See you around. I'll give you a holler if my guy comes through with more info about the shipment."

"I'll have additional deputies in or near Presidio. They were already on the schedule to be at the UFO conference. Hard to understand that's the date they're choosing…when we have *more* men posted there."

"My source is more reliable than they normally come. It ain't gospel, but it's close. Take care now." Cord closed the door of his truck and drove out on the broken trail.

Pete stayed put, leaning on his Tahoe, watching the first evening star shine in the darkening sky. Andrea would have been dropped off about an hour ago. His dad was driving her from the ranch to the observatory and a deputy would pick her up in the morning and drive her to the ranch.

He would have to talk to her sooner or later. They couldn't keep successfully avoiding each other. He finished his soda and crushed the can, tossing it into the back. A couple of minutes on the road and he could make a call.

"Dispatch, reassign the driver for Miss Allen in the morning. I'll be picking her up myself."

"You don't say," Peach answered. "I told Honey you'd come around."

"Thanks for the confidence."

"Well, we did raise you as a hero, not a coward."

"I'll be signing off now, Dispatch."

"'Night, Sheriff."

Not a coward. For the past three days, he sure as hell had been one where Andrea Allen was concerned. Dammit.

PETE WAVED AT Randy Grady still on his feet at the door where Andrea was working. "Didn't they have a chair for your shift?"

"I didn't want to get too comfortable and nod off. You said to stay on our toes. I thought your dad was picking up Miss Allen?" They shook hands.

"He had an errand this morning, so I'm filling in."

"How's the arm?"

Pete stretched it across his chest. "Surprisingly good."

"Heard you passed out." Randy snickered under his breath.

"More from a lack of sleep than this thing."

"Right." Randy sang a song as he said the one word, doubting. He trotted down the sidewalk and stopped. "She's a nice woman. Any chance this protective detail will be over before she blows town?"

"Don't think so. Not with her father."

"Totally understand. I'd keep her for myself, too. I'll head out, then."

"It's not like that." But at the back of his mind, he knew it was. Randy disappeared down the path, and Pete stopped himself from shouting a denial.

He watched the sky lighten in the east through the tree-tops. Andrea would be out any minute. Why had he decided to pick her up? The dare from Peach? He had nothing to prove. Andrea would be gone at the end of the week without a glance back in his direction.

She didn't need any of the complications that getting involved with him would bring. The door opened.

"Oh, hi," Andrea said, then waved behind her. "My ride's here, guys. See you tomorrow."

Pete scanned the perimeter, including the skyline for a possible chopper, avoiding eye contact with his assignment. There had been three days without a hint of an incident. None of the deputies had reported any unusual activity. No one had reported any unusual cars or visitors hanging around either Fort Davis or Marfa.

"I'm surprised to see you."

"Why?"

"Well, Randy was here earlier."

"He just left. I thought I'd give you a ride back to the ranch. Do you need anything else?"

"Nope, I've got everything." She patted her laptop bag. "Gorgeous morning."

"That it is." She was a step ahead of him. He could take a long, good look at her. Gone was the bandage around her wrist, and the bruise was fading. Tight-fitting jeans covered her slender figure. A McDonald Observatory souvenir T-shirt hugged a tiny waist, giving him a terrific view.

They both got inside the Tahoe, and he drove away from the observatory, watching for stalled cars or men on the road. He noticed Andrea's constant movement and glances behind them. "You seem kind of antsy. Something on your mind?" he asked after a few minutes.

"I was just waiting for you to drop the real reason you're personally picking me up. I know you've been avoiding me. Did something happen? Did they send a new threat?"

"Nothing like that. I thought I'd give you a chance to pick up anything you might need. Our schedules haven't been conducive for much socializing, that's all." *And let you know about the possible threat for the next three days.* But those words stuck in his throat.

"And whose fault is that?"

"I wouldn't place blame on anyone. It's just the way it happened to turn out." Peach's words argued with his conscience. If he did say something, what good would it do?

"So, did something happen? Do you have a message from my father?"

"Wouldn't Commander Allen be calling you directly?"

"I really don't know. This isn't exactly our normal situation. We normally don't talk that often."

"That's a downright shame."

Andrea laughed. "You've heard all about the educational differences I've had with my family. Now it's your turn to share."

"My dad and I get along just fine."

"You can't get off that easy. I've been living in your house. Joe's walking on eggshells and you guys barely say three words to each other."

"He had a heart attack, and I've sort of been busy."

"Oh, I know all about that. It's nothing to take lightly, but he's exercising and has lost seventeen pounds by changing his diet."

"How did you know that?"

"He brags about using a new belt hole all the time. You'd know if you were around him for more than five minutes.

Is it the upcoming election? Are you afraid he's going to be upset that you're taking his job?"

The desire to spill everything to Andrea was tempting. In spite of the nonstop chatter and her irresistible kissing ability, she was easy to talk with. He'd kept his dad's secret without saying a word for six weeks.

"I take your silence for a yes."

"Joe Morrison has been ready to retire. I know he'll miss the people, but he's been frustrated with the day-to-day stuff for a while now."

"He said you're running unopposed, so what's the problem? Why are you nervous?" she asked.

"You seem pretty cozy with my dad, but I'm not sure this is any of your business."

"What can I say? I like to talk."

"I've noticed."

"Are you mad at him because of me? I mean, Joe agreed to help the Commander. I know all this is an added strain. Especially having to drive me back and forth to the observatory."

"I have an idea. Why don't we listen to the radio and you take a break from thinking too hard on my problems."

"Okay, but I don't do country. Are there any classic rock stations around here?" Andrea turned away.

Pete immediately wanted to spill his guts. He'd been rude in order to stop himself from telling her everything. By the time they turned south into Fort Davis, he was ready to beg her to chatter again. He liked her voice and hadn't realized how much he'd missed it.

"You're right," he said, unable to take the silence.

At least she looked at him, eyebrows arched, waiting for him to continue.

"It's not…" Could he appease her curiosity without sharing all the details of his problem? No. In a very short time, this woman had gotten into his psyche. He wanted to be honest with her. But he just didn't know if he could be.

Telling anyone would be risking everything his dad had worked to achieve for thirty years.

"If things were different—" He clammed up…again.

"I get it. This is personal and I'm a stranger."

"Why is it so important to you?"

"You and your dad have been a big help this week. I owe you a lot. I hate to see your relationship strained because of me."

"It has nothing to do with you."

"Okay, I'd believe that. Except, after my dad formed this task force, you didn't want to have anything to do with me. And Joe said I should just ask you why. I would have sooner, but you made it pretty clear—"

"Wait a minute. Slow down. Dad told you to ask me why?"

"Yes, when he left the meeting Saturday, he said you had a good reason for acting like a jerk."

"He's called me worse."

Andrea turned a nice shade of embarrassed pink. "Sorry, that's actually my description. But you didn't even give me a chance to say thanks for saving my life before you completely brushed me off."

"I think we sort of saved each other. We made a good team."

"And that has to end?"

He took the vehicle through Marfa and made the last couple of turns to the ranch without responding.

"Look, Andrea, I don't see the point. You'll be on a military chopper out of here in four days. I have no doubts your father will keep you as far away as he can from Marfa, Texas, and this drug cartel. After that, you're trying to get a job on the other side of the world."

"Oh, so that's it. You're afraid of short-term relationships. Have you been burned before?"

He pulled past the front of the house, waving to his dad on the front porch. The grin and waggling eyebrows on his dad's face were enough of a sign that everything appeared normal. He parked, cut the engine and got a strange feeling his dad expected something to happen with Andrea and him.

She unbuckled, turning his direction. A playful grin replaced the serious expression from earlier. "I got the impression from the nurses the other night that you were a popular guy."

"Popular? I've had a few dates, nothing serious—"

"Hold that thought. Do you hear something?" She opened her door and hopped out before he could react. "Is that a helicopter? Was it following us?"

He drew his weapon as he jumped from the Tahoe, searching, seeing nothing. Andrea continued to the far side of the barn, her face turned to the sky.

"Wait! Don't run out in the open! Dammit, exactly like what you're doing."

## Chapter Eighteen

Andrea ran until she got a good look at the helicopter heading away from the ranch. A sense of relief that their day wouldn't be interrupted swept over her as fast as the pleasant northern breeze. She stopped, and a second later, Pete skidded to a halt behind her. He stretched out his arms to steady her but quickly dropped them to his sides.

"Still alive." She shrugged. Hopefully indicating that running had been the wrong thing to do. "We don't have to make a big deal out of this, Pete. I know I shouldn't run off like that. It won't happen again."

"When am I supposed to make a big deal out of it? After they succeed in abducting you?"

Andrea was tired of seeing Pete's face worried instead of smiling. In the past few days, when that deep furrow appeared across his brow it was because of her. She was also tired of avoiding her attraction. Deep down, she knew that part of the reason she'd stayed in the area was her attraction to this man.

There was just something about him. Something sweet about his silence, though he was strong to his core. She wanted to discover what centered him and made him so easily confident without conceit. Simply put…she wanted to know him better.

So it made perfect sense to kiss him again.

"Did I finally ask something you don't have an answer for?"

Shrugging a little, she couldn't help smiling at the confusion in Pete's eyes. His hat was already in his hand or she might have pushed it off his head to the ground. He took a step back. She followed with two steps, catching his shoulders. With one small twist, she had him next to the barn wall.

He knew what was coming. She knew because his head tilted sideways and his face dropped even with hers.

"This is a bad idea, Andrea."

"You've got to have a better reason."

There was a hairbreadth between their lips. They stayed there, taking in each other's air. The minty clean made her wish she'd taken him up on the lifesaver he'd offered in his car. His chest began to rise and fall quicker, matching hers. His hands tightened around her waist, and she draped hers around his shoulders.

"Bad, bad idea," he said before crushing his lips to hers.

Sheriff Pete Morrison might think kissing her was a bad idea, but the man hauling her hips to his… Well, he left nothing but good sensations behind.

"The suggestion that any part of this is bad…absolutely ridiculous," she whispered close to his ear. "You are such a good kisser."

"You make me crazy," he said. He smashed his mouth to hers again, not allowing her to respond.

The returning kiss she gave him should have been answer enough. She was desperate not to let him go this time. Her body needed him, and his needed her.

She pulled back, dipping her mouth, tasting the salt on his skin, nipping the curve where his shoulder muscle met his neck. She tilted her head back, encouraging him to taste the V of her throat, sending additional shivers of anticipation down her spine.

His lips traveled down her breastbone, lightly scraping his teeth across her sensitive skin. His tongue darted under the lacy edge of her bra. His hands stretched along her sides, then tugged at her T-shirt, making her wish she'd worn the button-up hanging in her bedroom.

Oh, gosh, a bedroom would be nice. They could take their desire to the next level. But they couldn't... They weren't alone. But that didn't stop the exploring.

Pete's cool hands slid under her shirt, up her back and to her sides. He skimmed her breasts, just the thin lace separated the tips of his fingers and her flesh.

More shivers. At this rate there would be endless shivers and no relief in sight. She wanted his shirt off, but it was firmly tucked into his pants. She settled for skimming the tops of his ears, dragging her nails gently across his scalp and filling her hands with his thick hair.

Pete caught her mouth to his again, plunging his tongue inside. He captured her whimper as their hips gnashed together again. Wanting more than either could deliver in broad daylight on the side of the Morrison barn.

"Ahem." Joe cleared his throat from the corner of the barn.

Breathing too hard to speak, Andrea looked in his direction and could only see the toe of one boot and a long, tall shadow.

Breathing a little hard himself, Pete dropped his forehead just above her ear. Then he whispered, "Very bad idea."

"Not at all," she whispered back, noticing his hands settled on her hips, his thumbs comfortably hooked inside her jeans.

"Um, son. Since you're going to be here with our guest, I thought I'd take Rowdy into town. We need feed and supplies. I have a few errands. We'll probably be gone a good three or four hours, so I thought we'd grab lunch at the café."

"You don't have—"

She placed a finger over Pete's lips, fearing he'd convince his father not to leave. She lowered her voice again. "I promise to be good…and not run away."

Pete dropped his head against the barn, then his eyes seared her with their heat. "Fine, Dad. I got this covered."

Yes, he did.

PETE NEEDED TO drop his hands and lock the county's guest in her bedroom. That would be the right thing to do. The responsible thing. The sheriff thing. He could try. But the way his body was throbbing it would take every ounce of control he no longer had.

Holding Andrea in his arms, he'd lost control. If his dad hadn't interrupted them, there was no telling what he would have done. His heart rate was still thrumming at top speed. If he didn't have a grip on her hips, his hands would be shaking.

The horn from the truck sounded a couple of blasts. A minute later he heard it leaving. He stayed put, reluctant to let Andrea go because he knew what needed to be done.

"We should get inside." He reluctantly dropped his hands, pressing them against the barn.

Andrea stepped to the side and picked up his hat. She handed it to him, then put her fists on her slim hips. "What's wrong? You embarrassed?"

He shoved his hat on his head and circled her wrist, tugging a little to get her started. "Inside and no. Or yes, a little."

Once they were around the corner and headed to the house, she twisted her wrist free. "I've been walking on my own for a while now."

"Come on, Andrea. You're under my protection. We

can't— I shouldn't let my guard down or take advantage of our situation." He opened the screen door, ready to let her go through and plant himself on the porch until his father returned.

Looking him up one side and down the other, she seemed to read his mind and paused. To add to his misery, she took a seat on the porch swing and gestured for him to join her.

The chain suspending the swing creaked above their heads in a gentle rhythm as they sat shoulder to shoulder, silent. The horses clopped around in the corral. The breeze was picking up and blowing the top branches in the tree. Then just like high school, Pete found his hand inching toward Andrea's, then lacing their fingers together.

"This is nice. My mom would love this porch. She'd decorate it with all sorts of plants and small statues. She loves statues." She didn't seem mad.

In fact, she seemed to be in a great mood. Just like before their make-out session. Man, she was completely different from any woman he'd ever met. Shouldn't she be furious with him instead of holding his hand, sending lightning bolts up his arm or making small talk?

"Plants don't do so well out here in the winter." He could make small talk and ignore the energy surging through his body at her touch. Could he ignore that they had the house to themselves for the next three hours?

"Your dad is convinced that your reason for halting a potential relationship between the two of us is *solid*, as he put it. I, on the other hand, am not convinced."

So much for small talk.

"I have a lot of good reasons." It was easier to remember they couldn't be together when he wasn't touching her. He just couldn't force himself not to enjoy the smoothness of her skin. In fact, the memory of her incredible breasts made it hard to keep his seat.

"Why can't you tell me, Pete?"

"It's complicated."

"Then why is your dad so eager for you to share these reasons?"

"I don't know."

"One more question and then I'll go to my room." She looked down, dragged her toes and stopped the swing.

"Go for it."

"I think I will." She arched those beautiful brows again and winked. "Does it really matter for the next three hours?"

# Chapter Nineteen

Pete watched Andrea's eyes slowly look into his and with his free hand, he tilted her chin until he could brush her lips again. Close enough to share her breath, her softness and her taste, and still far enough apart to quit. All he had to do was release her hand and let her go.

"What about all your reasons?" she asked.

His mind raced to find one legitimate objection not to finish what they'd started.

*They'd only known each other a few days.* That wasn't cause enough to stop. He felt drawn to Andrea like he'd known her all his life. And he wanted to know her better. Completely.

He wanted to taste the rest of her, working his way down from her slightly salty neck to her cute little toes. He wanted to find out if she was ticklish behind her knees or at the curve above her hip. He wanted to keep her to himself for a week of Sundays and forget the rest of the world and his list of reasons.

*He didn't have a future.* Hell, she only wanted three hours. The way his body was humming, he could guarantee that short time would be a long unforgettable adventure.

*He was in charge of her protection.* Her father working with Border Protection and Homeland Security still wasn't enough to make him stop. He'd take his chances.

But could the biggest reason on his list be ignored? *He was a phony.* He didn't want to lie to her, but it wasn't his secret. No matter how much she liked him, he couldn't take a chance telling anyone. Ever.

Pete stood quickly and jerked her into his arms. Her blue eyes were a perfect match with the sky. A perfect backdrop to kiss her again. He wanted to consume her, but he managed to keep his hands on her upper arms. He pressed his mouth to hers, coaxing her lips apart enough to enjoy the luxurious softness.

He wanted her with a fierce need that made nothing else matter. It had started in the hospital with each cheeky answer she'd given to his questions. And he honestly didn't see an end happening soon. It would, just not today. He'd already wasted enough of her remaining time in town. He tapered off their kiss in order to coax her to the door.

Andrea curved her hips into his, leaning back as she'd done on the far side of the barn. Her smile was sultry, sexy. "Does this mean you've changed your mind about the next three hours?"

With her looking like that at him, they weren't going to make it to the bedroom.

PETE KISSED HER hard and wrapped his arms around her waist as she wrapped hers around his neck. He moved toward the door, almost dragging her feet across the porch as he lifted her body next to his. Andrea didn't care. She was in just as big a hurry. Give the man too much time to think and he might change his mind.

Their limbs tangled as they helped each other take off their shirts. Hers pulled straight over her head, while she could only get his unbuttoned. Still kissing and touching, they dashed down the hall to the bedrooms.

"Mine," she said, bouncing against the closed door and struggling to turn the knob.

Pete didn't object. He skimmed her black bra—thank goodness she'd worn the sexy one—then traced her collarbone, moving higher until he cupped her neck with one hand and opened the door with the other. They backed into her bedroom, lips frantically finding each other again.

The belt holding his holster was unlatched. Andrea shoved his uniform over his shoulders and tugged his undershirt loose. Her hands skimmed his chest, hot flesh against her palms.

She returned his hard, deepening kisses, breaking long enough to stretch the white cotton over his head and let it fall to the floor. His hands slid down her back and seconds later her bra fell. Pete took a step back, his eyes smoldering as they saw her for the first time. She paused, letting him, not feeling vulnerable or self-conscious.

Andrea couldn't pretend to be a shy girl. She wasn't. Neither could she act coy and tiptoe around what she wanted. She'd wanted Pete Morrison since noticing his dimples back in the hospital. And what girl wouldn't want to make out with the man responsible for saving her life, not just once but twice?

"This has to be the *best* bad decision I've ever made."

"Oh, yeah?" She reached for the button on his fly and couldn't miss his physical reaction to her body as she unzipped his pants. "Then why are we slowing down?"

"Some things are worth savoring."

The smolder in his eyes turned to pure flame, spreading the heat to his entire body. He held her, letting her arch her back over his arm as he kissed and nipped a hot trail to her breast. By the time he reached the second, he laid her on the bed, taking his time to explore.

Pete stood between her legs, which were still encased in the heavy denim. His strong hands glided slowly down her thighs. If she hadn't been going crazy with anticipation, she might have screamed for him to hurry. But the anticipation was exquisite as he undressed her, giving a final tug to the tight jeans.

"You are more than beautiful. I could stare at you like this all day."

"You better not. What's good for the gander is good for the goose, you know." She winked suggestively and scooted farther onto the bed, pointed at his pants and propped her head up for a more comfortable look. "Strip, mister."

"Yes, ma'am."

Without much effort, Pete divested himself of all clothing and stood at the side of the bed a second before he looked uncomfortable. But that was only for a second. He got onto the bed, leaning on his side, and worked magic with his hands again.

Feather-soft strokes up and down her breastbone sent tingles all over her body. He drew concentric circles until her nipples drew tight, making her shiver multiple times. The strokes became longer, including her hips and thighs. Then tiny circles at the back of her knees.

"You've got a gentle touch," she gasped a little before he created a trail up her body with his lips. Then silenced her again with decadent kissing.

Andrea eagerly explored Pete's body, too. His sinewy muscles, long powerful thighs, lean hips and sheer strength left her breathless. When he reached between their bodies, she grabbed his shoulders, unable to keep her nails from lightly scraping into his skin. Moments later, her body hummed in fleeting perfection as she cried out.

Pete rolled to his side next to her, kissing her along her shoulder up to her neck, following the line of her jaw back to her lips. There wasn't an inch of relaxed parts on the man as she reached out and explored more.

It took a slight nudge to reverse their positions. Seconds later, Pete was on his back. She rose to her knees, massaging his chest, admiring the muscles extending to his hips.

She mimicked his technique of touch. She loved the fine dusting of manly hair on his legs, drew circles behind his knees, where he jerked away and laughed.

As much as she loved those dimples, another touch made him suck in his breath and tighten his abs. She shimmied up his body, her breasts sensitive as they flattened against his chest.

"I need my…my pants," he said, gulping air.

"Oh, no, you don't, mister. You aren't getting away now."

"Not…leaving." He smiled, pushing gently at her shoulders, then cupping her breasts, making her join him on a long sigh. Then he whispered, "Condom."

He groaned when she sat up, connecting them and then again when she left to retrieve his slacks. She tossed his wallet to him, repositioning herself across his thighs, hand extended for the foil packet. Once the condom was on, she was no longer in control. His smile was replaced with a look of longing. His gentle, slow touch was replaced with a frenzy she could barely control. He flipped her to her back and filled her.

Their joining was more than she'd thought it could be. They settled into a rhythm that belonged only to them. It couldn't be duplicated with anyone else.

"Meant to be" kept repeating in her head. No words were needed and none were said as their lips opened for each other just like their bodies. The perfection she'd experienced at his touch shortly before returned in extended stellar abundance. Pete joined her, tossing back his head as his body went supernova.

## Chapter Twenty

"Think you could tell me about your list of reasons now?" Andrea asked, her head nestled in the crook of his shoulder. Her body was only half covered with the sheet, so he could still admire her flawless skin and curves.

"I'd rather make love to you again before I go remembering why I shouldn't."

"Don't get all hot and bothered because you're my protection detail."

"That's easy for you to say. What am I supposed to write in the report?"

"You can say I spent a pleasant morning in my room. You don't really write everything down for my father, do you?"

He'd pass answering that question honestly because the answer had been yes until an hour ago. "So now you know the real reason why I've tried to talk us out of this."

She climbed on top of him, close enough to kiss, her breasts gently grazing his chest. "I really want to know, Pete. I meant what I said about staying in touch when I leave." She paused, her head cocking to the side with realization. "I thought you were kidding earlier about long-distance relationships. But you really don't want that."

He gently held her in place when she tried to roll away. "Just hold your horses. Before you start rapid-firing questions off only an assumption. I never said I didn't want a relationship, close or long-distance."

"Then what is it? I can tell that something's bothering you. Is it my dad?" She turned her head again. "I knew it. The Commander is such a turnoff to potential boyfriends. But good grief, Pete. You're the sheriff. You can't possibly think he'll find out something about you…"

He couldn't look into her eyes. She was reading his mind—or doing a dang good job interpreting his expressions. She scooted to his side, pulling the sheet higher and tucking it around her like a toga. He threw his legs over the side of the bed.

And once again, Andrea surprised him with a comforting hand soothing his back muscles. She didn't seem indignant or curious. She just ran her fingertips lightly up and down, giving him a chance to think of what he should say.

"I should have just made love to you again."

She laughed and pressed her body to his, her arms lightly circling his neck. Her tongue flicked out enticingly against his earlobe.

"You don't have to tell me anything else," she whispered. "I'm very happy to take you up on your offer."

He twisted in her arms and dropped them both nose to nose on their sides.

"This isn't about you or your father, Andrea."

"All right. Since you don't know me very well, perhaps I should inform you that I'm pretty good keeping a secret. I once kept a secret for my best friend for almost two years. That actually might be because I forgot about it, but it should still—"

"Shh," he said just before covering her lips.

The long kisses kept them both silent. He wanted to tell her. She deserved to know that it had nothing to do with her. The frenzy slowed but not the intensity. Soon he was kissing his way down her body and loving every part of her.

"THAT WAS INSANE," Andrea said, collapsing next to Pete. "I can barely breathe. How much of our three hours is left?"

She'd fallen for Pete faster than a shooting star fleeted through the sky. And she was glad. He was a complex man, very intriguing and just plain adorable. Plus, he was a heck of a lover. A seriously wonderful lover. She had to be careful she didn't meet the same fate as a shooting star and burn up when it hit the atmosphere.

"Enough for a shower and breakfast." He was propped on the pillows, the corner of the sheet modestly covering his vulnerable parts.

"You mean lunch," she teased.

"Or dinner if you look at the fact that we both worked all night and neither of us has slept in a while."

"Wow, Sheriff. You did all that on no sleep? I can't wait until you're functioning at full capacity." She laughed, but she was also impressed at how this man could be wide awake for just over thirty hours.

"Shower, food and sleep. In that order."

"Sounds like a plan. If I can move, that is. Maybe I'll just stay here for a couple of days and recover."

He pushed off the bed and she admired his backside as he gathered his clothes. "Race you."

"You're on. First one finished has to cook."

"I might have a better idea. We wash each other's backs, finish together and both cook." He caught her wrist and pulled her to him. His sexy definition of "cook" was pressed between them.

"I really am hungry," she said only because she'd noticed their time was running short. Otherwise she would have been all over the possibility of another romp. "Didn't Joe say they'd be back around one?"

"You're right. We'll save the shower for next time."

"I love a good plan of action." She winked at him as he patted her behind, then swaggered down the hallway.

He beat her out of the shower only because she made certain her legs were shaved again. Who knew? They might actually get time alone together before heading to work. She slid the understated tracking devices back into her ears and yawned. They needed something upbeat to keep them alert, at least long enough to eat.

Music. Shoot, hers had been stolen. Well, at least the device had been kept by the men in the desert. Fortunately, all her music was stored electronically and could be accessed via Wi-Fi. She grabbed the university-issued tablet from her bag and followed the aroma of sizzling bacon.

"Oh, my gosh, that smells delicious." She got close to Pete, stealing a kiss when he faced her. She didn't want him to retreat to their relationship status prior to the front porch. So she stood right next to him, hoping the popping grease wouldn't reach her bare arms.

"Nothing fancy. I'm too tired for anything other than breakfast." He pulled her close, then let her back away from the frying pan.

"I don't mind. I'm starving." She suddenly wanted to know more about him. What could he cook? What did he like to eat? There were so many unanswered, frivolous details. The only conversations they'd had were about parents or Sharon or madmen who might still be trying to abduct her. She powered the tablet on and set it on the table. "Hey, what kind of music do you like? Are you a good ol' country boy? A hard rocker? Oh, please don't be a closet classical music guy. That might just be a deal breaker."

He threw his head back, laughing. She loved getting that reaction from him and watching those dimples. Spatula in hand, he drew her into the circle of his arms and just looked at her. She dropped her head onto his chest, hugging him.

"You are so lucky you're the sheriff."

"What do you mean?"

"Well, my dad's probably running an extensive background check on you, verifying that you're good enough to date his only child."

"Are you serious?" He broke their embrace faster than she could wonder what was happening. "He can't. You've got to ask him to stop."

"What's wrong?" She knew something major had changed. The smile had disappeared and was instantly replaced with a look so serious it frightened her.

"I like you, Andrea. Give your dad a call, will ya?"

"I like you, too. I know my dad can be a bit overwhelming. This is no big deal. Really. He was probably already running one for the task force."

"I should have thought of that. Explain there's nothing between us, so he'll call off the background. I just hope it's not too late." He scooped the eggs out of the pan and set their plates on the table, treating his command like any other friendly suggestion.

He was clearly worried something awful would be revealed. But what? He couldn't be the county sheriff if he'd broken the law. That couldn't be a possibility. So what or who was he trying to protect?

"First off, do you really think I have that kind of control over the Commander? And second, I thought there was something between us. Am I wrong?"

"Go ahead and eat."

They both sat, coffee and breakfast growing cold while they sort of just stared at all of it. She didn't know what to do, almost afraid to say anything that might change his mind about telling her—whatever was horrible enough that he thought it would keep them apart. At least she assumed it would keep them apart. His seriousness seemed to indicate that, but it was hard to hypothesize correctly without any facts.

Silence was not her thing. She asked questions, got people to spill the beans all the time. Pete seemed to have mastered how to keep his mouth shut. How typical that she'd fallen hard and fast for someone who fit the strong-and-silent stereotype.

"Other than the professional reasons we shouldn't be involved, there's something very basic you should know," he finally said.

"Okay." That hurt. She really hadn't anticipated he'd say they shouldn't be involved. She better understood what biting your tongue meant. She literally bit the end of her tongue to keep her silence.

Neither of them lifted a fork. She was glued to the endless expressions crossing Pete's face. She might pass out from holding her breath waiting for him to talk.

"I can't leave Marfa."

"Is that all? I didn't expect you to. At least not now. If I do get the post outside the country, maybe you can visit. If you want to, that is. I mean, I'm not assuming anything because of what happened this morning." The words spilled out.

"I would if I could, but it's just not possible."

"Do you need a passport or are you afraid of flying?" He was so earnest and didn't seem as if he was going to explain the background comment. A million reasons popped into her head. Reasons she wanted to be true instead of the one thing that kept reverberating in the back of her mind.

"No and no." He shook his head and pushed his damp hair away from his face, clearly struggling with the decision to tell her.

She covered his hand, now on the table. "Whatever it is, you can trust me."

"Pete Morrison is not my real name."

"Honey told me about your adoption last week." She couldn't wait for his explanation and rushed forward, following the illogic of what he'd revealed. "So what is it? What secret are you protecting? I mean, you live here, everyone knows you. Those pictures back at the sheriff's office prove you grew up here. Your life looks like an open book."

"I'm not explaining this correctly."

He shoved back from the table and stared out the window. "God, I don't know why I'm trying to explain this to you at all. I shouldn't. I wouldn't have brought it up if you hadn't warned me about the background check. I need you to call your father before it's too late, but I can't tell you why."

"Oh, no, you don't. You can't just drop that kind of…of request and not allow a question and answer." She stayed remarkably calm. She didn't know how, she just did. Much the same way she'd encouraged him this morning to face his attraction for her. She wanted him to trust her. Becoming all shrewish wouldn't accomplish that. "I didn't mean to rush you. I'm overly curious, if you couldn't tell that from knowing me a few days."

Waiting, she forced a bite of the bacon down without choking. Then a sip of cooling coffee.

"It's complicated," he said, dropping his chin to his chest.

"All the better to talk it through with a person who has an objective mind and can be unbiased." *Be patient.*

"I can't. I want to. It would be easier, but I can't." He walked around the kitchen, agitated.

Andrea placed her hands in her lap and watched without anxiously following him around the room. Part of the question on her mind was why Pete wanted her to know something he was clearly conflicted about revealing. Then again, why was she so excited that he'd begun to share with her?

"Whatever your real name, it won't change anything about our...friendship." If not a relationship, they could at least be friends.

"Not even if I'm the son of a murderer and never legally adopted by Joe?"

She swallowed hard after realizing her jaw had dropped open, totally unable to believe his statement. He was the son of a murderer and never adopted? It was more than a little hard to believe. "Those exact possibilities never crossed my mind."

"Believe me, I thought Joe was delusional from the heart attack when he told me what he'd done." The hurt he experienced was easy to see. His entire body slumped as he sat in the chair.

Andrea wanted to pull him into her arms and hold on as tight as he'd let her. She couldn't immediately call her dad. He'd want to know why, and if he hadn't begun the background check already, he would as soon as they hung up. "I hate to ask, Pete, but I'll need details to convince my father. Have you talked about this with Joe?"

"We've managed to avoid the conversation for six weeks."

"I don't think I could have waited. I'm too impatient and would want answers."

"Yeah, well. I didn't wait. My job does have some advantages. With a little research, I could put the facts together. I just don't know why my dad doesn't think it's a big deal. It could ruin everything he's worked for his entire life."

"You're talking about the illegal adoption? Maybe there were extenuating circumstances. I'm sure he'd be forgiven."

Elbows on the table, Pete blocked showing his emotions to her by resting his head on his hands. There were very few times when she felt completely lost. This was one of them. Did he need comforting or someone to vent to?

He looked up, and his eyes sparkled with near tears. And she knew…no matter what he needed, she wanted to comfort him. She also knew exactly why it all mattered… she was falling in love with the whole man. Not just his dimples.

# Chapter Twenty-One

Stupid. He'd blurted out his dad's well-kept secret. Just spilled his guts to a woman he hadn't known a week. The daughter of a man who could dig into his past and destroy everything he knew. And everything his father had sacrificed for his entire life.

"Are you okay, Pete?" Andrea asked.

Yeah, he was okay. He wanted to be angry at his dad. He was angry. Then he felt guilty. That had been the cycle for the past six weeks. How could he blame the man who'd raised him with no obligation to do so? It hurt…the betrayal. Pete hadn't realized how much.

"I'm not sure I can forgive him. He's lied to me for over twenty-five years. Upholding the law has been his entire life. He made it my entire life. And yet everything's been a lie."

"Not the way he feels about you." Her hand rubbed his shoulder, trying to comfort him. "Anyone who meets the two of you can tell how much he cares."

"I don't want to be the reason he loses everything. Can you call Commander Allen?"

"I don't think it's a good idea to bring the situation to his attention. Maybe he's not digging into your past at all. He hasn't removed you from the task force, which would happen if he'd discovered your identity doesn't exist. Where did Joe get your birth certificate? Things like that?"

"I don't have one. That's what started this whole mess. County Administration entered my interim-sheriff status into the system and notified me they didn't have a copy of my Social Security card or birth certificate. Dad admitted that he twisted some arms to get me hired back before the updated system was installed. He also said my Social Security number is a fake. He bought it before I started school, so I had no idea."

Andrea's jaw dropped again. Sort of the way his had done when he'd found out.

She quickly recovered. "That seems…"

"Very illegal, as in he's bound to do jail time." Thus his dilemma. Having a government agency dig into his past would expose his father no matter what good intentions he had long ago.

"No wonder you're worried for him. He must have had a good reason to go to such lengths."

"I wouldn't know. I haven't asked."

"You have to be the least curious man I've ever met." She left the table to microwave her breakfast. "Obviously, you're going to ask him, right? I mean, you need to hear the entire story. Want me to heat up your plate?"

No longer hungry, he shook his head. If he didn't know how smart Andrea Allen was, he'd wonder about her stream-of-consciousness conversation. All in all, he liked it. More often than he'd admit out loud, he silently chuckled at how her mind worked and made him stay on his toes.

Every time he turned around he was amazed by how casual and accepting she was of their situation. Telling her he was the son of a murderer stopped her as long as it took to hiccup. Then she was asking to warm his breakfast.

Damn, the woman made him want more. More of her. More of life. Just…more. Until he'd met her, it had never crossed his mind. Now that it was out of his reach, he ached for a chance.

She was back at the table, silently eating and occasionally looking at him. He could tell she was dying to ask more questions. He didn't know if he was ready to answer.

"Do I smell bacon?" his dad asked as soon as the front door opened.

"In here, Dad."

He barreled around the corner. "Good, you're still awake." He looked at the table, grabbed a slice of bacon from Pete's plate and nodded toward Andrea. "I can see by the look on his face that you asked him. About dang time. You tell her?" he asked his son.

Pete nodded, and Andrea sipped the last of her coffee. He wondered how long her silence would last before she'd shoot a list of questions for his father.

"Good," his dad continued, twirling the chair around to sit. "We need to get this out in the open, and you need to stop trying to protect me."

"Outside." Pete liked Andrea, but this was private. He needed the reason before he shared it with anyone—if he ever shared it.

"You don't want her to know why?"

"I was just telling Pete that I'm really tired. You guys talk. I'm plugging in my earphones, turning on some music." She lifted the tablet and forced a yawn. "I'll be out before you can say right ascension." The blank look on his dad's face must have encouraged her to explain. "It's an astronomer's term that… Sorry, never mind me. I'm heading to bed."

Andrea backed out of the room. Her bedroom door clicked shut softly, and he was alone with his dad. Biological or adopted, legal or not—Joe Morrison would always be his dad. He'd already forgiven him.

"I shouldn't be surprised at not being able to follow her

talk too much. Andrea tried to tell me what she was looking at through the telescope the first time I picked her up. Couldn't make hide nor hair of it. She let me take a peek, though. It was almost as pretty as her." His dad poured himself a cup of coffee from the pot that rarely turned off.

"She's definitely a smart woman." Pete realized what he'd said and tried to ignore his dad's inquisitive raised eyebrow. "Yeah, you meant the picture in the telescope. I got it. But she is smart and gives good advice."

"Like…"

"Like how I should have asked you about my *adoption* as soon as you were out of the hospital. I can't believe that the man who preached at me about doing what was right my entire life had been breaking the law the entire time."

Joe leaned on the counter, just as Pete had earlier, talking to Andrea. He held his coffee cup the same way as his dad.

"The first four months you were here, I never had to ask for a babysitter when I went to work. The church organized it. You know, people say we look alike. It was easy for everyone to believe you were my grand-nephew. It was also easy for them to look the other way about certain things."

"Seriously, Dad, you risked everything. Why did you do it?"

"The why part is an easy answer. You. I did it for you."

"I need a little more than that, Dad."

"It was the right thing to do, son. And I'd do it again."

Joe sat at the table, taking Andrea's place. The tanned skin around his eyes crinkled with his smile. "When you said you knew who your father was, I'm assuming you figured it out after I said I arrested him."

"I figured it had to be someone outside Presidio County about the time I came to live with you. You only arrested three people. Two were transferred to San Antonio and one ended up in Huntsville State Prison. Philip Stanley sat on death row for eleven years. Just after my fourteenth birthday you took a trip to see him, didn't you? Did you go for the execution?"

"That's right." He sipped from the cup. "Sad day. He'd robbed a liquor store in El Paso. Shot and killed the attendant."

"The report said you talked him into releasing hostages at a house south of here."

"A family of four. They moved not too long after that. I think their five-year-old son made more of an impact on Phil than I did trying to get him to let them go. Something the kid did made him want you to grow up in a home and be happy. He loved you in his own way. He let the people go when I gave my word I'd find your maternal grandparents. His were already gone. I tried. Believe me. I verified straight off that your mother was deceased. It took nine months to discover that her parents had passed on before you were born."

"And I lived with you for that time? Why didn't you turn me over to foster care?"

"Gave my word I wouldn't. He was scared you'd turn out like him and made me promise no foster homes." He cleared his throat and leaned back in the chair. "I'd already told everyone you were my nephew. Hell, Sheriff Grimshaw is the one who encouraged me to give my word at the house. He's the one who helped me find information on your family."

"So Uncle Russ knew and even helped you."

"Yeah. He vouched for me and thought of you as part of his family, too. We convinced ourselves we were doing the right thing. Two old bachelors taking on a kid who we were determined would not end up like his old man. We thought about the foster program, but after you'd been here that long, they wouldn't have given you to me."

"How'd you enroll me in school? Didn't I need records?"

"We actually used his wife's Social Security number for

school. It's not so hard to enroll as long as you had shot records. Everyone around here knew your story by then. No
one pressed us. Russ got the county to hire you. I winked
a couple of times to make people forget your paperwork
was incomplete."

"You know you can go to jail."

"Son, no one cares. You're a good man. This won't make
any difference in you being sheriff."

"Dad, Andrea's father made me a part of his task force.
He's probably got people vetting me right now. That means
a background check. They'll find the falsified information.
Believe me, the government cares."

"I don't see why it should matter now. We can get everything straightened out, maybe legally change your name.
You haven't done anything wrong."

"Dammit, Dad. Don't sit there and act like this isn't a
game changer." He would have been yelling. If there wasn't
a guest in the house, he probably would have been ranting
a little at how nonchalantly his dad was accepting their
secret was out.

Yes, it was their secret now. People would assume Pete
had known about his adoption circumstances. As close as
he was to Joe, no one would believe otherwise.

His dad seemed remarkably calm when he turned to him
with no smile, just a gleam in his eyes. He looked free of a
huge burden. "Son, I know the gravity of the situation. I'm
accepting full responsibility. If the world finds out, then
the world finds out."

"They don't have to find out. I can resign, stop Commander Allen from moving forward with the vetting process."

"No way. Absolutely not."

"Dad, what's impossible is to ignore this ticking time
bomb. No ifs, ands or buts. It's going off. Only a question
of when."

"I disagree. There's—"

"Excuse me." Andrea dashed into the room. One ear pod dangling, one still in position, tablet in hand, looking as bright as sunshine. "I know you two need to talk, but this… It just can't wait. I'm so sorry for interrupting. But can I? Interrupt, I mean?"

"Sure," his father said. "Have a seat."

Pete would have rather finished their conversation, devising a game plan. Whatever she'd found, Andrea seemed about to burst with excitement. She probably couldn't wait.

"Oh, I can't sit, thanks. This is… Well, you have to read it for yourself, but I think Sharon was working with those men. Or at least it seems that way to me. Do you want to call the rest of the task force? Maybe get their take on it?"

"You might want to show us what you're talking about first." Pete tried to slow her down.

"Oh, I was doing it again. My apologies." Standing between him and his father, she set the tablet on the table and swiped the screen. "An email popped up addressed to Sharon from an unknown sender."

She touched the screen a second time, bringing up the email program.

We'll pay $500 if you get her on her own. Let us know when and where. Don't cross us, Sharon. You know what kind of trouble you'll be in if things go wrong.

"So what do you think?" she asked.

"This could mean anything," he answered. "Are there more emails?"

"A couple. She sent the information about me taking her place on Friday night at the Viewing Area, right down to the license tag on her car."

"Then you were set up."

"How did you find the emails?" his dad asked.

Andrea leaned on his shoulder. The movement was so casual he wasn't certain she knew she was there. Nice, yet very telling when his dad raised an eyebrow and the corner of his mouth in a half smile.

"This is a university-issued tablet. I've been utilizing it, inputting my data and notes. Those creeps stole my music last week, so I thought I'd listen from my cloud. I haven't been on the internet, since Dad asked me not to. But when I went to sign in, the device automatically logged in as Sharon. She must have been the last user and forgotten to log out." She shook his shoulders with her excitement.

Pete scrolled through some of the other messages. "Why wasn't this turned over to Commander Allen's team? They're better equipped to trace where the message came from. They collected her laptop and cell from the car fire— or at least what was left of it."

"I guess no one thought about the tablet. The University of Texas owns it and all the students use it."

"I'll drive the tablet over to Cord's place."

"Not so fast, please," Andrea said, trying unsuccessfully to snatch it from his grasp. They both held it inches above the tabletop.

The look on her face sort of shouted that she wanted to use the clue herself. "No way, Andrea. We've got to get this to Cord's team. I'm not putting you in danger again."

"We should check with the DEA agent at the task force meeting. Maybe she knows how to trace the sender or who to contact about it."

Pete stood, grabbing her shoulders securely enough to get her attention. "We are not tracking down whoever sent this email."

"But they might have Sharon."

"I agree. But it's not my job." He'd guessed why she'd stayed at the observatory just after her father left. He'd come right out and accused them of using her to draw

Logan's murderers into the open. But no one else had confirmed it. If they didn't give him a direct order, he could play along and focus on his assignment.

"You're kidding. Why are you on the task force, then?"

"To babysit."

His decision not to search for her friend wasn't the only contribution to her look of dissatisfaction. She was disappointed in him. And he could live with that. As long as it kept her safe.

## Chapter Twenty-Two

Studying the chessboards along the edge of his study was comforting. It took his mind off other problems and somehow helped him eventually resolve those problems. Then his eyes landed on Patrice.

Once again, she sat on the edge of her chair, sipping her wine, ready for his instructions. She'd behaved well during their last encounter, following his instructions to the letter. As a result, she was conducting herself with cautious obedience.

The delivery was scheduled to take place in two days' time. The details were complete, with the exception of Andrea Allen in his possession. The risks were much higher without her as a pawn. He kept reworking the board, wanting a different outcome.

The only way to guarantee victory was his original plan. Throw another distraction into the laps of the Border Protection officers and they'd weaken. If they were searching for their commander's daughter, there would be fewer officers searching for his shipment.

Yes, his tactics might need to change, but the fundamental overall strategy was sound and needed to stay in play. Therefore, it was essential to capture his opponent's queen.

"Do you still have the college girl?"

Patrice looked up quickly, setting her wine on his glass

table. "Yes, of course. You said to ship her south with the guns and let the men split the money when they sold her. Blondes bring a good price."

"Good. Good." He studied his third game board, anticipating a Steinitz strategy.

"There's one more thing, Mr. Rook. Our mutual friends would like you to oversee the transfer yourself."

"Certainly. Patrice, have I ever told you about Wilhelm Steinitz? He developed several rules of chess. The first states that the right to attack belongs to the person with the positional advantage. Since I am in the superior position of knowing what lies ahead, I believe I have an obligation to attack or lead. If I fail to attack, I deserve for the advantage to evaporate."

"I think I know what you're saying." Her look of utter confusion confirmed she did not.

"Steinitz thought the attack should always be made on your opponent's weakest square. Do you know what that is for the men trying to find us?"

She shook her head.

"Andrea Allen."

"She has around-the-clock protection. Do you have a plan to abduct her?"

"I do. And I'll need the university student. How soon can we have her available?"

"I can get her back by tomorrow. I'll need a drop-off point."

"Certainly." Ah, yes. If he moved his king's rook… "Hand me my phone."

She complied, and he texted the new position of his rook. If his opponent's moves were as predictable as he projected, in two moves he would run the board.

"Based on Miss Allen's personality and the inexperience of the new sheriff, I think our problem will be resolved soon. Let's drop her roommate near the abandoned southwest camp."

"And what then?"

"I'll provide you instructions. Do you need more wine?" She shook her head, and he locked the door. "After a very long week, I'm in the mood for a bit of fun."

There was a moment—just a slight raise of her delicate eyebrow—where Patrice had a look of calculated control. He didn't care to think about it twice. She unzipped her leather skirt and let it fall over her slim hips. She could make the arrangements for the girl's transportation soon.

The thought of Andrea Allen sitting in Patrice's place excited him to his core. Extracting his pleasure shouldn't take long at all.

## Chapter Twenty-Three

Father and son had both picked her up from the observatory this morning. They held a conversation in the front seat while Andrea stared out the window at the same rocks as yesterday and the day before and the day before that. Boring terrain? She wouldn't admit to anyone that she secretly loved it. Watching the sun rise here was different from anyplace she'd ever lived, and the stars... The stars were amazing. She could look at them every night for a lifetime.

"Not a word since I told her no yesterday," Pete answered Joe.

Joe had offered the front passenger seat to her, but she'd moved past him and climbed into the back. Alone, free from distractions. Without staring at Pete, she could search the sunrise for answers to all the confusing questions she'd been left with yesterday.

Search, but not find. She was still as confused as ever. Needing to be involved in finding Sharon. Scared that she might be allowed to participate. Frightened that she wouldn't. Ultimate confusion.

She forced herself to count the different varieties of trees instead of sneaking a peek at Pete. The conversation with his dad was obviously meant to pique her curiosity. Both men were blatantly attempting to get her to jump in and talk to them. She'd easily ignored them both yesterday afternoon, closed off in her bedroom sanctuary. Today would definitely be harder.

Especially when she wanted to ask if the task force had discovered anything from the tablet Sharon had used. Nope, she wasn't going to talk to him. She might ask Joe later, but he was helping Pete annoy her at the moment.

"I'm just doing my job. You'd think she'd understand how a protection detail works," Joe said. "Someone protects the gal needing protecting. The rest of the task force runs down the information about secretive emails implicating a missing student."

"Secret?" she began, then stopped herself. No talking. Pete had insulted her and hadn't bothered to apologize. Point in fact, when she'd taken her dinner to her room he'd shouted after she was around the corner that he wouldn't apologize for thinking of her safety first.

It was killing her not to ask a gazillion questions. Where was Sharon? Why hadn't Joe just legally adopted Pete? What made him lie all these years? But more important, how did Pete feel about his father's explanation?

It appeared that whatever the explanation, Pete had accepted it and moved on. His relationship with his dad seemed as strong as ever. Another reason she wanted to talk was that she had her own news to share. Each morning, she'd enjoyed filling Joe in on her project, even if he rarely understood what she said. It felt good to talk about the progress and the setbacks. Darn it. And last night had been one setback after another.

Pete made the final turn onto the last road to their house when the county radio squeaked. "Pete, you there?"

"Yeah, Honey. What do you need?"

"We've got a call here for Miss Allen. She still with you? Want us to patch it through?"

"Who's calling?"

"A woman just keeps saying it's an emergency and asks

for a number to reach her. I'd assume it's no one from her work, since she was there all night. Her parents have your number, right?"

"Patch it through and run a trace." Pete passed the microphone to her. "This doesn't seem right, Andrea. You will not give them a number to call you directly. Not until we establish who it really is. Got it?"

"Yes."

He pulled next to the barn when the radio crackled again. "Andrea?"

"Sharon? Thank God, you're alive. Where are you? What happened?"

Pete covered her hand and lifted her thumb from the microphone. "Let her talk, Andrea. We need some details."

"They won't let me go unless you bring…" Sharon whimpered. "I'm sorry, I don't understand."

Andrea was frozen with fear. She couldn't press the button to ask if Sharon was still connected. She could hardly breathe, wondering what demands these vultures were going to make. And she was scared to death she wouldn't be able to help.

All the questions from earlier dissipated into the ozone. They seemed petty in comparison to someone's life.

"Sharon? Are you there?" Andrea jumped when she heard a short scream, then crying. "Sharon!"

"Three thousand dollars. They want money…you and only you…" Sharon continued to cry. "Bring it at sunset tonight. The…coordinates… Oh, God, are you ready to write this down?"

Joe wrote the numbers on Pete's notepad he'd removed from the glove box.

"Do you know where you are?" Andrea asked, her eyes locking with Pete's.

"No." More crying. "Andrea, please come. I'll pay you

back, I swear." Sharon's sobbing was followed by another short scream as if she'd been struck.

"Whoever you are, the money's not a problem. Don't hurt her!"

"I'm scared." The static from the call stopped.

"We'll find you." She'd moved closer to the front seat and didn't realize that she was clinging to Pete's hand. "Do you think she heard me?"

"Yes," Joe said, patting her shoulder.

She kept her eyes on Pete. His lips flattened, and he nodded ever so slightly. He didn't like it. "Those coordinates sound like the box canyon on Nick Burke's place where they had the shoot-out with the McCreas."

"I was thinking the same thing," Joe said. "That means we need horses, and they don't actually expect her to be alone. I'll get in touch with Burke. I assume you're heading to talk to Cord. You taking Andrea?"

"Of course he is," she said to both men, who continued to ignore her.

"She's got to go somewhere. She won't be safe here alone."

"You know it's an ambush." Joe nodded, reaffirming his statement.

"I think they've had a reason for everything they've done." Pete kept hold of her hand. "This fits in with Cord's informant hearing something would be going down during the UFO Border Zone conference." He looked at her. "I meant to tell you about the potential threat yesterday, but we sort of changed the subject."

She liked the feel of his strong fingers wrapped around hers. She could get used to that feeling, the sense of having someone there for you. Even if he was carefully controlling his emotions and hiding behind circumstances.

"Son of a—" Joe mumbled. "That's a couple of thousand extra faces to sort through. Half of 'em will be in alien costumes."

"Does anyone care what I think?" Andrea asked. Father and son stared at each other instead of laughing outright. They were the ones with experience. She knew that.

Fortunately, their silent laughter was interrupted by another squawk of the radio. "We couldn't get a trace, Pete. You want me to bring the deputies in to help? What kind of support do you need?"

"Keep them in Presidio with the want-to-be aliens until McCrea orders otherwise." He set the microphone down and rubbed his chin.

"Why ransom the girl back today?" Joe asked.

Pete snapped his fingers. "Another distraction. The UFO Border Zone starts this afternoon. It's the perfect time to smuggle guns with all those aliens running around all night."

"Night of aliens?" The phrase popped into her mind and she knew exactly where she'd first heard it. "The undercover man in the desert said 'night of aliens' before he passed out. The camera was in the back with him."

"Maybe he tried to warn you or give you the group's location. Maybe he knew more and left the info on the camera after the accident. There was no way to know when he actually died, especially when they stole his body."

"If he did say something else, I don't remember. The recording would be on that missing camera. Didn't anyone look for it after the meeting?" She sat on the edge of the seat, then fell backward as realization dawned. "Oh, my gosh, whoever has Sharon must not have the camera or they'd know what was recorded, right? That's why they need me. To see if I know the plans. Do you think the agent could have hidden the camera and it's still in the car?"

"It's possible," Joe said. "We weren't looking for a camera at the crime scene."

"I'll have Hardy go over and take another look. Maybe he'll get lucky and we can get you out of this mess."

"You know it doesn't matter if he finds it." Andrea knew this was the reason she'd agreed to stay. "We don't have any choice. We still have to go or they'll know we've figured out their plans. Sharon will be at those coordinates and we need to save her. That's all that matters. Three men have died already. Sharon has her whole life in front of her."

"So do you," Pete stated simply. "You aren't going."

"I know, I know. Your job is to babysit me." She dropped the warmth of his hand, scooted across the seat and opened her door before looking his direction. "Look for the camera. I hope the information we need is on it. But I'm still going. You can't stop me."

"Is that a challenge?"

She wouldn't argue now. She knew how to defend a position and had even taken classes on the subject. Her dad's instructions were clear. She just needed to prepare her plan of attack.

"JUST WANTED TO say again how much I appreciate you coming here to the ranch, Cord." Pete was relieved he hadn't needed to demand the task force come to them. "I don't want to move Andrea yet."

"It made sense. Half of us were already here," Agent Conrad said, then shrugged.

Andrea smiled at him, suggesting her position on the task force had been confirmed.

"Miss Allen is not a member of this team," he corrected, and no one challenged him. "Did you discover anything about the emails?"

He moved behind Andrea, keeping his hands on the back of her chair instead of reaching out to touch the back of her neck. If he looked at her, someone might overanalyze how long he stared or why he felt such a strong urge to shout that she needed to be flown out of the area immediately.

"Mind you, I'm only working with this one account, but I don't think she meant Andrea any harm. At least it doesn't seem so. If I took a guess, I think the person making the suggestions to her is a female."

"How can you get that?" Cord asked.

"The sentence structure and choice of words. I've had a little profiling. In an earlier email, the sender states they're friends with you, Andrea."

Everyone looked first at Andrea and then toward him, standing directly behind her. Everyone, with the exception of his dad, who just shook his head and sighed.

"That's ridiculous. I don't know anyone around here and even if I did, does it really make sense to want to meet me in the middle of nowhere? I would never have agreed to that." Andrea tried to stand up.

Pete placed his hand on her shoulder, keeping her in the chair. They hadn't really spoken since the day before, but it didn't seem to matter. She immediately responded with a deep breath and seemed a little less tense. By Cord's compressed lips, he hadn't missed the gesture.

Agent Conrad sat on her hands. Her gaze dropped to her lap. She was busting buttons to keep herself from responding.

"I think Beth is implying that someone told Sharon they were trying to surprise you and not to ask you about it. And no one here thinks she did," his dad said to Andrea with complete calm.

Absolutely the calmest man he knew, Joe stretched back in his favorite chair, hands behind his neck, ankles crossed under the coffee table. He didn't seem worried that a woman's life was in danger. The others in the room might misinterpret his calmness for not caring, but Pete knew different.

In that moment, the clarity of how his father had been

over twenty-five years ago smacked into Pete. Calm and rational. Two things his father had always been. He would have been no different confronting a murderer and promising that man his son wouldn't face the same fate.

He would have meant every word. And then kept his word. And he had. The price just might be the expense of his entire career.

There was nothing Pete could do at the moment to help his dad. He caught his hands slipping toward Andrea's shoulders and pulled them away, tucking them into his pockets before taking a step back. He glanced around the room. Only Cord had a disapproving frown on his face.

Andrea popped up and went to the window. "I just need to get to a bank to withdraw the three thousand dollars."

"Why that amount?" Agent Conrad asked. "Does it strike anyone else as an odd amount for a ransom? I mean, it's not an overly large sum. Many would have that in their bank account."

"It's not a problem for me to pay."

"Why do you think it's a low amount?" Cord rose and guided Andrea away from the windows.

Her long sigh assured everyone in the room just how tired she was of being kept safe. Pete knew she was ready for the forced protective custody to be over. "Shouldn't we get started? It takes forever to get from place to place around here."

Cord swiped a hand over the bottom half of his face. "Nick's bringing extra horses and will help with the tracking—if necessary. We're leaving from here, Andrea."

"When? I need to change and then get to the bank."

"Cord brought the ransom. You're not going," Pete stated, again waiting for someone to tell him different. He knew the bomb would be dropped. Just not by whom.

"What do you mean?" Andrea marched toward him, sticking her hands on her hips, ready to do battle. "Of course I'm going. I have to go. They won't release Sharon if I don't."

"No. Agent Conrad's going in your place." He could try. They all knew why she'd stayed in Marfa even if no one said it out loud. She was the bait. But he could try to keep her out of the frying pan.

"Um, Pete," Cord interrupted.

At the same time, Beth Conrad shook her head. "I'm not sure that's wise."

Pete had made a decision. He no longer cared about being politically correct or following orders or whose orders needed to be considered. "My job is to make sure this woman stays safe. That's not going to happen taking her into a trap. We all know it's a trap. The responsible thing is to have her stay with my dad."

He wanted to be the one to stay with her, protect her, make love to her again. But safe with his dad and a couple of trusted ranch hands would have to do.

"The responsibility isn't yours," Andrea stated firmly. "You know what my father already decided."

"I don't know how to ride a horse," Beth Conrad mumbled behind him.

"She'll be safer with us," Cord said, clapping a hand on his shoulder. "We can't do this without her."

He shrugged out from under the hand of the official leader of the task force. "This is a joke. Plain and simple. What you really mean to say is that Andrea's father has already decided she should go. Does he have a death wish for his daughter?"

A red haze seemed to tint the entire front room. Pete's blood pumped loudly through his veins while he concentrated on relaxing the tightness in his chest. Nick's truck and trailer turned onto the driveway. They'd be leaving soon. All of them.

Overruled again. At least he'd made his objections well-known.

"Nothing good's gonna come from this. Nothing." He slammed out the screen door, taking a deep breath, surprised at how betrayed he felt. "Acting sheriff or actual sheriff. Makes no difference when no one listens to a word you say."

## Chapter Twenty-Four

They were on their way to rescue Sharon and had officially crossed over onto the Burke family ranch. Andrea had won and was with the rescue party. It was obvious to her that every person around her disagreed with the decision. No argument needed. Her father had left instructions that if the opportunity presented itself, she'd take an active role and try to lead them to the murderers.

So here she sat, sure to be saddle sore tomorrow even though the riding wasn't that difficult. Pete, Cord and the DEA agent—maybe even Joe—all considered her the weakest link. She knew that. The new guy who'd brought the extra horses, Nick, had raised a ruckus about bringing either woman.

None of them would allow her to carry a weapon. Ironically, her father had probably had a gun in her hands earlier than any of them. Well, maybe with the exception of Pete since Joe didn't have a wife telling him not to teach his son anything and everything.

The DEA agent tugged at the reins again, upsetting the beautiful sorrel she rode. Beth would be lucky if the mare didn't buck her off just to escape the woman's obvious inexperience. Then where would Sharon's rescue be?

"Loosen your grip and she'll follow the trail just fine," Nick Burke said to Agent Conrad.

"You're kidding me, right?" the agent replied, jerking the reins to the side. They continued arguing, exchanging little digs back and forth. Some under their breath, but mostly not.

"This will never work." Andrea was furious but kept her voice low enough for just Pete to hear her. "Agent Conrad might be the same height, but stuffing her hair into a hat won't fool anyone that she's me. She doesn't even know how to sit a horse. It's obvious to everyone she's petrified of the animal. It's old, as slow as Christmas, and she's still having trouble controlling it."

"We'll get there in time." Pete stayed calm and relaxed in the saddle.

In the week she'd known him, anxiety rarely showed through his controlled exterior. Stressful situations seemed to make him even more laid-back. He watched, waited.

And she was just the opposite. The more frustrated or excited she became, the more questions she asked. And at the moment she was very anxious for Sharon's benefit.

"What if they're watching us right now? I mean, anyone can tell she's not me."

He took a long look at Andrea's outfit. She knew exactly what he was thinking. They'd gone to great lengths to make her look like a guy, even setting her on a smaller, shorter horse so she'd look larger. The oversize Western hat on her head stayed in place with a leather tie.

"They don't know you're the one who can ride a horse. We're not certain they know about Agent Conrad being here at all. Keep your eyes open."

Beth Conrad's horse whinnied loudly and began dancing in circles. They'd never make it to the rendezvous point at this rate. Pete brought his horse closer. It was the first time since their task force meeting that the frown on his face had relaxed.

"Andrea, we won't be able to stop them from taking

you. Do you know that?" The concern on his face broke her heart.

It should have frightened her.

"Cord informed Dad's team. They're tracking me. It'll be okay." As hard as it was to say the words, it was harder to believe them while she looked at the worry on Pete's face. He hadn't smiled all day and probably shouldn't, but she missed it. Missed the man who had teased her to nervous, unending babble.

Pete leaned in close, tugging her even closer. If anyone had fallen for her outfit before, her cover was totally blown when his lips devoured hers. Excitement returned even with the cautioning clearing of Cord's throat.

"I know you think you have to go through with this, but you don't." Pete let his horse put a couple of feet between them.

"He's right," Cord added. "Say the word and we're heading back at a full gallop. There's no guarantee that Sharon will be released."

"But there's a chance."

Nick tried to help Beth by jumping off his horse and soothing the older mare.

"Very slim," Pete said.

"I have to do this. And we all know the real objective is to find their camp and the men responsible. We'll put a stop to the murders and find Sharon."

Pete exchanged a glance with Cord, making her feel naive. Well, maybe she was, but she had to try catching the person responsible for Logan's death.

"Remember what we said. Try to keep an idea of where you are. Landmarks, if you cross water, sounds like a train or lots of people." Pete rubbed her back. "If I can't stop you, just remember that I'm not far behind. I *will* find you. Got that?"

"Yes."

"Don't be a hero, Andrea. Just do what they say. Please," Pete whispered.

"If things don't go according to plan, just listen to us and do what we say. Okay?" Cord added. "You ready, Nick?"

Before Nick could respond, Beth exploded with confidence behind them. "I can do this!" But a loud crack sounding like a single gunshot echoed through the mountains, giving their horses a different opinion. While the rest of them regained control, Beth's old mare bolted into the open area toward the wider end of the ravine.

"Dammit, she's lost control of the reins," Cord said, rising straighter in his saddle as if he could see more than a runaway horse carrying away their bait.

"I'll get her," Nick exclaimed, taking off before anyone could object. "Don't wait for us."

"You want to wait here?" Pete asked. "Or do we turn around and forget this farce?"

"We can't." Andrea could only think of her mission. The shadows were growing long behind them as the sun sank lower on the other side of the mountains. "We have to keep going for Sharon."

She shoved the hat off her head, letting the leather string dig a little into her throat as the wind caught it like a sail behind her. She tussled her short hair around, fluffing it a bit to let anyone watching know it was her. Pete was still close so she leaned and kissed him with all the passion she could. He kissed her back and looked stunned when she sat in her saddle again.

"We have to find Sharon." She kicked her horse and took the lead, trotting up the trail they'd been following.

"Andrea! Wait!" Pete shouted. "What are you doing?"

Both men called for her to stop. She would, just as soon as she got over the next rise and it was too late to follow the DEA agent whose horse was still galloping in the opposite direction. She clicked to her own mare, kicking her sides just a little to get her to break the trotting motion. The path was smooth and level enough for a short, steady lope.

She topped the rise, slowing and coming face-to-face with six armed men. Horses and ATVs and gun barrels. No Sharon in sight. Her escort was several seconds behind her.

It was the trap Pete had anticipated. She'd been so de-termined—or stubborn—to save the young college stu-dent that she'd disregarded all the men's warnings. Midway in turning her horse around to get back to safety, a man leaped out and grabbed her waist. They fell to the ground and rolled, lucky four hooves didn't trample them. She kicked out, threw an elbow in the soft spot under his rib cage, but he held tight.

Nothing deterred him. They ended up with him on the ground, her on top of him. He slapped a dirty hand over her mouth tightly so she couldn't shout out and warn the men. She kept throwing punches until another man put his boot on her stomach and pointed his gun at her head.

"That's far enough," the man holding the gun said. "Throw your weapons to the ground. We don't want any death today."

At first, Andrea thought he was talking to her. Then she realized that Pete and Cord had topped the hill.

"Let her go," Pete shouted.

"We have your money. Where's the girl?" Cord's weapon was still holstered.

Pete moved, his eyes searching hers. They both knew that these men weren't there for a hostage exchange. They were there to abduct the daughter of the man in charge of border patrol.

The man holding Andrea released her to two others, who quickly yanked her to her feet and zip-tied her wrists behind her. Pete began to swing his leg over the back of his horse to dismount, but the man with the gun shoved it in her back, tsking.

Pete cursed and kept his seat.

"I'll be okay." She answered his unasked question. Her father would certainly be tracking her, but she could see the determination in Pete's eyes that he'd find her no matter what the cost. She knew he'd keep his promise.

Countless times she told herself to expect this scenario, yet it was still frightening. They wanted her alive, otherwise they would have shot them all earlier. Why was the million-dollar question that her father and the DHS needed answered.

The men half lifted, half dragged her to an empty ATV.

"Wait. Isn't there some deal we can make?" Pete asked.

"Don't you want your money?" Cord shouted.

"You keep your pittance. The women are worth a lot more to me. We'll get more for not taking your money." The one pointing the gun laughed at their attempt. He straddled the ATV in front of her. "You can get off your horses now."

Two other men on horseback pointed their guns at Cord and Pete, waiting for them to follow instructions. The weapons they'd dropped earlier had already been picked up. They bent low against their own horses, grabbing the lawmen's fallen reins and leading them away.

As the horses passed Pete, he lunged, catching one of the men off guard and pulling him to the ground. The big man giving the orders held up his hand to stop his men. All stayed where they were while the one closest to Cord put a gun to his head. He froze while the fight continued.

The man Pete fought was young and seemed inexperienced. Pete got two or three punches in for every one he took. A final uppercut to the younger man's jaw had him out cold against the rocky trail.

Pete took a deep breath and wiped a little blood away from a split lip. A pistol was quickly pointed at the back of his neck, keeping him from moving.

"That was quite a show. The fight was good experience

for my man and seemed only fair since he helped kill one of yours." He gestured for one of the ATV riders to drag the unconscious man to his vehicle. "Useless to make a move. There are many of us. Too many to fight, I think."

"No harm in trying." Pete spit blood toward the man who had murdered Logan.

"I think Jimmy would disagree with you."

"I will find you," Pete growled with confidence but kicked rocks with his feet. The leader laughed.

It could have been encouragement for her or a threat to the man calling the shots. She didn't know. His words gave her hope and she'd hang on to them as long as possible.

Both ATVs were started.

"If it were up to me, *amigos*, you'd never walk out of here. Not up to me today. Maybe next time. *Sí*?" He saluted Cord and Pete and put the ATV in gear with a jerk. "Take their phones."

Pete and Cord had brought hand radios, which the armed men tossed to the ground and smashed. She looked at Pete as long as she could. She knew he was yelling, but she couldn't hear his words over the ATV engines. Hoping above all else that this would end quickly and positively, she tried to get her bearings.

Then they were bouncing over rough terrain and all she could think about was hanging on for dear life. She barely had a grip on the edge of the seat with her hands tied. One good bump and she could be dead against the rocks.

They were on the north side of a state highway. So she doubted they'd be riding horses and ATVs all the way to the border. So where would they take her? They hadn't scanned her for tracking devices and she could only pray they wouldn't before they arrived at their destination.

And if they did?

Would she vanish like Sharon?

# Chapter Twenty-Five

"They lost one of the signals twenty minutes in. Just lost the second." Cord hung up the cell.

"Where? Where's the last place they had her?" The look on the Ranger's face told him he'd been instructed not to disclose that information. "Dammit, Cord. Tell me. You knew this was going to happen. We all did and we let her go through with it anyway. Stupid. I should have stopped her."

"Take a minute. You tried to talk her out of it."

"I didn't try hard enough."

"We're to wait here. Burke and Beth Conrad are still missing." Cord calmly pocketed the cell they'd picked up from his truck.

"Do you think they're dead? We didn't hear any shots. And if they'd wanted more hostages, why didn't they take us?"

"Too much trouble, I imagine. Same as killing us would have brought too many law enforcement agencies in here to muck up their plans. We sit tight and wait."

"No. Whatever's happening is going down in Presidio. That's what your informant said. You going to sit in the corner and accept your punishment or are you coming with me?"

"Now, hold on just one damn minute. We aren't being punished. We're part of a team." Cord defended the task force.

At the moment, the only loyalty Pete felt was to Andrea. He'd promised her. He wouldn't sit around and let that promise be broken by following orders. He'd already broken a couple.

"Well, this player's tired of sitting on the bench." He threw out the challenge, wanting the backup but willing to go alone. "You coming?"

Cord hesitated long enough to blink. "Yeah, I need my shotgun."

"Dispatch," Pete said into the microphone while he was waiting.

"Whatcha need, Pete?"

"Anyone heard from Hardy? I sent him on an errand and thought to hear back by now."

"I'll ask him. Be right back."

And what if they were monitoring the police bands? "Peach, have him call my dad at the house."

"You got it, Sheriff."

Pete pulled out the tracking device he'd borrowed from the county. He'd been using it with Andrea since dropping her off the first day at the observatory. "Good, it's still working."

"You can't be tracking Andrea."

"Nope. Do you think I risked getting shot in a fight I knew I couldn't win? I planted a tracker on that guy, Jimmy."

"You could have told us."

"What's the fun in that?" He switched the box on and watched for a light. Nothing. "If I had told anyone, Andrea would probably have found out. I didn't want her to give it away. I also wasn't certain you guys would approve. We need to get closer for it to pick up the signal."

"Or they found it and got rid of it just like Andrea's. The fight was risky." Cord shook his head in disbelief.

"But worth it since my tracker still has a chance. Let's get going."

It would be the fastest he'd ever driven the sixty miles from Marfa to Presidio. Also one of the blackest nights until the full moon came up. He passed one other car, his flashing lights lit the fields on either side. They were taking a risk. Mainly him. Not with just the speed of the Tahoe...

"What if they took her somewhere else? I should have stayed in the mountains and tried to track them."

"Don't second-guess your decisions, Pete. You took a big risk dropping the pocketknife during the fight, then kicking rocks on top of it. If you hadn't, we might still be waiting on Nick and Agent Conrad to untie us."

"I was lucky they didn't just shoot me."

"If they'd planned to shoot us, they would have as soon as we got within range." Cord glanced at his cell again. "Still no word from Nick."

"He knows those mountains as good as either of us. The DEA agent's horse looked pretty spooked. Probably took him a while to catch up." Pete couldn't put much thought into Nick's problems. Every thought came back to getting to Presidio fast. A plan wouldn't hurt, either. But he had nothing. "Do you think we should have stuck with tracking Andrea's abductors?"

"Forget it. You couldn't see a trail in the dark. They had horses and ATVs. Three each, three pairs or six different possibilities. Presidio is our best shot. We both know that."

It was worse than trying to find a needle in a haystack. At least you had the haystack right in front of you. This time they had a town and all the surrounding area. Miles of border and no way of knowing which way the illegal goods were crossing. Guns into Mexico or drugs into the States. There'd be mass confusion with too many law enforcement agencies trying to call the shots.

"What are we looking for when we get there?" He

knew it was a long shot. "Other than Jimmy's jacket that I'm tracking?"

"Your guess is as good as mine," Cord finally admitted.

"I was afraid you'd say that."

ANDREA WAS STILL WET. The men who'd abducted her had been prepared for any electronics that she carried. By dumping her in a barrel of water the tracking earrings her father had sent would be useless. They'd held her under until she'd almost passed out.

Afterward, the six men had split up. Their leader drove them both to an awaiting helicopter. They didn't bother to blindfold her for the first part of the trip, so she could see all the terrain. They hadn't crossed the Rio Grande, so they were still on the U.S. side of the border. That, at least, was something in her favor. The nearest town to the east would have been Marfa, but they flew south.

The only city or town that direction was Presidio. Once they landed they'd covered her eyes with a sleeping mask. She could see nothing but her feet. And there hadn't been one clue about Sharon. Nothing had been mentioned.

Cord's informant had been right. The undercover agent had been right. And Pete had definitely been right. She, on the other hand, had been terribly wrong. There was little hope that Pete or her father would find her. But hope was all she had…and her wits.

What could these men gain from her being here? Especially tonight?

Alone in a small metal room, no bigger than a storage crate, she could hear the low bass of a speaker. It wasn't coming from the other side of the door as she'd first thought. It was behind her, through the wall. Vibrating. She must be close to the concert in Presidio.

Low lighting from a battery-operated lamp. Two chairs and a card table. It didn't feel like a normal room. The low ceiling was made of the same material. She was in a storage container. Driving from Austin to West Texas, she must have seen hundreds of these containers transported by train.

If she could only get word to Pete. She didn't know how much time had passed while sitting there. She'd counted every rusty plank of the container and knew how many rivets held it together. Her wrists were numb, still tucked behind her back in the folding chair. It made it impossible to rest her head.

The door opened and in marched an unusual man. Unusual because he was tall, well-dressed in a very expensive suit and had white-blond hair. His hair among all the darker Hispanics in the city would stand out. He smoothed it flat before clapping his hands.

"Come now, don't tell me that no one cut your hands free." A guy appeared with a knife.

Who claps their hands for the hired help? But that's how he acted…as if everyone around him was beneath him. So far beneath him he didn't give any direction to the men who'd abducted her, just facial expressions that shouted to everyone.

"Who are you?"

"You may call me Mr. Rook."

A comfy armchair was brought in for him to use. Then a glass of wine. Andrea would have settled for a sip of water. Her mouth was so dry she'd seriously thought about sucking some of the water out of her shirt. Then she remembered the dirty barrel they'd tossed her inside.

Mr. Rook sat and sipped his wine while one of the hired help cut her restraints. A sigh escaped from her as she massaged life back into her arms.

"There's no reason to think about trying to leave. My men surround this little box. No one will hear your screams because of the concert. And no one will trace you to our little town on the border since we got rid of anything on your person."

"I…" Her hoarse voice sounded ancient. "I wouldn't be so sure of that."

"Yes, you think your incompetent sheriff will find you like he promised? We've taken every precaution to make certain he doesn't. And this time tomorrow, you'll be secured in my home away from home so I can make a longer-lasting deal with your father."

"And where's that?"

"You'll find out when the time comes." He sipped his wine again and didn't look the least bit rushed.

The crate door opened and a beautiful blonde in a tight-fitting leather skirt and jacket joined them. She slid a phone across the table without a word. Mr. Rook held it to his ear and locked eyes with Andrea. Her spine and body shivered. The polite captor had disappeared. Hate and disgust oozed from him.

"I have your daughter. Speak, Andrea." He didn't switch the speaker on. She could barely hear her father's voice asking if she was okay.

"Can you hear me, Dad? I'm fine after my short trip. You were right—"

The woman cut her off by pressing three fingers against the base of her throat, choking her. Andrea jerked away, finally knocking the woman's grasp loose. She missed Rook's instructions for her father while coughing and trying to get her breath back.

He placed the phone on the table. "Time to get started."

The woman left.

"Start what?" She searched the small opening, but the door quickly closed. She couldn't see a thing except the woman walking down the stairs immediately at the door. "What are you really doing?"

The man stood, slapping her left cheek. "Tie her up and store her in one of the containers."

Andrea averted her face and watched through the hair hiding her eyes. The blond man spoke well, wore the suit well. She remembered what Pete said how most criminals forgot the shoes. This man's shoes were old but expensive and well-kept. His nails were well manicured like a businessman's.

There would be no answers from Rook. Just like the man who had brought her here had no answers.

Two men in green alien heads blindfolded her, grabbed her arms and then hauled her out the door. They kept her tight between them, dragging her about fifty yards before throwing her into another dark container. Was it strange that they hadn't hurt her? At least not yet?

Once the door was bolted shut, it was blacker than the blindfold she'd removed. She was stuck unless Pete found her. Her father's hands were tied because of national security.

She had to have faith in Pete. She did.

The confidence that Pete would find her was the strangest thing she'd ever experienced. It was more than just attraction. She admired his kindness, his humbleness. She especially admired—maybe even envied—his relationship with his father and how he was determined not to ruin him.

The darkness didn't seem as dark. She was surrounded by wooden crates probably filled with guns heading to Mexico. Her father and his men would be watching for a truckload of drugs headed north. Not a cargo container filled with guns going south.

She climbed to the top of the stack to wait.

Pete would be there. She just hoped it was soon.

# Chapter Twenty-Six

Pete and Cord followed the tracking blip to the outskirts of Presidio. If they could find the man he'd fought with in the mountains, they might find Andrea. They were close. He'd been stopped about half a block from them for a while.

"Our chances are slim to none this is going to work." Cord adjusted the shoulder strap holding his weapons and slipped into his jacket.

"Better than just aimlessly searching through a thousand people dressed as aliens."

Cord's phone rang. "It's Commander Allen." He answered, "McCrea...Yes, sir." He punched the speaker button.

"He's using her to guarantee safe passage for a shipment of drugs," the Commander said. "Wants to drive straight up Highway 67 through the Port of Entry. He knows most of your men are here and wants me to personally wave the truck through. He's a brazen son of a bitch, that's for sure. When he called, I could hear loud concert music. He may be holding her at the festival like you thought. Can you find my girl before his truck gets away from us?"

Music? The band was scheduled to begin in fifteen minutes. Did they just want them to *think* she was at the concert?

"We might have a chance, sir. Pete dropped a tracker in

one of the men's pockets. It was risky but seems to be paying off. We're on his trail now."

"Good thinking, son. I'm less than seven minutes away via helicopter from the Port of Entry. Call when you find her. I want this crazy SOB alive to uncover the extent of his operation. He has to know that I can't let drugs through even to save my daughter. Out."

Cord stuck the phone back inside his jacket. Pete couldn't see his face, hidden in shadow from the brim of his hat. But that meant the Ranger couldn't see Pete's, either. If he could, it would be filled with worry and doubt.

It was up to him to save Andrea. The Commander had as much as said there was nothing he could do. He dropped his chin to his chest again to watch the green dot on his screen inch forward.

"He's on the move," Pete told his partner. They'd left the vehicle about half a block back. "He's heading for the festival. If he gets there, it'll be easier for him to disappear."

They turned and ran, this time with Cord driving while Pete watched the blip.

"Not if we have anything to do with it." Cord shoved his foot on the gas.

They both buckled up as they sped through the backstreets. They stopped midblock just ahead of whatever vehicle Jimmy—or his jacket—was in. An old pickup barreled down the street, skidding to a halt when its occupants spied the flashing lights.

Fortunately, it was late at night and Cord was a good driver. He spun the Tahoe, pushed the gas and missed the old vehicles on the side of the street. Within minutes they had Jimmy and his *compadre* in cuffs. Pointing the shotgun out the window at the driver helped.

"Hands flat on the dashboard, you murdering son of a bitch," Pete yelled from the window as he covered Cord heading toward the truck.

Both men complied. Jimmy was in the driver's seat. When he recognized Pete, his head dropped backward in defeat. Then he began chattering in Spanish to his passenger, who Pete recognized as one of the other horsemen at Andrea's abduction.

It didn't take long to get Jimmy's story. Hired help for a few days. The guy who had hired him for the trip to the mountains said to meet him at the festival. Everyone helping tonight was to wear an alien mask that covered their entire head. Those were the only instructions. Just show up.

Pete looked inside Jimmy's truck, picking up an alien mask. *Why the mask? Who does he need to hide from?* "Distractions."

"What?" Cord looked up from settling the second prisoner into the backseat. The Tahoe had been equipped with handles to handcuff passengers into place.

"Everything this head honcho has done so far has been about distractions. So why tell the head of Border Security that you're bringing a shipment into the States? Why abduct his daughter and threaten him when you could continue to sneak under the radar?" Pete looked at the crate in the pickup bed.

"If it's a distraction, then what's he really up to?" Cord asked, not dismissing Pete's theory. "Probable cause applies if we open a sealed crate."

Pete retrieved the tire iron from the Tahoe and jumped into the back of the truck. "We up the security coming into the country and don't concentrate on what's going out." He pried the top off the crate, then lifted a .38 Special to show Cord. "Second possibility is that he's ferrying guns south just like usual. There's a variety of handguns here. Not packed well. Probably straw purchases."

Cord slapped the hood of the Tahoe. "It's so simple it has to be right. That's why his men are meeting on this side of the border. Allen should be able to get some air support, but I don't know how quick. I'm guessing that you're going to search for Andrea."

"It's my job, my primary assignment."

"And the right thing to do." Cord clapped his shoulder as he walked around the front of the service vehicle. "I'll call Allen with the update. We shouldn't split up, but I don't see that we have a choice."

"I'll pose as Jimmy, find out what's going down and where if I can. But I will find Andrea." Pete dropped his hat onto the front seat for safekeeping. It wouldn't fit on top of the alien mask he intended to wear when he found Andrea. "Keep your head down, man."

"You, too, and good luck," Cord called out as he got in the Tahoe. He'd take Jimmy and his partner with him to the border crossing. He'd meet up with Commander Allen to see if either man had more information about their un-named opponent or his plans.

Saving Andrea was Pete's duty, but much more than that. He'd promised to find her and he meant to keep his promise. The first step was to infiltrate wherever they were gathering.

He drove Jimmy's truck to the outskirts of the festival. The concert was in full swing. If there were any people attending not in costume, he couldn't see them. But since both the men they'd arrested were supposed to wear identical masks, he'd look for more of the same. Jimmy was slightly larger around than Pete, but the extra fabric of his denim jacket covered the pistol at the small of Pete's back. He was ready to pull the mask over his head when his cell rang.

"Pete, I found it," Hardy yelled excitedly. "The camera was hooked under the seat and stuck clear up at the top of the metal springs. I guess it got wrapped there during the crash. There's a recording with a picture before the car rolls. Shoot, that dude was messed up bad. Then there's only sound… Man oh man, the guy you found had a lot to say about a drug operation and a Mr. Rook who runs the whole dang thing. He lives in Mexico, but he's supposed to be there in Presidio tonight. You want me to bring it to you?"

"Hardy, slow down. Lock the camera in evidence. Did he say where they're meeting?"

"Something about masked men and a stage. Oh, and the password is…I have it here in my notes. I wrote it down. There, king's rook checkmate."

"Thanks, Hardy. You've done a great job. Secure the camera and you can get back to patrol now."

"Yes, sir."

Pete stowed his phone in the truck along with his identification and county-issued shirt. His white tee fit in with the crowd better and he couldn't risk being spotted as the sheriff. He pulled the mask over his head and drove the perimeter of the parking lot, searching for more green aliens.

The plastic mask was hot, hard to breathe through and limited his line of sight. But it did its job protecting his identity. He passed right by two of his deputies without a second glance. The variety of costumes—some elaborate and some just face paint—were impressive. The people impersonating aliens posed for pictures with those who weren't. Some took it seriously, beeping a make-believe language in the background.

On the edge of the crowd, an identical alien spun full circle. Trying to find something or someone? Pete hung back, waiting for the fellow to lead the way.

A couple of minutes later he was following four or five little green men and a woman. These were most likely ordinary people purchasing guns with cartel money. The smaller crates they carried weren't disguised. No bogus labeling. Different sizes and styles. Most weren't crates at all, just plastic tubs. He stayed at the back of the group. No one asked him for a password. No one acted like he was there at all.

At the back of the stage were half a dozen men all in the same masks, loading wooden crates, boxes or tubs like what was in the back of Jimmy's truck into a twenty-foot steel shipping container. Mask or no mask, he recognized the big guy from the ATV earlier. He was wearing the same clothes and carrying the same shotgun.

Where was Andrea?

The boxes brought in were stored in wooden crates that were then loaded inside the steel containers on the big rigs. But where were the trucks going? No one would be stupid enough to drive across the border so openly. Of course, he wouldn't think that the cartel would so openly gather the guns they were going to smuggle at a concert where county deputies and Presidio cops were stationed.

"Hey, you," the big guy said in his direction. "Where's your shipment? Get it loaded in the second rig."

Pete acknowledged him with a nod and ran back to Jimmy's truck. He had to send a message to McCrea. He dialed, and another alien tapped on the window, and a guy pulled off his mask to talk.

"Hey, man. You need help carrying— You ain't Jimmy."

Pete dropped the cell on the seat and shoved the door open, knocking the alien back a step. "Sorry, man. Jimmy said I could charge my phone."

"You're lying. No way Jimmy lets you in his truck." The guy's alien mask dropped to the ground.

"No, really. I don't want trouble."

The man punched him hard in the stomach, stealing Pete's breath for a second. He straightened, fighting the pain. "You got this all wrong."

Pete didn't want any attention. If law enforcement broke up the fight, his deputies would recognize him. Then the smugglers would know. He'd never find Andrea.

Pete allowed Jimmy's friend to grab his collar and drag him back to the light of the truck cab. He reached for his gun when the man saw the badge on his shirt. Before the guy could open his mouth, Pete had the barrel shoved under his chin.

"Not a damn word. Where do they have the girl?"

His prisoner shook his head and shrugged. Which was probably the truth. The likelihood that she was here was slim to none. What was he going to do with him? He cuffed the guy's hands behind his back and shoved him to the pickup seat. "Now what?"

"Now you're a dead man. That's what."

"Pete? Did you find something?" McCrea had answered and was still on the phone.

Pete clicked the speaker button and shoved the tail of his shirt into his prisoner's mouth. "Yeah, they're smuggling guns across the border on big rigs. Don't know the route yet. Send men behind the concert stage and locate Jimmy's truck in the lot. Out." He tied the sleeves behind the man's head, effectively gagging him before he shoved the door shut and dropped the cell in the jacket pocket, then grabbed the guns.

This area would be swarming with law enforcement, alerting the smugglers to the bust. He had to find Andrea's location in the next few minutes or it would be hopeless. Disguised and carrying the tub of handguns, he fell into a short line and set it inside the shipping container. It was easy to get a good look inside in spite of the late hour because of the concert lights. But there was nothing but boxes of guns or ammo. Four steel containers and very few people in masks left around. He sneaked around to the opposite side.

"Andrea?" He knocked on each container, wanting to shout at the top of his lungs, but keeping his voice normal. "Come on, you've got to be in one of these."

The first rig pulled away, and Pete ran behind the second. If Andrea wasn't inside, he had to stay with the con-

tainers in order to find her. He pulled himself on top of
the second rig and used the tie-down straps to hold on. He
didn't wait long before the second truck slowly bounced
across the field, west a few minutes and then south onto
Rio Grande Road. The trucks turned toward the border at
the railroad.

Above the roar of the wind and road noise, he heard the
loud rotation of giant helicopter blades as the trucks came
to a halt before the ground dropped away.

He dialed McCrea. "They're at the burned-out rail
bridge. There's a heavy-lifting chopper hovering over the
water. How fast can you get here?"

"Back off, Pete. We're spread thin on four fronts. We can
notify the Mexican authorities to pick them up."

"I'm not leaving. She has to be here." He shoved the
phone in his pocket and pulled his weapon. He crawled
forward using the cover of the engines to beat on each of
the containers, shouting her name, "Andrea!"

"Pete? Pete! It's about time you guys showed up. Let
me out of here!"

"It's just me. Pipe down and hold on while I figure out
a way to get us out of here."

Men climbed atop the first container, hooking cables
so the helicopter could airlift it over the river. Pete ducked
his head, desperately trying to come up with a plan. Before he could free Andrea, he needed keys to the padlock
on the door.

Ten guys would come crashing down on him if he fought
the big guy shouting orders. He couldn't get close without
being recognized as the sheriff. He climbed down the tail
end of the truck. Mimicking the smugglers, he tugged at
the tie-downs, keeping his face hidden.

Across the river, he saw a train arrive. The chopper
stayed low until the last hooks were in place, then took off
transporting the first container to the train. At this rate,

the exchange wouldn't take long and the smugglers would be out of reach before authorities could track them down.

Pete didn't have much time.

Taking on the leader would only get his head blown off. The solution was dangerous. His timing would have to be perfect and he'd most likely get shot. But he was willing to risk it for Andrea. He couldn't live with himself if he did nothing.

He coiled a tie-down and casually dropped it by the last container. By the time Andrea's was being hooked to the chopper, everything was in place—including himself. The leader gave a thumbs-up to the pilot just as he had for the previous three containers.

Gun in hand, Pete tackled the leader to the ground while everyone was looking up. He threw a punch, connecting the grip of his 9mm with the man's jawbone. Pulling the key ring, he ran to the back of the container. It was a stretch, but he caught the loop he'd tied for a handhold.

Curses. Gunfire. Pings from the ricochets off the steel. He dropped the gun down his T-shirt so he wouldn't lose it while crashing against the side, then pulling himself to the top.

They were flying through the air. Andrea yelled below him, asking what was going on, but there was no time to explain. He slipped his arms through the loop and dropped slowly down in front of the lock. The Rio Grande was below him as he banged around. He finally reached the door, kicking it with his boots to get Andrea's attention.

"Grab hold of something, I'm going to open this thing!"

"Ready."

The lock fell, clanging against the train below. He pushed out from the container. Gravity helped open the door as the chopper got closer to the empty flat car of the train. The darkness helped hide him against the black container. Shots from below. Andrea's smiling face in front of him. Apprehension that he might fail stabbed at his gut.

"Do I pull you inside? Or do you have an escape ladder?" she shouted.

The container was almost in place. A bullet ricocheted too close for comfort. "Steel between us and them might be a good thing." His hand caught the opening, and she caught his waistband.

Once inside, she pulled him close, kissing him before he could get the loop from his body. "So, what's the plan?"

"This is as far as I got."

"Can anyone come to our rescue on this side of the border?" she asked, lifting a handgun, arming it and aiming behind him.

"Not officially. All we have to do is get to the Port of Entry." He pulled the tie-down loop off his body and caught men taking cover behind several vehicles.

"Well, there's plenty of guns and ammo in here." She turned over a tub similar to the one he'd carried to the smugglers. Then she sorted through the smaller boxes in search of the right ammo. "All we need is a getaway car."

"Are you hurt?" He tugged her back into his arms and searched her eyes while she shook her head. "It'll be risky. No brave stunts. You run and you keep running. No matter what happens."

"I promise." She softly touched his split lip, then brought hers to his, clinging for the briefest of moments. Then she darted to the other side of the opening, drawing a couple of shots. "Grab what you need before they shut the door and lock us both in here."

He found ammo, pulled his shirt from his pants and retrieved his weapon. He took another, quickly loading and dropping it in his boot. She was right. If the smugglers were smart, all they had to do was close the door. One thing to their advantage was that the chopper was still attached, so the container was still wobbling around a bit.

"I'll lay down cover while you get to the other side of the train."

"Then I'll do the same for you."

"Look, Andrea. This isn't the same as shooting targets."

"Come on, Pete, we don't have time for lectures. I got this." She placed one gun at the small of her back and had the second ready to fire. "I'll see you in a minute."

He fired. She jumped, rolling out of sight below him. He didn't wait, just reloaded, fired in the direction of movement and followed her.

Backs to a train wheel, Andrea pointed to floodlights from a helicopter hovering on the other side of the river. "Do you think that's my dad? Can we swim across?"

"We can probably walk." He dialed the cell. McCrea answered on the first ring. Pete stated their plans and disconnected. "They agree that it looks like our best way out without your father flying over the river and causing an international incident. Stay low, drop to your belly if you hear anything and don't say a word."

"Got it. But before I stop rambling, thanks for coming to rescue me."

"No problem. It was my—"

"Let's shut up now before you say it was just your job. Go."

She ran. It wasn't far, but it was dangerous. He kept a close eye on the activity behind them. The men at the railroad were no longer worried about the prisoner's escape. They were more worried about their own. Pete followed, knowing that as soon as they crossed that river, he'd lose Andrea for sure.

# Chapter Twenty-Seven

Andrea ran. And when her lungs were screaming, she ran some more.

There was very little ground cover, but apparently losing her as a hostage was less important than getting their train out of there quickly. No one followed her and Pete, and in no time at all they were back on U.S. soil. Her father was waiting, hugging her as soon as she sloshed out of the river. Publicly.

"You're not hurt? Thanks to heaven for that. Now your mother won't divorce me," he joked.

Andrea was handed a bottle of water and gulped it down. "What about Sharon?" she finally got out when her dry throat was soothed.

"She was with the men in the truck with the shipment of drugs—if you could really call it a shipment. We stopped it six miles up the road. She looks okay, but drugged so she would cooperate." Her dad squeezed her shoulder, pulling her closer to his side. "We rounded up more than a dozen men at the concert. All in all, I think we can call this a successful operation."

Sharon was okay. She'd helped find her. All the risk had been worth it.

The man who had abducted her on the ATV was lying on his stomach with the rest of the smugglers, hands behind

their backs. She felt safe next to her father, but she wanted
Pete. She watched him about twenty feet away accepting
slaps on the back from his deputies. Their eyes finally met.
She gestured for him to come closer. He stayed where he
was, his face full of sadness.

"And what about the guy who orchestrated it all?" she
asked her dad. "What happened to Mr. Rook?"

"Ranger McCrea radioed that they found him speeding
to Alpine and an awaiting private airplane."

"So everything's okay and I can go back to the observatory."

"Absolutely not. We don't know the extent of this operation. You're heading back to Austin with me. In about
three minutes. No arguments."

"Yes, sir." She knew Pete heard. His chin dropped to his
chest, but he didn't move.

There was so much she wanted to say.

"Pete?" She ran to him, leaving her pride behind. "Come
with us," she said, hugging him, not wanting to let him go,
wanting to beg him, knowing she wouldn't.

"I can't." He lowered his voice, his breath close across her
ear. "You know why, Andrea." He pulled back, his mouth
only a whisper away. "I'm resigning. I can't let my dad's
reputation be destroyed."

"But you love being sheriff. I could stay, I don't have
to go…"

Pete looked around her to the waiting helicopter and her
father. "Yes, you do, darlin', and I have to stay in Marfa. As
much as I'd like things to be different, they aren't."

"But I lo—" He covered her lips with a soft touch of his
fingers, stopping the words but not the thought. She loved
him. Yes, it had only been a week, but she was certain of
it. Her heart felt heavenly with the realization, then plum-
meted with the miserable look on his face.

"Don't say it," he whispered hoarsely. "I couldn't let you go if you said it."

"We can work this out. It doesn't have to be your father or me."

"Dammit. I'm not choosing my dad over you. It's just rotten luck that our fathers are who they are."

"You make us sound like Romeo and Juliet. This can all be worked out. Our families aren't at war. They actually like each other."

"That's just it. You can't lie to your dad. It wouldn't be fair to you. And I can't tell the truth. Not after everything my father did for me. I just can't turn my back on him. If they found him guilty of perjury or forgery, what then? Think of every criminal he's ever put away. They'd appeal their cases. They'd be out of jail faster than a jackrabbit back in its hole."

"I understand, but there has to be a better solution than never seeing each other again."

"Andrea, it's time," her father called behind her.

She wrapped her arm around Pete's neck and gave a little tug. He came closer—a willing partner, knowing her intention. He meant their kiss to be a goodbye. She couldn't stand that it was. Hot, hurried, desperate. Their bodies molded together. She didn't want to let him go.

She couldn't let him go.

"Please don't cry, Andrea," he said against her lips, wiping a tear that had fallen to her cheek. "You've got to go. He's waiting." He reached up, holding her hands as they slid across his chest.

She already ached to touch his warm skin and play with the hair falling across his forehead. She turned and ran, afraid to look back at him. She'd scream how wrong he had to be. Or she'd shout over the whirling blades that she loved him. Then everyone would know she'd been rejected, that he was letting her go, practically chasing her away.

The door of the chopper closed, and they lifted off.

"I was thinking about offering Pete Morrison a job," her father said without the benefit of the headset and microphone. No one else could hear their conversation. "Funny thing. Pete Morrison doesn't exist on paper. At least not the man you just desperately kissed goodbye."

"And you didn't arrest him?"

"I'm assuming there's a logical explanation. I don't know the particulars yet. Do you?" He smiled. Totally her father. The Commander was nowhere in sight. He could tell Pete was a good man.

"Dad, I have a huge favor to ask you as soon as we get back."

## Chapter Twenty-Eight

It was a night just like all the rest before Pete had met Andrea. He was in his service vehicle driving Highway 90. Everything was quiet. Too quiet. The quieter it was, the more he thought about the mistake he'd made letting Andrea go.

Would he be destined to live on the ranch alone like his dad? Keeping secrets, scraping together enough to keep a few head of cattle.

His father was angry with him and as a result so were Peach and Honey. His family. And they were all disappointed that he'd let Andrea leave and hadn't called her in the week since.

There wasn't another way round it. He couldn't ask her to live a lie with him. It was his burden to bear.

"That sounds so stupid. Just get a grip on yourself. It wasn't a mistake. You were protecting her." He hit the steering wheel, leaving the palm of his hand stinging.

"Sheriff?" Honey's voice came through the radio.

"Yes, ma'am."

"We have a report of unusual activity at the Viewing Area. Do you think the smugglers are back?"

"I'm heading there now. Out."

He was only a couple of miles away. Heading east, he couldn't see if the Marfa lights were visible behind him.

There wasn't anything to the south—at least not in his line of sight. He slowed his approach.

There was one car in the lot, one person standing on the platform. Tight jeans hugging a figure he remembered all too well.

Andrea?

That was wishful thinking. Her father would never let her set foot in this town again. He got out of the car, not mentioning to Honey that he'd arrived. His feet wanted to run and spin the woman around to verify what his heart told him. It was her. It had to be.

And in that moment he knew beyond a doubt that he couldn't stay away from her. He loved Andrea Allen. Sure, they needed to learn more about each other, but this was different than anything he'd experienced. And he wanted more.

"Did you call for assistance, miss?"

"No. Honey thought it would get you here faster." Andrea turned, leaning on the railing with a large envelope in her hand.

"What are you doing— Should you— Why are you here?" he stammered.

"I need to ask you a question."

"Right here? Couldn't you just ask on the phone?"

"No. I needed to see your face. But out here in only starlight might not have been such a good idea." She slid her fingers around the edge of the envelope, nervously touching every side as it rotated in her hands.

"What's your question?"

"To answer your second question, I didn't want an audience when I asked. Or when I gave you this."

"What's in the envelope?"

"First, my question. Do you like me?"

"Of course. Is there more?"

"Do you like me enough to give whatever's between us

a shot? I mean, if you're not forcing me to lie to my father. That was the only reason you gave, but it could have just been an easy way out for you."

"There was nothing easy about letting you get on that helicopter." Protective emotions slammed him. She shouldn't be anywhere close to Marfa and yet he couldn't let her go. Not again.

She sighed and turned to face the mountains. He didn't analyze his actions. He simply walked to her and dropped his arms around her waist, pulling her into the curve of his body. He wanted to spin her around and kiss her into oblivion, but that's where he stopped. She'd come a long way to say whatever she was trying to say.

"I could get used to this." She linked her fingers with his and rested her head on his shoulder.

He could, too.

"I thought the only thing I wanted was to make my own discovery. A distant star that no one had ever seen before. Then I came here. With all the stars up there to see every night, I ran out of reasons to find another." She twisted in his arms, staying close, then skimmed her fingers through his hair, ending at the back of his neck. The envelope stayed in her left hand, dangling behind his back.

"I missed you. Missed the conversations that I didn't totally understand. Missed smelling your shampoo and soap when the steam from your bathroom found its way into the hall. Everything you feel about stars…I feel about you. I—" He was choking up, but had to tell her. It might be his only chance, and she deserved the truth. "If things were different, I wouldn't let you go. I've never felt this way about anyone, Andrea."

He leaned in to kiss her, but his lips found her neck instead.

She tilted her head enough to meet his eyes. "I feel the

same and I'm so happy. I think you should know that I accepted a job."

Gut kicked. Stomped by a bronc. The pain shooting through him was worse. His lonely life passed before his eyes. He'd looked up just how far away those jobs were. They might as well be on one of those stars she studied, since he couldn't follow her.

"I'm not sure I understand. Why'd you risk coming here to tell me you'll be living halfway round the world?"

"It's actually not that far." Her voice had the twinkle in it that made his mouth curl in a smile.

But not today. He didn't have the patience for teasing. He gently set her away from him and saw the laughter in her eyes. "Just where is this job?"

"At the observatory. I never thought I'd enjoy teaching, but I love it. Love the kids and all their questions. The stargazing parties turned me on to a new way of seeing the sky."

"But that means—"

"That we can work on this chemistry we seem to have?" She tapped the envelope against her thigh.

"What's inside?"

"Well, turns out my father knew about your false identity."

His mind exploded, running every scenario through his brain at once. What would happen to his dad?

"Before you go off the deep end. After a conversation with Joe, my dad used some connections and fixed everything." She handed him the envelope. "Meet Pete Morrison. Passport, birth certificate, adoption papers. Don't be mad at your dad for keeping it a secret. I asked to be the one to tell you."

"I don't know what to say. I never thought…"

"I know. When I asked him, I didn't think he could manage all this. I thought he might smooth things over, keep it

out of the courts. But he does know some influential people who obviously believed in you both. You're completely
legit, Sheriff." She pressed the envelope to his chest.

"Come here." Capturing her lips under his reempha-
sized just what a fool he'd been. No other woman would
ever take Andrea's place. She was his, but more important,
he belonged with her.

"There is one little catch my dad insisted on," she whispered.

"Whatever he wants," he whispered back, "we'll manage. I'm not letting you go again."

"Good, because he's insisting I stay at your place and
act as if I'm under house arrest until your task force is finished."

"That's not a favor, it's a reward." He kissed her again
to seal the deal. "Are you sure you'll be satisfied looking
at the stars from West Texas?"

"As long as I look at them occasionally with the man I
love…I'll be more than happy."

\* \* \* \* \*

*Don't miss the next book in Angi Morgan's miniseries,*
WEST TEXAS WATCHMEN, *when*
THE CATTLEMAN *goes on sale next month.*
*You'll find it wherever*
*Harlequin Intrigue books are sold!*

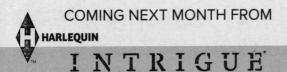

## COMING NEXT MONTH FROM

# HARLEQUIN

# INTRIGUE

### Available January 20, 2015

#### #1545 CONFESSIONS
*The Battling McGuire Boys* • by Cynthia Eden
Framed for murder, Scarlett Stone is desperate and turns to private investigator—and her former lover—Grant McGuire for help. If Grant is going to keep Scarlett at his side and in his bed, he has to stop the killer on her trail...

#### #1546 HEART OF A HERO
*The Specialists: Heroes Next Door*
by Debra Webb & Regan Black
Specialist Will Chase and trail guide Charly Binali race through the Rockies to stop a national security threat. When a single misstep could be their last, Charly must trust her life and her heart to this handsome stranger.

#### #1547 DISARMING DETECTIVE
*The Lawmen* • by Elizabeth Heiter
FBI profiler Ella Cortez's hunt for a rapist takes her to the Florida marshes, into the arms of homicide detective Logan Greer, and into the path of a cunning killer. Falling in love could be deadly...or the only way to survive...

#### #1548 THE CATTLEMAN
*West Texas Watchmen* • by Angi Morgan
Cattleman Nick Burke and DEA agent Beth Conrad are opposites—but they have to fake an engagement to trap gunrunners on Nick's ranch. Will they overcome their differences to close the case and find a love that is all too real?

#### #1549 HARD TARGET
*The Campbells of Creek Bend* • by Barb Han
Border Patrol agent Reed Campbell finds Emily Baker hiding out in a crate of guns smuggled into Texas. He knows keeping her safe will be hard—but keeping his hands to himself might be nearly impossible...

#### #1550 COUNTERMEASURES
*Omega Sector* • by Janie Crouch
Omega agent Sawyer Branson was sent to safeguard Dr. Megan Fuller while she neutralized a dangerous weapon that had fallen into enemy hands. Can Sawyer protect her long enough to finish the countermeasure, or will he have to choose between his agency and his heart?

---

**YOU CAN FIND MORE INFORMATION ON UPCOMING HARLEQUIN® TITLES, FREE EXCERPTS AND MORE AT WWW.HARLEQUIN.COM.**

HICNM0115

# REQUEST YOUR FREE BOOKS!
## 2 FREE NOVELS PLUS 2 FREE GIFTS!

### ⟨♦⟩HARLEQUIN®

# INTRIGUE®

## BREATHTAKING ROMANTIC SUSPENSE

**YES!** Please send me 2 FREE Harlequin Intrigue® novels and my 2 FREE gifts (gifts are worth about $10). After receiving them, if I don't wish to receive any more books, I can return the shipping statement marked "cancel." If I don't cancel, I will receive 6 brand-new novels every month and be billed just $4.74 per book in the U.S. or $5.24 per book in Canada. That's a savings of at least 14% off the cover price! It's quite a bargain! Shipping and handling is just 50¢ per book in the U.S. and 75¢ per book in Canada.* I understand that accepting the 2 free books and gifts places me under no obligation to buy anything. I can always return a shipment and cancel at any time. Even if I never buy another book, the two free books and gifts are mine to keep forever.

182/382 HDN F42N

| | |
|---|---|
| Name | (PLEASE PRINT) |
| Address | Apt. # |
| City | State/Prov. | Zip/Postal Code |

Signature (if under 18, a parent or guardian must sign)

### Mail to the **Harlequin®** Reader Service:
**IN U.S.A.:** P.O. Box 1867, Buffalo, NY 14240-1867
**IN CANADA:** P.O. Box 609, Fort Erie, Ontario L2A 5X3

### Are you a subscriber to Harlequin Intrigue books and want to receive the larger-print edition?
### Call 1-800-873-8635 or visit www.ReaderService.com.

* Terms and prices subject to change without notice. Prices do not include applicable taxes. Sales tax applicable in N.Y. Canadian residents will be charged applicable taxes. Offer not valid in Quebec. This offer is limited to one order per household. Not valid for current subscribers to Harlequin Intrigue books. All orders subject to credit approval. Credit or debit balances in a customer's account(s) may be offset by any other outstanding balance owed by or to the customer. Please allow 4 to 6 weeks for delivery. Offer available while quantities last.

**Your Privacy**—The Harlequin® Reader Service is committed to protecting your privacy. Our Privacy Policy is available online at www.ReaderService.com or upon request from the Harlequin Reader Service.

We make a portion of our mailing list available to reputable third parties that offer products we believe may interest you. If you prefer that we not exchange your name with third parties, or if you wish to clarify or modify your communication preferences, please visit us at www.ReaderService.com/consumerschoice or write to us at Harlequin Reader Service Preference Service, P.O. Box 9062, Buffalo, NY 14269. Include your complete name and address.

HI13R

SPECIAL EXCERPT FROM

**H** **HARLEQUIN**

# INTRIGUE

*Read on for an excerpt from*
*CONFESSIONS, the first installment in*
**THE BATTLING McGUIRE BOYS** *series*
*by* New York Times *bestselling author Cynthia Eden*

*Framed for murder, Scarlett Stone turns to the only man*
*who can prove her innocence, private investigator*
*Grant McGuire—the man who broke her heart years ago.*
*If Grant is going to keep Scarlett at his side and in his bed,*
*he has to stop the killer on Scarlett's trail…*

"I need you," she told him as she wet her lips. "I'm desperate, and without your help…I don't know what's going to happen." She glanced over her shoulder, her nervous stare darting to the door.

"Scarlett?" Her fear was palpable, and it made his muscles tense.

"They'll be coming for me soon. I only have a few minutes, and please, *please* stick to your promise. No matter what they say."

He shot away from his desk, his relaxed pose forgotten as he realized that Scarlett wasn't just afraid. She was terrified. "Who's coming?"

"I didn't do it." She rose, too, and dropped her bag into her chair. "It will look like I did, all the evidence says so…but I didn't do it."

He stepped toward her, touched her and felt the jolt slide all the way through him. Ten years…*ten years*…and it was still there. The awareness. The need.

Did she feel it, too?

*Focus.* "Slow down," Grant told her, trying to keep his voice level and calm. "Just take it easy. You're safe here." *With me.*

But that wasn't exactly true. She was in the most danger when she was with him. Only Scarlett had never realized that fact.

"Say you'll help me," she pleaded. Her tone was desperate. She had a soft voice, one that was perfect for whispering in the dark. A voice that had tempted a boy…and sure as hell made the man he'd become think sinful thoughts.

"I'll help you," Grant heard himself say instantly. So he still had the same problem—he couldn't deny her anything.

Her shoulders sagged in apparent relief. "You've changed." Then her hand rose. Her fingers skimmed over his jaw, rasping against the five o'clock shadow that roughened his face. They were so close right then. And memories collided between them.

When she'd been eighteen, he'd always been so careful with her. He'd had to maintain his control at every moment. But that control had broken one summer night, weeks after her eighteenth birthday…

*I can still feel her around me.*

"Grant?"

She wasn't eighteen any longer.

And his control—

He heard voices then, coming from the lobby.

"Keep your promise," Scarlett said.

*What the hell?*

He pulled away from her and walked toward the door.

Those voices were louder now. Because they were…shouting for Scarlett?

*"Scarlett Stone…!"*

"They were behind me." Her words rushed out. "I knew they were closing in, but I wanted to get to you."

He hated the fear in her voice. "You're safe."

"No, I'm not."

*Find out what happens next in*
CONFESSIONS
*by* New York Times *bestselling author*
*Cynthia Eden, available February 2015 wherever*
*Harlequin Intrigue® books and ebooks are sold.*

# JUST CAN'T GET ENOUGH?

Join our social communities
and talk to us online.

You will have access to the latest
news on upcoming titles and special
promotions, but most importantly,
you can talk to other fans about your
favorite Harlequin reads.

Harlequin.com/Community

Facebook.com/HarlequinBooks

Twitter.com/HarlequinBooks

Pinterest.com/HarlequinBooks

# JUST CAN'T GET ENOUGH
# ROMANCE
## Looking for more?

Harlequin has everything from contemporary, passionate and heartwarming to suspenseful and inspirational stories.

Whatever your mood, we have a romance just for you!

Connect with us to find your next great read, special offers and more.

Facebook.com/HarlequinBooks
Twitter.com/HarlequinBooks
HarlequinBlog.com
Harlequin.com/Newsletters

**HARLEQUIN**®

A Romance FOR EVERY MOOD™

www.Harlequin.com

"I thought it through, looked at it from all sides and I've decided that this is the right thing for me. For my life. For the life I want." Neha looked up with that defiant tilt of her chin. "I'm going to have a child."

It was the last thing Leonardo expected her to say. For a few seconds, he stared at her, his brain trying to catch up.

*She was pregnant? Had the man ditched her?*

"What is it that you want from me then?" he said, shock making his question curt.

Her teeth dug into that plump lower lip, and her tongue flicked over it, demanding, and getting, an unbidden reaction from his tense body. She turned a wayward lock from her braid behind her ear, each movement so feminine, so utterly taunting.

"Out with it, Neha," he said, corralling his own rioting reactions with a ruthless warning. He'd wasted enough time indulging an unlikely scenario between them that would never turn into a reality.

She stood up, and met his gaze head-on. "I would like you to father my child."

**Tara Pammi** can't remember a moment when she wasn't lost in a book—especially a romance, which was much more exciting than a mathematics textbook at school. Years later, Tara's wild imagination and love for the written word revealed what she really wanted to do. Now she pairs alpha males who think they know everything with strong women who knock that theory and them off their feet!

### Books by Tara Pammi

### Harlequin Presents

#### Conveniently Wed!

*Bought with the Italian's Ring*
*Blackmailed by the Greek's Vows*
*Sicilian's Bride for a Price*

#### Brides for Billionaires

*Married for the Sheikh's Duty*

#### Bound to the Desert King

*Sheikh's Baby of Revenge*

#### The Drakon Royals

*Crowned for the Drakon Legacy*
*The Drakon Baby Bargain*
*His Drakon Runaway Bride*

#### The Scandalous Brunetti Brothers

*An Innocent to Tame the Italian*

Visit the Author Profile page
at Harlequin.com for more titles.

# Tara Pammi

---

## A DEAL TO CARRY
## THE ITALIAN'S HEIR

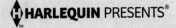

HARLEQUIN PRESENTS®

Recycling programs
for this product may
not exist in your area.

ISBN-13: 978-1-335-47885-6

A Deal to Carry the Italian's Heir

First North American publication 2019

Copyright © 2019 by Tara Pammi

Printed in U.S.A.

www.Harlequin.com

# A DEAL TO CARRY
# THE ITALIAN'S HEIR

To my endlessly patient and brilliant editor: Laurie. Thank you so much for your guidance on a superfun but complex Presents.

# CHAPTER ONE

"ARE WE REALLY supposed to think he's given up his twisted revenge scheme?"

Leonardo Brunetti, CEO of Brunetti Finances Inc., asked the question of his younger brother, Massimo, about the man who had done too much damage over the last few months to both BFI and Massimo's brainchild, Brunetti Cyber Securities.

Contracts had fallen through at the last minute, their father Silvio Brunetti's embezzlement from BFI and his corruption—everything Leonardo had cleaned up in the last decade since he'd taken over as CEO of BFI—was being recycled in the news again and again, and even worse, Vincenzo Cavalli had hired a consortium of hackers from the dark net to hit Massimo and his wife Natalie's multilayered security design for a billion-dollar contract for BCS.

They had almost lost that contract, too, except Natalie's genius had saved it at the last minute. And now, Vincenzo had disappeared. They both knew better than to think the man was done, not after his brutal tactics to bring everything related to the Brunettis down.

"What happened to the financial trail that Natalie gave us?"

"The investigator found only one small nugget of information. That account has ties to Mario Fenelli."

Mario Fenelli was one of the oldest members on the board of BFI, one of the old guard, a relic left over from when their father, Silvio, had ruled the board, and the staunchest, most vocal opponent of Leo.

While Leo, with his grandmother Greta's and Massimo's help, had cleaned up Silvio's corruption and ousted him from the board, BFI's founding board were members of Milan's upper echelons of society. Old money, old power—men who didn't want to give up what they had in the name of Leo's financial reform and ethics that he'd brought to the firm.

Vincenzo's actions had already had far-reaching consequences.

Contracts falling through, the cyber-attack on financial information of BFI's clients, leaving BFI's and BCS's cybersecurity vulnerable, and then leaking the information to the board—Mario had been one step behind with his accusations that Leonardo was following in Silvio's footsteps, creating an atmosphere of doubt and confusion among their clients, breathing rumors that Leo was just as corrupted.

It was because of the unprecedented growth and revenue BFI had seen under his leadership and the fact that the Brunettis—Greta, Leo, Massimo and their father, Silvio—still held the majority of stock in BFI that Leo hadn't been forced to step down.

With the financial connection between Mario and Vincenzo, it was clear that Mario had been bought.

"Mario Fenelli is a greedy bastard," said Massimo with a bite to his words.

"There has to be something in the old man's history that we can use against him," Leo said. "And if we can find Vincenzo through him, we can finally put an end to this."

"Ms. Fernandez is here," came his assistant's voice through the intercom.

"Neha is here to see you?" said Massimo, his brow tied. Neha Fernandez, Leo's oldest friend, was Mario's stepdaughter. "You're not involving her in this thing with Mario, are you?"

Leo wasn't insulted by Massimo's accusation. If he'd turned into the man that Silvio had brainwashed him to be, he wouldn't have hesitated to use Neha.

Massimo and he had made a pact to run BFI with ethical and clean practices—basically, to be the opposite of what their father had been.

But Massimo had had the influence of a mother who had tried her hardest to fight their father's corrosive and toxic influence on her weak son. A mother who'd strived to make sure that Massimo understood what was right and what was wrong. A mother who'd put up with an abusive husband because to leave would've been to give up on her son. Massimo's ill health, while making him the subject of Silvio's vicious rants, had also kept his father away.

Leo, on the other hand, had worshipped his father until he'd learned what Silvio was capable of. His mind had been filled with bitter poison against the woman who had walked out on her young son in the middle of the night by an infuriated Silvio.

"No, I'm not," he finally said.

Neha was the one woman with whom Leo's association spanned the longest. The one woman he respected and admired. The one woman he'd always been intensely attracted to but hadn't pursued because he wasn't a relationship kind of man.

The tentative friendship had built the first day when Mario, a new board member of BFI, had brought Neha with him on his trip to Milan, and Silvio had brought Leo.

While her mother and stepfather had postured about their wealth and connections, Neha—even then a quiet, sharp, pretty girl—had arrested his attention. She'd already been running her late father's bakery singlehanded, and had been full of ideas for new branches. Leo, meanwhile, had been roiling with anger and rage—he'd discovered that week that not only was BFI in ruins, but that Silvio had been abusing Massimo emotionally for years, and that the man he'd worshipped for all his life was nothing but a bully all around.

Neha had listened to him rage about his father, the devastation he'd felt. She'd clasped his hand shyly and said, "But all you have to do is tell your brother that you're sorry. That you do care about him. That… You love him." He'd vowed that when he returned home with Silvio, he'd do just that.

In the meantime, he'd distracted himself by offering Neha ideas about how to raise seed money to expand her business.

And through the meteoric rise of her fame, from winning a local English village baking show contest at sixteen to transforming a chain of baking goods she'd created into a multi-million-pound business, Neha had come to him for advice and Leo had given it to the best of his ability.

Mario had spotted the extraordinary talent and work ethic his stepdaughter had possessed even at that young age and monetized it so fast that within just a few years of Neha winning the contest and creating the first line of confectionary goods, Mario had launched her as a child prodigy that created delicious confections. He'd made her into an international brand, franchised her talents so far and so wide that So Sweet Inc. had become a world-renowned business.

"Why is she here, then?" Massimo asked, pulling Leo from the past to the present.

"She asked to see me. As soon as possible."

Massimo waggled his brows, doing quite a good imitation of a schoolgirl. "Is it really business, though? I've always sensed something more between you two."

Leo kept his expression implacable. Neha was forbidden to him, would always be. "It's pathetic to see you act like a matchmaker just because you are blissfully in love." He strode to the door and opened it. "Now, go back to Nat and leave me to my business."

Mouth twitching mischievously, Massimo walked over to where Neha waited, and hugged her with all the easy energy of a man who didn't have the complication of wanting her and keeping her at a distance, as Leo had done all these years.

Through the open doorway, Leo could only see the clean lines of Neha's profile: her long neck, her brown hair tied back in a braid that highlighted those cheekbones, the elegant white sheath dress draped over her curvaceous body and the yellow pop of her pumps. It was her public persona. White dress, yellow pumps and a strand of pearls at her neck. Red lipstick that made her lush mouth look like one of her delicious creations. A dimple in one cheek and laughter in those light brown eyes.

All that creativity and passion wrapped in unruffled composure, all those voluptuous curves with the hidden sensuality buried in the elegant, girl-next-door package she presented to the world. That subtle lure of wanting to delve beneath the elegant persona she showed the world, to ruffle all that composure… It had started on the eve of her twenty-first birthday party.

Overnight, she had transformed from a shy, pretty teenager into a gorgeously sexy woman. The urge to undo all that elegance, to reach the woman beneath, was as fresh and urgent and intense as it had been that day. For a man who went after his goals with single-minded ruthlessness, Neha was the one thing Leonardo had had to deny himself.

Their relationship, as much as it had stayed inside the unsaid boundaries they'd both set, and as much as it defied the media's incessant efforts to label, was important to him. Against all the odds for a man who had problems with trusting the opposite sex, Neha had become the one genuine friend he possessed.

He could never risk that.

Massimo asked her how long she meant to stay in Milan, because he wanted to introduce her to Natalie. Neha's gaze flew to his.

Leo stilled; every bit of his attention arrested at something inexplicable that flashed in her eyes. He frowned.

She turned back to Massimo. And gave him a circular non-answer. Thanked Massimo with a graceful smile before saying goodbye.

Leo's curiosity deepened as he drank the sight of her in with a greed he knew was useless to try to curb. She stood there, framed by the arch of his door, her lower lip caught beneath her two front teeth.

Afternoon sunlight from the high windows behind him gilded her in golden light, tracing the curvy contours of her body with the same delight and thoroughness that he wanted to. He'd seen her in a million variations of the same color scheme and makeup. And yet the white dress ending a couple of inches above her knees, the high-necked bodice that showed off the swell of her breasts, the tight dip of her waist…everything that was familiar about her spiked his awareness.

So thoroughly mesmerized was he that it took him a few moments to notice the hesitation in her gaze. The rigid set of her shoulders. The tension emanating from her.

"Neha…" he said softly, and she snapped into the present. "Do you plan to stand there for the rest of the day?"

She entered his office without answer, closed the door behind her, still not quite meeting his gaze.

In the wake of Massimo's jokes, the silence was thick, awkward.

She walked toward the sitting area of his office, poured herself a glass of water from the carafe. Her knuckles showed white on the glass while her gaze stayed on the streets of Milan's business district rendered colorful on a bright afternoon.

They had always been courteous to each other through the years, close without getting personal. He'd been there when she'd called her wedding off eight years ago—calm, quiet and yet somehow devastated. He'd never asked her why, only given his support when she'd asked for his help to curtail the media swarming in like locusts at the prospect of drama and tragedy beneath the elegant, sweet public persona of hers.

He'd never let on that she was the one woman he wanted with a desire that seemed to span years, when usually his lovers had a shelf life of maybe six months.

As she grew older, she'd become even more irresistible. More beautiful, more elegant, more composed, which taunted his base impulses because he wanted to see beneath that perfection. He wanted to see her undone. In his hands.

"Thank you for agreeing to see me on such short notice. I know how busy you are," she finally said, turning to him.

"Why are you being so formal?" he countered. "Is everything all right?"

"Everything's fine," she said, raising her brown gaze

to his, not quite smiling, not quite serious. She studied his features with something almost bordering on desperation, searching, as if she meant to see through to his soul. It was unnerving, and yet not…unwelcome.

"Sorry, I'm just… I don't know where to begin."

"Take your time, then."

She put away the empty glass, dropped her white clutch down on the coffee table and then rubbed her palms up and down her hips. Inadvertently calling his gaze to the thoroughly feminine swell.

His gaze traveled from where her hands rested, up, up, up her hips, to the thrust and fall of her breasts, the pulse beating away at her neck to the plump, glossed lips, to collide with her stunned brown gaze.

A sudden shimmer of awareness—bright as a bolt of lightning in a dark sky, sizzled through the air around them. Condensing the expansive room, the world, to just the two of them. Her gaze dropped to his mouth, for an infinitesimal second, before she pulled it back up. The moment was weighted, tangible, as if she'd pressed her mouth to his. But it was enough.

Enough for him to know that the attraction he'd denied for years wasn't just one-sided. Enough for his muscles to jerk and tighten in anticipation, in need. Enough for the rational side of him to issue warnings.

"I came to ask you something. Something very important." The words rushed out of her. "It's a big thing."

"*Bene,*" he said, reaching for her, but she jerked back.

"No, it's a huge thing. Don't laugh at me, yeah? No, wait, I don't care if you laugh at me. Just don't dismiss it immediately, okay? Please, Leo." Desperation filled her words. "I went through every means available to me and I come to you after a lot of thought. Please promise me you will consider it."

"Neha…"

"I mean, you know me, yeah? For what? Sixteen… No, seventeen years! I've never done anything impulsive or rash or reckless. Head down, I worked just as hard as you. Harder even, because life's not easy for women in the business world. I've never…" When her breath became shallow and her eyes filled with an alarming combination of panic and fear, he grabbed her hands and tugged her toward him.

"Calm down, *bella*," he said, keeping his own tone steady.

She was the most levelheaded woman he knew. This panic, this anxiety…was bizarre. Alarm bells went off in his head. Was she in some kind of trouble? Not financial, because he would've heard of it. He had a huge stake in So Sweet Inc.

*Was it…a man?* The thought jarred him on too many levels.

"Make me that promise first," she said in a demanding, petulant, possessive voice that was completely uncharacteristic of her.

"I can't make a promise without knowing what you're asking me for." His words were clipped, curt, tangled up in his own reaction. It had always surprised him that after her broken engagement, Neha had never been involved again with another man. Or at least he hadn't heard about it. He shouldn't be this shocked that she was involved with a man now.

"All I'm asking is for you to consider my request first. I have gone over all of my other options. Coming to you is the right choice." She sounded like she was convincing herself, too. "This is what I want."

"Fine, *bella*. I promise to consider your request. Now, out with it. All the suspense is giving me a headache."

"Whatever your answer, will you please keep this whole thing from Mario? This is personal, this is about my future."

Leo nodded, shoving away the flicker of distaste.

*It was about a man.*

Why else would she not want her mom or stepfather to know? Was he good enough for her? Had he already deceived her? Did she know what kind of fortune hunters her wealth could attract?

She slumped down onto the sofa with a harsh exhale. The afternoon light caught glints of copper and gold in the thick, silky strands of her hair. Fingers, clasped tightly together, rested in her lap. "I thought it through, looked at it from all sides, and I've decided that this is the right thing for me. For my life. For the life I want." She licked her lips, a fine line of sweat beading about her upper lip. Then she looked up with the defiant tilt of her chin. "I'm going to have a child."

It was the last thing he'd expected for her to say. For a few seconds, he stared at her, his brain trying to catch up.

*She was pregnant? Had the man ditched her?*

"What is it that you want from me, then?" he said, shock making his question curt.

Her teeth dug into that plump lower lip, her tongue

flicked over it, demanding, and getting an unbidden reaction from his tense body. She tucked a wayward lock from her braid behind her ear, each movement so feminine, so utterly taunting.

"Out with it, Neha," he said, corralling his own rioting reactions with a ruthless warning. He'd wasted enough time indulging an unlikely scenario between them that he would never turn into a reality.

She stood up and met his gaze head-on. "I would like you to father my child."

# CHAPTER TWO

IF ALL HER hopes and dreams hadn't been hanging on his response, Neha would have laughed at the astonishment on Leonardo's face. Like a typical man, he looked baffled by the concept of pregnancy. Or was it the forthrightness of her strange request?

Unlike any other man, however, he recovered fast and pinned her with his penetrating gaze.

"You're not pregnant already?"

"What? No!" She looked away, refusing to let her imagination conjure a quality to his question that wasn't there. "Of course I'm not pregnant. I haven't been with a man since…" She flushed at the sudden gleam of male interest in his eyes.

Clearing her throat, she slowly unlaced her fingers, forced herself to look up at him. "I'm not pregnant. But I want to be. That's why I'm asking you to… Be the father. To my child. So that I can be a mum. I want to build the family that I've always wanted. So that I can be…happy," she finished softly.

She grabbed her clutch and pulled a tissue out of it. Just to have something to do. He kept looking down at her, unblinking. Not betraying his thoughts. A stranger for all that she'd known him for so long.

Lord, she'd appeared on network shows, giving speeches at conferences with CEOs and entrepreneurs, and this, the most important thing of her life… She was making a total mess of this.

Even the practice sessions she'd done in front of the mirror in her bedroom didn't help. Because she couldn't recreate the most important facet of their relationship by herself in front of the mirror.

This pent-up, unwise attraction of hers that had taken root years ago. Leonardo was the one man who teased and taunted her dreams for so long, who made her want to break down hard-won defenses she'd built, for one taste of that carved, sinful mouth.

It didn't matter…it didn't seem to matter to her body how many times she told herself that Leonardo was out of reach.

For one thing, even if she could come out and ask him outright if he was attracted to her—and he amazingly said yes, Neha couldn't take him on because he was too…*important* to her.

For another, she knew what Leonardo thought of women in general and how far down his priorities romantic relationships were. He didn't believe in love and marriage any more than she believed that another man like her papa had been—loving, warm, unconditional in his love for her—existed.

In short, Leonardo was the last man on earth for a woman to build her future around. Not that he wasn't a good man. He was the alpha in any situation—a protector at heart—and he extended that protection and care to maybe two other people in the world.

She desperately wanted to be counted among them.

That first day when they'd met she'd still been grieving over her papa, and he'd been...ragingly angry about how his father had emotionally abused Massimo for so long. That regret and pain in his eyes that he hadn't protected Massimo... Neha had never forgotten that.

For a gorgeously striking young man with the world at his feet, there had been such dissolution in his eyes when he had to face the stark reality that his father was a brute who crushed weaker people. That he'd worshipped a man who was so far from being a hero that he'd have to question everything he knew of himself.

Wondering how many lies the foundation of his life had been built on.

It was the only time Neha had seen that vulnerability in him. The only time she'd seen beneath the ruthlessness, the arrogance, the aura of power that surrounded Leonardo Brunetti.

Once their careers had taken off, they had met a few times each year. In the beginning it had been accidental— bumping into each other at some conference, traveling at the same time. She'd started using him as a sounding board for her own business ideas. As the years went by, he'd started asking her to dinner every time he was in London. She'd begun stopping in Milan whenever she had the chance.

She had obsessively followed his relationships from that first day on social media, and in glossy magazines, feeding her addiction about his life, wondering if between all the women he seemed to sleep with and dump eventually, he remembered her existence. But whoever the current woman in his life, Leonardo Brunetti, CEO of BFI, would meet his close friend Neha Fernandez, CEO of So Sweet Inc., on his every trip to London.

For a confirmed bachelor, who couldn't be pinned down by even the most beautiful woman on earth, Neha had become a permanent fixture in his life.

Their friendship had deepened while morphing into a legend with the media. Their relationship had been analyzed and criticized and praised and "shipped" by some of Neha's fans.

And she was putting all that on the line. But her resolve didn't falter.

"You want me to…make you pregnant, so that you can have a baby, which in turn will make you…happy?" Leo finally said, every word enunciated in a biting tone.

She held her composure, barely.

"That is the request you want me to consider before I reject it outright, *si*?"

"Yes," she replied, squaring her shoulders.

A violent energy imbued his movements as he raked a hand through his hair and stepped away from her. "An innocent life is not a thing you go looking for because you're bored, or because you're unhappy, or because it's the latest celebrity bandwagon to jump on—"

"You've got every right to question the sanity of my decision. Every right to be shocked," Neha cut in, determined to make her point. His concern for a hypothetical child told her how right she was in her choice.

When it came to protecting an innocent life, Leonardo would always be a protector at heart.

"But don't think I came to this decision lightly. Or that it's some biological-clock-induced crisis I'm acting on without thought. And you know me better than to think it's for a publicity stunt." Her voice rose on the last and she took a deep breath to calm down. "I've always wanted a family. A man I'd respect and love, children, a house with a backyard and a huge kitchen while I do my best to be a good mum and run a bakery." A lump sat in her throat.

"Sometimes I wonder if I fell so fast and hard for John because he came with a ready-made family. His daughters, so young, needed a mum and I bought into the fantasy without knowing what kind of a man he was. The dream of fitting into that family blinded me to what I should've seen from that first day." She took a deep breath. "My dream has become impossible to achieve. One—" a bitter laugh fell from her mouth "—I can't afford for all the millions I've made." She'd morphed from a young girl, full of dreams, to a cautious, burned-out shadow of herself.

The anxiety attack had come out of nowhere but had been years in the making. Once she'd gotten over the shock and fear, she'd seen it for what it could be—a much needed wake-up call to fix her life.

It had given her the kick she'd needed to do something about getting the life she wanted.

"You never told me why you called off the wedding," inserted Leo, pulling her away from the whirlpool of her troubled thoughts.

Everything in her protested at having to share the shame of her naiveté, of her desperation.

But telling him why she'd called off her wedding was important now. For the most important decision she'd ever taken in her life. She had to strip her armor and bare herself. To a man who'd never be vulnerable in front of her, or anyone else, for anything in the world.

"John told me the night before the wedding that Mario had been pulling his strings all along."

Leonardo's pithy curse did nothing to salvage the pain of that meeting. The wound it had left in her. "What did the bastard tell you?"

His anger on her behalf sent heat prickling behind her eyes. Made her weak. And she'd promised herself that she would never be weak again. That she would never tangle herself up in fantasy so badly that she couldn't see the truth in front of her.

"Exactly five weeks to the day before I met John, Mario and I had a huge row.

"The company's IP hadn't been public yet. That first chain of bakeries we opened…it had become such a success in such a small span of time that I couldn't believe it. Mario's investment had come at the exact time. After the third bakery I'd opened, I was stretched to the max financially. I couldn't believe that he shared the same vision that I had had. It snowballed into a monster I couldn't keep grasp of soon after.

"Before I knew it, we were franchising my brand. New lines of goods were launched, only half of which I had designed. I signed with an agent, who in hindsight never shared my vision. I started to appear on network shows and then we released a line of baking tools. More and more things that I hadn't approved of. There were days when I hardly had any time out of meetings. But business was booming, and Mum was deliriously happy for me and so I let Mario steer the ship.

"I didn't quite have the guts to face up to him when I couldn't exactly pinpoint the source of my own frustration.

"Then I got a call from the CEO of a small American bakery goods company. He'd seen me on one of my shows and asked me to come take over his company's European branch. Offered me carte blanche—the vision, the line of the goods, a new bakery chain, everything would be up to me. It was exactly the break I needed from…" She looked away from him, refusing to share the complex relationship she had with her mum. "Anyway, it was the perfect time for me to start it.

"I gave myself six weeks to start tying up things with So Sweet Inc. before I accepted the offer. One week in, John joined my division. I found out later that Mario had appointed him to work exclusively with me. He seemed to be the perfect man—funny, kind, a wonderful father to his girls, and he believed in love. He wanted to settle down, get married and have more kids. Tailor-made for me because Mario had designed him like that.

"He'd been coaching him, pulling his strings, playing with my dreams and fears all along. John proposed within a month and I was more than happy to say no to the American's offer, to put everything I wanted on the line for the life we'd build. Mario got what he wanted.

"But the deceit turned too much for John. He came

up to my suite the night before our wedding and came clean. Apparently, he'd been in dire need of funds since his wife had passed away and the medical bills had piled up. Mario offered him the position of chief of division if he played the part of my husband."

Leo cursed again. "Why the hell didn't you confront Mario? Why continue to work with him?"

"Mario and I had a nasty argument after everyone left. I told him I was walking away from So Sweet Inc. after his manipulations."

She looked away, the pain of the blow that had come after still echoing within.

Her mum had refused to walk away from Mario. She hadn't seen what was wrong with what Mario had done with John to keep Neha home. "It's not easy to break those ties," she added softly.

"I'm the last man a woman with your…dreams should proposition."

Neha moved to stand in front of him, letting him see her conviction. "I'm not that naive to think a man and love are needed for happiness. I don't think I can even trust a man to have my best interests at heart anymore.

"Success is a double-edged weapon, yeah? I've enjoyed all the perks it's given me. But I'm ready for the next stage. I want to share my life with a child. I want to give him or her my love, nurture it, build a relationship like the one I used to have with my papa. I want more than I have now and I'm going after it the best way I know."

The space around them reverberated with pain and hope and sincerity.

He sat down on the opposite sofa, his right ankle propped on his left knee, his face thoughtful. "Why not an anonymous donor?"

Even having been prepared for that question, the quality of his tone sidetracked her. Distrust? Suspicion?

"Why me? What do you want from me?"

Neha forgot all her resolution to present a rational, cohesive argument. "For goodness' sake, Leo, you can't think I'm out to trap you.

"I might not be the heir of some centuries-long aristocratic Italian family, but I've got a fortune of my own. You know I've invested wisely. I can stop working tomorrow to have the baby and live comfortably for the rest of our lives.

"Granted, I won't be able to fly to Milan on a private jet or afford a chauffeur-driven car or live in a mansion in the middle of London, but I never needed those things."

"So you're not after my wealth. What do you think is the one thing that most women that I have had a relationship with hope for?"

Sheer outrage filled her. "You think I want to marry you?"

He shrugged. The man's arrogance apparently knew no bounds.

"Your romantic relationships are designed to last no more than three months at the most. Massimo cares more for those hounds of his than you do women. You think I want a piece of that?

"And not every woman's dying to marry you, Leo. I definitely remember the scientist, and who's the other one…? The CEO who publicly quoted her outrage when the trashy article implied that you'd dumped her," she finished with savage satisfaction.

His blue gaze danced with amusement. "A good thing you keep such good track of my love life, *bella*."

So he knew she was obsessed with his love life. So what?

Rugged masculinity, charming smile, unlimited wealth and power and a smoldering sex appeal meant half the women on the planet were obsessed with Leonardo Brunetti.

"So we've crossed off my wealth and my suitability as a husband. Maybe all this is a ruse to gauge my interest in you. To lure me into bed with you."

*Lure me into bed with you…*

A veritable cornucopia of images downloaded into her brain. Bare limbs all tangled up on pristine white sheets, of him bending that arrogant head to taste her lips, of him driving that rip-cord-lean body into her over and over again, of touching him intimately, of kissing that hard chest and lower, driving him crazy… Her skin prickled, her breasts swelling with an unspoken ache.

She couldn't look away from him, from the dawning desire in his eyes, from the acknowledgment curving his sinful, arrogant mouth, from the heat radiating from his powerful body. Her chest rose and fell as she forced herself to breathe in a long gulp. "If a red-hot affair's what I really wanted, I would've proposed that."

His eyes gleamed with a fire she'd never seen before. "Would you, truly?"

"No," Neha said, swallowing the *yes* that rose to her lips.

A flicker of disappointment in his eyes.

How had they arrived here, of all places? How did such a small thing that Leonardo was attracted to her send her sensible nature off running into the clouds?

For years she'd kept a lid on all her fantasies starring him, locked away all the feelings he'd evoked in her again and again, and now, when it came to the most important thing in her life, she wasn't going to let them create an obstacle for her.

"Don't mock this. Please."

"Why ask me and put yourself in this vulnerable position?"

*When she'd ever been anything but...with him especially.*

The ugly truth of her burnout, her inability to walk away from So Sweet Inc. all these years, the shame of her complex relationship with her mum… All these were vulnerabilities she loathed baring in front of him.

But Leo would not settle for half-truths. That he was a man who'd do anything to protect the people he cared about also meant that he'd strip her bare and leave her defenseless if she wasn't careful.

"You're the one man that Mario's always been wary of," she said. "My mum…she's the tether that keeps me tied to Mario and So Sweet Inc.

"In all these years, I haven't been able to figure out how to save my relationship with her, and walk away from his toxic presence. Mario rules my life—my day, my social life, my vision, my work, even how I dress and what I say outside the walls of the office..."

She rubbed her fingers over her temple, even talking about it bringing on a pounding behind her eyes. That powerlessness gave birth to anxiety that could choke her breath.

Hand on her tummy, she forced herself to breathe deeply, to anchor herself on one point in the room to focus on. To fight the wave that could overwhelm her so easily.

His hands as they poured a glass of water for her... she focused on them. Large, square tipped, and yet she knew, if he touched her, they'd be gentle.

And just like that, the encroaching darkness got pushed back. Knowing that she could control it, knowing what triggered it, made it less scary than that terrifying first time.

Knowing that she was taking the right steps to wrest her life back under her control, knowing that she was building a future she wanted helped.

"This last year...it's become imperative that I have to prioritize what's important to me.

"The pace that Mario sets for me, I can't continue and be sane. The entire board is in his pocket, even though I'm the CEO. Even though I own the IP to that first line of products that launched So Sweet.

"If I have a child with an anonymous donor, not only am I leaving myself more vulnerable to Mario's passive-aggressive tactics, but my child becomes a new weapon to manipulate me.

"Because, believe me—" a hysterical laugh left her

mouth as she imagined the aftermath of the bomb she was going to drop on Mario soon "—he's going to try and come at me with everything he's got over the next few months. I refuse to let my child become a pawn."

"Are you sure you're not overestimating the threat he might pose?"

"Said every man who claims he's a friend to a woman in distress." The bitter words rushed out of her on a wave.

Leo raised his brows and waited.

Neha flushed at the infinite patience reflected in his gaze. "I'm sorry. That was uncalled for."

Leo waved it away. "I shouldn't have doubted you. You would not concoct fantastic scenarios."

His fingers landed on her shoulder and squeezed, concern expressed in an ephemeral second and then gone. As if he couldn't let the contact deepen. As if he couldn't linger even for a moment.

"There is more, *si*?"

She nodded, not surprised at the depth of his perception. "I plan to retire soon. I have a legal team going over a million little things so that it can be a painless process. I plan to make a public announcement in a week or two."

"What?" He sat forward in his seat. "That soon? Don't make an emotional decision."

"I'm not."

"If this is about being a good mother—" admiration glinted in his eyes "—I have no doubt you can do both, Neha. And well."

Her entire being warmed at his words. It felt immensely good to hear another person talk about her future with a child in it as a real possibility. "Thank you for the vote of confidence. I want to be a hands-on mum. But this pace I've been working at for the last decade, I can't continue like that. Not if I want to have a healthy life, be a happy, strong mum to my child.

"Not if I don't want to end up..." She swallowed away the darkest of her fears. "If the child is yours, Mario won't dare to cast his shadow near him or her.

"So what I need is for you to create an illusion of standing beside me while I build the life I want.

"Can you do that, Leo? For me?"

Neha's laughter—loud, full-bodied—hit Leo like a sound specifically created to awaken every nerve ending he possessed. His hand stilled with his coffee cup halfway to his mouth. He had convinced her to stay at his family's villa by Lake Como for the weekend because he'd wanted to keep an eye on her.

It was a familiar sound—a glimpse into the funny, witty woman beneath the elegant facade. But so out of context here, in his home, where he had never invited a woman. Silvio's multiple affairs, paraded shamelessly in front of Massimo's mother, had been enough drama to last a lifetime.

He hadn't sought her out in the two days she'd been here, leaving her in Nat's capable and kind hands.

Ignoring his *nonna*'s complaints about the upcoming celebrations for her eightieth birthday in two weeks, he stood up and walked across the vast balcony.

A weak November sun cast a soft, golden glow around the gardens surrounding the villa that were his pride and joy. The villa had been a stalwart presence in his life when he'd been devastated as a young boy— confused, distraught and lost. The centuries-old legacy, the Brunetti name, thousands of people who'd always depended on the finance giant BFI for their livelihood, the tens of thousands of people who'd put their hard-earned income into the Brunettis' hands for safekeeping, an anchor that had kept him going straight.

But it was the gardens that had given him a sense of belonging.

He'd always been able to will the most reluctant, the most stubborn, flower into full bloom with his hands. For a long time, he'd believed this was his contribution to the Brunetti legacy. Well, this and the fact that BFI had flourished under his leadership for the last two decades.

Vaguely, he remembered following a fragile, delicately built woman around the same gardens with a plastic pail and spade in hand. With a sense of delight that hovered at the edge of his subconscious mind. Soft laughter, sweet words...a memory buried in the recesses of his mind.

Another laugh from Neha pulled his thoughts from murky, unreliable memories. More than relieved to leave the past behind, he studied the woman who continued to intrigue him. The same woman who'd rendered him sleepless for the two days that she'd spent under his roof. Roused protective instincts he'd never even known before.

Neha stood on the sloping path that led to Massimo's custom-built lab. Peach-colored trousers hugged her hips and buttocks, the fitted white shirt displaying the outline of her breasts perfectly. Hair high up in a ponytail that swung playfully as she walked, her smile glorious amid the riotous colors of the gardens.

*I want you to father my child.*

Even now, the fierceness of her expression when she spoke of a child that hadn't even been conceived amazed him. Then there was the very existence of another image in his head—unbidden—of a boy or a girl he'd try to guide and protect while Neha nurtured with unconditional love.

"She looks much happier just after two days of being here," said Massimo, joining him.

"You think so?" Leo had noticed something off with her but had put it down to the strangeness of her request. It wasn't every day she walked up to a man and asked him to father her child.

"You didn't notice?" Massimo wasn't being facetious for once.

"Tell me what you noticed," Leo invited him.

Massimo cast Leo a curious look but obliged. "She has such dark circles under her eyes her makeup can't hide it. I haven't seen her in…eighteen months, but she's clearly lost weight. I know these ridiculous magazines call her fat and plump—"

"Her brand is successful because, like her products, she's authentic, real. She eats like a real person and has curves like a real woman." Leo heard the vehemence in his voice only after the words were out.

Massimo raised a brow. "It isn't just her physical appearance, though. She doesn't have that glow that lights her up from the inside, that genuine quality of hers. Instead, there's a fragility I've never associated with her." Massimo's tone became softer, gilded with worry. "I remember Mama like that, before she left. As if she were at the end of her rope."

*Success is a yoke that can stifle every other joy.*

"But the two days here seem to have made a world of difference," Massimo added.

Again, true. Each hour Neha spent here in the villa seemed to restore a little bit of sparkle to her eyes. That innate joy.

"She wants to have a child. With me." The words came easy because somewhere in the last two days he'd come to a decision.

Massimo's sharp inhale jarred alongside his own steady breathing. "I didn't know you two were involved."

"We aren't. Until now."

"You're considering this," Massimo said, astonishment ringing his tone.

Leo's smile dimmed, his chest tightening with an ache that was years old, that he wanted to shove aside as he'd always done. But today, he couldn't. As much as he wanted to leave it there to rot, the past had a way of shaping the future. He couldn't make a decision without making sure no innocent, and there could be two if he agreed, got hurt.

"Go ahead, play the devil's advocate," he said, inviting his brother's opinion on a matter he didn't discuss with anyone.

Massimo turned around and leaned against the balcony. Studied Leo for long moments. "You're considering having a child with a woman who's the one constant in your life, a woman you respect and admire, a woman who's the real thing. I think it's *fantastico*."

Leo tried to swallow the shock that filled his throat.

"Shades of Silvio's ruthlessness and abusive mentality could be in both of us. That does not mean we'll prey on innocents," said Massimo, who preferred computers to people, perceptive when it came to this.

"You had a mother to teach you right and wrong," Leo whispered, the words coming from a dark place he'd shoved deep inside himself. From a hurt so deep he'd tried his damnedest to bury it. "A mother who taught you that it wasn't weak to…feel."

What he'd had instead was a father who had filled his formative years with poison against the woman who had walked out on both of them. Greta wasn't cruel but she hadn't ever been comforting to her grandsons, either. At least, not until she had married her second husband, Carlo, the first person who'd tried his best to teach them what it meant to be a good man.

But Leo had already grown up by then. Had been filled to the brim with bitterness against a woman whose face he didn't even remember.

"But I almost lost Nat with my own hang-ups, *sì*?" Massimo's gaze gentled. "You reached out to me when you discovered what a brute Silvio was, even though he taught you nothing of what makes family. You made him back off, you encouraged me to follow my passion. You believed in me and brought millions in seed capital when I'd have sold those designs for peanuts.

There's a reason a smart, levelheaded woman like Neha picked you."

Leo had no words to express the gratitude and the indefinable emotion that pressed down on his chest. He hadn't needed Massimo's reassurance, but it felt immensely good to have it all the same.

"The only thing I would worry about in this whole scenario is...how the both of you will make it work." Massimo grinned. "Nat and I will watch from the sidelines, popcorn in hands. She's going to love seeing Neha bring you down a notch."

Leo smiled. His sister-in-law was determined to see him defeated. In something, anything. "All Neha literally wants is to put me to stud, Massimo."

Massimo burst out laughing, then sobered up when he realized Leo was serious. "What?"

"She wants the child because if I'm the father, Mario will think twice before he comes near the child. He's got her all twisted inside out. She doesn't want a coparent. Much less a relationship."

"You're okay with that?"

Leo didn't answer, his gaze caught on the beautiful woman who had turned his life upside down with a simple request.

He was going to be a father, yes, but he wasn't going to do it all by her rules.

Neither was he going to be tempted into a relationship with a woman he'd share a child with, with his history of relationships. Agreeing to Neha's request meant he could never satisfy the deep hunger she evoked in him.

# CHAPTER THREE

NEHA KNOCKED ON the thick wooden door. When there was no answer, she turned the gleaming metal handle and stepped into Leonardo's bedroom. Uninvited.

The suite was twice the size of hers. Hers was thoroughly feminine with soft pink walls and bedspreads; this was a thoroughly masculine domain.

A dark oak desk sat in one corner of the room with a large monitor and papers neatly filed while comfy sofas and a recliner made up a cozy sitting area around a giant fireplace. Original, priceless artwork hung on the cream walls, a casual display of the Brunetti wealth—an overarching theme over the entire villa.

Dusk hadn't fallen completely yet and the high windows filled the room with an orange glow. One portrait hung on the wall—Silvio sitting in a vintage armchair while Leo, no more than six or seven, stood next to his father, dressed in a matching three-piece dark gray suit, his thick curly hair slicked back, his baby-blue gaze full of grief and an ache he hadn't learned to hide yet.

A jarring contrast to the powerful, impenetrable man

he was today. Neha traced her finger over the little boy's face, a host of emotions running through her.

She called out Leo's name a couple of times and heard nothing back. Drawing a deep breath, she ventured farther in. There wasn't so much sunlight in the bedroom and there was a coolness to the room, the air filled with that masculine tone she associated with him. The walls were a light gray with light blocking shades on the windows while a massive king bed sat against a high-ceilinged wall.

A huge upholstered headboard and pristine white sheets made the bed look like an ocean of welcoming comfort and warmth.

She could picture Leonardo sprawled in the middle of that bed, taut muscles relaxing after a long day, languid mouth stretched into an inviting smile, waiting for her. Her breaths came shallow, her fingers reaching out as if she could...

Leo walked in through a large door she hadn't noticed, rows and rows of expensive, tailored clothes behind him.

Any sense she did possess before, any air left in her lungs, rushed out.

His magnificent chest was bare, tailored black trousers hung low on his hips. His jet-black hair, thick and wavy, was damp from the shower.

Neha couldn't even pretend to look away. Every inch of him was chiseled to perfection like one of the life-size statues littered throughout the estate. She knew he worked out with that same ruthless discipline he applied to everything else in life, but dear God, she could spend hours just looking at his body, imagining all the things she would love to do to it.

Miles and miles of tautly stretched skin beckoned her touch. The broad sweep of his shoulders, the jut of his collarbones, the solid musculature of his chest, the slab of rock-hard abdomen…he was intensely male, an utter contrast to her soft curves.

His chest was liberally sprinkled with hair, and she imagined the sensation of that rough hair abrading her silky skin, over her sensitive nipples… An ache filled her breasts, narrowing down into her lower belly.

Every inch of him was defined and all she wanted to do was test the give of all that toned muscle with her teeth.

A single drop of water plunked onto his chest from his wet hair and she followed its trail from one neatly defined pectoral to the dip, through the tight planes of his abdomen and into the line of hair below his navel and into the band of his trousers.

"Should I wait a little longer before I put on the shirt?"

His voice—ringing with a husky wickedness—jerked Neha out of her greedy feasting. Heat rushed up her neck and into her cheeks.

Blue eyes danced with a roguish glint she'd never seen in him before. His sculpted mouth was turned up at the corners, his smile—a rare, genuine flash of teeth digging a groove in one cheek—a beautiful thing that could pull her out of the darkest of pits any day.

She looked away and then back, utterly incapable of coming up with a reply that wasn't a *yes, please*. He was flirting with her and how she wanted to retort in kind. But it could lead everywhere *and* nowhere…

"Massimo said you're leaving for Milan again. That you're off to Paris from there. I didn't want to miss seeing you," she babbled, trying to gather a little sense. "We hadn't talked again and I thought I should…"

He waited silently. And that bubble of intimacy pulled her, deeper and deeper.

"I'll wait outside. Can we talk while you walk to the helicopter?"

He leaned against the big bed, his shirt thrown casually onto it. His glorious chest still bare. "I wasn't going to leave without talking to you."

"Oh, okay," she said, suddenly feeling superconscious of her own attire. The see-through cover-up she'd pulled on in a hurry stuck to her damp skin while barely skimming the tops of her thighs. She pulled the sheer fabric away from her skin and his attention, arrested on every breath and movement of hers, made her shaky all over.

"I just wanted to reiterate that—"

"I have made a decision."

She swayed, her knees refusing to prop her up. He reached for her immediately, his long fingers grasping her elbow in a firm grip.

"I'm fine," she said, snatching back her arm. Forcing herself to breathe in long, deep gulps. "I'll let you finish dressing." She'd barged into his room and now she couldn't wait to escape. If he said no…

"I'd prefer to talk here," he said, pushing off from

the bed. "And I'll put on the shirt if it makes you uncomfortable."

"Not uncomfortable, no. After all, it's your bedroom. Just distracting," she said in a half-snorting, high voice, panic letting her thoughts out in a rush.

His laughter was delicious, sexy, rubbing against her skin, winding her up. Heat washed over every inch of her, the very idea of licking up that hard chest sending a rush of desire through her.

"As you wish," he said with a devilish smile, and reached for his white shirt.

Neha watched, shameless and bold and greedy, as he raised his arms and let the shirtsleeves slide down his corded arms. A mole on the underside of his right bicep, a small scar under his left pectoral—details she didn't need to know about him and would never forget.

She followed him into the seating area, too agitated to sit.

He took mercy on her and said, "We need to set expectations."

She nodded. "I'll sign any document you put in front of me that I'll never seek financial assistance. I'll never hint, twist or manipulate you for marriage. Or demand that you be involved in the child's life. I—"

He leaned forward in the sofa, all the humor gone from his face. "That's not what I meant."

"I just want to make it clear that I won't be a headache for you, Leo."

He pressed a finger to his forehead, as if he was exercising patience he didn't have. "In doing so, you're insulting me."

"What? How?"

"You want me to father a child, face off Mario, all the while offering no emotional or financial or even moral support?" His taut expression highlighted the rugged beauty of his features. "That makes me such a shining example of what a man should be, *si*?"

"I'm not sure I follow."

He sighed. "It's a little…disturbing to be thought a man who thinks nothing of fathering a child as a favor and moves on."

Shock rendered Neha silent for long minutes. That was the last objection she'd expected. "You told me once that you innately don't trust women, and when I said that that was horribly sexist, you said you didn't have the slightest inclination to examine it, much less fix it.

"You said…love was for fools who willingly bought into a bunch of compromises and then glorified it. You told that reporter you were ecstatic to let Massimo propagate the great Brunetti line further.

"I assumed from our long association that being tied down isn't in your future plans."

He ran a hand over his jaw. "Being tied down to a woman is one thing, a child, completely another."

"What does that mean?"

"If I father a child, I will *damn well* be involved in that child's life. Our long association should have told you that."

His softly spoken words packed a punch. Neha swallowed the defense that rose to her lips, slowly realizing that this wasn't about her.

It was about *him, his…feelings*. And he was right—in

all the myriad scenarios she'd foreseen she hadn't considered his feelings at all. "It wasn't meant as a statement on what kind of a man you are.

"I chose you because you're the one man I know who'd do anything to protect an innocent in your sphere."

His gaze held hers, as if to see through to the truth of that.

After a long time, he nodded and she let a breath out. "What does this mean, then?"

"The child and its well-being is the most important thing in all of this, *si*?"

"I'll love my child more than anything in the world. I'd do anything for her or him."

The hardness edged away from his eyes. "That's the only reason I've come this far, *bella*. But you need to accept that I will never be an absent parent or a stranger.

"I know what goes through a child's mind when a parent abandons him or her. I can imagine what this child will hear from friends, well-wishers, every cruel, hard word and taunt. I will not willingly put any child of mine through that."

He had every scenario their child would face covered so thoroughly that Neha stared.

How could she have forgotten that Leonardo's mother had left in the middle of one night, leaving her five-year-old son to his father? How could she have forgotten the fact that she knew better than anyone what a wound that had left in Leo's life?

*If Leonardo was a father in the true sense of the word...*

Mario's shadow wouldn't touch her child. He or she would have Leo's guidance and support, Natalie and Massimo's affection, be a part of a family. Everything she'd always wanted would be her child's.

The prospect of his involvement was such a tempting offer that Neha had to force herself to think of other implications. "Our relationship—"

"Will be defined by the fact that we want what's best for our child."

She nodded, the confidence in his tone building her own. They were rational adults, they knew each other's strengths and weaknesses—they could handle this rationally.

"You said conditions. What else?"

"I want you to postpone the announcement about your retirement. And, if required, your retirement itself. By a few months."

"No, absolutely not."

Her refusal rang around the room. It knocked Leo off axis to see the sudden fear and distrust in her eyes. Addressed toward him when he'd only ever seen respect.

"Neha," he started softly, reminding himself that, for whatever reason, she was fragile right now, "hear me out."

She stayed at the window, the waning sunlight from the skylight gilding her body in a golden outline.

Even in the tense situation, he felt the tug of awareness on his senses that she so easily provoked.

The loose white sheer tunic had a low neckline that presented him tantalizing glimpses of the upper curves of her lush breasts. The sheer fabric showed silky brown skin, and the shadow of her orange bikini, skimming the tops of her long, toned thighs. Pink nails peeked through the sandals she wore, completing a picture of such sheer sensuality that she took his breath away.

From the moment he'd found her standing inside his bedroom—staring at his bed—he'd had the most overwhelming urge to pull that tunic up and away from her body until he could feast on the sexy curves underneath. With his eyes, hands and mouth.

Damp hair stuck to her scalp, highlighting the classical bone structure of her face. He wanted to run his hands all over her, learn if she was as soft and silky as he imagined.

She stood up from the sofa, walked to the door and back, to the windows and then back again, every step conveying restless energy. Without that elegant facade she put on like a second skin, he could see now what Massimo had seen. Shadows hung like dark bruises under her eyes and there was a pinched look to her mouth.

When he went to her, she turned, her entire body trembling. He wrapped his hands over her palms, keeping the distance between them. She smelled like vanilla and sunlight and an intoxicating mixture of both. Against his abrasive fingers, she was silky soft. "Neha, look at me. I would not ask something of you unless it was important."

Her expression cleared. "You're right." She sat down on the coffee table, her knees tucked between his own. "Tell me."

"You already know a little about the cyber-attacks on BCS, right?" He waited for her to follow along. "But the cyber-attacks on Massimo's firm were just the tip of the iceberg.

"We had three deals in our pocket that fell through. Sylvio's colorful, abusive past keeps being recycled by the media and the press, dragging news of his embezzlement, and how he evaded incarceration because I bribed the pertinent officials.

"Alessandra's personal life, her past, her family—they keep getting exposure in trashy tabloids," he said, mentioning his grandmother's stepdaughter. Neha had met the beautiful top supermodel Alessandra Giovanni a couple of times during her long acquaintance with Leo. And for all her harshness and rough edges, Greta was a different woman with her second husband's daughter. Carlo had been gone for a long time, but Alex had become a part of the family.

"But Alex isn't even a Brunetti," Neha said, frowning.

"Massimo and I think she's been attacked because Greta is close to her. All of us have been featured in the news cycles over the past few months—always some sort of scandal or sensationalism attached to our names. Reputations have crumbled, businesses been ruined, for less in the finance industry."

"So everything is connected?"

He nodded. "Natalie was hired to bring down Massimo's security design. The clients' information was left vulnerable to attack, but she didn't steal it."

"That's how Massimo met her?"

"*Sì*. And thanks to the fact that she's crazy about

Massimo, she's given us a name. Vincenzo Cavalli. He's bent upon a revenge scheme, determined to cause as much harm as possible to the Brunettis.

"When Massimo's design was hit, only four of us knew. Massimo, me, Natalie—who'd attacked the system—and the man who'd orchestrated it.

"Yet somehow Mario leaked the news of the attack to the BFI board. He's been riling them up, calling for my resignation. That I'm not unlike my father, that in the end, I will bring ruin to BFI like Silvio had done once. Most of the board members remember the destruction Silvio caused."

A shadow of fear crossed Neha's eyes. "So Mario is involved with this man?"

"We found a financial trail between him and Vincenzo. Mario's as power hungry as it gets. He saw a chance to push me out of the CEO position and he's taken it."

"But what does my retirement have to do with it?"

"You are Mario's golden goose. Your retirement is my currency against him."

Her fingers were tangled so tight in her lap that they showed white. "Currency in what way?"

"Will you promise to not freak out first?"

"I'm still here, aren't I?" she said, some of the fight back in her eyes.

"We will pretend to be a real couple, make all those predictions that have been flying about us real. If I know how Mario's mind works, he will hate us taking our relationship to the next level. He won't like it that there could be another man—especially a man like me, arrogant and powerful as you said—who could control you.

"Everything you've told me about how he has tried to manipulate you all these years tells me that he will do anything I ask to make sure he doesn't lose you."

"So you'll use me like a puppet between you two?"

"To create an illusion that I have control over you, yes. To put pressure on him. If that doesn't work, then yes, I'll hint that I'm pushing you toward retirement."

She shook her head, shadows in her gaze. "I can't postpone it. It's not something I decided easily."

"I know that."

"I don't think you do. I don't trust you with this, Leo."

He sat back slowly, trying to digest the shock those words caused. Disturbing him on more levels than he liked to admit to himself. "Then none of this will work."

"You don't take this retirement thing seriously. You think this is some sort of temporary insanity phase. How can I believe that you'll put my well-being before your need to crush Mario or your need to stop this... Cavalli guy?"

True, he had mostly discounted her claims about wanting to walk away from an empire that had been built over two decades. He'd thought it was her need-to-be-in-control nature that was making plans for the future that weren't quite necessary. But Leo had always been willing to admit to his faults. "Yes, I did think that. But I would never do anything to harm you. Especially now, when our future will be tied together forever, when I'm agreeing to have a child with you.

"All I want to do is put the pressure back on Mario, get him to spill about Vincenzo before he does irreparable damage to my family.

"The fact that you and I will have a child together is going to make Mario nuts."

"Do you want to risk infuriating him with the decision to retire on top of that right now?"

"He's not going to like it," she said softly, running her hands over her neck. "Mario's going to be apoplectic at our…new relationship."

Leo took her hand in his and squeezed, willing her to trust him. All he wanted to do was kiss that tension off her mouth, to hold her until he could feel those lush curves against his, until he could calm her down like she had done him so long ago. But…if he did that, it wouldn't stop there.

He would seduce her, and he knew without being arrogant that she would reciprocate.

And then what? What would happen when he lost interest and moved on? When hers was the face he'd have to disappoint?

Neha pulled her hand back slowly. He didn't miss that she rubbed that palm against her hip. Or that she remained wary of the distance between them. "Okay. I agree to your plan."

"Good," he said. He could always count on her to be logical and rational. "What's next for your plan, then?"

"You have to have blood work done. Mine's done. I'll have a couple of appointments with the IVF specialist first and then we can decide the logistics of when and where…"

Embarrassment dusted her brown cheeks a slight pink, but Leo refused to break eye contact. There was something incredibly satisfying to his male pride to see her blush like that. To see that composure of hers falter at such an intimate subject at least.

"When and where I make my *contribution*. Does that work?"

He smiled when she nodded.

"I don't know much about it, but you have to take hormone injections, *si*?"

"Yes. It's a…little bit invasive and painful but I want to do this."

"I've never doubted your resolve, *cara*. You will call me if it gets too much or if you need a supporting presence there."

"Will I?" she said, a naughty smile dawning in her eyes, unfurling a beauty that made his body hum with desire, ache for contact. "Don't get all arrogant and commanding on me, Brunetti."

"Don't forget this is a partnership, Fernandez," he replied in the way they used to tease each other a long time ago. *Dio*, the woman had always been so strong. And it was the strength that attracted him, that will to keep going on in the face of adversity. "Everything will be all right, Neha. I'm glad you came to me."

"I hope so. I…"

Eyes wide, breath hitching loud enough for him to hear, she came at him. And hugged him. Hard. The press of her body against his was a pleasure of mere seconds, gone before he could revel in it. The scent and warmth of her fleeting heaven. Her hands on his shoulders, she kissed his cheek, and a shiver of anticipation built inside him. Anticipation that would never deepen into more. "I don't know how to thank you," she said, pulling back. "I promise you, Leo. You'll never regret it."

Leo pulled her arms from around his neck and took a step back. Putting distance between her and him. Giving his discipline a fighting chance.

Every muscle in his body flooded with the awareness that here was a woman who was his match in every way. A woman who'd never ask him for more than he could give, a woman who would be the absolute best mother to any child they had, a woman that would always make him laugh and want.

Awkwardness flashed in her eyes before she fiddled with her clutch again.

As he watched her walk out of his bedroom, Leo stayed leaning against the bed. He turned his neck around, tension clinging to his frame.

*Cristo*, now even his bedroom smelled of her.

The rest of the day, he wondered if he would come to regret his decision. Because he had tied himself irrevocably to the woman he desperately wanted and could not have.

# CHAPTER FOUR

NEHA WALKED ONTO the picture-perfect balcony attached to her suite and took in the astonishingly beautiful view of the grounds surrounding the villa and the glittering lights of Lake Como. After a relaxing day at a luxurious spa and lunch at a café overlooking the beautiful canal district of Navigli with Natalie's irreverent companionship, Neha was equipped to face the evening.

Greta's eightieth birthday celebrations—the perfect event for Neha and Leonardo's first public appearance as an official couple. Today, they'd confirm the rumors that had already been whipped into a frenzy by Leo's carefully orchestrated trips to her offices, even at the opening of a new, trendy café in London.

They'd seen more of each other in the last two weeks than they had in the last fifteen years. He was doing it for the press coverage, but she struggled mightily to not fall into the fantasy right out of her head.

Like sending her favorite exotic orchids the day after she'd returned from Milan.

Like showing up at work last night and packing her off to Lake Como so that she could attend Greta's party and get a weekend away in the process. Neha had protested at first—it was a whole extra day she didn't need to bunk.

"You expect me to accept the fact that you want to retire seriously, and yet you won't cut yourself a break after an eighty-hour week," he'd said, his powerful frame shrinking the size of her vast office. The broad sweep of his shoulders had electrified her senses after a long day, the reality of seeing him in her space making everything she'd set into motion achingly real.

The attraction she felt for him all the more painful to deny for he was just as out of reach now as ever. But he'd been right about her needing a break.

The two weeks since she'd returned had been packed with back-to-back meetings, a visit to a newly launched bakery in east London where she hadn't been allowed inside the huge, state-of-the-art industrial kitchen but posed for pictures with delicious treats she hadn't created, and reading hundreds and hundreds of pages of contracts with the legal personnel for a book deal she was going to sign soon.

A cookbook with her brand name but the actual recipes had been created by a team of world-class chefs.

She'd been thrust right into her soul-sucking life and desperate for escape, but Neha had given in. Even as the cautious part of her whispered that running away *with Leo and to Leo* was a dangerous habit.

Every free moment of the last two weeks had been spent replaying that scene between her and Leo in his bedroom. She'd fantasized in the most wicked detail what it would have been like if she'd taken his mouth for a kiss she'd wanted for so long. If she'd asked him to conceive their child by making love to her...

Her cheeks heated. Would he have taken her up on that offer, too? Did he feel this awareness that seemed to hum through her when he was near?

But she was also painfully aware that it was time to bury what had been her heart's desire for so long that it was a part of her.

They could never be lovers now, not with their lives entangled around an innocent life. Not an easy decision but done.

As the horizon shone brilliantly in the evening sky, for the first time in years she was hopeful for the future. With Leo by her side, she could finally build the life she wanted. And her baby would have everything she had known once—a doting mother, a caring father, a loving family.


"She's refusing to join us?" Massimo asked as Leo walked into the lounge, having spent more than an hour with Greta, who was acting like a petulant teenager instead of the Brunetti matriarch celebrating her eightieth birthday with Milan's upper crest due to appear in less than an hour to honor her.

Leo took the tumbler of whiskey Massimo offered with a grateful nod and downed it. He sighed. "She's not just acting out this time. She's really upset that Alex is not here."

"It's not like Alex to disappear like this without a word to any of us, for months at a time."

Leo agreed. While their grandmother's stepdaughter,

Alex—Alessandra Giovanni, one of the top supermodels in the world—had family in the US and regularly disappeared from Milan for months at a time for her shoots, on a given day, they'd always known where she would be. More importantly, Alex never went more than a few weeks without dropping by to visit with Greta.

But this time, even Alex's mother had no idea of her daughter's whereabouts.

Greta, having lived through the path of destruction her son had blazed through her life, had never been soft or loving with Leo or Massimo. But she had stood guard over her grandsons, helped them overthrow her own son when it had been clear Silvio would destroy BFI.

Only with her second husband, Carlo, whom she'd lost after a precious few years, and his daughter, Alessandra, had a different side emerged of Greta.

He knew Alex felt that same love toward Greta, knew she felt like she belonged here with Massimo and him, more than she did with her mother's family. So why disappear like this? Where was she?

He was about to suggest they reach out to Alex's agent when Neha walked into the lounge.

Looking absolutely ravishing in a fetching pink creation that left her shoulders bare, kissed every curve like he wanted to, molded to the swell of her hips. And yet, somehow, she managed to look elegant and stunning, too. Her hair in an updo showcased the beauty of her high cheeks and strong brows. Mouth glistening a light pink, she reminded Leo of a ripe, tart strawberry. A strawberry that he wanted to bite.

She took one look at them and stilled. "Sorry, I didn't mean to intrude on you two. I can come back."

There was a hint of shimmer on her neck and the valley of her cleavage when she stood under the crystal chandelier, beckoning a man's touch. Leo could no more stop watching her than he could stop breathing. *Dio*, he couldn't remember the last time he'd been this mesmerized by a woman. Maybe never. "Of course you're not intruding," he said.

Maybe a little too sharply, because her gaze jerked up to his.

He cleared his throat and went to pour another drink. He needed the extra fortification if he had to spend the rest of the evening with her—looking but not touching, enveloped by the warmth of her, pretending to be a couple in front of the world. But not doing all the things he wanted to do to her.

"I'll talk to Greta," Massimo said.

His younger brother had that mischievous smile that Leo had rarely seen growing up. Massimo stopped in front of Neha, put his hands on her bare shoulders and pulled her to him. An indulgent smile on those pink lips, Neha let him embrace her and then kiss her cheeks. Which he did with quite a relish.

Stepping back, Massimo smiled. "You look utterly enchanting, *bella mia*. If only you'd reciprocated my interest in you, we'd have been something. But alas, I remember you rebuffed me, of course without breaking my heart."

Neha laughed. And the sound of it snuck into Leo's

every pore. "*Per favore*, Massimo. Stop flirting with me, you wretched man, and go find your wife."

"*Sì,*" the rogue said with a smile, then bowed elaborately, which made her laugh harder.

That thick silence descended on them again, ripe with tension.

"Are you scowling because he was flirting with me?" Neha said, keeping her distance. As if he was dangerous.

"Massimo has eyes for no one but Natalie. That whole thing was for my benefit."

"Your benefit?" she said, her eyes growing wide in confusion. "What do you mean?"

Leo shrugged. He wasn't going to explain that his brother thought it was hilarious how attracted Leo was to her. Especially when he was determined to not do anything about it.

"You want a drink before the hordes descend on us?" he finally managed in a polite voice.

"Just some sparkling water, please," she replied.

Leo opened a bottle of sparkling water and offered it to her.

She took the glass from his hands, somehow managing to make sure their fingers didn't touch. "You didn't tell me how I look," she said in a soft, quiet voice characteristic of her. Not petulant, not demanding, just a simple, rational question. Maybe he could handle this better, then.

He let his gaze rove over her again. "I didn't think you were the type who needed compliments or a boost in confidence."

Irritation he'd never seen before flashed across her face. "There are two things wrong about that."

"Two?" He raised a brow, liking that he was getting under her skin. "Explain, please."

"First of all, I don't think I've ever met a woman who wouldn't welcome a compliment from a gentleman friend. No matter how gorgeous or successful she is."

"Touché," he said, raising his glass to her. "'Gentleman friend' has such…an old-world ring to it, *bella*? Is that where we're settling for?"

"Define this—" she moved her arm gracefully in the distance between them, distance she seemed determined to maintain "—any other way you want."

"And my second offense?" he taunted back.

"This is uncharted territory for me. So yes, I'd like to know what you were thinking for a change, instead of having to guess what your expression means."

"What is uncharted territory?"

"Playing your piece in front of the entire world."

Something in her tone snagged at him. But for the life of him, he couldn't put his finger on it. It felt like all the safe, neutral ground they'd carefully trod for so many years had disappeared, leaving them in a minefield. Filled with sexual tension and something else.

Were they foolishly, knowingly mucking up a relationship they'd built?

"Why is this so hard, Leo?" she said softly, a beseeching look in her eyes that shamed him instantly. *Dio*, did the woman have any idea how beguiling she looked like that? How much he wanted to remove any and every problem if it meant she'd smile at him like she did with Massimo?

He was man enough to admit that it was his fault. He'd purposely held back the words that had risen to his lips when she'd walked in. Made it awkward by behaving like a randy, churlish youth who had been denied the one thing he'd wanted the most.

He finished his drink and went to stand in front of her. Tucking his finger under her chin, he raised her face. His heart thudded as she met his gaze, his match in every way. "You're the most beautiful, poised, smart, courageous woman I've ever known in my life."

She laughed, swatted at his shoulder with her hand and stepped away. Leo buried the pulse of irritation at her need to put distance between them. "Are there any adjectives left?"

"You don't think I'm serious?"

"It doesn't matter, really." A tightness to her words. "I think I've indulged myself enough for one evening," she half muttered to herself. When she looked at him again, there was nothing but that serenity, that composure, he'd known for so long. "Natalie told me it was you who'd arranged such a lovely day for us. Going as far as to hound her into accompanying me.

"Just as you'd told me that she needed my help in picking a dress for tonight."

"She's got terrible fashion sense. You, on the other hand, never look less than stunning."

She laughed, and he basked in it. "You manipulated us both."

"I saw two hardworking, stubborn women who needed a break."

"It was exactly what I'd needed, and I didn't even know it. So, thank you."

"It was my pleasure. When I arrived last night, you looked like you were ready to drop." He'd been alarmed by how dull she'd looked with dark shadows under her eyes again. "Haven't you been sleeping well?"

She tucked a wisp of hair that wasn't in the way, and he knew she was going to lie. "I was fine. I just had a brutal week."

"Did Mario say anything about my visits?"

"We had a few meetings scheduled but he... Damn it, I'm nervous. About this whole evening."

He frowned. "Why?"

"I just... I wish we hadn't decided to make this whole thing public today. Although that's probably just me wanting to delay the inevitable." She laughed at herself, turning the glass in her hand around and around. "Now you think I'm a little cuckoo."

"No. But I'm definitely beginning to believe that saying you're stressed is an understatement. Are you having second thoughts about this whole thing?" He carefully controlled his voice, loath to betray the pang in his chest that she might have changed her mind.

This had to be about her, always.

"Of course not!" Her chest rose and fell, the thin chain at her neck glinting under the light of the chandelier. "Not at all." When he just stared at her, she sighed. "If you must know, I mostly avoided Mario this past week. I stayed at my flat the whole week, which I never do because I like to see Mum at least every other day—running away when I knew he might be looking for me, canceling on a one-on-one lunch saying I had a checkup, that sort of thing."

Anger flared in Leo's gut. He took her hand and was startled to feel her long fingers tremble. "Neha, are you scared of him? Has he caused you physical harm?"

"God, no. I'd like to think if he'd ever raised his hand to me, at least then my…" She cringed and snatched her hand back. And he wondered at how much she kept to herself, how little she showed of her true feelings. "If he had, I'd have knocked him down in return," she said fiercely. "Mario thinks too much of himself to stoop to what he'd call vulgar behavior. His tactics are more… insidious. I didn't tell you this, but I had an argument with him before I came to see you about this new book deal we're signing and it just blew up.

"I'm sure he thought I ran to you to complain about it. After leaving it like that, you showing up at work in the last week and me avoiding him, he'll be bursting to have a go at me."

"Then why avoid him? Why not face him today when I'm here, too?"

"It's just that…every time he and I get into it, it's Mum who suffers. It's Papa's birthday next week and she's always extra fragile on that day.

"Usually she and I spend the day together, donate a week's worth of meals at this shelter Papa used to volunteer at…help out the whole day. And then we have dinner with a lot of his friends and family, just remembering him. I prep for it for days, take the entire day off, and it almost feels like…she and I never drifted apart." The wistfulness in her eyes tugged at him before she blinked it away. "If I have a massive row with Mario now, it'll bleed through to her. She'll worry that the both of us are fighting and I don't want to make Papa's birthday extra hard for her."

Leo voiced the question that came to him instantly, his tone a little bit sharp. "And in all this, who looks after you? Even I know that you still miss your papa."

She frowned. "I look after myself. My mother has always been emotionally delicate—I don't think she ever recovered from Papa's death, and yes, sometimes I wish…" Guilt shone in her eyes before she sighed. She fiddled with a ring she wore on her right hand. "I don't like talking about all this with you."

"Why not?"

"I feel guilty for talking about her. And I definitely don't want to lose your respect. I know you abhor emotional drama of this sort."

"Because you have a complex relationship with your mother?" he said, swallowing away the stinging words he wanted to use. Like *toxic* and *harmful* and *soul-sucking.*

"I think you have made a lot of extrapolations from whatever the media reports about my relationships with women." For some reason he couldn't fathom, every time Neha made even a fairly reasonable assumption about him, it riled him. He wanted to be…the perfect man in her eyes.

*Cristo! Where was this coming from?*

"What did you think raising a child together was

going to entail? Whether we like it or not, whether we want or not, our families and our history are going to feature in our child's life."

"And it doesn't bother you?" she said, searching his gaze.

"I forgot *extremely stubborn* in the list of adjectives earlier," he said, taking her hand in his. "Believe me, *bella*. We're in this together. There's nothing you need to hide from me.

"In the meantime, I'm more than happy to play your hero."

She rolled her eyes and laughed. "I don't need a hero, Leo. I just want you to pretend to be one." Her fingers dusted at some imaginary speck on his jacket and his heart thundered under the casual touch. Her gaze ate him up. "But yeah, I'm glad you're on my side."

# CHAPTER FIVE

Two and a half hours into the party, Neha was glad she'd let Leo convince her to stick to his side.

There was a power high in being the woman that Leonardo Brunetti couldn't keep his hands off. Oh, she knew that all the long, lingering looks and touches—she loved the feel of his palm against her lower back—were for the benefit of the couple of journalists he'd told her were present through the crowd.

It was about making a public statement without actually standing in front of a high-focus lens and admitting that yes, after years of platonic relationship, they were taking their relationship to the next level. But she couldn't stop herself from enjoying the thrill of the moment.

The warm, male scent of him was both familiar and exciting. Every time he wrapped his arm around her waist, or squeezed her shoulders, or pulled her to his side, she felt a little tingle pulse up her spine, filling her veins with electric charge.

She loved hearing her name on his lips as he introduced her around to the extended Brunetti family, to the powerful board members of BFI. Clung to his every word, loved the secretive smile he sent her way when someone commented that the most untouchable bachelor had been finally caught.

But it wasn't just the electricity arcing between them.

There was a sense of strength in his mere presence at her side. She'd been self-sufficient, emotionally and mentally, for so long that to have him at her back felt like a luxury. An echo of a need that had gone unanswered. She had someone in her corner finally to face Mario.

Even the sight of Mario's scowl when his gaze landed on Leo's arm around her waist, the way his sharp gaze followed them around, couldn't dilute her enjoyment of the party.

The entire grounds around the villa had been lit up until it was reflected on the waters of the lake. Pristine white marquees caught the overflow of guests from the villa. Cream-colored circular lanterns hung from the ceilings while beautiful white lilies made up exquisite centerpieces on round tables. Strategic ground lights added nightly splendor to Leo's gardens. With the backdrop of Lake Como's lights, the estate glittered.

The only strange thing was Silvio Brunetti's conspicuous absence from the celebrations, and Alessandra's, too, who was close to Greta, even more than her own grandsons.

A small dais had been raised at the center of the marquee where the matriarch, Greta, came onto the dais and delivered a speech in Italian that was too fast for her to follow. She invited her family to join her. Neha sat stunned when Leo walked up to her and reached out a hand to her.

For a few seconds that felt like an eternity, she could feel every single gaze trained on her, the silence deafening. Yes, they were putting on a show for a variety of reasons. Neha had never expected to be counted as one of the Brunetti family.

But even her hesitation hadn't thrown off the resolute look in Leo's eyes. Bending down from his great height, the broad sweep of his shoulders cutting off the entire world, his gorgeous, rugged face filled her vision. The focus of that gaze—all on her—was addictive. "I thought I had made this clear between us. Whatever happens in the future, or doesn't happen—" a twinkle appeared in his eyes "—my child, and therefore you, will always be a part of this family."

"You don't understand," she'd whispered, putting her slim hand in his huge one. Shivering at the abrasive slide of his palm. "They'll think it a declaration neither of us intends."

"I do not give a damn, as you say, *bella*."

After that, she hadn't even cared how Mario was taking the whole thing.

There was an exhilarating kind of freedom in letting Leonardo shoulder her burdens, at least for the evening. She danced with Massimo once and then twice with Leo, and tasted so many delicacies while laughing with Natalie.

After a long stretch of loneliness, life felt good, real.

Having just touched up her makeup, she walked out into the small sitting lounge with full-length mirrors and a soft white leather sofa when she realized she wasn't alone.

Everything in her braced to face the vitriolic attack that would come from Mario. Instead, her mum stood inside the room, her delicate face pinched with worry and distress. Dressed in a cream pantsuit that set off perfectly against her fair skin and pearls at her throat, she looked exquisitely lovely in a frail way. When she'd been a teenager, Neha had wished she'd been more like her mum with her petite, feminine frame, the silky dark hair, the delicate, sharply set features.

But now… Neha was glad she'd inherited her dad's build and his resilient nature.

"Hello, Mum," she said, leaning down and kissing Padma's cheek. A subtle scent of roses filled her nose, instantly plunging her into that twisty, minefield she'd been navigating for too long. "I was hoping we could have a quick catch-up before you left. Especially since I hadn't seen you in a while. Sorry, I didn't come sit by you tonight." She hated this, this distance that came between them, all because of Mario. "Leo had all these people he wanted to introduce me to, and Natalie dragged me into the photoshoot—"

"I thought you were past this rebellious phase where you do things just to annoy your stepfather," Padma said. Launching directly into attack.

No question about why Neha hadn't come to see her in two weeks. No question about the sudden change in her relationship with Leo. That cold knot in her chest squeezed painfully even as that wet, helpless feeling filled her throat. "Mum, what are you talking about?"

"This…thing with that man."

"What about it?"

"Leonardo Brunetti is your stepfather's enemy. You know he causes all kinds of trouble for Mario. Of all the men in the world, Neha…have you no loyalty for Mario? After everything Mario's done for us, after he made sure we didn't wallow in poverty, after he built this empire with your face, after he's treated you as if you were his own…" A long, rattling sigh shook her slender shoulders, and she reached for the wall behind her, her breathing shallow, her pretty face crumpled.

Panic filled Neha's limbs. "Mum, please don't stress yourself like this. You know it's not good for you. You'll have an asthma attack and I—"

Padma jerked away from her touch. "Then you should've thought of that before shacking up with a man Mario can't stand."

"Mum, listen to me. It's not what you think. I'd never do anything to hurt you. This is something I needed to do for myself…" Neha pushed her shaking fingers through her hair, fighting for composure. Fighting the anger and helplessness rising through her, the selfish need to demand her mum's support when she was weak already. "To build the life I—"

"You've chosen to go against the man who gave you everything. And when Mr. Brunetti breaks your heart, and Mario says he will, who do you think will pick you up again? Who do you think looks out for you in all this?

"Your stepfather, that's who." Her mum took her face in one hand, fingers tracing her jaw tenderly, her gaze taking in everything. "Walk away from this man, Neha." Tears made her mum's words a soft, beseeching whisper. "Come home with us, now, tonight. Mario's generous. He'll forgive you the simple mistake of falling into Leonardo's trap."

Of course he would. He'd riled up her mum to see only an enemy in Leonardo. A selfish woman in her own daughter, a naive fool who fell for a man's sweet words. Still, Neha tried. "Mum, I haven't done anything to be forgiven for. I've stayed all these years even though—"

"No, stop." Padma took a deep, shuddering breath, her mouth trembling. Ignoring what Neha was saying. "It pains me to see you at such cross-purposes with him, darling."

"Mum, I'm doing this for me. No one else. For my future."

"Please stop this before you hurt yourself and us, too."

"And if I don't?"

Padma stepped back from Neha, a resolute look in her eyes. "Then I know that Mario's right that you've never accepted him. That you've never forgiven me for choosing to marry again when your papa passed away. That all these years, you've resented the place he's taken in my life."

The dark midnight sky was a star-studded blanket as Leonardo made his way through the well-worn path to the greenhouse that had been abandoned for more than two decades.

He had engaged a crew to renovate the greenhouse,

but apart from stepping in there with the architect for a quick inspection, he hadn't been here again. He wanted the renovated greenhouse, not a desolate, haunting monument with memories that could steal his sleep.

Nothing but Massimo's knock at his door, his face concerned, well past midnight, as he'd been getting ready for bed, could have brought Leo to this place. For years, he had ignored the presence of the abandoned structure, refusing to step foot even in its shadow.

But he'd realized that it was silly to let a child's confusion dictate the rest of his life. An utter waste of time and energy having something new designed when a perfectly old structure was sitting right in his backyard.

He keyed in the security code that had been newly installed and pushed open the glass door. The rise in temperature was instant—a blast of warm, wet air hit him in the face.

Surprise filled him at the progress the team had made. Most of the overgrown shrubbery and vines had been cleared and new temperature-controlling tubing had been installed all over the ceiling. A huge industrial-size porcelain sink sat along one wall with gleaming granite counter space.

That, along with the perfectly placed overhead lights in a crisscrossing design through the center line of the high ceiling, made it eons different from the abandoned shell he'd discovered months ago.

There was one corner of the huge greenhouse where the overgrown, climbing vine had been left in place. The small area stood like a piece of the past he never seemed to let go of.

*Cristo*, he was in a strange mood tonight.

The lounger he'd ordered in a moment of self-indulgence stood like a throne in an abandoned castle. Her gray sweatshirt lay discarded on the lounger while Neha walked around the long aisles, drifting aimlessly, in deep thought. Even the ping of the door hadn't disturbed her. Leo took the time to just watch her.

The rational part of him wanted to turn around and walk out, leave her to her midnight rambles. She'd made it clear before the party tonight that she was never going to cross that line that she had drawn around herself and let herself be vulnerable to anyone, much less him.

The loose, sleeveless T-shirt and cotton shorts she had on should have looked anything but sexy. But the slightly damp fabric stuck to the outline of her curves and the shorts—*Cristo*, her legs were long and lean, packed with muscle.

He'd never gone for the delicate, wispy, stick-thin kind of women. He liked curves, and from every glimpse he got of Neha's, it felt like she was tailor-made to fit into his hands.

Her face scrubbed free of the makeup only highlighted the dewy silkiness of her skin. Her wild hair had been braided into submission into a single braid, already half undone and framing her face.

It was only when she raised her gaze to his and gave a soft gasp that he saw the wet tinge to her eyelashes. *Cristo*, she'd been crying?

He pushed away from the wall, all thoughts of leaving her to her own problems fleeing. "Neha?"

She scrubbed a hand over her face. "What're you doing here?"

"That is for me to ask." He tucked his hands into his pockets. She looked crumpled, a little broken, and the last thing she needed was for him to paw at her. "Massimo told me he found you walking out here. That he gave you the code."

"Oh." Her fingers played with the hem of her T-shirt. "I couldn't sleep and was walking the grounds. I can't come down from the high of the evening that quickly, y'know? Especially when... It was a lovely party, yeah?" He didn't for one second believe the glassy, too-bright smile. She looked around herself self-consciously. "I'm sorry for intruding. *Again.*

"Massimo thought it was better if I wandered inside here. I gathered from what he said this greenhouse... is off-limits to guests. But he wouldn't leave my side until I went in or returned to my bedroom.

"I didn't want to lie down when my head's spinning."

"This apologizing of yours is becoming a bad habit, *cara.* You're welcome to walk into any part of the estate."

"I think I've done enough midnight meandering. I'll wish you good night."

"You are upset," he said, reaching for her arm as she passed him. He kept his grip slack. She didn't pull away and, this close, he could feel the tension emanating from her. All his protective instincts went into overdrive. "Did Mario get to you? I made sure he came nowhere near you. And when I was busy with Greta, I asked Massimo to keep an eye. What did he say? Did he scare you?"

"No, he didn't. It's not that," she said, stepping back from him, trying to hide her face in the shadows.

Leo was in no mood to be fobbed off.

One hand on her shoulder, he gently tugged her toward him until the overhead lights illuminated her face. He clasped her chin. Her eyes were puffed, her nose slightly red at the top.

*Dio*, the woman gave new definition to self-sufficiency. Usually he was the one who maintained those boundaries in a relationship religiously.

"Keeping the lines between us separate is one thing. But this isn't just about you anymore, even before a child comes into the picture. I dragged you into this battle against him, *after* you told me it's been near impossible to decouple yourself from him.

"So tell me what happened. The last thing I think right now is that you're weak. Infuriatingly stubborn, however, comes to mind."

She bent her forehead to his shoulder, her body shuddering with shallow breaths. Running his palms over her bare arms up and down, he waited. In the damp air, the faint vanilla scent she used mingled with her skin to create a musky fragrance that filled his nostrils. Her warm breath coated his neck. He gritted his teeth, willing his body to not betray him.

"You're right. I've got to talk about this."

When she pulled back, she looked composed, strong again. And he realized how similar they were.

"Mario didn't get to me," she said, her long lashes looking thicker with wetness. "I saw his ugly scowl the moment they arrived and stayed well out of his way. The last thing I wanted was to make a spectacle at Greta's celebration. Even when I saw your exchange with him, I ignored it. But Mario is nothing if not clever."

Leo knew what she was made of, and he knew that the ache in her eyes had its origin a long time ago. He waited patiently, understanding in a way no one could how hard it was to show vulnerability when you spent most of your life making sure there wasn't any.

It only made him respect her more.

"But he got to her."

"Your mum?"

"Yep." A smile that was nothing but a caricature of the usual loveliness twisted her mouth. She ran a hand through her hair, a violent physical energy vibrating from her frame. "Frankly, I'm a fool to be surprised by this. I know the kind of hold he has on her. I know how his mind works. But she…" She swallowed, and then looked up at him. "After a long time, today I realized how nice it is to have someone in your corner. I know it was all for show but still it felt good to belong with people who like and respect me, with whom I don't have to walk on eggshells.

"And bam! She ruined everything."

Leo wanted to tell her that it hadn't been for show, that he did have her back in all this. That inviting her to be a part of his family's celebration while the whole world watched had come naturally, easily. That with every deeper glimpse into her, he wanted her by his side. The strength of the urge was inexplicably overwhelming.

Physical attraction was one thing…this quite another.

"Mario constantly feeds her lies and she swallows it all. Apparently, the only reason you could be interested in me is to get at him. The only reason, after years of a purely platonic relationship, that you're taking this to a new level.

"For so long, I tried to be strong for her. I let him manipulate me, twist me inside out. I let him run my life because I was afraid of hurting her. And the one step I take to build something for myself, to reach out for something I want...

"She actually asked me to leave with them tonight! She thinks I'd...tangle myself with you out of some petty need for rebellion? It's like she doesn't realize I have my own dreams and needs," Neha finished. "She'll never realize that I have my own life to live."

There was anger in her voice now—anger that reverberated within him, a hundred times stronger, calling for action. And Leo knew she would come out of this fine. Anger led to action whereas grief just left one powerless. Under someone else's control.

Like love.

*Dio*, how could Padma miss the ever-present shadows of anxiety in Neha's eyes? How could she put Mario ahead of Neha?

"Then it's time to remove that toxic presence from your life," he said softly.

Her head jerked up. "What?"

"Mario's not at the root of that grief in your eyes. Your mum is. So don't give her that power anymore."

Her eyes widened. "I can't just cut her out."

*"No?"*

She sat down on a cement bench, her bare legs stretched out in front of her. Her gaze turned thoughtful, her chin rising in that stubborn way. "What would've happened if Massimo had decided you should be cut out of his life all those years ago, just when you wanted to build a relationship with him? What if he'd decided you weren't worth it?"

The question stopped him in his tracks.

*If Massimo had refused his olive branch...*

Leo's isolation would've been complete. Silvio would have succeeded in turning him into a mirror image of the power-bloated monster he was. The idea disturbed him on so many levels that Leo couldn't curb his harsh words. "I'm not the one questioning every choice I've made over the last decade."

Neha fidgeted where she sat, the awkward silence building into something she couldn't break through. His harsh tone shouldn't have surprised her, but it did. Because she'd never been on the receiving end of it.

Her question had disturbed him. And he had shut her inquiry down. Neither was she unaware that they were discussing her own family's shortcomings...but instead of resentment, she felt a sense of kinship with him.

What kind of a man would Leo have been if hadn't been tempered so harshly by the discovery of what kind of a man his father was? If he hadn't had his fundamental beliefs shaken so early in life? If he hadn't had to shut down a vital part to survive another day?

So many years of knowing him, learning him and

wanting him…a lifetime of watching him like this, and she'd never have enough.

From the thick slashes of his brows to the deep-set eyes with long lashes he used to hide his expression, the deep scar on the left cheek and the thin-lipped mouth, combined with that weather-beaten quality of his skin— the gardens outside were clearly a labor of love—he was not classically handsome. But the ruggedly hewn features, that sense of calm confidence in his broad frame, the power of aura that radiated from him…the appeal he held had intensified as he grew older.

Where there had been a cocky, the-world-is-mine kind of arrogance to him when she'd met him all those years ago, the fierce discipline with which he ruled those around him, and himself, had entrenched into his features.

Her mum's marriage to Mario had changed the course of Neha's life, too. Carved away her choices bit by bit until this version of her remained. How much longer?

"I've lived almost fifteen years of my life walking the tightrope of wanting something and being afraid of the blowback to her. Afraid that Mario would use my actions to drive a wedge between us. I turned myself into something even I don't recognize."

Leo covered the distance between them, shaking his head. "You're being too hard on yourself."

She swallowed the lump in her throat as he took her hands in his and squeezed tight. She'd been so lonely. But it was Leo's touch that jump-started something that had been dormant inside her for too long. "Yeah?"

"You took the first step toward building the life you want despite knowing what the consequences will be. Not only did you approach me with your...request but you knew what to say to convince me. You didn't let your mum frighten you off today." His gaze searched hers, as if he was seeing her anew. "Despite the emotional toll it's taking on you." A lone tear tracked down her cheek, the tenderness in his words a balm to her soul, the sheer conviction in his voice a steely source of strength.

He pulled her up to face him, and Neha could have drowned in the emotions swirling in those blue depths. His grip on her hands was the only anchor in a collapsing world, the warmth radiating from his solid body the only reality she could hold on to while she built a new foundation for her future.

With infinite gentleness, he flicked away the tear. "Do you remember the heated arguments we used to have about my opinions of women?"

She nodded, wondering where he was going. "You were a budding sexist."

He laughed and she watched that stark, serious face bloom into gorgeousness that shook her knees. "You've been the biggest, most positive influence in my life, Neha. Like a river carving away at the bedrock of a mountain, you cleared so much anger I'd harbored toward women, just because of what one woman did to me when I was a child. You helped me realize how irrational and hateful I could become if I didn't let go of it. Watching you become this woman of grace and courage and beauty...helped me in ways you can't imagine.

"So don't you dare say you're a coward because that's my friend you're trashing."

A sob rising through her, Neha threw herself at him. And luckily for both of them, the giant of a man that he was, he caught her. The strength of his arms rocked her as she tried to curb the emotional storm unleashing within her.

She kissed his cheek and whispered a hundred thankyous. The scent and warmth of him was a cocktail she felt drunk on, the muscled wall of his body a heavenly slide against her own. Her arms vined around his neck, she pulled back and looked at him.

Nostrils flaring, eyes shining with desire, he radiated the same kind of energy she could feel thrumming through her veins.

A ribbon of awareness whipped around them as her gaze fell to the languid curve of his mouth. It was a matter of seconds, maybe, but it felt like an eternity as Neha pulled herself closer. Their breaths were a harsh symphony around them. She moved her hands down to his chest, scrunching her fingers in his shirt.

She'd spent an eternity wanting this man…wanting one kiss, wanting to be the woman he needed. And now she couldn't turn away even if her very next breath depended on it.

After years of living in a prison she'd made for herself, Neha stepped into her own life. And took Leonardo's mouth in a kiss she'd needed for more than a decade.

Lips that were both firm and incredibly soft met hers. That first contact spread warmth through her, unraveling in spools through her limbs, leaving her trembling, stomach tightening with anticipation, standing on the cliff of something new and painfully exciting. He was unnaturally still, not rejecting her, but being a passive participant that was nothing like the man.

She flicked her tongue over his lips next, tracing the defined curve while the rhythmic in and out of his breath coated her skin in soft strokes. A continuous thrill thrummed through her veins as she fit her mouth this way and that, teasing and tasting, tugging on that lower lip with her teeth, licking her way into his mouth and touching the tip of his tongue with hers before she retreated and started all over again. And again gorging herself on him. Breathing him in.

*And still, he held himself rigid, his hands not holding her but not pushing her away, either.*

He tasted of whiskey and maleness and Neha reveled in the high of having him like this—hers to pet and play with, hers to ignite. Hers to rumple. When she dug her teeth hard into his lower lip, his chest rumbled. Her own need deepened at the utterly masculine sound drawn out of him despite his control.

Dampness bloomed at her sex, every part of her aching to be touched and stroked and possessed. She ran her palms down to his neck and pulled at the lapels of his shirt until the buttons popped and she could sink her hands inside.

Her groan was joined by his, creating a symphony of need and desire.

Defined pectorals and warm skin, the sensation of the springy hair under her palms, the tight points of his nipples—his chest was an endless delight to her quest-ing hands. She touched him all over, loving the hard clench of his muscles, the feral sound that fell from his lips. This time, when she explored the moist cavern of his mouth, she tangled her tongue with his, sucking it into her mouth. Playing hide-and-seek with it. Digging her teeth into the soft inside of his lower lip.

Her breasts ached to be touched. Her hands roamed restlessly over his hard body, across his broad chest, back onto his rock-hard abdomen, her fingers dig-ging into the waistband of his trousers. She dragged her mouth from his, trailing kisses over his rough jaw, down to his throat, and pressed her tongue against the hollow there.

Salt and sweat and incredibly male—he was heaven on her tongue.

The growl that fell from his mouth reverberated up from his broad chest, shaking her with its ferocity. Like an earthquake rearranging everything beneath the ground on which she stood. His powerful body shud-dered around her, and then he was jerking her up to him, his fingers sinking deep into her hair, and his mouth crushed hers.

The kiss was raw, fiercely honest, and it whipped her into a frenzy of sensations. Not a single one of her dreams had done justice to what the man could do with his mouth.

There was no exploration in how he took her mouth, no tentative melding to see if it could be anything more than a pleasant experience. No gentle welcome or a soft landing. No initial awkwardness that came with two people kissing for the first time, no searching for rhythm, no place for anything that was remotely rational.

The savagery of the need between them…this need that had been building for a long time, it tossed him around just as it did her.

He devoured her lips with his. Hunger and heat and hardness… Neha drowned in a surfeit of sensations he seemed to evoke so easily with a masterful glide of his lips, or a sensuous nip with his teeth or a rough, needy dance with his tongue. Everything she'd done to him, he paid back a hundred times over—sometimes smooth and slow, sometimes hard and demanding. Leaving her mouth stinging, her nipples taut and needy, her body scandalously ready for his possession.

A needy groan fell from her mouth when his arousal—thick and hard—rubbed against her belly, sending sparks of renewed need. She stole her hands down his body, desperate to trace that, desperate to feel what she'd done to him. He grunted in denial, his fingers arresting her questing hand. *"Basta, cara!"*

Neha felt his soft whisper like a cold lash against her skin. Her body cooling off in a matter of seconds into a frigid cold despite the warm air currents, she stepped away from him. "I'm sorry." She ran a hand through her hair and bit her lip. Which was swollen and tender. The memory of digging her teeth into his lower lip and his answering growl…it was a sound she'd never forget. "I'm… I've no excuse for attacking you—"

"You didn't attack me!"

She looked at him and away, but not before noticing

how devastatingly handsome he looked with his hair all rumpled up, by her fingers. The flaps of his shirt open and baring that magnificent chest covered in hair. "I've been so up and down tonight, and I—"

"Look at me, *cara*! I knew what you were doing, and I was a more than willing participant."

"Still, I'm sorry, Leo. I'm—"

"Stop saying sorry. All you did was make the first move. One nanosecond later, I would have been all over you. *Cristo*, do you have any idea what watching you in that wet shirt sticking to your body is doing to me." He thrust his hand roughly through his hair, his breaths harsh. "Do you have any idea how long I've wanted you? *Dio mio*, it seems wanting you has become a part of me. If not for the fact that you're very important to me and my lovers don't last long, I wouldn't have mustered the sense to put a stop to it, *cara*."

The raw emotion in his voice gave her the courage to stop lying. To herself and to him. To face what had been staring at her from the moment she'd gone into his office with her bold request.

Her gaze fell to the swollen curve of his lower lip and something fractured within her at the blazing passion of their kiss. The rightness of this moment between them. The reality of the future she wanted to build with him. Something that took wings and wanted to fly. "I want to do this the real way," she blurted out, one of the biggest decisions of her life falling into place as easily as her next breath.

So easy, yes, but so, so right, too.

"What?" Leonardo looked at her with that penetrating gaze. Giving nothing away. Already retreating from that fracture in his impenetrable self-control.

*Wanting you feels like...it has become a part of me.*

A new sense of freedom ran through her limbs. There was a high in standing here, staring at him unabashedly, and glorying in it. In acknowledging her desire for this man.

His face one of those bulletproof masks that no one could break through. And that mask was doubled down right now. She was finally beginning to understand the real man beneath the larger than life figure she'd built in her head.

He'd been attentive and filled with concern from the moment she'd walked into his office. Playing the role of a man pursuing her perfectly for the public. At her back the whole evening tonight because he'd decided she needed protection from Mario. And she had no doubt he'd do the same for the rest of their lives with their child and, by extension, her.

Whatever she needed—physically, emotionally, mentally—he'd be there.

But to give her a part of him—to let down that guard that surrounded his mind and his heart, to show a little vulnerability—was unacceptable. To need her even in a small way was unacceptable. It would always remain a weakness.

That admission that he'd wanted her for a long time—had it been too much already?

She wondered if she'd have understood him so perfectly if she hadn't built that same armor around herself for so long that she'd ended up choking herself within it.

The intense loneliness, the craving for connection, the long, silent nights blending into farcically busy days, always alone, even in crowds… She was finally breaking through those chains she'd bound herself with and she wasn't going back into them willingly.

She wanted to live her life. She wanted this man. She wanted to create a child with him doing what would bring them both incredible pleasure.

There wasn't a moment's doubt in her mind that what she was starting tonight had a very definite endpoint. Having that endpoint made it easy to push away her fears. Leonardo and she were rational adults with very clear boundaries.

"I want to conceive *our child* the traditional way."

When he stared back in mute silence, she huffed, "You. Me. Sex, Leonardo."

## CHAPTER SIX

LEO JUST STARED, his mind filled up with images of their naked limbs tangled, slick and moving together. The woman he'd wanted forever, finally within his reach.

He shook his head, as if he could simply dislodge those images. "You've had a very emotional evening." He ran the pad of his forefinger gently over the dark shadows under her eyes. Amazed by her resilience and the strength of her resolve. Aroused by the boldness of her gaze. "On top of a manic two weeks. On top of a stressful last decade."

"Leo—"

"Tomorrow, you'll regret it. Tomorrow, you'll panic that we've blurred the lines. I will not take advantage of a weak moment."

She pulled back, a flare of anger in her eyes. "Ah... this is you being all honorable and letting me down gently, isn't it? I'm a big girl, Leo. I can take it."

"I have no idea what you mean."

"Just say you're not interested in sleeping with me. Especially after learning that I'm not as rational and robotically perfect as you thought I was," she said, a flash of self-doubt in her eyes.

"*Maledizione!* You think I could want you less because you stuck to your guns in the face of emotional blackmail from the one person who should be protecting you from that bully Mario? You think years of want goes away in a single evening? If only it were that easy, *bella*."

Silence descended on them, fraught with the energy of an attraction that was all out in the open now. She licked her lips, the pulse at her neck drumming away madly. "I believe you. Now will you do me the courtesy of taking me at my word?"

"I always have."

"Good. I feel as if the fog I've been living in is finally lifting. I'm sick of living afraid, always calculating risks, always worried about the outcome. I hate that I let Mario win all these years. I hate that I've used him as an excuse to give up so many things that give me joy, pleasure, excitement."

*But no more.*

"I want to leave all thoughts of ovulation kits and basal temperatures and IVF out of this. I want to conceive our child doing what I desperately want."

Her husky demand carried over the damp air currents in the greenhouse, the naked want in it echoing around them. And Leo knew his reasoning capability was crumbling to dust. That in the face of her bold demand and perfectly outlined reasons and the heat of their kiss singing through his veins, he was going to give in. Still, he looked for reasons to make sure this was exactly what she wanted.

"You can't do this because you're angry with him."

"Let me come closer."

Neha kicked at his feet and he spread his legs apart in response and she moved into the gap, closer and closer until her thighs grazed his hard thighs and the tip of her breasts were a mere inch away from his chest and the deepening scent of his skin filled her nostrils.

She moved her fingers from his chest—his racing heart gave her courage—up the corded column of his neck, to the raw stubble already coming in at his jaw, winding around his neck until her nails were sinking into the rough hair at his neck, scraping at his scalp. Digging for purchase. Determined to stay.

She bent closer, her mouth inching toward his. His hands stayed on her shoulders, pressing lightly, stopping her from covering that last bit of distance between them.

"If you think this is some twisted way to get back at Mario or a petty rebellion against my mum, you've got it all wrong." She shook his hands off her shoulders and pressed up snug against him. Heat and hardness, he was a perfect fit for her, and she shuddered at how good it felt. "I had a huge crush on that hot twenty-year-old who walked into my life that day. In a parallel universe, I grabbed that boy, and planted a kiss on him that sent him to his knees. If I could tell my younger self one thing, it would be to go after that guy."

She wiggled against him, trying to get closer, and he cursed softly. She felt his arousal against her belly, incontrovertible proof that sent shivers up and down her spine. Her lips close to his, she licked at the corner of his mouth. "This is all about me and you, Leo. I want this for no other reason than I need to desperately know how it will feel to have you inside me."

"Let me look at you, then, *cara mia*."

Neha pulled back from him, her heart still racing. Her body already mourning the loss of warmth from his. "What?"

"That damp T-shirt has been tormenting me ever since I walked in." Wicked light filled his eyes—a flash of that Leo he must have been before he'd had to bear the burden of the Brunetti legacy. "I should very much like to see you properly."

"You mean...here?"

"*Sì.*" Unholy amusement curved his mouth. "You said tonight. I say here. Now." He looked around the greenhouse, that hardness that was an intrinsic part of him etched on his features again. Lost to her in those few seconds. "This ghastly place needs new memories, anyway. I can think of nothing better than walking in here a few years from now and picturing you, all damp and naked and waiting for me."

That glitter in his eyes at his imagined image of her was incredibly sexy. "But—"

"Second thoughts, *cara*?"

Neha shivered at the blatant hunger written over his features. At the dawning resolve in his eyes. At the unspoken challenge in every pore of his body. It wasn't enough that she'd thrown herself at him, was it? He would strip her bare, of clothes and defenses, until there was not even a sliver of doubt that she'd walked into this with every sense alert, every cell desperate for it.

Leonardo Brunetti wasn't a man who would give

anything of himself without demanding everything in return.

"I'm more than ready to persuade you, like you did me. Unless you prefer the dark and a bed, then, we will walk back to my—"

Neha tugged the hem of her T-shirt up and over her head in a smooth movement that surprised the heck out of even her. The appearance of the lacy baby-pink bra and how it cupped her breasts, the way his eyes drank her in, pushed away the hesitation that came with baring her body to a man after a long time. To the man she'd always be attracted to on so many levels.

"I forgot there's a reason you've held my interest for so many years, despite my every effort to suffocate it, *sì*? *Dio en cielo*, you're sexy and bold and you will be the death of me, *cara*."

Every word out of his mouth bucked up Neha a little more.

She didn't wait for another order. *In for a penny, in for a pound.* Not that her heart wasn't beating at a pace that might send it careening out of her chest. But Neha had never lacked for guts once she'd set her mind on a goal. Never lacked the gumption to see things through thoroughly.

While the media regularly published articles about how she'd gained weight or that her body type wasn't currently in fashion, Neha had never let the criticism get to her. Thanks to her mum's constant positive dialogue and praise when Neha had complained as a teenager that she was too big, everywhere, she'd developed a healthy appreciation for her body early on in her life.

Reaching her hand behind her, she undid the clasp of her bra. An expansive sigh drummed up her chest as her heavy breasts were freed from the metal underwires of her snug bra. Dark color streaked Leo's cheeks as he watched the gentle bounce of her breasts.

Her spine straight, she threw her bra at his feet, reveling in the naked desire chasing away every other shadow from his face. The damp air currents swirling around the greenhouse kissed her nipples, making them rigid. Her skin was damp, and hot, and felt far too tight to contain her.

Holding his gaze, she kicked off her shoes. The smooth floor was surprisingly cold against her bare feet, a welcoming contrast to her overheated body. Then she peeled off her shorts and stepped out of them, standing in front of him in white lacy knickers. She'd never been more glad of her expensive lingerie habit—her one decadent indulgence.

He made a thorough inventory of her—as if he was determined to not miss an inch of everything she had bared. Her heart thudded so loudly in her ears that she could barely hear herself think.

"I'm glad you waited to take this chance with me, *cara*. I'm glad you decided I wasn't worthy of you back then. That twenty-year-old, he was full of arrogance and ego and vigor. He didn't have enough sense to appreciate—" his gaze touched her everywhere: her bare breasts, the firm and yet soft curve of her belly, her muscled thighs, the white lace barely covering her sex "—everything about you. He wouldn't have known what to do with a bold, sensual creature like you. But me, now… I can appreciate everything you are. I can appreciate what a gift you are."

And just like that, Neha knew she'd picked the right man to do this with. She mock frowned and licked her lips. His gaze zeroed in on the action. "Are you saying the thirty-six-year-old man has all the sense but lacks in vigor?"

A flash of white teeth against dark skin that gleamed with such masculine intent that some places in her body tightened and some loosened. He undid the rest of the buttons on his shirt and shrugged it off those broad shoulders. "Why ask questions when you're about to try it, *tesoro*?"

Between one blink and the next, he was all over her, a violent storm of need and demand that pulled her in.

His mouth crushed hers, his arms were steel bands around her body and his hard thigh was lodged in between hers, almost lifting her up, rubbing exactly where she needed contact. She dug her nails into the bands of muscle in his back and rubbed herself shamelessly against the taut clench of his thighs.

"*Cristo*, you're wet already," he whispered, licking into her mouth just as eagerly as she clung to him.

The slide of his rough chest over her sensitized nipples was a sensation she'd remember to her dying breath. His hands seemed to be everywhere on her body and yet landed nowhere. Not for enough time. Not to her satisfaction.

His hands patted every inch of her back, his teeth tugging and his tongue licking at the hurt, and then moved to her chest. The graze of his callused fingers over her swollen nipples sent a needy moan rippling out of her mouth. Learning her, drawing on her body's cues, he rolled the tight knots back and forth between his fingers, tightening the arrow of need concentrating in her lower belly.

Pleasure flew in rivulets up and down her body, there one second, fleeing to a new part of her the next, driving Neha to near madness.

When he bent her over the counter that he'd been leaning against and brought his mouth to her breast, Neha jerked at the wet warmth. He licked around the center begging for his attention in mind-numbing circles. Blew hot air, plumped and shaped and caressed the soft weight with such exquisite skill that Neha arched into his touch, begging for more and more. Again and again his clever fingers and his cleverer mouth ministered to her, noting her responses, driving her wild, waiting for the wet lash to reach the place where she needed it the most.

"I've had dreams of touching you like this. *Cristo*, I've brought myself to…"

He stopped when Neha jerked her head up, his words just as arousing as his caresses. "You what?" The thought of Leo taking pleasure in an image of her was like a hot cinder going off in her entire body.

Color streaked his cheeks and those thick lashes hid away his expression. She rubbed his lower lip with the pad of her thumb. "Show me," she said, knowing that he'd always be a man of actions and not words. Never words. Even if every cell in her wanted to hear all the intimate things he'd thought of her through these years. "I'm in your hands, lover. Do whatever you want with me."

"*Sì?*"

"*Sì.*"

"What do *you* want?" he asked, his hands never stopping in their exploration of her body. Cupping her buttocks, tracing the line of her spine, palming her breasts, nipping her lips. On and on and on, he kept the fever building in her.

"Your mouth, now, here," she demanded boldly, cupping her breast and raising it up to his mouth like a prize.

His nostrils flared, primal male satisfaction in every carved angle. "*Dio*, only you could demand and yet somehow give, *cara mia.*"

She didn't have enough brain cells left to figure out his cryptic remark. All she cared about was that he...

And then he was there. The cavern of his mouth was there, surrounding the hard tip of her nipple. Wet. Warm. Welcoming. First this breast and then its twin, until her nipples were gleaming with wetness and exquisitely sensitive even to his warm exhale.

He licked and stroked the nipple with a thousand lashes of his tongue, pressing up against it in such a cleverly wicked way that each swipe of it sent a current of need down to her sex. And then he closed his mouth around it, and he sucked in deep, drawing pulls that made her sex twitch with growing need.

"*Dio*, you'll climax if I continue this," he whispered against her neck, almost to himself. "You're extra responsive here." He tweaked a nipple and she felt an answering jolt in her pelvis.

Neha nodded, engulfed between ropes of sudden shyness and a desperate desire to climax.

Baring her body to a man she'd known for fifteen years hadn't given her a moment's doubt. But this intimate dialogue between them, the look in his eyes when he so thoroughly studied every inch of her damp skin, every rise and dip of her body, every jerk and twitch when he touched her somewhere new, as if he was cataloging it all away for future reference, this made a fragility she didn't like fill her up. Fragility that would let fears in, that would make this moment into more than what it was right now—utterly perfect.

"Please, Leo." She pulled at his hair, forcing him to lift his mouth from her tender nipples. "I need you… now."

"Not yet, *cara*." The sheer masculine arrogance in his tone scraped at her skin, winding the knot in her lower belly tighter. "Not until I have touched and kissed and learned every part of you." His palm was on her belly now, inching lower and lower. The tips of his fingers played hide-and-seek with the flimsy seam of her knickers. In and out, in and out, covering more ground every time, stealing her breath on every dive inside.

"Not until I'm inside you and we're moving together, *si*?"

She shivered at the rough promise in his words. Drank in the sight of him—damp hair sticking to his forehead, muscles bunched tight in his shoulders, that hard chest breathing harshly as if he'd been running, greedily. "I think that's setting the bar a little too high for the first time."

"I like high bars—" a rough tangling of tongues and teeth "—and bold challenges issued by a bolder woman—" a wet lash against her turgid nipple "—and I want to be inside you when you come so hard that you'll burst out of your skin."

Neha jerked at the first touch of his fingers against the folds of her sex. Light and soft and oh, so gentle that she was ready to scream, he explored every inch of her. Drew a line around her opening with his finger and brought the wetness up to the bundle of nerves desperately waiting for his touch.

When he rubbed her there in a soft, mind-numbing circle, Neha cried out at the burst of fiery sensation. Heart in her throat, her breath coming in a harsh rhythm, she lifted her pelvis, chasing his clever fingers. He repeated the action, until she thought she would go mad with wanting.

Wanton, incoherent cries fell from her mouth. She was writhing under his careful, crafty caresses, begging him with her body. Reduced into nothing but a shivering, spiraling mass of sensation and pure pleasure.

Every stroke of his finger, every kiss he showered on her breasts, every breath he exhaled into her skin, every word out of that wicked mouth, drove her higher and higher until release was a shimmering mirage beckoning her fast. She gripped his wrist when he'd pulled away, her limbs honeyed, her entire being pressed down under a languorous weight. "I'm so close, please," she said, and his husky laughter enveloped her in its embrace.

"No, not yet." His smile was wicked, his rough tongue-and-teeth kiss purely possessive.

"I hate you," she whispered, sweat dripping into her eyes, her body unwilling or unable to follow her brain's simplest commands.

He pulled her up gently, as if she were a treasure he meant to hoard all for himself, his mouth curved into a dark smile, his eyes dilated, tension radiating in waves from his powerful body. Large hands clasped her chin, pulling her closer. He kissed her softly this time, less lust and desire and more…affection and connection. If her heart had ever been at risk, Neha knew it was then. His desire and his ultimatums and his possessiveness… she could handle all of those. His tenderness, however, would be the ruin of her.

"You trust me, don't you, Neha?"

"Always, Leo."

His face broke into a radiant smile that washed away any misgivings on her part. Washed away the frustration inside her limbs, flooding her with a renewed sense of wonder. She loved seeing him like this—demanding things of her—loved being with him in that moment, sharing this intimacy.

He tugged her with him, and she went without protest.

The lounger she'd noticed earlier came into her vision and dissolved like every other thought that didn't concern her eyes when they could gorge on the supremely male specimen in front of her.

Any thoughts of even intrusive shyness disappeared as he undid his trousers. And his black silk boxers.

A soft gasp built up and out of her chest as her gaze lowered to where he couldn't hide his desire. She could stare at him for the end of time and still not have enough. His thighs were thickly muscled, covered in hair, while his hips were leanly sharp planes, his skin lighter there than the rest of his body.

Neha licked her lips, her gaze once again going to his arousal, and a growl rumbled up from his chest. While she watched him, he hardened and lengthened. Her core dampened, as if in perfect answer.

"Come to me, *cara*," he said in a wicked tone that promised to make every fantasy of hers come true. Flushing, Neha lifted her gaze to find him seated on the lounger, his long legs on one side, utterly confident in his nudity.

Neha went to him, her skin damp, every muscle shivering, her heart overflowing with the rightness of this moment. With the conviction that she was exactly where she wanted to be in the entire universe. Naked, wanton, with the one man she'd wanted all her adult life. Living her life purely, simply, fully, in the moment.

# CHAPTER SEVEN

SHE CAME TO HIM, her lush breasts bobbing, her small waist and wide hips calling to be held, her strong thighs and shapely calves utterly feminine. Her light brown skin glinting like burnished gold with a damp sheen, her hair tumbling around her face in a messy tangle, her eyes filled with a deep hunger that mirrored his own. Plump brown nipples shone with the wetness from his mouth. He gripped the lounger on the sides of his thighs, his hands already missing the voluptuous dips and valleys of her waist and thighs.

Her underwear was a narrow, white lace thing that just covered her from him.

He felt painfully hard, desperate to possess this woman who challenged him every step of the way. Who met his desires with her own, who it seemed was determined to carve away a piece of him without asking but by simply giving and trusting and wanting.

Strength and sensuality roped together in an irresistible combination, she was unlike any woman he'd ever known.

*Cristo*, he'd always known Neha was a force to

reckon with. Everything about her shouted incredible confidence and innate sensuality and a strength he found utterly arousing.

She'd knocked him over with her gutsy plan to build a life she wanted, she amazed him the way she'd looked at her own flaws and decided to change her life and now...now she matched him hunger to hunger, demanding boldly and giving everything in return. He had a feeling he'd never hold a woman like that ever again. That he would never forget tonight, whatever juncture life brought them to in later years.

And he wanted to make tonight unforgettable for her, too. Every time she laid eyes on him, he wanted her to remember tonight. If ever she went to another man after tonight, he wanted the memory of this encounter to be the one she measured it against and found lacking. He wanted to be the man she measured every other man against.

His gaze caught on the flash of a thin gold chain around her ankle, a detail he'd overlooked before. And he didn't want to. He didn't want to miss an inch of her gorgeous body, or her smile, or a nuance in those expressive eyes. He didn't try to curb the urgency pounding his every muscle and instinct as she reached him. He knew it would be a useless attempt.

The scent of her hit his nostrils first—vanilla mingled with the smell of her skin, becoming a richer, deeper scent he would always remember when he stepped into the greenhouse. He spanned his hands around the sharp dip of her waist as she came closer, humbled again by the beauty and grace of the woman who was his match in every way. "You're trembling," he said, pressing openmouthed kisses to her soft belly.

"You're the reason I'm shaking like a bloody leaf in a storm," she said, her arms coming around his shoulders, her fingers sinking into his hair. Her nails scraped at the nape of his neck and Leo's body hardened between the slick rub of their bodies. Her voice caught on those words, a smoky quality to them, as if she'd ill-used her throat for a long time. "Make it better, Leo."

Instead of giving her more promises, Leo showed her he would. Worshipped every square inch of her gorgeous body. Set his fingers, his mouth, to working her into a deeper fever, kissing every inch of her silky-smooth skin, palming the globes of her breasts, raking his nails down those turgid nipples, stroking and kneading every inch of her supple flesh. Giving her everything she'd dealt him a thousand times back. Driving her as mad with need as she was doing to him.

"Naked, now," he said in a husky, demanding tone even he'd never heard before, pushing her away from him.

Dutifully, she stripped off her knickers, her brown eyes drugged with desire, her breaths coming in shallow and fast.

One hand on a hip, she stood before him, naked. And it was the honesty in her eyes that undid Leo.

She was the only woman in his entire life that aroused every primal instinct in him. That made him want to rumple her up and bend her to his will and also, in contrast, made him want to protect her with everything he had in him.

Pulling her to him, he filled his hands with her buttocks, dug his teeth into the tight flesh of her hip. When she jerked against him, he held her immobile with his arm around her. "Open your legs for me, *bella*."

She did and he was dipping his fingers into her folds, reaching for that wet warmth that had welcomed him earlier. *Merde*, her damp heat drenched his fingers.

He cursed hard and long, every inch of him shaking with need. He pushed one finger and then two into her and she cried out and rubbed sinuously against his hand. Taunting him. Teasing him. Half mad with the same want, he smiled.

*Dio*, she was more than ready. And after so many years, Leonardo was ready. For whatever this was. Because he had no doubt that something was beginning tonight. Here, in this moment. Something he didn't even fully understand.

"Leo, enough games. Now, please," she said, half sobbing.

Lust riding him hard, he pulled her on top of him until she was straddling him on the lounger. He sank his fingers into her thick hair, took her mouth in a hard kiss. Adjusting her body slightly, in one smooth thrust, he was inside of her. A filthy curse fell from his lips as she fit around him like a snug glove.

With a soft gasp, Neha stiffened in his arms, her spine bowing back, her nails sinking into his shoulders.

Stars blinked out behind his eyes at how incredibly good she felt. *Cristo*, he'd never felt anything remotely like this before. He'd never had sex in his life without a condom, he instantly rationalized. He'd never let a woman seduce him like Neha did and she had, so thoroughly tonight, even though he'd taken the ropes from her in the end.

As much as he tried to, he couldn't pin down the gloriousness of being inside this woman to some rational reasons. He buried his face in her neck, breathing her in, listening to the racing of her heart, letting emotion after emotion run through him, trying to center himself. Trying to not let it unsettle him.

Or was it the fact that there was an element of the emotional commitment already between them? Something he'd never let enter his relationships with women. The simple fact that while he always made sure there was an expiry date to his relationships, here, in every look and touch and caress, there was that awareness that they were tangling with each other for more than one night and not to just satisfy their desires.

But in an incomprehensible way, it felt more than just good. It felt right. It felt right that his experience with Neha should be different from any other sexual experience he'd ever had. It felt right that the woman who would bear his child should somehow be different. Be more than all the women he'd been with in his life before that.

"Are you well, *cara*?" he asked belatedly, aware that his accent was thick, aware that every inch of his body was drawn tight into a sharp point of need and desire and an unknown quality he didn't want to put a finger on.

When she looked down, her eyes held the same wonder Leo was sure his did. Her face glowed from within, a tentative, slumberous smile touching her pink lips. "You know how there are moments in life you want to use fancy words to describe how…big and grand they are and then you suddenly realize no language has a word that could ever encompass the enormity of everything you feel and yeah…"

He crushed her tart mouth with his, needing the anchor of her taste. Needing to know she was just as lost as he was. The kiss went from soft to devouring, morphed with the sure knowledge of how good it was between them, becoming something neither could corral or define.

Every simple touch turned into a conflagration. Passion ebbed and flowed between them in perfect rhythm, sometimes he the aggressor and sometimes she, and Leo knew he could spend an age kissing her like this, breathing her in, joined in the most intimate way possible.

Soon, he was dueling his tongue with hers, her teeth were scraping at his jaw, their bodies slick with sweat sliding and gliding against each other in an instinctual rhythm that defied something as rational as good sex. Arms vining around his back, she snuggled closer, her breasts rubbing up and down his chest. Pleasure came at him in waves, building up into unbearable pressure in his pelvis, a tingling storm sweeping up the backs of his thighs.

Hands on her hips, he gently pulled her up and down, testing the fit. A spark of sizzling sensation raced up his spine and he closed his eyes, as if he could will the climax coming at him hard to slow down.

A soft cry fell from her mouth as she wriggled in his hold.

"I don't remember it ever being this good, Leo." A bemused, overwhelmed quality clung to her words.

Leo ran his hands over all of her again and again, not getting enough of her supple, sweat-slick skin. All the while, she moved forward and backward, up and down, kissing his mouth when she came closer. The friction was incredible. Sweat beading on his brow, he willed his self-control to last just a little bit more when all he wanted to do was pound into her.

Eyes wide open, she held his gaze as he trailed his hand behind a bead of condensation tracking all over her skin, and reached the curly hair at her sex.

He dipped his thumb and found the slick bud throbbing for his attention. He saw her swallow, her breath coming in shallow bursts. Every time he stroked that bundle, she tilted her pelvis up and down, sending friction down the length of him. Every muscle in Leo's body screamed for release. She was so close he could feel her body clamping down on him, contracting and expanding, and he wanted to push her to the last edge.

"Look at me, *cara*," he said, and she tilted her head down. "Cup your breasts for me." He wanted to give her what he'd promised.

Eyes wide in her face, she raised her breasts to his face. Leo rubbed his stubble against the tender nipple and then flicked the tight knot with his tongue while he kept his finger on her and worked her over and over. Soon, she was writhing and twisting and moving up and down on him and then with a cry that shot shivers down his spine, she orgasmed.

Her muscles spasmed around him, setting off his own climax.

Leo rode the wave of it with her, pushing her down onto her back. Wild and abandoned, she was the boldest creature he'd ever seen. And all he wanted was to lose himself inside her. He pounded in and out of her with a savage need he didn't even recognize. Her eyes flew open, she clasped his jaw, and when she pulled her upper body and took his mouth in a shuddering kiss, she sent him over the edge faster than he'd ever known.

His climax swelled through him, splintering pleasure far and wide. His breath was so deafening in his ears that Leo could see or hear nothing for a long while. He was still shaking with the force of his release when he opened his eyes. Sweat dripped from his forehead and fell on her neck, and the drop pebbled down her damp skin. He followed the drop with his finger, a fierce possessiveness filling him.

Her eyes closed, her head tilted away, she was a study in sensuality. Leo ran his knuckles over her cheek before turning her to her side and joining her on the lounger. She was damp and trembling and warm when he wrapped his arm around her waist. Tenderness filled his chest and he gathered her to himself. For himself as much as her for he needed a physical anchor right then.

It was a long while before the high of his release and the glut of emotions that had overpowered him ebbed. And in its wake an unusual knot formed in his stomach.

Leo couldn't shake off the sense of alarm that he'd

gotten more than he had ever bargained for. And yet, as he tucked her into his side and wrapped his arm around her trembling body, he didn't want to leave her.

Not tonight. Not for a long time.

Her body's unfamiliar aches in new places woke Neha up when she tried for a more comfortable position on the lounger. A deep languor thrummed through her, as if her limbs were filled of honey.

The first thing that struck her was the delicious kind of soreness between her legs. Enough to short-track the details of where and what had led to it. As did the scent of what they had done thick in the air around her.

She tried to sit up on the lounger when firm hands on her bare shoulders pressed her back down. "It's okay, *cara*. I'm here."

Her chest ached at the tenderness in Leo's voice. Neha stretched her neck back. To find herself looking up into that impenetrable gaze that she'd have known in the midst of a dream.

His thick hair formed a wild halo around his face; his mouth was a little swollen, his expression as always hidden. Leo sat leaning against the back with one foot dangling down and the left folded at the knee, while her head lolled about on his thigh. He'd put both his trousers and shirt on, though the latter was unbuttoned. All she wanted to do was sink her fingers into his thick hair and pull him down to kiss her.

She kicked back up into a sitting position. "How long did I sleep?"

"Thirty minutes, at the most."

A shudder of relief passed through her as she noticed that her bare torso had been covered up with the T-shirt she'd discarded. Her shorts hung loosely on her hips.

"You put my shorts back on me?" she said, not quite meeting his eyes.

She was aware of his shrug from her side vision. *"Sì."*

"You should've left me here."

He turned her to face him with a rough grip. "And leave you to find your way to your suite at the crack of dawn? I know you have this idea that I'm allergic to being tied down, but it doesn't mean I treat women like trash."

"That's not what I meant." It was exactly what she meant. Heat washed over her. "I'm sorry for—"

*"Dio mio!* Stop apologizing. It was either cover you up or wake you up for session two. You were exhausted after everything from the evening and that was the last thing you needed."

A rough shove of his fingers through that thick hair. Which like hers had taken on a life of its own thanks to the humid air. This version of Leo—hair wild, shirt unbuttoned—the intimacy of seeing him all rumpled and sexy, broke the tension choking her.

"I wouldn't have minded session two," she said, tongue in cheek.

His expression didn't relent. If not for the muscle jumping in his cheek, she'd have thought he was already regretting everything. Did he regret admitting that he'd wanted to make love to her again? Or was he wondering if she'd make it all awkward and weird now that it was done?

No, she wasn't going to go digging for things that weren't there. Overanalyze what was there. With a man like Leo—who exercised the utmost self-control and discipline—it was his actions that mattered. What he chose to say would always be more important than what he left out.

She'd gotten more than she'd ever dreamed of having of him. If she lived to be a hundred, this would remain the most extraordinary night of her life. She'd found not only incredible pleasure but an inexplicable joy in what they had shared.

Time to make a graceful exit. Without wondering what could be or what it hadn't been.

"I only meant to stay horizontal for a little while." She looked down and up into his eyes again. "I've read that it's good to prop your hips up after…to increase your chances of conception." He folded those corded arms and waited. "So I didn't immediately get up and then I fell asleep."

"You do not need a reason to not run away as soon as we're finished, *bella*."

She nodded and pushed to her feet. He stood up, too, and all Neha could see was the broad sweep of his shoulders, the delineated line of his muscles, the lean tapered waist, the strong, hard thighs that had cradled her.

Hand on his chest, she rose up on her bare toes and kissed him on the cheek. "Thank you, Leo."

He took her wrist in his hand and slowly returned it to her. His gaze studied her as if he meant to look beneath the amiable expression she was determined to keep. As if he wanted to know everything she was neatly stashing away to be explored later. Or never.

She tossed around in her head for some mundane topic while looking for her shoes. "What's going on here?"

His head tilted down, he was buttoning his shirt. A slightly reddish mark above his pectoral winked at her. Furious heat climbed up her cheek when she realized she had raked his skin with her nails.

She watched greedily until the last patch of olive skin stretched taut over hard muscles was covered up. Fisting her hands, she swallowed the longing that rose through her.

Asking him to sleep with her so that they could conceive had been easy. But now there was so much more she wanted, so much more she still didn't have. Small, intimate things she wanted to share with him—like buttoning that shirt, or pushing that thick, unmanageable hair away from his forehead, or kissing away his frown…those would always be out of her reach.

She looked away barely a second before he faced her. "With what?"

It took her a few seconds to trace back their conversation. She walked around the lounger and ran her hand over one of the vines that had crawled up all the way to the high ceiling. "The greenhouse."

"I'm having it restored."

"Why did it get to such a dilapidated condition in the first place?"

There was a tenuous quality to his silence behind

her that raised the hairs on her neck. A cold remoteness entered his eyes. Those rough fingers moved over and over on an ancient-looking ceramic pot with two handprints on it—one adult and one child.

*"This ghastly place needs new memories."*

Realization slammed into her. Her throat closed up, words coming and falling away to her lips.

"It belonged to my mother."

"Oh." There was a violence to his contained stillness, a restless energy that would only singe her if she ventured closer. And yet she couldn't help it. "You must have got your green thumb from her, then. Massimo says there's not a flower in the world that won't blossom in your care."

A shrug that conveyed so much without saying it.

"Do you remember much—?"

"After she left, it went to hell," he said, cutting her off. It was as if a door had slammed in her face. The tender lover of just a few moments ago was gone.

"When I realized I wanted a greenhouse, I asked the architect to build a new one in the same spot." He passed her and opened the door. "He said it would be a waste to gut the structure. He's restoring it instead."

There was no doubt left that he'd preferred to have it ripped out. Maybe remove any sign of his mother in the process, like he'd done in every other area of his life. Like he'd advised her to do earlier.

And yet, Neha intrinsically knew she'd never be capable of that. Removing the bad stuff meant removing the good stuff, too, and she could never sterilize her life of her mum's presence. Before it had all been destroyed with her papa's long illness and death, she had known happiness with her parents. She'd been loved by her mum, before her papa's death had broken her, had changed the course of their lives permanently.

The moment she stepped out of the greenhouse behind him, Neha took a bracing breath. The dip in the temperature outside had her shivering.

Leo tucked her under his arm as they walked, their thighs wedged close all too comfortably for her.

She knew she was dangerously skating over the invisible boundary he'd always drawn around the topic of his parents, but Neha couldn't keep quiet. Couldn't bear to know that it had affected him but had never been addressed.

Because who would do that for him? Not his father, who'd been an abusive man. Not Greta, who knew no tenderness. Leonardo had always taken the role of the head of the family and the burden that came with it whether he wanted to or not…but had anyone ever asked him what his mother's leaving had done to him? Had anyone even wondered?

"I didn't see any pictures of her in the villa."

"I have an early start tomorrow and I'd really like to get to bed now."

"Of course," Neha replied, keeping her tone steady, even as tension swathed them. She wanted to push—she had a feeling he'd talk about it to no one, but the last thing she wanted was to be told it was none of her business.

Physical intimacy didn't equal emotional intimacy. Especially with Leo.

Finally, they reached her suite. He turned the knob but didn't release the door.

"I didn't mean to be so curt," he said, his hand on her lower back, his breath raising the little hairs on her neck. He was a wall of warmth and want behind her.

She nodded, refusing to give in on the issue but accepting his apology. Years of habits couldn't change overnight, and she wasn't even sure she wanted Leo's secrets. That way only lay more blurring of lines and emotional labor she didn't want to pay.

"Everything is okay?"

"Yes." She turned her head and laughed softly. "Don't worry, Leo. It's not going to be awkward between us. I won't let it be."

She didn't wait for his answer as she went into her bedroom and headed straight for the shower. Even though she wanted to linger in the scent of him still clinging to her skin. She wasn't going to turn what had been a fantastic evening into what could only be a dream made of cards.

# CHAPTER EIGHT

IT HAD BEEN three days since Leo, for the first time in his adult life, had woken up late, sunlight streaming onto his huge bed the morning after the party, and felt a strange reluctance to begin his sixteen-hour workday. He had wanted to revel in the complete languor that had filled his mind and body. Three mornings ago, since he'd wandered through the villa only to discover that Neha had caught a lift with Massimo to London.

He had no idea how the woman had found the energy to disappear the morning after what had to have been an eventful, emotional night for her. But then Neha had always possessed a no-nonsense, pragmatic approach to life.

Three days in which he'd thought of her every hour, on the hour, as if someone had set an alarm in his head. Of how pliant and responsive and eager she'd been in his arms. Of how she'd felt around him, her gaze boldly holding his. Of how she'd tried to assure him that he had nothing to worry about.

If he were honest with himself, he hadn't needed that cheeky reassurance. Taking his honesty a step further, he even admitted to himself that he'd been annoyed by her reassurance that she wasn't going to act the part of a clingy lover.

He'd never had a connection like that with a woman even during sex before, the connection that had gone a little beyond the physical.

Whatever the reason, he was finding that one evening hadn't been nearly enough. If anything, seeing how incredibly good it had been between them, Leo wanted a lot more of her.

He had a million things on his calendar to take care of—he'd been postposing his visit to his father. Silvio's health had taken a rapid downturn in the last month. Alex was still acting strange even though she'd had the sense to call Greta the night of the party, and he had a meeting with Mario. A confrontation that had been coming for months that he needed all his wits for, and yet, here he was thinking of Neha in the middle of the afternoon.

*Basta!* He'd never been a man to sit and wonder why he wanted something. He'd just gone after it.

He picked up his phone and clicked on Neha's dimpled smile on the screen.

A flurry of voices accompanied her greeting. He heard the click-click of her heels and then quietness. "Hey, Leo."

Just her voice sent memories of remembered sensations rushing through him.

*Cristo*, she'd openly admitted she wanted him. He didn't have to stand here and moon about that one experience like a teenager. He could simply arrange to see her again. And take her to bed. "I called to see how you are."

"Oh, thanks. I'm good, yeah? Y'know, the usual. Back-to-back meetings, morning to night, but I'm okay." A pause, and he could feel her hesitation through the space. "Did you get a chance to talk to Mario?"

"No," he said, instantly alert to the ragged quality to her question. "Did he confront you again? Did he send your mum?"

"No. I called her, but I haven't heard back." The ache in her words made him feel entirely too powerless. He had the overwhelming urge to hold her close in his arms, to tell her in person that it would be all right in the end. "I just…was wondering where we're at. In the scheme of things."

"I have a meeting with him in two days," he said, and could practically hear the relief in her sigh. "I can't look overeager to wave the proof of our relationship in front of him. Mario's clever. I have to keep him thinking he has the upper hand in all this for now."

"Do you want me to be there?"

*"No."* The last thing he wanted was to rub Mario's face in it or expose Neha to the man's temper any more than she already was. "If he asks you about us, just say that we've been spending more time together. Don't go into any kind of detail about BFI or even my family. The press coverage tells him enough, *si*?"

Just as he'd expected, the media was going gaga over the two of them finally heating up the relationship. His asking Neha to join the rest of his family on the dais hadn't been lost on the media or Neha's fans. The only thing missing was a statement from So Sweet Inc.'s publicity team.

"Okay, yeah. I've been trying to keep my meetings with my lawyer on the down low just in case he—"

"You didn't have to sneak out the morning after the party." He finally gave voice to the one thing that had been bothering him.

He could imagine her leaning on her desk, worrying her lower lip, wondering what to say and what not to. "I thought it was better that way, to have some distance. Because, as good as it was, it was also…a bit emotional for me. It's been a while and it came on top of everything. I don't want to make you feel as if I want more than you're willing to give. I never—"

"*Cristo*, Neha! Did it occur to your overthinking mind that I wanted you there the next morning?"

He'd no idea what to make of her silence except that he'd stunned her. "I told you in the greenhouse that I was okay. It would have been just…" A sigh and then the sharp inhale. "Leo, I… The truth is I've been only with two other men in my life and I thought I was going to marry one of them. Sex is emotional for me, and with you, it's like a minor earthquake, both physically and in other ways. I needed the distance. To keep things in perspective."

"I wanted to take you to bed again, a proper bed this time. If you were still willing."

Another silence. Another few seconds wondering what she was thinking. "Oh."

"Instead, you ran away with Massimo."

"I didn't run away, I just—"

"I want to see you this Friday. Be ready, I'll pick you up at work."

Another long pause.

*Cristo*, he should have just flown into London to see her instead of engaging in this conversation over a ridiculous phone call.

"I have plans on Friday. Saturday, I'm meeting with the publicity department to shoot some pics for the new book, and then in the evening—"

"You're the boss. Take one Saturday evening off."

The urge to ask her to make herself available rode him hard. He held himself back.

Why couldn't he? Was it because they hadn't established that this was a relationship? He had no hesitation to call it that because he wanted her.

"I can't take any more days off because I already flew twice to Milan and…" He heard someone call her name and then she was rushing through her words. "I'll look at my calendar and text you."

"You'll text me a fifteen-minute window where we can conceive our child in the most efficient way possible?" He regretted the words the moment they were out.

*Dio*, he sounded like a spoiled, privileged, puffed-up man determined to have his own way.

But instead of being offended, her laughter filled the line. "I like you like this, all grumpy and…frustrated?" When he grunted, she laughed again. "My calendar is full just as yours is, you know that. To beat a dead dog, this is the reason I'm trying to revamp my entire lifestyle."

God, the woman was as graceful as she was beautiful. "My continued frustration because of your un-availability will mean everything will go too fast when you're in my hands, *bella*."

She gasped—that hoarse, throaty sound that played over his nerves as if she'd run those long fingers over his clenching muscles. "Then we'll go fast to relieve your...frustration the first time and then take it slow.

"Now, unless I want to scandalize my team by sprouting more sexual innuendo over the phone and give them enough to sell to a tabloid, I really must go."

"*Bene.* Remember, don't engage with Mario without me."

"Okay."

"Call me any time you need me. If you can't reach me, call Massimo."

"I will."

"*Ciao, bella.*"

"Leo?"

"*Sì?*"

"Thank you."

"I don't think I've ever been thanked so many times for sex, *cara*. It is annoying the hell out of me."

She laughed and the carefree quality of it made him smile. "No, I'm not thanking you for the mind-blowing sex. Although you give it good. I meant...for checking up on me." A catch in her throat.

He waited, instinctively knowing that this was harder for her to do than ask him to make love to her. Knew that she'd gone so long without leaning on anyone that it had become a way of being. Because he was exactly like that.

"I feel a little less alone than I've felt in a long time, like the future I want is really in my grasp. We work really well as a unit. On so many levels, y'know. I'm just…"

Leo stayed silent, trying to dislodge the unfamiliar tightness in his chest. He didn't know how to give voice to emotions. Even with Massimo, it was only this past year, once his brother had fallen for Natalie, that they'd put into words the divide their father had caused between them and all the steps Leo had taken to build a bridge to Massimo.

Even that night in the greenhouse, all Neha had done was to broach the topic of his mother. Not so out of context because, *Dio*, he'd commanded her to cut her own mother out of her life. He had shut her down so curtly that it was a surprise she hadn't taken it as an insult. But in that moment, like right now, Leo couldn't open up.

Couldn't tell her that he liked hearing her say it so openly. Liked that she'd always been honest with him.

He had a sense of what was right and wrong, though he didn't know where it came from because all Silvio had taught him in his formative years had been how to wield power. Greta had taught him how to do the right thing by the Brunetti name no matter what. Greta's second husband, Carlo, had tried to nurture the little good that had been in Leonardo.

But no one had taught him how to let another human being close, how to process, much less express, emotions like fear and need, so he'd simply buried them all for the sake of survival.

And now, Leo wanted to say something meaningful, but all his energies went into burying the weight he felt on his chest. On fighting the web into which Neha drew him so easily, so effortlessly. So he stayed silent and he sensed her confusion in the pause.

"I have to go now," she whispered softly.

Without a reply, Leo hung up. And for the first time in his life, he wondered if there would come a day when Neha would ask something of him and he couldn't give it.

Even having been prepared for the meeting, Leo felt a strange reluctance when Mario walked into his office at the appointed hour wearing a self-satisfied smile that Leo wanted to wipe off with his fists. He had never liked Mario—too smooth in hiding the oily nature beneath, even when he'd been Silvio's cohort in any number of activities.

Mario's true nature had been revealed when, at the first sign that Silvio was going down all those years ago, the man had immediately cut any ties and jumped ship. Leo had always wondered how much Mario had known about and hidden Silvio's activities even then, but there had never been any proof of his complicity.

Now, knowing how the older man manipulated Neha, using her affection for her mum, Leo knew his estimation was right. Mario was of the same ilk as Silvio, a man who preyed on weaker people. Except much cleverer.

With a full head of gray hair, strong, sharp features and a fit body, at sixty-five, Mario was considered a handsome man.

"It is a good thing you scheduled this," he said, strolling in and going straight for Leo's leather chair at his desk. The CEO's chair. While Leo stayed at the sitting area. "Ever since the spectacle you made of her at the party, I've been meaning to have a word with you."

"A spectacle of whom?" Leo asked.

"My stepdaughter, Neha, that's who."

"I don't understand."

Mario grunted, coming away from Leo's desk. "Her mother and I worry about her. She hasn't been—" he pretended concern so well here that if he hadn't known his true colors, Leo would have bought it "—well these last few months. She's not operating at full judgment."

"Are you saying something's wrong with Neha?"

"Ah, so she didn't let you see that, did she?" he said with unconcealed satisfaction. "But no, the girl hasn't been well."

"She's not a girl, Mario. She's the CEO of So Sweet Inc. She's the engine that keeps your empire running."

Pure evil glinted in Mario's eyes. "Neha hides it well, even from her mother, but I know something's wrong with her. Clearly, these anxiety attacks have messed with the good sense God gave her."

"Anxiety attacks?" Leo asked, stunned.

"She had one a few months ago, when she was in China. Her assistant told me even though Neha ordered her not to.

"She's not operating properly. Or she'd have realized you're just playing with her. That you're using her to get at me. And that she'll be shown to be a fool in front of the whole world when you dump her and move on." The pure cunning in Mario's shrewd gaze sent a shiver even through Leo. "Maybe I should just wait for this whole thing to play out to its natural ending. Let her learn that lesson publicly, despite her mum's constant worries."

So her mother did worry about Neha. That would be of consolation to Neha, but it wasn't anywhere near enough to cancel the pain the woman caused her own daughter. "What lesson would that be, Mario?"

Mario waved a hand through the air between them imperiously. "She's always had a thing for you. Follows your affairs quite religiously. Thinks the world of you, thinks she has you in her corner, *sì*?"

Fury rose through Leo and he barely stopped himself from turning away in disgust. What kind of a man betrayed his stepdaughter's confidence like this to a man she was in a relationship with to be used as ammunition? What kind of a woman tied her daughter up in such a man's toxic shadow? *Dio*, how had Neha stayed sane all these years?

*"She looks like she's falling apart at the seams. That joy, that sparkle of hers is gone."*

Massimo's words came at him with a painful clarity he had been missing before.

"I'm not surprised you figured out her little thing for you and decided to use it to advantage," Mario went on, without missing a beat.

Leo held up a hand. "You think I'm using Neha's... admiration for me to lure her into a relationship to some nefarious purpose?" That the man had hit his eventual goal on the nail only made Leo's hackles rise.

Mario shrugged. "It's what I'd have done. Your plan has one big loophole, though. You will tire of her when you realize she gives you no leverage with me and then dump her. The girl will be heartbroken and then she will know where her loyalties should lie. A lesson she needs reminding of."

That Mario would relish Neha's downfall with such glee sent bile through Leo. All his careful plans crumbled to dust in the wake of the fury coursing through him. "I wouldn't be so quick to decide that," he said, the words sticking to his throat like thorns. But a man like Mario only understood his language.

He wasn't going to betray to this snake of a man what regard he had for Neha, how she consumed his every waking thought and how that regard for her was only growing with every glimpse into her life. "There are many advantages to be had in an ongoing association with a successful, beautiful woman like Neha. Especially a woman who would go to any lengths for me, it seems." He mentally apologized to her for it. "I wouldn't make bets on how long our relationship will last, Mario."

Mario's handsome face transformed in a mere moment into something ugly. Somehow, he wrangled his temper back under control to say, "What will it take to…shorten the duration of your relationship with her?"

"How did you know that BFI's systems had been cyber-attacked two times?"

"A rumor."

"Impossible. Only four people knew about it. Me, Massimo, the woman who did the attack and the man who engineered it. Which means the source had to be that man."

"This whole meeting is a waste of—"

"What did Vincenzo Cavalli offer you? BFI's CEO chair? More stock in BFI?"

Mario examined his buffed nails at leisure. "I've no idea what you're talking about."

"*Basta*, Mario! If you know what's good for you, tell me where I can find him and why he's bent on ruining BFI."

"Or what?"

"Your golden goose is in my hands, Mario. I can turn her head whichever way I want."

"What the hell does that mean?"

"You and I both know Neha's tired of it all, *sì*? Of the rat race, of the eighty-hour-week grind, of you running her life… What do you think it would take for me to nudge her into taking a more permanent holiday from So Sweet Inc.?"

A vein dangerously popping in his temple, Mario looked ready to explode. "Neha would never do anything that would hurt her mother."

There it was… Mario's means of manipulating her again and again. "Not the first time a weak woman's so in love with the wrong man that all sense deserts her, is it?" Leo said.

Mario's skin flushed, confirming his own awareness of his wife's sheer inability to see what Mario was doing to her own daughter. "So you're your father's son, eh? You would use a foolish woman for your own power play, then? Is it any wonder Cavalli is out to ruin you all? Don't forget I know all of Silvio's secrets, Leo. Secrets even you don't know.

"I can lead you or Cavalli to them. It's your choice.

"Dump Neha. Walk away from anything to do with her. End this thing publicly. And maybe I'll think about what I can tell you."

Leo stood up from his seat. There was only so much he could pretend before his skin crawled. Only so much he could do to turn a snake like Mario. "I'm nothing like my father. I don't make deals with bullies."

"He's got it in for your entire family, and he's not stopping any time soon," Mario retorted, finally showing his true colors. "Think about it, Leonardo. Think about what your temporary association with Neha will cost you.

"You consider yourself honorable, *si*? Think about what this association with you will cost her...because both you and I know, in the end you'll move on to the next woman.

"She's already crumbling. Where will she be when you've dumped her and she's all alone in the world?"

With that warning, the hateful man exited his office, leaving Leo shaking with fury and guilt.

It took Leo more than a few minutes to calm down, to bring his mind back to rationality. *Maledizione*, he hadn't meant to throw Neha's retirement plans in Mario's face so soon. But the way the man had spoken of Neha, Leo couldn't regret his loss of temper.

Mario's words only confirmed Massimo's and his suspicions.

Their father was at the heart of all this.

Leo needed to visit Silvio, ask him to remember the Cavalli family, get him to sign the will transferring his stock to Leonardo and Massimo equally.

It was also the only chance to ask Silvio about something that Leo had buried deep down for years. A chance to open up the past again and let it rake its fingers through his present.

*Cristo*, but he was sick of having to deal with the fallout from his father's actions. *Dio*, all his adult life he'd spent rebuilding what Silvio had destroyed, cleaned up what Silvio had corrupted, had taken on the responsibility of BFI on his shoulders.

No, he wanted to leave the past where it was. He had never wanted less to see the man he'd worshipped for half his life and abhorred the rest of it. He refused to let the past leave a mark on him. Or on Neha for that matter.

*She'd had an anxiety attack...*

It was the last piece of the puzzle of those shadows in her eyes. But Leo couldn't muster anger that she'd hidden it from him. Could understand the kind of defenses Neha had built around herself after being let down by a parent...

All he felt was a certain resolve that she needed his protection. Especially now that Mario knew of her retirement plans.

From her own stubborn clinging to her self-sufficiency to begin with. From her mother's manipulations.

Their child, whether she retired in a few weeks or not, would always need protection from Mario's hateful shadow. From Neha's own inability to cut her mother out of her life.

And there was only way to achieve it.

The idea of marrying Neha, instead of knocking him

back, built in his head like a tsunami, gaining momentum with each passing moment. It was Neha herself who'd made that decision so easy.

She'd never ask him for what he couldn't give. She'd proved in the last two weeks how rational she was. They'd have a solid foundation for a marriage—respect, passion and a mutual desire to do the best by their child.

Suddenly, there was a future he could see when he closed his eyes, a future he wanted for himself. Not just the ashes of the past. Their child would be part of a family unit and have everything Leo had never had and desperately craved for as a child.

Leo stood inside the grand entrance hall of Neha's Mayfair apartment complex and studied the high, domed ceiling and the dark stained oak curving staircase with pleasant surprise. The expansive cream Nettuno marble floor with the black onyx squares popping the monotony screamed understated luxury.

He'd recommended the property a few years ago when she'd asked him about investment advice, since Mayfair had been on the cusp of rivaling Knightsbridge as the area for luxury residential homes. The value of the two-bedroom flat she'd purchased had only gone up.

After facing down Mario two days ago and still digesting the disgusting lengths the man could sink to, his admiration for Neha grew boundless.

How much of a fight had she had to put up to buy such expensive property in her own name? What had Mario already unleashed in the last week that Leo had been gone?

He had the concierge let her know that he was waiting in the lounge, aware with every breath that the sense of urgency he felt to see her, touch her, was something he'd never experienced before. Now that he had a plan in hand, Leo couldn't wait to put it into motion.

His breath caught when she stepped out of the lift, her hair shining like a silky black curtain.

She was wearing a blouse with a long shawl draped over it and a billowing skirt underneath—all in the same cream and gold silky, flowing material that made her look like some beautiful princess stepping out of a fairy tale.

Large earrings with a cluster of pearls bobbed when she moved her head. A black dot took the pride of place between her eyebrows, and her eyes, lined with kohl, were huge in her face.

Her mouth was painted a light pink shade that reminded him of those decadent, pink confections she had once asked him to taste-test when he'd found her in the industrial kitchen at one of So Sweet Inc.'s branch of bakeries. The bracelets she wore on each arm shimmered gold.

She stilled, her gaze running over him like a physical caress, a warmth in her eyes that he couldn't help but bask in. "Will I do?" she said, reminding him of his pithy text that she should dress up.

He nodded, something primal and possessive rising inside him.

"Will you tell me the surprise now?" she asked, her hand reaching his hair and pushing away at a lock. And, just as fast, snatching it away. The subtle scent of vanilla and something sweet filled his breath, his body desperate for more.

He pulled the tickets out of the inside pocket of his jacket and waved them in front of her. "We're going to a *tabla* concert, although I'm not sure if 'concert' is the right word? By your favorite maestro."

"My God, Ustaad Atif Hussain? That's why you asked me to dress in traditional clothes." Her eyes widened as she grabbed the tickets from him and scanned them. She vibrated with excitement. "I was too late to get tickets for it. Wait! It's a super-exclusive invite-only event because Ustaadji doesn't perform for crowds. He's supposed to be super-private… How did you…? I can't believe you remembered how much I adore his music."

"You told me once you'd always dreamed of taking your papa to see him. That he and you used to spend hours in the bakery working with the *tabla* records on in the background."

Tears filled Neha's eyes. "I never got a chance to bring Papa to see him." She lifted those beautiful eyes to his, and a tightness filled his chest at the emotion in them. He grunted when she threw herself at him and hugged him with all the strength she had in her. He laughed when she kissed his face, sputtering thank-yous in between, with all the enthusiasm of the younger Neha who had stormed into his life one summer.

She pulled away suddenly and stared at him. "Why did you do this?"

Leo didn't hesitate. "I know how upset you were that your mum canceled the whole thing you do for your father's birthday. I know how hard this is hitting you. And it's kind of my fault."

"That's not possible."

"Mario knows about your retirement plans. I knew he was going to come hard at you. I just…"

"You just didn't expect that she'd break such an important tradition at his behest? Neither did I. But there it is."

Leo clasped her chin, guilt coursing through him. "I'm sorry I went off script, *cara*."

She clamped her fingers on his wrist, sinking into his touch. "No, this was going to happen, anyway, remember? But I'm not alone to deal with it, at the least."

"No, you're not." The ache in her eyes was like a fist to his gut. Ache he still felt responsible for. "I thought this would be a perfect way to pay a tribute to your father's birthday…maybe even become a new ritual?"

She nodded, something flashing in her eyes he couldn't recognize. "Time for new things, yeah." Her chest rose and fell with a deep breath, the tinkle of her bangles a sound he'd never forget. "I don't know how to thank you."

"Just enjoy the evening. Mario and your mother and BFI can all wait for a few hours, *si*?" He ran his thumb over her lips, unable to hold back. "After all these years, I thought we deserved a normal date."

She nodded, that sparkle back in her eyes. "I'm game. No talk of dysfunctional families or careers or vengeful enemies." She tucked her arm through his. "But you don't even know if you like Hindustani music."

"If you can sit through the opera when you hate it,"

he said, mentioning the time they'd attended the opera at La Scala and she'd barely sat still, "I can sit through this."

"Oh, the opera's got nothing against Ustaadji's fingers on the *tabla*," she said.

"No worries, *bella*. I'll find a way to exact some kind of compensation in return if I do find the maestro boring," he whispered, and laughed when she instantly got his meaning.

Suddenly, the evening ahead felt incredibly long when all Leo wanted to do was to bring her upstairs, slip the ring in his jacket on her finger, find that bedroom and claim her.

# CHAPTER NINE

LEONARDO'S PRESENCE STARTED a thrumming in Neha's veins. He walked around her home—her pride and heart and her first big victory against Mario—stopping here and there to study artwork she'd collected on her international travels.

She'd been telling herself that the time in the greenhouse couldn't have been as spectacular as she remembered. That she wasn't that wide-eyed teenager who still nurtured a fragile hope that Leo would want her in his life. But tonight...tonight that hope had come roaring back into life.

Tonight, all the lines between them were blurred. And she wasn't even afraid.

God, he'd been the most amazing companion through the *tabla* concert, going as far as encouraging her to talk to Ustaadji after. Dinner had been a noisy affair at an outdoor café, and she'd talked and talked about the exquisite music they'd heard. And now...now that he was inside her flat, she had no energy to hold herself aloof. No way to stop what the evening had meant to her, what his actions meant to her, from drowning her in a surfeit of emotions she didn't know to handle. Even knowing that it was mostly guilt that had motivated him.

He'd been right when he'd said she'd run away. She had. She'd resolutely buried the longing she'd felt, the insane urge to ask him when she'd see him again on the phone. How was she to fight it now when he was the most perfect man she could've asked for?

While he looked at the gallery wall she'd decorated with a number of pictures of her and her parents through the years, she stole the time to study him to her heart's content.

He'd shrugged off the charcoal jacket he'd been wearing, and the very breadth of his shoulders made her palms itch. He was a giant of a man and a primal part of Neha loved that he was so big that he made her feel feminine, fragile, sexy.

The sky-blue shirt fit his torso perfectly. With no tie and three buttons undone, he looked less the suave businessman and more the rough and tumble gardener who loved getting his hands dirty. Whose fingers had felt so abrasively delicious against her skin.

She let her gaze traverse to his lean hips and the taut behind. Her fingers curled as the memory of sinking her nails into his buttocks while he'd pumped into her came at her fast.

He turned at that exact moment. His gaze dipped to her mouth and lingered. Awareness enveloped them in a world of their own, taunting with memories of that night.

"I'll change and then we'll talk. I made a list of things to run by you," she added, suddenly feeling incredibly vulnerable, "when you said you'd be coming over."

"You don't need a reason to have my company."

"Or to simply have you?" she taunted.

He caught her wrist, arresting her between his legs in a sudden move. A sensual smile curved his lips. "Or to have me, *sì*."

Rough fingers abraded the plump vein at her wrist, pulling her down, down until she rested her hands above his knees. His thighs were rock hard under her fingers. Her hair fell forward on both sides of her face like a shimmering curtain, blocking the world out.

"I don't have the emotional energy today to walk away when we're done," she said, offering them both an out before she gave in.

"I never asked you to, *cara*." Each word pelted her skin like a caress, drawing a shuddering response. This close to him, she could see the lines carved into his rugged face, feel the heat radiating from his powerful body. "You're so busy acting how you think I want you to act that you're depriving us both of what we really want."

She gasped as he held the *dupatta* in one hand and pulled sharply. It fell away with a silky hiss, leaving the deep neckline of the blouse and, with it, her cleavage exposed. Dark eyes tracked the rise and fall of her flesh like a hungry hawk. His fingers landed on the patch of bare skin between her blouse and the skirt, and she had to fight to not sink into his touch.

His mouth covered hers, swallowing away her confusion and vulnerability and in turn giving her pleasure and joy and warmth. In the beat of a harshly drawn breath, she was in Leo's lap, her legs draped over his, her flowing skirt and all, and his mouth continued to devour hers. Neha sank her fingers into his hair, loving the rough texture of his hair. Soft and firm, his lips laved and licked, his tongue teasing her into such erotic play that she writhed in his lap. He gave her everything she wanted without being asked for it.

It felt like heaven. Like coming home. Like a safe place to land. After that first demanding taste of her mouth, he groaned against her quivering lips. "That's all I've wanted to do for days now."

He explored her mouth softly, slowly, as if he had all the time in the world to learn her anew, as if he was determined to know more of her than anyone ever had. His fingers held her with infinite gentleness, his body a haven of warmth she didn't want to leave.

There was already a sense of familiarity in how they melded their mouths, in the pull and push of their lips and breaths, and yet there was that thrill making her blood rush, her nipples knot, her body melt with each increasingly clever touch of his.

His long fingers left striations of heat on her belly and back, inching up and up under the loose blouse. His hands busily roamed her torso, plumping and squeezing, stroking and pinching. The pad of his thumb unerringly found the tight knot of her nipple and Neha arched into his touch.

She palmed his shoulders with her fingers, exploring every tense muscle in his neck and shoulders and back, while he ravished all her senses. With him so solid in her hands, it was hard to fear the future. So deliciously demanding against her mouth, hard to stay rational, sensible.

She was falling, falling, and yet didn't care about anything but the thrill of his hot mouth and roving hands and warm body.

His large hands encircled her waist, pulling her closer and closer, his desire a hot, hard throb against her hip. All Neha had to do was undo the zipper on her *lehenga* and slide it off her legs, and straddle him until her warm core was notched against that hardness. The world disappeared when he was inside her. She could escape the pain of the increasing rift between her mum and her; she could escape the seesaw of her own emotions when it came to this man.

But when it was done, he would leave and…tonight, she felt too raw to face the rest of the night alone. Lord above, please help her that she'd already conceived, and these were hormones taking over her body and not something else. How many months of this could she take if they didn't conceive immediately?

Would she be able to keep her emotions separate from her desires when it was Leonardo? It was such a scary thought that she pulled her mouth away from his. She buried her face in his neck, willing her breath to even out. Every inch of her shivered with longing and something else she didn't want to identify. "I'm afraid this is getting too hard," she said, opting for honesty. She could never play coy or tease, especially not with Leo.

"What is?"

"This…you and me." She tugged her gaze to his face and felt a tug in her chest that had nothing to do with attraction and desire or dreams she was determined to realize. This was all about the young man she'd adored once and the perfect man she admired so much today. This was about wanting so much more than what she already had. Of him.

His fingers played on her cheek. "Tell me what's going on in your head."

"You'll think I'm changing the rules on you."

"Because you want me for more than one stolen night in a greenhouse?"

"I don't know what I want anymore. Or how much. That's what's scary."

His fingers clasped her cheek gently. "This was never going to stop only at sex and conception, *bella*," he said, shocking her with his perceptiveness, the scent and feel of him a warm anchor in the maelstrom of her emotions. "We've known each other for years and it could never be just that, *si*? I don't think we established rules in the first place, *tesoro*. Not for any of this. So how about we address it now?"

Neha nodded, her eyes still closed, a rush of warmth filling every inch of her. God, how did he know to say the exact thing she needed to hear?

He crossed his legs with a grimace, and she laughed. A wicked hunger shone in his eyes, making promises that didn't need words. "I have the perfect solution for our situation, but first, let's talk about Mario. That should cool me down like nothing else."

She studied her hands, willing the shaking that began deep in her soul to subside. "I didn't think Mum would cancel our day together for Papa's memorial. When I called, she wouldn't even come to the phone. He's completely cutting me out of her life and there's nothing I can do."

His fingers squeezed her shoulder. "Mario's every bit the monster you said he is. I'm sorry for doubting your fears for even a moment."

She frowned, something in his tone tugging at her. "What did he say?"

"A lot of posturing…but the most important thing was that you had an anxiety attack when you were in China. Why didn't you tell me, Neha?"

"I told you everything but about the attack. And it was a full-blown panic attack actually, the one when I was traveling. It scared the hell out of me, but it was the kick I needed to make much needed changes. I promise, Leo, my health—physical and mental—is my top priority. I wouldn't put our child in harm's way."

"I never doubted that." He squeezed her fingers and Neha had to swallow the lump in her throat. "Have you spoken of it to anyone? Your mum?"

"No. I… There was something to deal with when I came back and—"

"You're struggling with a very serious problem and you hadn't felt like you could confide in her?" He nudged her in that infinitely patient tone.

Neha sat back in the sofa, a tremble in her very limbs. As if a truth she'd been trying to escape hit her in the face.

There was no excuse that she could offer that answered his softly spoken question.

He was right. She should've been able to confide in her mum, draw on her support. She'd been close to falling apart, and still, she'd had to make allowances for her mum, instead of the other way around. That the attacks could be used by Mario as some sort of weapon meant she'd had to hide it from her parent.

Her chest tightened at the pain of that final thread breaking in her heart. She couldn't fool herself that if just given a little more time, her mum would do the right thing.

Her mum might never do the right thing by Neha.

"New things don't grow unless everything that is dead is pulled away at the roots, *sì*?"

Neha flinched, an ache that had been building for years and years settling like an unbearable weight on her chest. "She's hurting me with all this, yes, but she does love me. Neither can I stop loving her, Leo. Love can't be calculated like a transaction."

"Tell me this, *bella*. If you had any inkling that our child was struggling with something like this, for instance, what would you do?"

"I'd fight the entire world to protect her or him. I'd take on anyone. Even you." The fierce quality of her answer was inescapable.

"Tell me what the doctor said."

"That it was chronic fatigue. I know the signs of an impending attack now and I've been trying really hard to avoid the triggers. But it's not going away until I fix the root of the problem. I work eighty to ninety hours a week doing things I have no interest in. I have no life outside of work, no companions, no friends."

"Which is why you want to retire," Leo said, concern in his eyes.

Neha hadn't cried even when she thought an attack had been impending, but hot tears filled her eyes now. And crashed down her cheeks, her control in shreds.

She turned away from him, embarrassed beyond measure, but he arrested her, his arms like steel bars around her, crooning to her as if she were a fragile thing. Whispering to her that she'd never be alone again. That he'd always be there to catch her if she fell. That she was the most beautiful, most courageous woman he'd ever known.

God, she should've had this with her mum. This outlet to let all her fears out, to sob through the crippling fear, to have the plain comfort of another person's touch…there was nothing to be gained in hanging on to a relationship that only brought grief. "You're right. I need to let her go. But I can't do it overnight. I…just can't."

"I know, *cara*." Arms tightening around her, his mouth warm against her temple, Leo just held her for a long time, his body a haven of tenderness. "Describe the attack to me."

She took the rope he threw her with overflowing gratitude. Words came so easily then, piling on top of each other, as if they'd been waiting to be let out.

"I'd been working without a break for months. We were shooting a segment for my guest appearance in between my tour in Beijing. I'd barely eaten and I still hadn't adjusted to the jet lag. When the lights came on, I froze for a few minutes. I…had no idea where I was or what I was doing. I could hear people calling my name, but it was like I was in a separate world.

"It felt like someone was cutting off my breath. I fell to my knees and stayed on the floor until it passed. I… It was exactly the wake-up call I needed."

He held her like that for she didn't know how long, and Neha stayed there. Long fingers clasped her cheek, fanning out in a caress. "For future reference, I would like for us to not have any more secrets, *sì*?

"Your health, your finances, your business—anything and everything that concerns you, your future, this baby, I want to know. I want you to come to me if you need help. If you need a sounding board. If you—"

Neha placed her finger on his mouth, smiling at the pure arrogance in his tone. "That's a tall order. You can't just order me to open my life up to you with a command."

"I believe I just did."

"It doesn't work that way," she said, fighting not him but her own weaknesses.

She wanted to feel the tensile strength of him beneath her fingers any time she reached for him; she wanted to escape the increasing rift between her and her mum in his arms every night. She wanted to ask him to hold her until all the destruction she had begun was done and she could see the light at the end of it and maybe even beyond. "You don't want a woman completely dependent on you, Leo."

"Do not tell me what I want or do not want, *cara mia*. You shouldn't be under any pressure. Dealing with Mario and your mother is enough to begin with."

"But—"

"Learn to ask for help. Learn to take it when I give it."

Neha nodded slowly, knowing in her heart that he was right. She hadn't even conceived yet—she had resolutely kept away from the dozen or so pregnancy kits she'd stashed in the cupboard under her bathroom sink—and already she was on an emotional seesaw from morning to evening.

She looked down at her hands and then back at Leo. "I've spent years making myself self-sufficient. I can't undo it in a few days."

A nod of concession. "Tell me one of these things you outlined for us."

Neha pulled the laptop forward on the coffee table and pointed to the browser. "I'm going to put the flat up for sale soon."

Leo didn't even look at the browser. "Why? Its value is only going to go up."

"I've been doing my finances, and retirement means my income's going to be fluctuating in the near future. Also, I don't want to raise the baby in a flat. And since I have plans to experiment with some new recipes and start a baking school, I figured it would be a good thing if I buy land and have a house and an industrial-size kitchen custom-built. All that's going to need a lot of capital—"

"If you raise the child outside of London, I'll barely be able to see him or her."

The vehemence of his tone took Neha aback. "I understand that but—"

"Move closer to me. Whatever property you want or capital you need, I'll provide it. Keep the flat."

"That's not a good idea. Everything will get too complicated then and—"

He stood up so suddenly that Neha lost track of what she was saying.

"I made it very clear that I won't play the role of a stud that provides you with genetic material. This is a partnership and you have to start treating it as such."

Neha had never seen that hardness directed at her before.

Her guarded nature, her fears that she'd want more and more, would always come between her and the future she could have with him. And she was sick of living in that fear. She wanted to take more than one step toward him. She wanted to carve a place for herself by his side; it was all she'd been able to think of this past week.

She went to him and took his hand in hers. "It's not my first instinct to ask you for help or even accept it when you offer it but I'm learning to navigate my way through this. I'm learning to find a way to you. Uprooting my entire life, however, just so you can be near—"

"You began uprooting your life before I came into the picture, *cara*. Do you truly have such a full life in London that you can't turn your back on? We can't move forward with our lives with you determined to keep all the lines, Neha."

Neha smiled at the impatience peeking into his tone.

She didn't want to be alone anymore.

She'd need him more and more in the coming months, especially because she wanted his advice on some of the legalese around her retirement and IP associated with So Sweet Inc. And because her growing hormones would only make her more susceptible to another attack. She couldn't forget that stress could always make her anxiety worse.

He'd already more than proved that she could count on him, that he'd be there for anything she needed. And yet to uproot her life in London and move to Italy on the strength of his words sent her heart palpitating. To see him with another woman down the line, when they called their own affair off, God, the emotional stress of that would be too much…

"What happens when there's another woman in your life? Can you imagine how awkward it will get with me trying to cling to the fringes of your life? I don't want to presume a place in your life—for me or for the child—and then be made to feel that I took more than was mine. I couldn't bear to—"

Leo placed his finger on Neha's lips, cutting off her rambling protest.

"No woman will come before you as my child's mother. I give you my word on that."

"It's not possible, even for you, to predict the future. You might fall for another woman, you might get bored of being a parent, you might want to escape with a—"

He pulled her to him by her shoulders, needing to feel her soft body against his. "None of these scenarios will happen because we will marry as soon as possible."

"What?" She stepped back, her frame radiating emotion. "Marriage is not a small thing you decide on on impulse, Leo," she said, mirroring his own words.

"It's not an impulse. I've been thinking about it for more than a week."

"But…why?"

"Think on it, *cara*. What we have between us—respect, admiration, an attraction that's not going anywhere soon and clear expectations of each other…it's more than most marriages have. We share the common goal of doing everything right by our child. Why not just make it official, then? Why these arguments over logistics when a simple, convenient solution is right in front of us?

"Both of us are too wise to get embroiled in love and all that entails. Instead, we can build something even better."

"But what will it mean between us?"

"It means fidelity and respect. It means we'll build a family, *cara*. Isn't that why you started this?"

Her brown eyes flashed with an emotion he couldn't recognize. "I have to think on this. Will you give me time?"

Leo nodded. He wanted her acceptance more than anything he'd ever wanted in life before.

For now, he decided to be satisfied by the lack of her objection. And really, she was a sensible woman and he hadn't expected her to jump with joy. He knew she would weigh every pro and con just like he'd done. And she would come to the conclusion that they were a perfect fit, just as he'd done.

However, he'd never been one to leave things to chance, either.

He reached for her from behind and drew her into his body. She smelled like the most decadent treat, her body warm and curvy and so soft against his. He shuddered at the press of her buttocks against his front. He caught his hips from thrusting into that behind with the last inch of his control.

*Dio*, the day she discovered the power she could wield over him with that sexy body of hers…

She didn't stiffen or pull away. Leo leaned his chin on her shoulder, his palms settling on the almost flat curve of her belly. The very idea that she might already be carrying his child filled him with a joy he had never known.

*Mine*, a part of him wanted to growl. *All mine*. It felt as if a part that had been missing from his life for so long had finally settled into place.

He pushed away the silky curtain of her hair and rubbed his stubble against her soft cheek. Sent his fingers questing up the dips and valleys of her curves until they rested right beneath her breasts. "While you decide whether you want to accept my proposal or not, there's no rule that says we can't indulge ourselves, is there?"

He couldn't see if she smiled or not, couldn't see if those gorgeous brown eyes had flashed with want that she had boldly shown him that night. But he felt the rise and fall of those gorgeous breasts, felt the tremor that shook her luscious body. He trailed soft, slow kisses along the line of her jaw.

She pressed her behind into him, and he hissed at the tight groove he nestled against. "I want to be inside you, *cara mia*. Desperately. In every way possible. And it has nothing to do with business empires, or twisted revenge schemes, or even conception.

"Just you and me and what's been there between us for so long. Say yes to this at least, *carissima*."

Her whispered, "Yes," was barely out before Leo clasped her chin and took her mouth in a kiss that told her he had no doubts about their future.

# CHAPTER TEN

SLEEPING WITH A man wrapped around her—a mansion of a man at that—was a sensual feast Neha would never get enough of. As dawn filtered orange light through the windows, her entire body ached with the good kind of soreness; a lethargic sense of well-being, like honey, filled her limbs. They'd spent most of the last two days in bed—after almost a decade of wanting each other, getting the edge off took a long while.

While the attraction between them still amazed with its intensity, Neha was also aware that Leo was very systematically seducing her into accepting his proposal.

The space he created around them was like a cocoon of warmth and laughter and security and thrill. To reach for him in the middle of the night and find solid, dependable, utterly masculine Leo at the tips of her fingers—whether she wanted comfort or closeness or this mind-bending physical intimacy that was so good between them—it was a potent, addictive feeling.

With Leo there would never be a doubt that he had her best interests at heart.

She would always know exactly where she stood.

There was a such a sense of security in that and a sense of freedom, too, especially after the minefield of emotional dependence she'd been navigating with her mum for so many years.

A real family with Leo was more than she'd ever even conjured in her wildest dreams. So why was she hesitating so much?

Why did her heart stutter when he outlined all the rationale as to why they'd be a good fit? Why did doubts engulf her when she was away from him?

Was there still some naive part of her that hoped for the happiness that her parents had shared once? For all the pain her papa's long illness had caused them, she was sure her mum wouldn't trade the number of joy-filled, loving years they'd had together.

If she went into this with Leo, that naive part had no place in her life. She could never hope for more for this relationship than what they had now. And there was something very heartbreaking about that.

She reached out with her hand and found the other side of the bed empty. Burying her face in the pillow, she breathed in the scent of the man who consumed her thoughts to distraction.

She pushed up on the bed just as Leo walked back into the room, his hair gleaming black from the shower, already dressed sharply in black trousers and a neatly pressed white shirt that made him look painfully gorgeous.

His gaze took in her bare torso, and the heat in his eyes stopped her fingers from pulling up the duvet to cover herself.

Any awkwardness Neha would have felt over being naked with a man she'd admired for so many years, a man she'd always told herself wasn't for her in that way, had disappeared after Leo had pushed her to new realms of pleasure with his carnal demands.

Sitting on her sofa with her bum pulled up to the edge and her legs splayed open in shameless abandon, while Leo on his knees pushed her over the edge with his mouth and tongue and fingers, left no place for awkwardness.

Having sex on the rug in front of a cozy fireplace on her hands and knees, his powerful body thrusting into hers while she urged him on to go deeper and faster, dissolved any self-consciousness.

Being taken care of afterward with tender, apologetic words in lilting Italian, masterful hands wielding a washcloth with tender care she couldn't ever have imagined him to possess, did away with lingering doubts.

Laughing about the rug burn on her knees and being fed crisp grapes and apple pieces by a half-naked giant of a man removed every rational defense and argument against not doing this for the rest of her life.

*"Buongiorno, cara,"* he said in a voice that sent ripples down her skin, even though his blue eyes seemed alert, almost distant.

"Hey," she said, nothing more coherent rising to her lips. "You're already dressed."

"I had the chauffeur bring me some of my stuff. I have to catch a flight to Bali. Sorry if I disturbed your sleep."

"Is the honeymoon already over?" she teased in reaction to his curt tone.

"It wouldn't have to be if you agreed to just move

into the villa immediately." A pithy curse followed the sharp retort. "The last thing I need right now is to worry about what Mario will do to you while I'm on the other side of the world."

"Stop treating me as if I were another obligation."

"What do you think the future we're building together means, *cara*? I'm obligated to worry about you, and you're obligated to stop being your old stubborn self and make things easier on both of us."

"You know it's not that simple," she said, sticking to her guns about not moving to Italy for a couple more months. Her fingers finally found the loose T-shirt she'd discarded only a few hours ago and she pulled it on. "Is everything okay?" she asked, not liking the sudden distance between them. And yet wary of trespassing where she wasn't wanted.

"Nothing that I can't handle," he said, turning away from her. "But I would sleep better while I'm gone if we make the announcement official. If you refuse to move there, I'd have to simply ask Massimo or Nat to keep you company while I'm gone."

"That's not necessary," she added, trying to understand that behind his high-handedness he was worried for her. That he had felt her fear when she'd described the panic attack.

"What's not necessary, *cara*? The announcement or the engagement itself?" he said in a rising voice that reverberated around them.

The tight set of his shoulders chipped away at her own rising frustration. She wanted to spend her life with him building the family they both wanted; she knew he would never hurt her…so why was she still punishing them both with her stubbornness?

Once upon a time, marriage and a husband and real, messy love were all she'd wanted. But Leo would never offer that. Did that make everything else less real?

Neha went to him and wrapped her arms around his wide frame and pressed her cheek into his back. Uncaring that she was mussing him up. She was slowly realizing she didn't want the perfect, larger than life, arrogant Leonardo that had dazzled her back then. She wanted the real man beneath that—the man that was determined to do the right thing despite the odds, the man who fought every inch of himself he gave. She shouldn't, but Lord help her, she did.

"You insist this is a partnership and yet, when it comes to your personal matters, you push me away. You don't share what's going on with you, you…you keep those boundaries around you so very tight, Leo." Her heart ached at how alone he always seemed, at how much burden he carried on his shoulders. "What is the point of getting married if you won't even share what's on your mind? If you're determined to keep me in the same box after all these years. Talk to me. Please. Share your burden, if nothing else."

"I'm not used to it."

She smiled into his back. "I'm not used to a giant of a man ordering me about in my own flat. But then I remind myself of what the giant can do with his crafty fingers and how he holds me when my mum's breaking my heart and how he finds ways to let me know I'm not alone anymore and I go…okay, I can compromise.

"I can let go of stupid, girlie dreams and reach for what's real. I can have an imperfect but real future instead of fluffy, romantic fantasies.

"I want you to be my husband. I want to make a promise to you that I'm committed to the life we build together. Watching my parents together all those years ago, marriage is the most honorable thing for me. If I make that promise to you, if I agree to be your wife, I take everything that comes with it very seriously.

"We've been good friends, lovers, we trust each other, but being a husband and wife…there's something about that holy bond that changes everything. I want to be the best wife I can be, Leo," she said, trying to articulate some of her fears into words. "But I can't if you shut me out at every turn."

He turned around, pressed a kiss to her temple. It lasted only seconds, but when their gazes met, she saw that her words had registered. That she'd surprised him with both her vulnerability and her opinions about marriage. "For me, marriage is a logical step. A way to make sure history is not repeated with our child."

She nodded. To hide the sudden shaft of pain that pierced her heart. "It is, for us. But it also means a lot more to me."

His frown slowly morphed into a smile and he clasped her cheek. "Of course. I should've known you won't enter into anything without planning to give it your everything." And then a hand through his hair, his only tell, before he leaned back against the wall, putting distance between them again. "What do you want to know?"

Neha lowered her arms, glad that he was at least talking.

"You never even told me what Mario said about that man and what he's up to."

"Just a lot of threats about what this Vincenzo means to do to our family."

"Any light on why he's targeting you?"

Leo shrugged. "Vague hints at how all roads eventually lead to my father."

"To Silvio? This is all connected to your father?"

"*Sì*. All these attacks seem personally motivated. Other than maybe a spurned girlfriend in Massimo's case, we haven't harmed anyone, on a personal or a professional front. That was a conclusion Massimo and I drew weeks ago."

She knew she was venturing into dangerous territory but she had to try. "Then why can't you simply talk to Silvio? Tell him about this Vincenzo's mad campaign against all of you. He can shed light on the whole matter. And you can clear it up with some sort of…reparation to this man, can't you?"

"You think a man who has continually launched attacks on BFI, BCS and on personal fronts on me, Massimo, Greta, even Alex, will accept reparation and move on?

"Not knowing what Vincenzo wants, waiting for him to make his next move while being unable to do anything…it's the most powerless I've ever felt.

"As for Silvio, my father is not one who will willingly come clean about every crime he's perpetrated in his life. The only communication he and I have is the deal we made years ago. He gives me proxy power over his shares, and I let him out of that clinic once a year and let him keep his friends. We've shared nothing more in a long time, *bella*."

"Leo, that's not…healthy. I know what an awful man he's been his entire life, but have you never wanted to ask him about your mother? Never wanted to find out why?"

"And play into the old man's manipulative games again? Do you think he'd tell me the truth, or some twisted version he could use against me? Men like my father only understand power. Do you think it makes a difference to me now? She left me with him, *cara*. I made my peace with it a long time ago."

"Have you, though?"

Blue fire glittered in his eyes. "*Sì*. And you get nothing by excavating a topic better left in the past. You know me better than anyone, Neha. Please don't assume I need a heart-to-heart about all this to get in touch with myself better. I want to solve this Vincenzo thing once and for all and look to the future. Not get mired in the past."

But was anything ever untouched by the past? Could anything new ever grow when everything that was hard, and painful, had been buried underneath? When emotions were stifled because they would bring pain?

Because that's what Leo was doing. Without pain and ache and fear, could there be joy and contentment and peace? Without the risk of vulnerability, could there ever be love?

There wouldn't be. Because Leo had closed himself off to all of it a long time ago.

And yet, she couldn't bring herself to voice those fears. She couldn't push when he wanted to leave it where it belonged. When he was determined to not let it mar the future.

His, and now hers. Their future child's.

"This trip to Bali…is it to find Vincenzo?"

"*Sì*. Massimo and Nat found financial details for an offshore company that originates there from the transaction to Mario."

"What if you can't catch him there, Leo? You can't go chasing this man around the world, can you?"

"But he's not all I'm chasing. Last I heard from her agent, Alessandra has been in Bali this whole time."

A soft gasp escaped Neha's mouth as she thought of the genuinely lovely Alessandra within this… Vincenzo's reach. "You don't think it's a coincidence?"

Worry etched into Leo's brow. "No. Neither does Massimo. Since the last organized dark net attack on BCS, we've been waiting for his next move. It's been months and he's been quiet and then we learn that she's been in Bali this whole time… Greta is going mad with worry.

"I have to find Alessandra and make sure she…stays clear of him." *If it wasn't already too late…* Neha heard his unspoken fear.

And now, after knowing how many things he handled, she couldn't blame him for being short with her. "I'm sorry I added to your worries."

"That's the deal we made, *bella*. But this is an obligation I chose for myself, Neha. Not had thrust upon me. Can you remember that?" He reached her, his fingers sinking into her hair at the nape of her neck. She nodded, her heart jerking in place at the distinction he'd made. "I don't like having to leave right now when Mario's furious with me. He'll manipulate you and use your mum to do it."

"I'm through with her," she said, swallowing the ache

in her throat. "She's going to miss our wedding. She's lost her chance to be a part of her grandchild's life. She…" A sob rose through her, but she killed it. She'd shed enough tears over her mum. "There's nothing he can hold over me. I promise you. Go, do this thing and be back soon."

*"Bene."*

Neha rubbed her face against his chest, loving the solid musculature of him against her cheek. Knowing that it was useless to deny herself and him. She wanted this future with him. She wanted whatever little he had to offer.

She swallowed away the lingering doubts and pressed her mouth to his. "I want that future with you, Leo. For the first time in so many years, I feel like I'm alive. I wake up with joy and expectations and…yes, I'll marry you."

His kiss said everything she knew he wouldn't say. It was warm and desperate and full of a longing that was more than just physical between them now. The velvet box glimmered in the soft morning light. Her breath lodged in her chest as he tugged her left hand up, and placed a warm, lingering kiss at the center of her palm.

His breath was a symphony against her skin as he took her mouth in a devouring kiss. The platinum set, princess-cut diamond winked at her in the weak morning light, and turned her into an inarticulate jumble of emotions.

"You play dirty," she finally said. *This was for convenience*, she chanted to herself as if it were a mantra, using it to corral her runaway imagination.

"That's a serious accusation."

She laughed at the seriousness of his tone. "You misunderstand. I'm not talking about that diamond. I'm talking about seducing me all night and then springing the ring on me when I have no defenses or rationality left. I'll agree to anything."

Her fingers trembled as he slid the ring on, and it fit perfectly. She kissed him this time, needing the intimate connection that came when they communicated with their bodies. Like every single time, the simple contact flared into something more, so much more, until they were both breathing hard.

When he looked at her like that, Neha could almost trick herself into believing he genuinely cared about her.

No, he did care about her.

"This feels right, *bella*. Everything I do with you feels easy…uncomplicated, in a way I've never expected.

"For the first time in my life, I'm building something for myself. Something tangible and real for the future. You, this child and what we build together…it's mine, all mine. *Only mine.* Untouched by my family's dirty legacy, untouched by the ugly past. A fresh start. There's a powerful quality to new beginnings, it seems, that even I can't resist."

Neha stood leaning against the bed for a long time after Leo left, his words ringing around in her head. On paper, she and Leo could have the perfect marriage. No lofty expectations of each other. No messy emotions. No high highs and low lows.

But life, she knew, was never that simple or easy to be ruled by logic and boundaries.

Even with all her rationale in place, she would always be vulnerable when it came to Leonardo. Already, she was far too invested in his every word, look and gesture. In what he said and everything he didn't say. And for all the distinctions he made, she was another obligation to a man who had spent most of his adult life shouldering numerous ones.

And yet, Neha knew it was too late to walk away from him. Knew her vulnerability to Leo meant her heart was already in danger.

Just as Leo had predicted, Mario walked into her office on Tuesday afternoon, his mouth curled into a sneer. Neha sighed, thankful that he hadn't brought her mum along at the least.

From the moment the news of her engagement to Leo had gone viral, she'd been on tenterhooks, her heart jumping into her throat every time her phone rang, hoping it was her mum. Hoping she'd at least begin to see that Mario hadn't been right about everything.

The glass door to her office barely closed behind her when Mario erupted. "Have you no loyalty? No shame? Are you that desperate for him, for his attention, that you'd let him manipulate you?

"Have you no shame in selling out your own family?"

Neha let him spew his poison, let him vent it all out, before she said, "Are you through?"

"No. You'll wish you hadn't taken me on when you see what I can do. You think you have it all neatly tied up, don't you? Your retirement, your IP from the company, your engagement to Leonardo…you've no idea how fast he'll dump you when I bring my full might onto his precious company and—"

"Enough, Mario! I've heard enough. For years, I shut my mouth because I was afraid you'd twist Mum against me.

"So many years, so many wasted opportunities… and you know what?

"The worst is done. Despite my every effort, you've created a rift between us. No, she let you create a rift between us. She gave you that power and I'm done.

"Tell her that, won't you?" she said, tears streaming down her cheeks. "Tell her I'm done being the sensible one, the adult, the strong one. Tell her that I'm done putting up with her bully of a husband just for her sake." She swiped at the tears on her cheeks and took a calming breath. Still, her voice reverberated with conviction and strength. Strength Leo had given her.

"And you've lost any leverage you had over me. By threatening Leo, by threatening me, you've lost any chance I might have given you because you're her husband.

"I'm through with you and I'm going to take every penny that's mine from you."

For the first time in her life, Neha saw shock descend into her stepfather's eyes.

She walked around her table and opened the door. "Get out of my office. And if you threaten me like that ever again, if you come near me, I'll let Leo do what he really wants to do to you," she added for good measure.

In the ensuing silence, Neha slumped onto her chair,

a sense of relief and freedom engulfing her. She lifted her cell phone with shaking fingers, her vision blurred.

"Neha?" Leo's voice came through clear and concerned.

"I told him off, Leo," Neha whispered, tears clogging her throat.

"Of course you did," Leo said with such conviction in his tone that Neha thought she might have lost a little of her heart to him on that phone call. "You must have been spectacular."

She laughed through the tears. "I was. Truly. But he's not going to go away calmly. On second thought, I don't know if I should've enraged him like that."

"You had every right, *bella*. And don't worry. I'll deal with whatever he brings, *sì*?"

"*Sì.*"

"Will be you okay?" he said with a smile in his voice.

"Yes. But come back soon to me, won't you?" she said, letting the longing she'd always felt for him pour into words.

"*Sì, bella.* Soon."

Neha sat in her chair for a long time, the phone pressed to her chest. She looked around her office but there was nothing she was attached to here.

One chapter of her life was done. And one would begin soon. And she couldn't wait to start it with Leo at her side.

Standing in her underwear in front of her bathroom vanity, Neha checked the small plastic stick resting on the dark marble surface again and again.

*Pregnant.*

The world seemed blurry and distorted to her tear-soaked vision. She hastily scrubbed her eyes, afraid the word might change to something else.

It didn't.

It was her sixth pregnancy test and none of them had changed the verdict on her. And slowly, the truth sank in, filling every cell and pore in her.

God, she was pregnant.

With Leo's baby.

*With Leo's baby...*

Pregnant by the man she'd wanted for so long that every time he looked at her with that dark, knowing gaze now, she had to remind herself that it was real and not just a fantasy out of her head.

They were going to be a family, support each other, shower their child with love. After being mired in loneliness for so long, the dream of being a part of something would finally come true.

A shiver swept through her as she imagined the future, an intense rush of emotions and thoughts stealing her breath. Fingers holding on to the marble, she ducked her head, focusing on taking deep, long breaths. As she pushed her hair away from her sweaty forehead, her gaze caught on the diamond glittering on her finger.

It had been a week since the night since she'd agreed to marry Leo, caught up in the warmth of his sexy body and his clever caresses. And ever since that day, she'd been waiting to wake up to some kind of reality check. For some rational voice inside of her to say this was madness.

Instead, the weight of the ring on her finger had become familiar already, an anchor to ground her, a comforting, caring voice in her head when the madness of her unraveling life threatened to overwhelm her.

Like the explosion of media and fan interest after her and Leo's PR team made an official announcement. But in the effusive rush of well-wishes from her fans, Neha hadn't let herself forget that the rushed announcement was more for optics.

He was committed to a future with her and their child, but it didn't mean he wouldn't use it to put pressure on Mario. To show Mario that Leo was in Neha's life and he intended to stay. To push Mario to the edge where he might cough out any information he had on Vincenzo Cavalli.

A stark reminder that Leo was still unswerving and strategic when it came to achieving his own ends, that he didn't forget for one minute that this was a convenient arrangement on so many levels.

She ran her palm over her bare belly repeatedly even though it was too soon to tell. She couldn't wait to share the news with Leo. Couldn't wait to say goodbye to the pieces of her life that brought her pain and nothing else.

In the meantime, she still had to deal with the consequences of her confrontation with Mario, face whatever it was he threw her way.

Just a few more weeks, she reassured herself as she dressed in a white dress shirt and black trousers. She'd just finished her smoothie and put on her jacket when her phone rang.

She frowned as she saw Massimo's face on her screen. "Massimo?"

"Hey, Neha." His greeting was subdued. "How are you doing, *bella*?"

"I'm fine. Is everything okay with Leo? What happened?"

"Leo's fine, *cara*. He's just busy dealing with things here at the villa…"

"Oh. I didn't know he was back from Bali already," she said, fighting the shaft of discontent settling in her chest. Why hadn't Leo called her as soon as he was back? After being worried that he was leaving her alone to face Mario at that. When they were so close to knowing whether they had conceived or not.

Her practical nature asserted itself in the next minute. Honestly, she couldn't expect him to remember the dates of her cycle as obsessively as she did. The man not only ran BFI but managed a thousand other responsibilities. Sometimes, she wondered how Leo had sustained it all for so long.

"Neha? Are you okay?"

"Yeah, of course. Sorry, I just wandered off." She frowned as she sensed his hesitation. "Massimo, why are you calling me?"

"Leo had to cut his trip short since we got news the previous night that my father…our father had a cardiac arrest. Silvio passed away late yesterday afternoon at the clinic. Leo has been dealing with all the arrangements and, of course, Greta, and hordes of my father's old friends descending on us.

"None of us have had a moment to process it yet. Natalie reminded me that you probably didn't get the news yet."

Neha pushed away the niggle that Leo hadn't even thought to inform her. This wasn't about her. This was… about Leo. And his complex relationship with his father. This was about being there for a man who'd always been there for her, a man who seemed as if he'd never need anyone. A man who'd shown he was capable of incredible kindness and yet shared nothing of himself.

"When's the funeral?" she said.

"Tomorrow afternoon."

"Can you make arrangements for me to fly out there immediately, Massimo?"

Neha heard Massimo's relief in his long sigh.

"I just… I don't want to deal with Mario right now," she added when he remained silent.

"Of course. I'll have the pilot contact you directly."

"Thank you, Massimo. For remembering me," she added, knowing that for all the dysfunction behind closed doors, the Brunettis had always presented a united front to the world. Whatever his sins against his sons, Silvio Brunetti had been shielded by them. By Leonardo.

"I have my own selfish reasons for hoping you'll come, *cara*," Massimo said, throwing Neha for a loop.

"What do you mean?"

"I want Leo to have someone by his side. Even if my brother acts like he needs nothing and no one."

Neha stood at the same spot for a long time after Massimo hung up, thinking how right Massimo was.

Whether Leo wanted her or needed her or not, she would be there by his side.

# CHAPTER ELEVEN

NEHA WALKED AWAY from the last, lingering group of guests as the sky shimmered orange at the end of the day, pleading the excuse of a headache, which was quickly becoming more than real. She'd been up since dawn after a bad night's sleep, and worrying about a showdown between Mario and Leo had stolen the rest of her sanity.

Most of the guests had already left—including Mario and her mum. Just seeing her mum while she had this momentous news to share but not being able to…it had taken everything Neha had to maintain her equilibrium. Not for a moment had her mum strayed far from Mario's side *even if* Neha had wanted to talk to her. With so many guests' eyes on her, in the end, Neha had simply been glad that Mario hadn't created his signature drama again.

But of course, he'd been busy in other ways, as she'd realized the moment she'd arrived.

In the two days since she'd arrived at the Brunetti villa, she'd been mostly on her feet, holding the fort on the home front with extended family and close friends descending on the villa—discussing the meals with the housekeeper, having to arrange rooms for their stay at a neighboring villa, keeping well-meaning but curious relatives away from Greta, while Leo and Massimo dealt with the massive media ruckus following Silvio's sudden death.

By the time the helicopter had dropped her off, the whole household had been in uproar in the wake of a rumor that Silvio had died leaving or selling his stock in BFI to an unknown third party in the weeks leading up to his death.

Neha had a feeling she knew the source of the nasty rumor that had been making the rounds among BFI's board members. It was clear Mario was still not backing down. For who else would get such a piece of news to go around and around? Especially after the showdown between him and Neha herself.

Couldn't the circling hyenas keep their hungry noses away from his sons at least on the day of their father's funeral? How had Leo dealt with this for so long?

Greta, who'd always come off as the strong, implacable type with boundless energy, had been close to a nervous breakdown when Neha had checked on her upon arrival. Natalie had pulled Neha aside to tell her that the Brunetti matriarch had gotten other distressing news from her stepdaughter, Alessandra, who was still worryingly absent, on top of her son's death. Finally, Neha had called her physician, who'd recommended a mild sedative for Greta.

Natalie herself was young, inexperienced in real-life situations, so Neha took the ropes of handling people at the home front with Massimo's help. For all that Silvio

Brunetti had brought BFI to its knees once, he'd still had a huge network. There were a lot of families and powerful figures that wanted to pay their respects to the family, including one cabinet minister.

At least Neha hadn't received strange looks or comments about taking over the hostess duties. Not that she'd give a damn about anyone's opinion except the one man who had maintained an aloof distance the whole time.

She only saw Leo in passing the first day and he'd done no more than acknowledge her presence with a nod. Most of the first night, she'd spent it in a restless slumber hoping he would join her, only to find out that Leo had only retired to his bedroom past dawn.

He had so many things on his mind, she knew that. And she'd never be the clingy, needing-reassurance-for-everything kind of a woman, but oh…she just wished he'd said something, anything, to her.

She'd have had a hint of where his mind was at. Instead, he'd given off the clear vibes that he wasn't available or willing to have even a quick conversation. The last thing she could do was throw the news of their pregnancy at him…in the midst of it all. She hated it but there was even a part of her that was afraid of what his reaction would be to the news in the current situation.

So, she'd acted like nothing was wrong between them and done everything she could to let him know that she was there for him. Having been burned so many times by her mum's fluctuating moods, Neha had stayed out of his way, like a docile puppy. When she was anything but.

That little niggle grew into resentment, with herself that she'd let him discourage her, with him for treating her as if nothing had changed between them, and morphed into a pounding headache.

Her pasted smile and polite words took too much out of her. She grabbed a glass of water and guzzled it down, remembering that she needed to take better care of herself. That tranquil quality she'd cherished so much on her first trip returned to the villa as the guests became scarce, but it couldn't restore her own spiraling mood.

Most of the staff was well trained under the efficient housekeeper, Maria, and wouldn't need further instruction. After thanking her, Neha checked on Greta—who still looked pale but rested— one last time and walked back to her suite.

Wondering all the while what was going on in Leo's head.

She wanted to hold him, and she needed to be held. She wanted to tell him about their child already growing in her belly, day by day, moment by moment. She wanted to see that glow in his eyes when he talked about their future together. She wanted him to tell her what his father's death meant to him, if anything. She wanted to talk about how close she'd come to pulling her mum away from Mario and spilling the news of her pregnancy. She wanted to talk about how scared and alone she felt when she saw that distant, aloof look he got in his eyes sometimes.

As if she were alone again... No, she couldn't tell him that. She couldn't throw her niggles and fears at him at a time like this. As long as he came to her, she'd somehow deal with it.

But would he?

From everything she knew about him, Leo was a man who retreated in times of grief, or pain. That glimpse she'd gotten so long ago was a one-off. Until he processed what Silvio's death meant to him and how little it should, he would hold her at a distance.

Thoughts in a turmoil, she unzipped her black sheath dress and moved to the closet.

And came to a standstill.

Why was she letting him decide how this would play out? They wouldn't have much of a relationship if she treated it like a paint by numbers canvas. Things had changed between them. It wasn't all sex and conception and business between them…wasn't that what he'd said? And when she'd needed him, he'd been there, so why couldn't the reverse be true?

She understood he'd been too busy to call her once he'd returned from Bali, too busy fighting the rumors that he wouldn't stay CEO of BFI much longer to give her two minutes of his time, but enough was enough. He wasn't going to compartmentalize her role in their relationship before it had even taken off.

She wasn't going to wait for his time and attention like one of Massimo's affectionate hounds.

She didn't want to sleep in an empty bed, not when he was only a few rooms away.

Not when she missed him like a physical ache. Not when she was dying to share the most important news of their new life together. And she sure as hell wasn't going to let him go to his room alone. If he was okay with her taking over at the villa, with acting as his hostess, then he needed to be okay with her moving into his suite.

Because that's exactly what she was going to do.

Never again in her life was Neha going to wait for someone to tell her what her place in life should be. Never again was she going to let someone else decide where she belonged and where she didn't. Not even Leo.

Zipping the dress back up, heels hanging from her fingers, she walked out of her assigned suite.

She found Maria, told her she'd be in Leo's suite and begged for a snack. Once in the massive suite, she stripped, showered, fished for something to wear inside Leo's closet and crawled into bed. The sheets were luxuriously soft around her as she sat cross-legged in the center of his bed and ate the bowl of fruits Maria had sent up. Stomach full, she pulled up the shirt and studied the curve of her belly for a few moments.

Joy was a visceral thing inside her chest, a tremendous force of emotion for this child and the man who had given her everything she'd asked for and more.

Her heart felt overwhelmingly full, tears filling her eyes. This house, this family, the man at the center of it…she wanted this for her, this future, so badly that her heart raced at an alarming rate in her chest. She'd do anything to keep it, to hold on to it. To build it.

She grabbed a pillow, buried her nose in it and was rewarded with the lingering scent of the man she never wanted to let go. Beneath the overpowering surge of emotions that took over every time she thought of the child in her belly, there was also a pulse of something else, softly calling her. Something that utterly terrified her.

She closed her eyes, tried to order her thoughts and frantically prayed to God that this was just her hormones already in play, that this seesaw of emotions was just the consequence of having to keep mum about her pregnancy for forty-eight hours. She wasn't resentful because Leo hadn't given her something she didn't even know she'd wanted. She couldn't be.

Her last thought before she drifted off to sleep was wishing he'd come to her for whatever it was he needed. Share a little more of himself with her.

Because she could walk into his bedroom and his life and take what she thought was rightfully her place, but his heart…his heart was always going to be out of her reach unless he gave it to her. Unless he let her in.

Leo walked into his bedroom after midnight had come and gone, his fingers wrapped around the slender neck of a two-thousand-euro bottle of whiskey. Half of it was already in his bloodstream but the liquor hadn't done a thing to numb him so far.

He had maintained his usual implacability in front of Massimo and fobbed him off because the last thing he needed right now was to be studied under a microscope of brotherly concern. Not that he didn't want it, but because he wasn't sure what Massimo would discover if he delved too deep. There was a volatility to him that he didn't want anyone exposed to tonight, not until he had it under control.

Everything felt upside down, and he hated that feeling.

A mere forty-eight hours ago, the news had reached him that Silvio wanted to speak to him urgently. But he'd put it down to Silvio having one of his tantrums and decided not to expend his energy and time on it.

Within a blink of an eye of that decision, Silvio had died of a cardiac arrest.

If not for the coroner's report and his father's physician's diagnosis that Silvio had been having a lot of breathing trouble for the last week, Leo would have expected foul play. Because it was so convenient for his father to drop dead right after he'd decided he didn't want to bequeath his stock in BFI to Leo and Massimo, after all.

Now there would be more investigation while the lawyers picked up the trail to figure out who Silvio had sold the BFI shares to.

For once in his life, Leo realized he couldn't bring himself to even care about who had bought Silvio's shares in the company or who was masterminding the whole thing, or what it would mean for his CEO position.

*Cristo*, he was bone-tired physically after two nights of practically no sleep and keeping his family's name above the rumor mill. Of course his father hadn't made it easy on Leo and Massimo even in this final step— the bastard. All he wanted was to numb himself until rationality and balance and his composure returned.

For his mind to stop going in circles looking for an answer to a question that was forever lost to him now.

Moving into his bedroom, he shrugged his shirt off, undid the button of his trousers. His eyes—gritty from lack of sleep and out of focus—took a few seconds to get used to the darkness. And then his gaze found her. His heart jolted like a drowning man given a benediction.

In the center of his massive bed, fast asleep.

Everything in him drilled down into a laser-like stream of focus on the beautiful, sexy woman, all troubling thoughts fleeing, all concerns dying, until nothing but she remained. Like walking into a dream where no questions existed, no doubts remained, no possible answers haunted him—only the present mattered. Only she and her sensuality, and her passion, mattered.

Moonlight drenched her body in sweet, pale light, and he fisted his hands, fighting the memory of how soft and responsive she'd been to his slightest caress.

She slept on her side, one arm tucked under her head, long, bare legs flung in opposite directions, her silky hair flying rhythmically with each exhale. Her lashes cast crescent shadows on high cheekbones. The shirt rode up high on her thighs, giving him a glimpse of a pink-lace-clad curve of one buttock, while the collar fell open to reveal her breasts pressed up together in a tempting invitation.

A flood of carnal hunger surged through him, washing away what even alcohol couldn't. Leaving nothing but the primal need to claim her.

Putting the bottle away, he moved to the head of the bed. His breath punched through him as he realized that the shirt she wore was his. It threw him, in his current mood, her clear claim to him, here in his bedroom and outside over two days.

Not for a single second had Leo been unaware of how seamlessly Neha had fit into his life in the past two days. Of how easily she foresaw people's needs and met them with an effortless grace. Of how calmly she'd handled Greta's impending breakdown with no input from either himself or Massimo. Of how strongly she'd faced her mum while he knew it had to break her inside for not being able to reach out to her.

She'd been there all day at the back of his consciousness—a calming presence, a landing place, when he wanted to keep the world at bay, centering him, even when he avoided her, with the practicality of her calm nature. It hadn't been easy to shut down the urge to follow her into that bedroom and let her see the growing void he could feel in himself and ask her to soothe it away with whatever magic she weaved.

Somehow, he'd fought it.

But now, seeing her sprawled like a queen at the center of his massive bed… As if she belonged there. Daring him to face her and the vulnerability he'd never been able to shed within himself. Forcing him to face things he'd rather stayed buried.

A soft moan left her lips and the husky sound went straight to his groin.

He knew he should walk away right then, knew that what he wanted to do to her, with her, was wrong after he'd purposely avoided her for two days. *Dio*, the bastard he was, he hadn't even asked how she was feeling.

Somehow, he pulled himself away and almost reached the door when he heard her throaty, sleep-mussed voice.

"Leo?"

The rustle of the sheets made him think of the soft fabric gliding up and down her body doing what he wanted to do. Giving up the fight, he turned around.

Hair in a rumpled mess, knees tucked together and away, the shirt—his shirt—unbuttoned all the way to her navel and falling off the smooth, rounded shoulder he'd sunk his teeth into the other night, she called to every masculine instinct in him.

"Go back to sleep, *cara*," he whispered.

She blinked, pushed her hair away from her face and looked around. "It's one-thirty in the morning. Where are you going?"

He shoved his fingers through his hair, his entire body thrumming with sexual hunger and the tension that came with denying himself. "I'm not... I don't think I can sleep tonight."

He swallowed the need flaring through him as her gaze swept over his bare chest like a physical caress. So openly she devoured him. Such hunger in that sensual body for him.

*Cristo*, he felt it a thousand times more. Especially now, when he knew that the fire between them only flared hotter and higher every time they came together.

"Okay, that's fine." Her words were soft, soothing, as if she were gentling a wounded animal. *Dio*, he hated this so much, hated his inability to accept the haven she offered. But he just couldn't bare himself to her now. "We can just talk."

"I'll only disturb you if I stay," he said through gritted teeth, his impatience and need swirling through the air. "And the last thing I want to do is talk."

She tossed the duvet aside, and threw her long, bare legs over the side.

Lifting the bottle to his mouth, he took a long sip. Her eyes followed the drop that fell on his chest with a lingering fascination that corkscrewed through his body.

"You're drunk," she said, her eyes widening, her fingers scrunched tight around the duvet. "But you never drink to that point. You hated Silvio's alcoholic rampages. You'd never willingly give up control like this. Leo, please—"

"You know me so well, *sì, cara*?" he said in a mocking tone that rendered her pale. "I'm drunk because I wanted a moment's peace from the million obligations that choke me at any given moment. Which is why I'm going to find a different room."

"I'll be damned if I let you call me an obligation."

God, even spitting mad, the woman was simply magnificent. "I don't really care what you get from that."

"Wait, Leo—"

"*Merde!* Let it go, Neha! Get some sleep. You've been on your feet constantly for two days."

"I didn't think you noticed," she said with a flash of vulnerability that pierced him.

"I notice everything about you, Neha." The words rushed out of him, emotion ringing in them.

"So you kept me at a distance on purpose," she said, the shadow of hurt in her eyes lingering far too long for his comfort.

Maybe it was better that she understood that he'd

purposely avoided her. Knowing her and how strongly she prided herself on her emotional self-sufficiency, she would back off now.

"Yes. I had a lot on my mind, and I didn't have time to coddle you."

"Ah... I see now why you shouldn't drink. The ruthless bastard, the arrogant jerk version of Leonardo Brunetti, comes out to play."

Despite the dark mood clouding his better judgment, he smiled. "Now you know. I'm a mean drunk, just like him."

"Are you mad that I snuck into your room? Your bed?"

*No, you were born for that role. For my bed. For my life.*

The words stuck in his throat, like acid he couldn't swallow or spit out.

Everything he'd wanted with her tilted on its axis in the current state of his mind, everything that had been easy and good now felt as if it could choke him with all its myriad possibilities...everything she made him feel yawned open like a dark pit from which he might not pull himself out if he ventured further.

The Brunettis had a dark history of abuse and dysfunction. Massimo had changed it by reaching for Natalie and he'd wanted to do the same. Because it would take a woman like Neha to break that cycle, to rewrite a new chapter, a different ending.

Until yesterday, he had wanted that new beginning... but tonight, today...

"I'm not mad," he finally said, "but I wanted privacy tonight." He knew he sounded like a petulant boy.

In the blink of an eye, Neha was in front of him, a solemn expression in her eyes.

"I'm sorry about your loss, Leo. I know you didn't have an easy relationship with him. I know he was a beast of a father but—"

"No. Don't give me that. *Cristo*, not you, too, with lame condolences, not when you know how little I care.

"I don't feel anything at his death, Neha. Don't you get it? I don't feel…*anything*. He was a monster who ruined so many lives. When I got the message that he wanted to see me urgently two days ago, I brushed it off as if he were an annoying ant.

"Even knowing what happened after, I don't regret that decision.

"That's how ruthless I'm.

"This is the man you've invited into your body, into your life. I don't feel anything. I can't feel anything. There? Are you happy now? We've talked about it."

Tears filled her eyes and the concern in them almost undid him. "Is it really that simple? Then why get drunk? Why those shadows in your eyes? Talk to me, Leo. Burying your pain does nothing but damage us irrevocably. Believe me, I've done that to myself for so long until nothing but a shadow of me remained. I understand at least some of what you're going through. I want to—"

"*No*, you don't! You can't."

Pain burst open in the void of his chest, everything he'd buried his entire life flooding into this moment, this night cloaked in the dark, into the present he wanted with this woman, poison fouling up the very air between them, running unchecked, messing with his head.

He rubbed his hand over his temple. "You can't imagine what it is to be a five-year-old boy who wakes up one morning to find his mother's room deserted, who frantically searches her closet, every nook and corner of an eerily empty villa, who rifles through her drawers to find her things are gone, who runs around between the villa and the greenhouse and the grounds, panic beating out of his chest, short legs eating up the distance, terrified that if he stopped looking, she'd really be gone, terrified that if he stopped running, his world would crash down around him…who kept running until the physical pain buried the emotional.

"And today, when I face the question I should have asked him once—a single time, over all these years, the question that haunts me, the question that changes nothing of the past or the future or my present…"

And still the words came, into the stunned silence. As if he couldn't lock them away now that they'd been released.

"Why did she leave? Did he drive her away with his rages and his abuse? How could she go when it meant leaving her son with the same monster?"

"What is wrong about wanting to know?" Neha said, her palms on his chest, rattling him, rumbling him, still determined to get through to him. Her tears drew wet tracks on his chest, drenching him, crying for him when he couldn't for himself, her shoulders shaking against him. Grieving for him. Fighting for him, he realized with a strange fascination. "She was your mother! What's wrong with wanting to think maybe she'd had a horrible reason for deserting her son? With being hurt by their selfish actions—either as a boy or a man?"

He pressed his hands to her shoulders, feeling spent. Feeling that void take over again. Feeling the blessed relief of numbness starting to descend on him.

"Would Silvio's answer have changed anything? No.

"No little kernel of truth is going to shine a light in the closed-off quarters of my heart. I will never be vulnerable like that again, because I don't know how to be. This is who I am. Nothing will change the man I've become. Nothing will turn me into that boy again, open to hurt."

Tears poured down her cheeks and even now, when he should walk away from her, Leo reached for her.

"Shh…don't cry, *cara*. Don't waste your tears on me."

"I'm not crying for you."

He bared his teeth in a sneering facsimile of a smile. "*No? Then do you cry for yourself, cara*? That you get a damaged man who will never let himself be vulnerable with you? That you made a commitment before you realized what you were truly getting? Are you thinking of going back on our deal now?"

She wiped her face, a resolve in her eyes that threatened to knock the blessed numbness. "I'm not going anywhere."

He raised a brow. *"No?"*

Stepping back from him, she looked up. "No. However, since you've made it very clear that you don't want me here tonight, I'll go back to my bedroom and you can—" her gaze swept over his face and then dismissed him "—continue your drinking binge or whatever you want to do with yourself. When you're in a… better mood, come find me."

His heartbeat kicked up. Even ravaged with the ache she felt for him, her eyes smudged with tears, her mouth pinched and trembling, she was the most beautiful woman he'd ever seen.

And still, he wanted her.

She grabbed the duvet and wrapped it around herself, covering up the lush beauty of her body. "Good night, Leo."

"No," he said, grabbing the edge of the duvet, challenge shimmering in the very air around them. He tugged at it and she came with it, unwilling to give it up, fiery and sexy and every inch his deepest fantasy come true. "I want you to stay."

"Why?"

He needed anesthetizing from whatever she had made him spill. He needed to bury the overwhelming emotions in his head. He needed to isolate the scab and cauterize it forever.

He threw the bottle in his hand carelessly behind him and it fell with a hard thump against the sofa. "You want to make me feel better, *si*? You want to be there for me? That's why you were here, in my bed?"

She licked her lips, and he tightened painfully at the memory of how she'd licked him up one night. It was a magnificent thing to be with a woman who went after what she wanted.

Sex with Neha wasn't just sex anymore. It was… something else, something that defied definition. Something he was already addicted to. Nothing, it seemed, was simple or easy anymore. And yet, in this, he couldn't make himself retreat.

If he'd expected her to flinch away, he'd have been disappointed. Shoulders straight, gaze steady, she was awe-inspiring as she said, "Yes."

"Then kiss me. Go to bed with me. Give me your body tonight." Arrogant demand reverberated in his voice and Leo hated himself for what he was saying, the reckless cruelty it seemed he was capable of toward the one woman who'd tried to reach the darkness in him.

*Maybe the apple didn't fall far, after all.*

He braced himself for a slap. For stinging words. For the fury that he could see brewing in her eyes.

The duvet fell to the floor in a silky hiss.

Her fingers went to the last three buttons on her shirt. No hesitation in those eyes or her fingers. She wriggled her shoulders in that way of hers that made her full breasts bob up and down, until the shirt fell off, clinging to her wide hips for a few more seconds and then to the floor in a whispered hush.

Desire hummed through his body, not even the alcohol in his blood curbing the anticipation swelling his desire.

Miles of smooth brown skin stretched taut over supple curves. The slopes of her breasts partially covered by strands of silky hair, the sweep of her hips, the soft swell of her belly, the muscled length of her thighs… she was a goddess he didn't deserve.

But she'd come into his life and he was damned if he'd let her go.

"Sacrificial lamb, *bella*?" he said, even knowing that he'd take her however she came to him.

A soft laugh from that incredibly lush mouth. A fire in her eyes. "I told you. I'm done with living my life for someone else. I came to your bed because I wanted to be here for you, *yes*. But I also came because I didn't want to sleep alone.

"I've already gotten used to having you next to me—hard and warm and solid and real." Such naked need in her eyes that it pinned him to the spot. Such vulnerability she exposed that it humbled him. "I want you. Inside me. Over me. Any way I can get you."

He undid his trousers, pushed them down and stepped out of them. Covering the distance between them, he pulled her to him roughly. One hand around her nape, he held her open for him, while he devoured her lush mouth. Her moans were a balm to his frantic need.

The other hand, he sent it questing—to cup her plump breast, to rub the pert peak, to follow the lush lines of her body, to trace the curve of her hips, to dip into her folds, to stroke and caress her core, to press against the bundle of nerves he loved to taste, to make her ready for his ravenous possession.

And as always, she rewarded him. So quickly, so easily, so generously. Her nails dug into his shoulders, her teeth digging into his bicep, her leg opening around his hip when he slid a finger into her wet warmth.

His heart raced, his body throbbing almost painfully. He kissed her with a bruising need that showed no sign of abating any time soon. He filled his hands with her buttocks, brought her to the edge of his bed. She wrapped her legs around his hips, her skin damp, her eyes drugged with desire.

Leo took one more look at her face, then another and then another. Pushing her thighs indecently wide, he entered her without his usual finesse, his need far too urgent.

Somehow, from somewhere, he gathered enough sense to help her reach climax, moved her back onto the bed. Urged on by her throaty moans he climbed over her and slid inside her again. Fast and hard, he used her body to race toward their climax.

And finally, on the heels of his own thundering release, wrapped in her arms, her breath stroking his damp skin, came the quiet and calm he'd been seeking for forty-eight hours. And with it came the determination to keep the one good thing that had walked into life with him whatever the cost.

Leo didn't sleep at all. Neha had slept on and off between his urgent demands for more and more of her, as if he could chase away whatever demons prowled after him tonight.

"We're pregnant," Neha said into the quiet, inky depths of the pitch darkness of the dawn, a few hours later.

She was lying on her front, her face to the side, his body covering most of hers. His hand in her hair stilled; his heart might have come to a screeching halt, for all the breathlessness he felt in his chest.

"What did you say?" he said, wondering if he was making the whole thing up.

"I took the test before I left London. And then five more. They were all positive."

With shaking hands, he turned her, with none of the tenderness his mind was screaming she deserved. The shadows under her eyes were even more significant now. But her eyes were alert, studying him. And wary, too, as if she was unsure of his reaction.

Could he blame her when he'd behaved like a beast? *Cristo*, did she think he regretted this, her, them?

"Why didn't you tell me?" The question shot out of him like a bullet.

But of course, there was no answer she could give.

First, he had avoided her, then when she'd confronted him, he'd mocked her concern and then used her body through the night. Had she come to him hoping to share the news? Needing him to share in the happiness he heard in her tone?

Instead, he'd all but bitten her head off.

*Cristo*, he was a bastard.

"How do you feel?" he asked now, a hint of wonder he was beginning to feel creeping into his voice.

"Good. Mostly good." Her voice caught on the last part. Her gaze held his, asking questions he didn't understand. "You still want this?"

He cursed, instead of giving a straight answer. And still she didn't flinch. "Of course I do. Nothing has changed between us, *cara*," he said, knowing full well that the words were a complete lie.

Something had changed. In him. Between them. He

just didn't know what it was or how to handle it or how to bring everything back to how it had been before.

"This is good, Neha. This is *perfecto*," he added with emphasis, and finally the wariness in her eyes receded.

She pulled his palm to her belly and it felt as if he could breathe again. He spread his fingers over the soft, lush swell of it, a sense of wonder and inadequacy surging up inside him.

"This is our future, Leo. All ours. Just ours," she said with a tremulous smile, before pulling his head down and kissing his mouth. A promise in the kiss, a demand in the thrust of her tongue, an anchor winding around him when he felt as if he was drowning.

Leo nodded, and took over the kiss, needing her, needing this. For the first time in his life, he felt as if he didn't know a way forward, but he wanted to let her guide him. He wanted to let her hold his hand and pull him along for the ride, but the gnawing in his gut wouldn't ease.

Tenderness and fear roped together to beat an incessant tattoo in his chest. Gathering her to him, he kissed her temple. Her nose. Her cheek. Her mouth. The crook where her shoulder met her neck. Everything in him shuddered. "Talk to me, *cara*. Tell me your plans for us, for…our child. Tell me your hopes and your dreams and your wishes. Tell me every single thought that comes into your head about our baby. *Please*."

And as she talked about their family and their future, Leo listened, hoping that her voice and words would wash away the vulnerability that threatened to open up within himself again.

Hoped that the future she so clearly envisioned for them and their baby was all in his power to give.

"Massimo said you're leaving? Again?"

Leo looked up from his computer to find Neha standing at the entrance to his study, a soft, white nightie falling to below her knees, making her brown skin look strikingly gorgeous against the thin straps. She looked incredibly beautiful and utterly rumpled, though he had left her in their bed not an hour ago, her hair a cloud framing her face, her eyes full of that challenge he adored.

"*Sì*, I have to."

"Why? Exactly, do *you* have to, I mean?" Her question exploded into the silent midnight just as the door banged behind her with a loud thud.

He closed his laptop and sighed. Damn Massimo and his big mouth!

"Why are you up at this time, *cara*? The OB-GYN asked you to rest as much as possible after your high blood pressure numbers."

"Resting is all I've done the past week, Leo. And please don't treat me as if I'm a child who would endanger her health. Nothing is more important to me than this baby."

He nodded, greedily taking in the fierceness of her expression. *Dio mio*, she got lovelier day by day, fiercer minute by minute, when it came to the child she carried and Leo didn't know how to stop from wanting that same fierceness for himself, how to stem the desperate need to see the same wonder and adoration in her eyes when she looked at him.

For a few scattered moments here and there, he'd even caught himself being envious of that innocent life they'd created together. Had wondered if his mother had ever loved him like that, for a second. Had wondered if Neha would ever... *Basta!*

He had more than he'd ever wanted in his life and this fixation had to end.

"Leo?"

He rubbed a finger over his brow. He hated disappointing her but until he found some kind of balance in his head, he had to stay away. "What do you want from me, Neha?"

She flinched as if he'd raised his voice to her. "If you maybe take the time to answer my questions properly, instead of playing hide-and-seek with me, I can rest better. It doesn't help that I have to chase poor Massimo through the villa and the lab for information and that you keep enrolling him to be some sort of bodyguard for me while you go chasing shadows across the world."

Despite his reservation, he went to her, as if he was pulled by a magnet. "We still haven't identified who the new stockholder is. Alessandra is still MIA. Mario's rallying board members behind him, using your retirement announcement as some kind of backstabbing play from me. Until I discover who'll be coming onto the BFI board in Silvio's place, every rogue on the board thinks the position of CEO is up for grabs."

"I know all this. What I don't know is why you have

to be the one to solve it all." Her fingers tapped at the shadows he'd glanced under his eyes earlier. "Why you have to be the one who shoulders all this. Why can't Massimo go for once?"

*Because I need the distance from you.*

"Because Massimo hates dealing with bureaucracy and strategic moves. And if it were up to him, he'd let the whole Brunetti legacy burn to the ground with Vincenzo and Mario and the whole lot..." He saw the question in her eyes and answered it. "As much as I hate my father, I can't be that reckless, *bella*. Thousands of people depend on BFI for their livelihoods. I simply can't let a madman with a thirst for revenge tear it up."

"Sometimes I hate that you're so honorable." She looked up at him then. "If you're not going to be here, why can't I just go back to London? I feel like a third wheel with Massimo and Nat, and really, if you're that busy, we should postpone the wedding. I'm really not sure if we should even be having a wedding this soon after your father's death."

He barely kept the bite out of his tone. "It's a small civil ceremony, *bella*. And for the thousandth time, I refuse to let his death have any effect on my life." He sighed, hating the wary look that entered her eyes. "Think of it this way, *cara*," he said, lying through his teeth, hating himself for what he was doing, "the sooner I figure out all this, the freer I'll be when the baby comes."

Her arms vined around his waist, her face pressed up against his chest, she stole the ground from under him. She gave her body, her thoughts, her loyalty, and yet it felt like he didn't have enough. "And that's all it is, Leo?"

"Sì."

He nodded, sinking his fingers into her hair. Wanting to run away from this moment as much as he wanted to stand there and hold her for all of eternity. Wanting with everything he had to tell her about the turbulence inside him.

The solid foundation they'd built with years of friendship was still there. He trusted her more than he had anyone else in his life. And yet...there was a new intimacy between them that scared him. A sense of everything not being in his firm control, himself included. A weight on his chest as thoughts of past and future wrapped up in a vicious cycle.

As if she'd weaved some kind of magic and created a chink in him. As if she'd unearthed a weakness in him, a vulnerability no one else had.

And he hated being vulnerable. He found himself at the oddest of moments wondering at how all this had started. He hated that she'd come to him because he could stand up to Mario, that she'd come to him because he was wealthy and powerful enough to protect their child, that she'd agreed to be his wife only for the child... God, he was all twisted inside out.

And until he figured out how to put himself back together, until he rid himself this ridiculous vulnerability, he needed distance.

# CHAPTER TWELVE

See you the morning of the twelfth.

THE MORNING OF the twelfth was the morning of their wedding.

Neha stared at the message on her cell phone, frustration and anger rising like a tide through her throat. She threw the phone onto the sofa, and plonked down next to it, her hand on her belly. Tears prickled behind her eyes. Slapping her head back, she closed her eyes to stem the confusion overwhelming her.

They were going to be married in two days, and he told her over a pithy text that she wasn't going to see him before that? After another week of barely giving her any time and attention? And where the hell was her own self-sufficiency? Her composure?

God, she was too tired of wondering whether she was overreacting. If it was just her hormones or if it was truly Leonardo retreating from her. From their relationship, even before it took off.

The tears she'd been holding back for a long time drew tracks down her cheeks. Already, she felt heartsore from all the guessing, walking on eggshells because she didn't want to upset him, afraid what she might say that would be too much.

It had been three weeks since the day of Silvio Brunetti's funeral and she was at the end of her tether. She had meant to wait before telling him about the pregnancy.

But wrapped in his arms, her body sore from his fierce lovemaking, her heart tender and desperately needing an anchor to bring him back to her, to the common footing they had started this with, she'd blurted it out.

And he'd responded as she'd hoped, in a moment that had clearly been hard for him.

He'd kissed her with a tenderness that had her heart bursting, asked so many questions, kept her on the topic for so long that she'd gone to sleep a little worried about him, yes, but her heart full of hope that things would work out.

But the day after, he'd barely said goodbye before he'd left on another trip.

She'd given Leo time. She'd given him of herself when he'd been so angry and hurting and grieving, when all she'd wanted was to run away to her previously sterile and safe life. Where boundaries were not blurred and he'd been the immovable rock in her tumultuous life, her safe harbor when everything was sinking.

But now, he was the rocky outcropping she'd have to save herself from.

She honestly hadn't even minded that after that emotional outburst, after plainly rejecting her offer to talk, he'd wanted sex. Forget not minding, she'd needed it, too. She'd needed to feel close to him after seeing the pain of his childhood rip him open like that, knowing it was the only way he would let her comfort him. She'd needed to know that beneath the hurting, lashing out, he was still the Leo she trusted above any other man.

If he wanted to use her body in times of ravaging grief, she was more than happy to be used.

Because that's how much he meant to her. Because that's what she wanted this relationship to be—them holding each other through the worst that life threw at them, that was the family she'd always wanted to build.

But the aftermath of that night, the aftermath of her impulsively whispered admission in the dark of the dawn, nothing had been right.

They hadn't come through that night intact on the other side. Something had been broken. Or reality had changed. For her.

Their lovemaking had a deeper level now, some-times torrid, sometimes his tenderness brought tears to her eyes, and yet the rift between them seemed to grow increasingly wide, almost insurmountable. If she'd thought giving herself to him freely in his moment of pain would fix anything, it had done the opposite.

He'd retreated from her so far and so fast, as if he'd betrayed far too much of himself that night.

Oh, he was polite, and concerned for her. He watched over her like a mama bear, he granted her wishes before she could even think of them; he was the perfect lover, the perfect companion, and when they married in less than two days, he'd be the perfect husband.

The perfect husband, the perfect father, the perfect provider, and yet it wasn't what she wanted at all. Not anymore.

What he had promised, what she had wanted, was not enough anymore.

Pushing away from the sofa, she walked into the closet where her wedding dress hung. Panic was a bird in her chest, wings fluttering incessantly—night or day, wondering if she was making too much of nothing. Wondering if she was making a huge mistake. Wondering when he would do or say something that would bring her out of this misery.

The expensive, ivory silk rustled with a quiet whisper when she ran her fingers over it.

All the arrangements had been made for a quiet civil wedding, with only family present, but Neha hadn't been able to give up on the wedding gown. The minute she'd expressed a long-buried wish for an intimate wedding with a beautiful gown, Leo had made it come true within hours.

A custom design by an A-list designer specially commissioned for Neha. The straight lines of the dress highlighted her bust, falling into a loose drape from there as her belly was already rounded, to her knees. Stylish and elegant, it was Neha to the T.

It wasn't the traditional style or length but it suited them perfectly, she'd thought then.

Because she and Leo hadn't started in a normal way, either, but their relationship, she'd foolishly hoped, would only go from strength to strength.

A diamond necklace had been delivered yesterday—

tiny, multiple diamonds delicately set into platinum wire—so exquisite that Neha was afraid to take it out of its plush velvet bed.

*For my beautiful bride*, the note had said.

And a week ago it was the tour of the ten-acre small-ish estate he'd found on the shores of Lake Como where, if she wanted, he'd have the waiting architect design and build a state-of-the-art, industrial-size kitchen for Neha to play in. Mountains in the background and the lake on the other side, it was the most beautiful place Neha had ever seen. And only ten minutes from the Brunetti villa.

Interviews for nannies, a horde of lawyers to better settle the IP of So Sweet Inc., a twenty-four-hour companion/nurse to stay with her for the duration of the last two months and after—something she'd fought for instead of starting now. There was no end to the number of things he had arranged for her.

And yet…

Will you be at the villa tonight?

She texted him standing in her closet, her chest heavy with a weight she couldn't shift.

If he was there, she could ask him if everything was okay. She'd let him hold her, like only he could, and they would talk. And maybe she'd tell him that she…

The answer came after a few minutes.

No. I won't be.

I can fly to wherever you are tonight.

There wasn't even that bubble that said he was typing.

We've hardly seen each over the past two weeks.

Her heart crawled into her throat, thudding, as she waited.
Nothing.
She sent another, something in her chest cracking wide open.

I miss you.

Most of her life, she'd spent it on eggshells with her mother, wondering if she was asking too much, wondering if she should be even stronger, waiting to be loved. God, she couldn't spend the rest of her life like that, too.
She didn't want her future to be like that. She wanted to tell him how much she missed him, how much his withdrawal hurt. She wanted to demand he open up to her, she wanted to tell him how much she...how much she loved him.
*God, she loved him.* She'd loved him for so long. She'd loved from a distance. She'd seen him grow into the most honorable man she knew, and today, she wanted a part of him. She wanted his heart.
She texted again, her fingers slipping on the smooth screen, her thoughts unfurling, her emotions unraveling like the spool of a yarn her mum used.

I want to be near you.

His answer came finally.

Only a few days and then we'll be a family.

A family? But this wasn't the family she truly wanted. This distance between them, this game he played with her, these doubts and confusion, this misery in her heart…

She wanted more, she wanted everything—she wanted his heart.

She jumped as her phone chirped. Fingers shaking, she swiped to answer.

"Neha, what is it? Are you unwell, *cara*?"

"No," she said, the urgent concern in his voice jolting her rationality. "I'm fine. I have an appointment in a week but everything's good."

The silence on the line stretched from relief to tense in that awkward way she hated.

"I just… I'm not feeling good today. In my head, I mean. This wedding and us… I barely saw you the last few weeks. I know, I know, you're busy with figuring out the identity of new stockholder and I just…this doesn't feel right, Leo."

"Are you having an anxiety attack about the wedding? I told you we should hire that companion full-time starting now."

Whatever choke hold had been gripping Neha, whatever second-guessing she'd done over three long weeks—castigating herself, telling herself that she shouldn't demand too much of his time, his emotional energy, pulling herself back, wondering if they'd return to that open, honest place before that night—all of it collapsed into dust at his careless question.

Fury vibrated through her so hard that for a few seconds she couldn't even breathe, much less speak.

"Neha, *cara*, if you're—"

"Will you come if I'm having an anxiety attack?"

"What kind of a question is that?"

"It's an honest question. Answer me, Leo. If I was frothing at the mouth having an attack, what would you do?"

"I would be there as soon as possible."

"Because that falls within the purview of the boundaries you've drawn in this relationship?"

"Neha, you're worrying me."

"I don't want your bloody worry, Leo. I want you."

"What's the distinction?" she heard him say and then sigh. "You don't sound like yourself, *cara*. I'll be there in a few hours. In the meantime, I want you to call Nat and talk to her."

"I'm not having a breakdown here, Leo. So stop. Just stop." A laugh fell from her mouth. "In fact, after a long time, I'm shedding that final shackle around my heart."

"What are you talking about?"

She knew she had to do it like this. Take the coward's way out. Because if she saw him, if he touched her, if he held her, if he looked at her with those beautiful eyes that promised so much and yet gave nothing, she'd never be able to walk away.

She'd spend the rest of her life, loving him so much, waiting for the little crumbs he gave her, wondering what would be too much to ask, wondering what was too little to take, wondering if she was settling again.

She flopped to the floor in her closet, her knees unwilling to hold her up. Her body shaking. Her heart breaking into so many pieces. "I can't do this, Leo."

"You can't do what?"

"I can't marry you. Not like this."

"Not like what? Neha, what's going on? What has got you upset like this?"

"I'm in love with you. So much. I've loved you for so long that you're a part of my soul. A part of me. And you…"

*I'll never be vulnerable like that…*

The words he'd said that night reverberated in the distance between them, mocking her.

She rubbed at the tears on her cheeks but more came. The silence was so deafening, as if she had said the words into a bottomless abyss and they would never be returned to her. They would only be swallowed up.

"It's so strange, isn't it?" Her voice was unbelievably strong, clear, in contrast to his silence. "I was so determined to keep this all rational and in between the lines. I thought, *I'm prepared for whatever little he gives me.* I have wanted you for so long, from a distance, and there you were, offering me everything, and honestly, I couldn't believe that this dream I had was coming true. But then I realized your everything is really…not much, is it?"

"So you'll walk away from this after all the promises you made? You'll bolt at the first hurdle just like my mother once did, like a coward? Will you make me a stranger to my child?" His voice was piercingly cold, soft. As if he were determined to remove any emotion from it.

"How dare you? How dare you call me a coward? How dare you turn this on me when you can't even acknowledge the hole she left in your life?

"And no, I'm not backing out, Leo. I'm doing what you taught me to do. I'm standing up for myself. Dead things should be cut away, *si*?

"You're stunted. Your heart is dead.

"Even in your weakest moments, you never reveal yourself to me. Any time I get close, you run away. You will never be vulnerable. You will never go through that pain she caused you again, you won't even risk it.

"A month ago, even a week ago, I was okay with that. I was going to have this family with you. It was more than I'd ever imagined having...

"But I love you so much and I want to be able to say it. I want to be able to show it. I want so much, and this little, it's not enough.

"This is me doing what's healthy for me and our baby. This is me putting myself first.

"I can't marry you and lose the rest of myself. I can't spend the rest of my life loving you and resenting you for it. And believe me, our child will be better off with two parents who live apart than two who would stay together and destroy each other."

Neha cut the call and in the terrifying silence gave into the sobs crashing through her.

Leo waited in the gleaming white marble lounge the maid had shown him to. It had been three weeks since

Neha had called off their wedding. Three weeks since he'd discovered what Vincenzo Cavalli had been up to in the last two months, while Leo's own life had been turned upside down by the one woman he'd trusted more than anyone.

And yet, a day after the realization that Silvio's stock was firmly in Vincenzo's ownership, Leo found he didn't give a damn anymore. The man could raze BFI to the ground for all he cared right now.

"Hello, Mr. Brunetti."

He turned when he heard the soft voice. It was the first time he'd taken the time to study Padma Fenelli. Her hair was cut into a fashionable bob and she wore a beige pantsuit that was expertly cut.

The woman was a complete contrast, even physically, to Neha, from her fair skin to the fragile, almost elfin features to the carefully but expertly applied makeup. She looked like an exquisite doll that might break if handled even a little roughly.

Leo found himself greedily looking for signs of Neha in that beautiful face. But there was not the fire in Padma's eyes that Neha's held, no strength of character in the thrust of her chin, no fierce sparkle to her smile that Neha's crooked one had.

"Mario's not here," the older woman said, a small flash of belligerence in her eyes.

"I know," he said, wondering at the way she squared her shoulders as if she could take him on. "I came to speak to you. About your daughter."

Her fingers fidgeted relentlessly with a napkin in her hand, her diminutive frame shaking with alarming tremors. "What's there to talk about with me? You've ditched her just as my husband predicted, as soon as she's of no use to you. She deserves better. Lord, she's been strong for so long and she deserves better than all of us. And with all the social media sites positing that she's expecting, how could—"

"It's not a rumor. Neha's expecting. My child, yes. That's how this whole thing began." Even to his own ears, Leo sounded infinitely weary. The weight of the past few weeks without Neha had gouged a hole in him. "She wanted to have a child and she thought I would be the only man who'd take on Mario and keep him out of the child's life.

"That's the only reason she came to me. That's why she chose me."

Even as the last words left him, Leo realized how much bitterness he had amassed in the last few weeks at that. Yes, it had started like that, but *Cristo…*

*I've loved you for so long…*

The older woman crumpled as if she were built of cards, and despite his aversion to theatrics, Leo couldn't help but reach a hand out to catch the woman, couldn't help but feel that her worry was genuine.

"Oh, God, she's pregnant! My darling girl's pregnant? When is she due? How could she not tell me? How could you have abandoned her at such an important time? I have failed her, haven't I? I'll be a *nonna* and she hates me, my own daughter hates me and it's all…my fault. Her father would've been so disappointed in me."

Leo escorted her to an armchair and patiently waited for the woman to find her calm.

Her ramblings were incessant, the sobs rising up through her chest violent enough to make Leo realize how hard it must have been for Neha to walk away from this tiny, weak woman. To understand that for all the years of mistakes she'd made, she could still have a good heart.

Just like another woman who'd abandoned him long ago might have had. A sense of calm descended on him as if the small acceptance had burst through the darkness he'd built up inside him for so long.

He buried his face in his hands and let the pain of that boy steal through him. He'd never be at peace with that piece of the past but acknowledging the hurt lightened his chest. Cleared away so much baggage he hadn't realized he was carrying.

*You can't even acknowledge what a hole she left in your life.*

Neha had told him again and again and he'd just refused to listen. Because he'd been scared. Because he'd been afraid he wouldn't be enough for her in the end.

The fire in Mrs. Fenelli's eyes when she looked at him had him recalculating his opinion of her. "You're just as despicable as Mario said you were."

Leo shook her head. "I didn't call our wedding off. Neha did."

"Why?"

"It doesn't matter why, does it? Neha's the most courageous woman I know. But she still needs you, Mrs. Fenelli. Especially now. That's why I'm here. She believes that you deserve another chance. That if only you could be made to see how Mario has manipulated her behind your back all these years, you would not let her—"

"It's too late." Fresh tears poured down Padma's cheeks. "I confronted my husband last week. I watched the interview she did for that network, speaking out about her retirement and her anxiety attacks and being so brave in front of so many people, going it alone, again. I did that to her. I was so angry with myself and with Mario. I asked him why he'd hidden it all from me.

"For the first time in all these years, I argued with him, and in a matter of seconds, I could see the manipulative monster I'd subjected my child to for so long. My darling girl needed me, and I let her down. Again and again. I'm so ashamed of myself."

"Then go to her. She still loves you. And more than that, she believes in you. She believes you deserve her love even though you've wronged her. Even after you let her down countless times. Even after you..."

Even after he'd pushed her away again and again, from that night in the greenhouse to the night of his father's death.

*I love you so much...*

Leo stood up and walked to the French doors that opened up onto a beautifully manicured garden. For all the trust he'd claimed to have in her, he hadn't believed the simple thing she'd told him, had he?

She loved him. And Neha's love, like her heart, was all-encompassing, forgiving, strong. And he'd wanted it from the beginning. He'd wanted everything with her.

And because he'd been afraid of realizing that, he'd

avoided her, retreated from her, trying to get a better handle on his own emotions.

On the slow but irrevocable discovery that Neha was the one woman who could make him vulnerable again like that boy. That she could make him hurt again. She'd held him and loved him when he'd been the lowest denominator of himself.

But what he hadn't realized was that it had been too late already.

He'd always loved her—wasn't that why he'd never gone near her?

Because with her, he'd want everything. *Dio*, look how eagerly he'd jumped into the idea of marrying her, of having her by his side for the rest of his life.

The knowledge came so easily now, so freely, as if the huge weight that had been crushing him had been released.

Maybe the past was truly gone. Maybe his father's death meant he was free of the questions he'd never asked. Finally, he was ready, he was enough to love the precious woman that had chosen him, even before he had chosen himself.

Or his happiness.

Now he had to make the same choice. For her, for them. For himself.

# CHAPTER THIRTEEN

NEHA HAD WALKED back to her flat from her yoga class and was about to jump into the shower when the doorbell pinged. She frowned, wondering if her mum had already packed up her things at the mansion, even though it had only been yesterday that she had confronted Neha in the street market, tears in her eyes.

A smile curved Neha's mouth now as she remembered how much her papa had loved Mum's dramatic bent as he called it. It might have taken her mum years to realize how much distance Mario had created between them, but damn if she hadn't jumped in a taxi and accosted Neha the moment she had realized.

Not bothering to pull on shorts, Neha walked to the door in the loose, sleeveless pink tee and opened the door, a welcoming whoop on her lips.

The smile dropped from her face and something like a balloon filled her chest, stealing her breath. Sending tremors rippling through her frame.

His shoulder pressed against the door frame, Leonardo stood there. His unruly hair looked even more rumpled, his light blue shirt fit snugly across that chest that had held her so securely, his jeans highlighted the power in his thighs. He looked broad, rugged and painfully handsome at her front door. *Where he belonged*, the stray thought lodged in her head.

Fingers gripping the wood tightly, she stood there, unmoving, staring at him, while her body combusted with myriad chemical reactions. Every inch of her flooded with longing—a desperate weakness she'd foolishly thought she'd buried.

His gaze held hers for what felt like an eternity, unspeaking. A caress running over her face, her neck, her body. Down her bare, clenched thighs, to the gold chain she wore around one anklet, to her pink-tipped toes and then back up again in what felt like a rite in fire to her.

That magnetic gaze lingered on her belly, her breasts and then rose to meet her face again. Heat swept her damp neck and into her cheeks. Her head was dizzy beneath the desire humming into life as if she were a generator that had been plugged into the power socket.

God, all it took was one look from him and she was melting from within...

"I didn't know you were coming to London," she said into the thick silence, just to break the tension.

Because honestly, she'd done everything she could to keep him out of her life. Out of her thoughts. Out of her near present.

Which was damn hard with the fact that he'd sent Nat to her in London at the crack of dawn after she'd broken everything between them on that phone call. Damn hard to do when he called her like clockwork every two days to inquire how she was doing.

She'd been far too miserable to not have expected something like that from him. Just because she'd called off their wedding didn't mean Leo would stop looking after her. Or that she would stop hating it this century.

Keeping him out of her heart was another matter completely.

Because she still wasn't in a good place to deal with him. Still felt this powerful tug toward him. Still harbored anger and resentment and pain over what he wouldn't give her.

She wanted to be rational and clearheaded and reasonable in their partnership. Because he was still the father of her unborn babies…

Her composure nearly broke at the thought of the small clip sitting on her cell phone.

"Hello, *bella*," he said finally, his voice husky and rough, like it got when he was inside her. When he felt some strong emotion he usually buried deep inside. When he was so fiercely pursuing his pleasure that he had no control over himself.

Every inch of her skin tingled in response to that tone, her body loosening itself in some sort of ritual, awaiting the pleasure he gave so skillfully.

"It felt like a good time for a visit. We finally discovered who the new stockholder is."

"Yeah? Who?"

"Vincenzo Cavalli.

"Somehow he's managed to get his hands on Silvio's stock. Massimo is investigating if it will hold up in court."

"What does it mean for BFI, then?" she asked, knowing how much of himself he'd poured into the company.

He shrugged and her eyes widened. "Massimo and I can take on whatever he brings, *sì*? If Vincenzo razes BFI to the ground, we'll just build it bigger and better. I've decided to focus my energies on other things for now."

"Oh," she said, still struggling to swallow the overwhelming urge to throw herself into his arms.

She hadn't seen him in four weeks. She'd imagined how this conversation might go, she'd steeled herself for the impact of seeing him. But God, nothing was ever going to prepare her for the sight of this man. She was never going to look at him and not want to hold him with such force that it was an ache in her belly.

"Can I come in?" His voice was polite while his gaze felt hot, greedy, on her skin. Like in those beginning years when they'd still been learning each other, testing each other, starting to like each other.

She nodded and stepped back.

He passed her and the scent of him—so familiar and wrapped up in so many good things in her life—gripped her hard, like a vise clamping down on her chest. She felt the heat of his body surround her.

His fingers touched her cheek gently, tenderly, and retreated when she stiffened.

"You okay, *tesoro*?" Again, that husky shiver in his tone.

Or maybe she was going mad with longing and imagining things that weren't there. God, he hadn't uttered a word when she'd poured out her heart. She was crazy and hormonal to think something had changed.

"Fine. Great," she added for good measure.

She walked into the kitchen, aware of his eyes on her back. Pouring herself a glass of cold water, she downed it in one go. She walked back into the living room but kept the length of the sofa between them. "I'm meeting Mum for lunch and I don't want to keep her waiting," she fibbed.

"She came to see you, then?"

Something in his tone snagged at her. "Yeah. She… kinda accosted me when I went to the local market, crying. She apologized for years of not realizing what had been right under her nose. Said she was leaving Mario, if you can believe it. She said all those years ago, she'd only even accepted his offer because she knew she was too weak to look after me, because she thought I would need at least one strong parent… All these years, so many times, and for her to realize only now how much Mario harmed me…" Neha gasped, her hand rising to her chest.

"What?" Leo said, his tone urgent. "*Cara*, are you unwell?"

"No. I was so happy that she finally came to me, so happy that she… I never asked her. You…*you* did it. You went to her and told her what's been happening? You went to my mum and told her what's been going on all these years? You told her how much she hurt me? You…"

Her heart beat so rapidly that Neha thought it might

rip out of her chest. God, was there no end to this stupid thread of hope?

She reached out to him, and he stepped back, as if he was afraid she might assault him.

"*Sì*. I did. Even before you broke things off, I knew how much pain she was causing. I was so sure you were better off without her. But you...you love her so much and I thought there must be a reason for that, other than the fact that she simply gave birth to you. I thought if Neha loves her that much, then there must be something redeemable about the woman.

"You were right. She loves you just as much as you love her. She's just not as strong as you are. No one is, *cara*. All she needed was some reassurance."

He'd gone to her mum for her. He'd convinced her mum to see the truth even when he didn't like her. Her throat tight with tears, Neha blinked. "Reassurance about what?"

"That I...was here. To protect you against any blowback you might face from Mario when she left him."

And just like that, he shattered her all over again. "Oh, of course. Thanks for that. For everything. You didn't have to come all the way to London to tell me that."

A shadow crossed his face. "What the hell does that mean?"

Her head jerked up. For the first time in her life, Neha saw beneath the polite, calm facade he wore like a second skin. Some emotion darkened those eyes. That flash of emotion exhilarated her, winding her up, breaking the tight hold she had on her own emotions.

"I just don't need a regular reminder that I'm an obligation to you, Leo. One of the million you carry on your broad shoulders."

"Is that what you think? That you're a responsibility to me?"

"Yes. And to be honest, I'm quite tired of it. I know—" she cut him off forcefully when he'd have argued and knew at the back of her mind that she was being completely irrational, but man, she was tired "—I know that I asked for your help. I invited you into my life. I opened the can of worms that's my family. But I'm honestly beginning to develop an aversion to the way you see me."

"And what way is that, *cara*?" His voice went dangerously low, and if she had any sense, Neha would've remembered that the more furious Leo got, the calmer he looked.

"As another thing to protect. Now doubly so, because I'm the mother of your unborn children."

A pulse in his jaw ticked dangerously as he waylaid her. His fingers on her arm were firm, and yet somehow so gentle. "You said children...why children?"

She buried her face in his chest. "Twins. We're having twins. A boy and a girl. I saw the ultrasound yesterday."

"And you didn't call me?"

"I was going to. I so desperately wanted to... But if I had... I was so desperate to hear your voice, to tell you the news, to ask you to..."

"Ask me what, *cara mia*?"

"I wanted to be held, Leo. I wanted to be kissed.

Where does that fall in your duties? Will you kiss me out of obligation? Will you sleep with me because I'm extra turned on because of this pregnancy? Where does your obligation to me end? Do you see what I've gotten myself into? Do you think I want you to—"

"Shh...*tesoro*. No more. Shh..." A torrent of Italian flew from his mouth—lilting and gentle and a litany of warmth and joy. He kissed every inch of her face— her eyes, her temple, the tip of her nose, her cheek and then, finally, her mouth.

Her body arched into his, as if he were her homing beacon, her home, her salvation. He kissed her with a desperation that mirrored her own, sweeping into the warm cavern of her mouth, his hands incredibly gentle as they moved all over her body, his mouth breaking into tender words in between. "I love you so much that it terrifies me, *si*?

"You declared so boldly that you loved me and I ran even from that. I went to talk to your mum and I realized the weight of your words to me...

"I loved you for so long, always, maybe. But I didn't know what love was. I couldn't see it even when you told me. I couldn't see past the fear that if I opened myself up, you might leave me. You might hurt me.

"Loving you...it makes me quake in my handmade loafers." He was laughing and Neha was crying and she didn't know if it was a dream or real.

His rough hands clasped her face, pulling her up, and when she looked into his eyes, Neha knew it was all real. "But loving you also makes me joyous. I'm finally at peace. Like a piece I hadn't known was missing has been slotted in. Like I could finally let go of the past.

"I wake up in the morning and dream about our future. Loving you makes me stronger and yet somehow weaker at the same time.

"But if you will have me—only because I couldn't bear to spend another day without you—I will spend the rest of my life proving to you that I'm enough to love you, *cara*."

Neha pressed her mouth to his and tasted her own tears. "Of course you're enough, Leo. All I wanted was a tiny piece of your heart. All I wanted was a foothold, my love."

"You helped me discover my heart is whole. It is all yours."

Tears overflowed from her eyes again and Leo wiped them away, his own alarmingly wet. Hands on her shoulders, he held her at arm's length and let his gaze take her in.

*Dio*, this incredibly gorgeous, strong woman was his. All his. He fell to his knees and placed his forehead on the swell of her belly. Then he kissed it, wonder filling him at the change in her body. Then he looked up into those beautiful brown eyes. "I had nothing until you came into my life. Thanks for loving me, *bella*, for choosing me. For you. And for these babies."

She came into his arms like lightning and took his mouth in a hot, possessive kiss that got his blood thrumming. "I'll always choose you, darling. Always."

# EPILOGUE

*Three years later*

NEHA PULLED THE fresh batch of cinnamon rolls out of the monstrous oven that she still hadn't gotten used to, and placed them with great care onto a ceramic plate. It was a waste of time and effort, she knew, but she still liked seeing her handiwork beautifully arranged, even for a few seconds.

Even if her audience hadn't developed an aesthetic sense along with a palate.

She poured cold milk into the glass carafe and carried the whole thing out into the backyard, which had a view of beautiful Lake Como.

She'd barely put the tray down when two pairs of grubby hands reached for the rolls and her carefully crafted tower was demolished into a blob. When she'd have run after the screeching toddlers with a roll in one hand and a plastic shovel in the other, strong arms gripped her from the back and held her arrested in a cocoon of heat and hardness she couldn't resist to this day.

Maybe never.

"Let them be," Leo whispered at her ear, and then buried his face in the crook of her neck. The press of his warm mouth at her pulse sent shivers spewing over her skin. "Your mum will watch them."

"My mum's a fragile, delicate thing and those children of yours are two monsters. Maya, somehow, you can still reason with. But Matteo... God, Leo, he's already a little terror the way you let him do whatever he wants."

"He's two, *cara mia.* I don't have the heart to tell him to stop digging for treasure or tell Maya she's responsible for her brother. He'll learn when it's time how to behave. Let them be children. For as long as possible."

Neha sighed and swept her arms around his neck, sank her fingers into his hair, knowing that her husband was a marshmallow when it came to their children. And a natural at it, too. "Fine. Don't come to me when he's a moody, spoiled teenager."

Leo's hands pushed up her blouse until his roughened hands reached the skin beneath. He stroked her skin, the fingertips reaching up and up until she heard her breath hitch. "Maybe what they need is company. You wouldn't be up for another set, would you?"

"Another set of what?" Neha demanded, even as she pressed herself shamelessly into the hardness nestled between her buttocks.

"Twins, *cara mia.* We'll ask Massimo and Nat to babysit, go on a proper honeymoon this time and get to working on that. *Sì?*"

"*Sì,*" Neha whispered before turning her mouth for his voracious kiss. "*Sì* to anything you suggest, darling," she whispered, and he laughed, those blue eyes shining with love. And Neha knew that even thirty years later she'd still be shaking at the knees when he looked at her like that.

*"Ti amo, tesoro,"* he whispered before he claimed her mouth with his.

\* \* \* \* \*

*If you enjoyed*
A Deal to Carry the Italian's Heir
*by Tara Pammi*
*look out for the first instalment in*
*The Scandalous Brunetti Brothers trilogy:*
An Innocent to Tame the Italian,
*available now!*

*And why not explore these other*
*Tara Pammi stories?*

Bought with the Italian's Ring
Blackmailed by the Greek's Vows
Sheikh's Baby of Revenge
Sicilian's Bride for a Price

*Available now!*

# WE HOPE YOU ENJOYED THIS BOOK!

**HARLEQUIN** *Presents*®

Get lost in a world of international luxury, where billionaires and royals are sure to satisfy your every fantasy.

Discover eight new books every month, available wherever books are sold!

Harlequin.com

## COMING NEXT MONTH FROM

### ⬦ HARLEQUIN
™

# *Presents.*

### Available December 17, 2019

### #3777 THE ITALIAN'S UNEXPECTED BABY
*Secret Heirs of Billionaires*
### by Kate Hewitt
Mia is wary of trusting others, so when Alessandro coolly
dismisses her after their night together, she dares not tell him
she's pregnant! But on learning her secret, he's *determined* to
legitimize his child...

### #3778 SECRETS OF HIS FORBIDDEN CINDERELLA
*One Night With Consequences*
### by Caitlin Crews
Overwhelming. Irresistible. Off-limits. Teo was all those things to
Amelia. Until she attends his luxurious masquerade ball, and they
share a deliciously anonymous encounter! Now Amelia must tell
brooding Teo he's the father of her unborn baby...

### #3779 CROWNING HIS CONVENIENT PRINCESS
*Once Upon a Seduction...*
### by Maisey Yates
Nothing surprises Prince Gunnar, until personal assistant Latika
asks him for help—by marrying her! Recognizing her desperation,
he protects her with his royal name. Yet the biggest surprise isn't
their sizzling chemistry, but how dangerously *permanent* his
craving for Latika feels...

### #3780 CLAIMED FOR THE DESERT PRINCE'S HEIR
### by Heidi Rice
When Kasia comes face-to-face with Prince Raif at a lavish party,
he looks furious—and dangerously sexy. For Kasia can't hide the
truth...after their desert encounter, she's pregnant. And this time
Raif won't let her go!

HPCNMRA1219

## #3781 BILLIONAIRE'S WIFE ON PAPER
*Conveniently Wed!*
### by Melanie Milburne
Logan can't lose his family estate. But to rescue it, he must wed! He avoids real relationships, having failed at love before. So when housemaid Layla suggests he take a convenient wife, he's intrigued...and proposes to her!

## #3782 REDEEMED BY HIS STOLEN BRIDE
*Rival Spanish Brothers*
### by Abby Green
Having stolen his rival's fiancée, billionaire Gabriel is blindsided by his powerful attraction to innocent Leonora! He believes he can offer her only passion, but Leonora knows her proud husband could offer so much more than pleasure...

## #3783 THEIR ROYAL WEDDING BARGAIN
### by Michelle Conder
Princess Alexa's strategy was simple: avoid an unwanted union by finding a short-term fiancé. Notoriously untamable Prince Rafaele seems her safest bet...until the king demands they marry, for real!

## #3784 A SHOCKING PROPOSAL IN SICILY
### by Rachael Thomas
To save her penniless family, Kaliana needs a husband—urgently! So she shockingly proposes to billionaire Rafe. Yet Rafe has his own agenda—a marriage could secure his rightful inheritance, but only if it appears to be real!

# Get 4 FREE REWARDS!

## We'll send you 2 FREE Books plus 2 FREE Mystery Gifts.

**YES!** Please send me 2 FREE Harlequin Presents® novels and my 2 FREE gifts (gifts are worth about $10 retail). After receiving them, if I don't wish to receive any more books, I can return the shipping statement marked "cancel." If I don't cancel, I will receive 6 brand-new novels every month and be billed just $4.55 each for the regular-print edition or $5.80 each for the larger-print edition in the U.S., or $5.49 each for the regular-print edition or $5.99 each for the larger-print edition in Canada. That's a savings of at least 11% off the cover price! It's quite a bargain! Shipping and handling is just 50¢ per book in the U.S. and $1.25 per book in Canada.* I understand that accepting the 2 free books and gifts places me under no obligation to buy anything. I can always return a shipment and cancel at any time. The free books and gifts are mine to keep no matter what I decide.

Choose one: ☐ **Harlequin Presents®**
Regular-Print
(106/306 HDN GNWY)

☐ **Harlequin Presents®**
Larger-Print
(176/376 HDN GNWY)

Name (please print)

Address                                                                 Apt. #

City                          State/Province                    Zip/Postal Code

## Mail to the **Reader Service:**
**IN U.S.A.:** P.O. Box 1341, Buffalo, NY 14240-8531
**IN CANADA:** P.O. Box 603, Fort Erie, Ontario L2A 5X3

**Want to try 2 free books from another series!** Call 1-800-873-8635 or visit www.ReaderService.com.

*Terms and prices subject to change without notice. Prices do not include sales taxes, which will be charged (if applicable) based on your state or country of residence. Canadian residents will be charged applicable taxes. Offer not valid in Quebec. This offer is limited to one order per household. Books received may not be as shown. Not valid for current subscribers to Harlequin Presents books. All orders subject to approval. Credit or debit balances in a customer's account(s) may be offset by any other outstanding balance owed by or to the customer. Please allow 4 to 6 weeks for delivery. Offer available while quantities last.

**Your Privacy**—The Reader Service is committed to protecting your privacy. Our Privacy Policy is available online at www.ReaderService.com or upon request from the Reader Service. We make a portion of our mailing list available to reputable third parties that offer products we believe may interest you. If you prefer that we not exchange your name with third parties, or if you wish to clarify or modify your communication preferences, please visit us at www.ReaderService.com/consumerschoice or write to us at Reader Service Preference Service, P.O. Box 9062, Buffalo, NY 14240-9062. Include your complete name and address.

HP20